Severed by Vengeance

THE SEVERED SIGNET BOOK ONE

ELLE MALDONADO

Authors Note

Severed by Vengeance is a dark romance. It contains explicit content and depictions that some may find triggering.
It is intended for readers 18+.
A complete list of triggers can be found here:
https://tr.ee/m-kuu-R8Rz
Or visit my social media:
https://www.instagram.com/authorellemaldonado

*To all my readers who long to be devoured in the flames
of passionate and all-consuming love.
But also crave to be ravaged.
Taken.
And disrespected in the best way.*

Chapter One

Derek

Killing my father was a reckoning seventeen years in the making. I was just a boy the day I decided he would die by my hand. And I spent the years since envisioning every twisted way in which I'd make him beg for the mercy he'd refused me as a child.

Nothing I'd do to him today would erase the past or ease my trauma. None of that shit mattered. My motive was sheer self-satisfaction. I'd take pleasure in watching him breathe his last breath, cry out to whatever God he thought would save him, and cower as he looked into my eyes, knowing I'd come like a reaper to collect what was owed.

For the past hour, I stood in his living room. Waiting. Adrenaline pulsing, the pent-up anticipation of years culminating all for this very moment. Everything was set. All he had to do was walk through the goddamn door. While James was a man of strict structure, tonight, he was late.

Drawing a deep, irritated breath, I roved over the picture frames lining the mantle of a brick fireplace. Most were of James, who smiled like a smug bastard while receiving awards and accolades. In others, he posed at banquets and charity auctions as strangers stood beside him, oblivious to the darkness he kept hidden under the façade of philanthropist and good doctor.

A gold rectangular frame caught my attention, one where he posed with a young woman, her head leaning affectionately against his chest. She was beautiful: long dark hair, olive complexion—and those damn dimples. Her piercing brown eyes bore through mine as I momentarily lost myself in their depths.

Who was she? A lover?

Unfamiliar voices poured in from behind the front door, and I quickly slid into a shadowy hallway across the foyer.

"Eva!" he said, sounding equal parts surprised and excited. "What are you doing out so late?"

James stepped through the threshold with his guest, the lock clicking behind them—an unexpected turn of events.

But I was a patient man, and sometimes collateral damage was part of the job.

"I got off early and came by to check on you. Heard you haven't been feeling well."

Her voice.

It wrapped itself around me. The rasp it held was soothing and husky. And damn if it wasn't sexy as hell.

"Don't you believe a word Franco says. You know how he exaggerates."

The mystery woman laughed in response, and I'd be lying if I said the sound hadn't stirred something inside me.

As their voices carried over into an adjacent living room, I caught a fleeting glimpse of her reflection in a hallway mirror. Eva was the woman in the photo, though the picture hadn't done her any justice. She was fucking devastating.

"Sit, Eva. Can I get you a glass of water or something to eat? Have you been taking care of yourself?"

"Hey, I'm here to check on *you*, remember? And I'm good. My levels are perfect, promise."

Levels?

I could hear the smile in her voice, and I berated myself for craving to see it.

"You should come around to visit this old man more often. I mean that." His tone turned serious. "I miss our chats. You know you're like the daughter I never had."

The goddamn audacity.

A scoff escaped my throat, and I stilled my breath, muscles tensing at my slip. But James's cheerful, grating voice echoed like a fucking bullhorn in my ears. The gun holstered inside my jacket suddenly felt hot and weighted as he unknowingly carved his name on the lead of every bullet.

"I promise to swing by more often. I've been meaning to, but you know work can be unpredictable."

"I completely understand. So, when do I get to meet a potential son-in-law?"

The woman laughed outright. "Well, I'd have to find him first, then we can plan dinner and set a wedding date."

It was the asshole's turn to bellow a laugh.

The dynamic of their relationship confused me. James hadn't only been a deadbeat father; he was corrupt and black to the core as much as I was. Living among soulless sacks of shit had given me the instinct and wherewithal to recognize demons hidden beneath the surface.

Guilty men—like me, like James—with buried skeletons and

blood-stained hands would forever bear the weight of their sins.

But Eva—she was something else.

Their conversation continued, and I waited, biding my time. It wasn't long before they drifted back into the foyer as she said her goodbyes.

"Text me so I know you made it home," he said, waving her off and closing the door.

Once it shut, I stepped out from behind the curtain.

"Well, that was touching." James froze. "She's really something, isn't she?"

He turned around slowly, his graying brows pulled together in confusion.

"Who the fuck are you, and what are you doing in my house?"

I strode into the hallway, the sides of my mouth tilted into a devious grin.

"What, you don't know who I am? You don't recognize me, Dr. Ford?"

"Listen, I don't know what you're playing at, but you need to get the hell out of my house before I call the cops."

Fear tainted his voice. Good.

"No offerings of water? Food? My, my, James, where are your manners?"

The coward took a step back, body tensed against the door as he reached blindly for the knob. His breaths were shallow and fast, sweat already beading his forehead.

James Ford might not have been aware of who I was, but the guilt festering in his conscience was seeping through every pore as if I'd already gutted him.

An innocent man would have offered everything at his disposal to spare his life. Or hell, even put up a fight. Instead, our eyes had been gridlocked, each waiting for the other to make the first move.

"What do you want? Money?"

Ah, there it was.

He turned the knob.

"I wouldn't do that, Dr. Ford," I threatened, voice menacingly calm. "Step away from the door and put your phone on the table. I just want to talk."

"Fuck you."

My grin widened. "Now, that's no way to treat a guest. I'm offended I don't get the same courtesy offered to—what was her name—Eva? Mm, now that is one fine piece of ass."

James schooled his shoulders, as if suddenly feeling brave, and stepped toward me, mouth twisted into a grimace.

"Leave her out of this."

I rounded him like a predator would its prey.

"Do you even have a clue who I am?"

He took a moment to examine me from the bottom up. James wasn't stupid. He knew I wasn't your run-of-the-mill burglar looking for some random shit to pawn.

"You here to blackmail me? You think you have something on me I can't bury by morning?"

I arched a brow and scoffed. "I haven't needed a damn thing from you my whole life. What makes you think I'd start now?"

There was a twitch in his jaw, his eyes narrowing as they centered nervously on my face.

"Yeah, almost there. I can see the pieces falling into place. Notice anything familiar in the shape of my jaw?" His focus dropped to the bottom half of my face, then back up to meet my eyes. "These baby blues have really been a hit with the ladies. But I'm sure you know all about that, don't you?"

James's mouth fell agape, eyes doubling in size. "You... you're... *Derek*," he stammered.

"*Surprise.*"

He shook his head incredulously. "I thought you—"

"What? Got lost in the system?"

Of course, he'd be disappointed I wasn't dead.

A gloved hand fell over the hilt of my blade. There was nothing I desired more than to stain the air with the scent of his blood.

Hurried footsteps and subsequent knocking had our heads whipping toward the door, jarring me from my bloodlust.

Our joyful little reunion would have to wait.

"Uncle James! My phone must have slipped out of my pocket. Can you open the door?"

Eva.

James's brows shot to his hairline, chest rising and falling in rugged pants.

"If I don't answer, she'll think something's wrong. Please, don't hurt her," he begged, face flushing red.

"You are a master at playing the part of doting uncle," I whispered, pulling my HK from its holster. "Her life depends on your last performance, so make it count."

The blood on my hands was thick with the souls of dead men. Each one another notch, another number to the tally. But for reasons I refused to examine further, the thought of hurting this woman twisted something deep in my gut.

Stepping back into the cover of shadows, I watched as James huffed out a long, shaky breath of air before opening the door.

"Evangelina! I'm sorry, I was upstairs. You said you left your phone?"

Careful to stay hidden, I observed as the woman nodded slowly.

She seemed to scrutinize his flustered appearance and the subtle nervous tells of his body language. Perceptive, I'd give her that.

Evangelina.

I rolled that name around in my thoughts.

"Is everything… all right?" she asked, leaning forward.

My eyes lingered on her plump mouth.

"It's nothing. I just got winded, running down the stairs. I might be decrepit, after all," he said with a wary laugh.

Evangelina flashed him a smile that didn't quite reach her eyes as she walked past him, patting his shoulder. "Sounds like you need to get some rest."

Once she disappeared into the living room, I stepped under the glow of a wall lamp, and James and I locked eyes. The good doctor rubbed a rough hand through the once sandy blond hair I remembered. Thick streaks of platinum now in their place were a testament to his absence and the years gone by.

He was frozen to the spot. Watching. Probably trying to come up with ways to escape or sway me.

They always tried.

As the woman's footfalls neared, I shot him one last implicit glare, then slinked back into obscurity.

Stopping a few short feet from where I was hiding, she leaned a shoulder against the wall, and I closed my eyes, daring to breathe her in. Her scent was intoxicating. My fingers curled into a fist, and I swallowed the urge to run them through the dark waves falling like a curtain down her back.

But James quickly approached, and with a protective arm around her shoulders, he led her away.

A weakness.

"Promise me you'll take it easy," she said, rising onto her toes to press a kiss to his cheek.

The woman was short. Probably no taller than five foot two.

On the wingtips of that thought, my eyes journeyed up her toned legs, stopping to admire how her jeans hugged the perfectly rounded globes of her ass. Rogue thoughts of Evangelina's lithe body wrapped tightly around mine had me shifting my weight, feeling the strain of my cock against the zipper.

Yeah, it would be a damn shame if James blew our cover.

"Eva love," he croaked, voice on the verge of cracking.

"Uncle James? What's wrong?" Her tone was tinged with worry.

Holding her gently by the shoulders, he feigned a smile. "Don't pay me any mind. Truth is, I was looking at photos of Pam. Of our wedding. I miss her; that's all."

Evangelina's voice softened. "Talk to her, Uncle Jay. I know she still loves you."

"Don't you concern yourself with Pam and me. She's much better off, trust me. Now, get out of here. It's late. Don't make me worry about you."

"I face the worst of society every day. I'll be fine."

"I'll always worry, no matter how capable you are," he said with a proud tone. "But evil lurks in every corner, Eva. Never let your guard down."

His cryptic words only seemed to set off more alarms. She bit down on her lip. "Uncle Jay, are you sure you're all right?"

"Go now, Eva," he urged.

A soft sigh blew past her lips, and she nodded, turning to leave.

I released the breath I'd been holding until he stopped her again, and an exasperated growl threatened to claw up my throat.

Fucking let her go.

"Eva? Remember what I said. Be careful out there. Always trust your instincts. You're so smart, so beautiful—I love you."

She leaned her back against the door, skepticism cutting across her features, and for just a moment, her anxious brown eyes found mine through the veil of darkness, piercing through me and briefly causing my breath to hitch. I wasn't sure if the fear of being caught, or something more, had induced my reaction.

"I love you too. But I'm checking on you first thing tomorrow." James forced a nervous laugh. "Sleep well," she said, regarding him one last time before slipping out the door.

I let James stew in his misery for several moments before slow-clapping and stepping into view.

"Bravo. No wonder my mother fell for your bullshit." Raising my weapon, I motioned for him to move. "Living room. Now."

James hung his head and cursed under his breath. He walked like a resigned man, accepting his judgment and the fate he'd sowed decades ago when he'd laid eyes on my mother, destroying everything she was or could have been. The domino effect of his cruelty poisoned me as well.

"You don't have to—"

A silencer suppressed the loud popping of two bullets as they left the chamber of my gun, cutting into his flesh in quick succession. James dropped, a howl erupting from his throat as blood soaked into the beige carpet beneath his mangled legs.

"You… crazy bastard," he heaved, tears welling in his anguished blue eyes.

"I won't deny that. That's exactly who I am. But you made me this way, James."

My boot connected to his jaw, and blood spewed from the split lip.

"Please, stop. I'm sorry! I was a different person back then," he sputtered, covering his face with both arms.

"I bet the fuck you were." My knuckles tore the skin above his right brow. "Now, you're the loving Uncle James, aren't you? The successful doctor." Another right hook whipped his head back against the couch.

"Derek, please. If I could go back, I—"

"You'd do *what*?" I shoved the suppressor into his mouth. "Not leave your bastard son to rot in the system?"

He was breathing hard through flared nostrils, tears running down his cheeks. I leaned close to his bloodied face, a sadistic grin on my lips.

"Tell me, James, who is Evangelina? And what is a pretty little thing like her doing with a piece of shit like you?" He thrashed beneath me, his cries muffled by the hot titanium searing his tongue. "I know she's not your niece."

Saliva sputtered out of the corners of his mouth as he shook his head in defiance. "I'm losing my patience, James."

Several teeth fell into his lap when I tore the gun from inside his mouth and pressed it to his temple. Blood ran down his chin, staining the front of his shirt.

The man was a sorry fucking sight.

"Don't you touch her. She has nothing to do with any of this. Kill me. Just me."

"Oh, that's still the plan. But death is much too easy for what I endured because of you. No, you don't just get to close your eyes and die in peace."

"God, Derek… I'm so sorry. I really am!"

I fisted the collar of his shirt. "I've been a man for a very long time. Never once heard shit from you. So, goddamn you and your apologies." Pushing his head against the hardwood, I growled through clenched teeth, "Who is she, or so help me—"

"My goddaughter! She's the daughter of a colleague and close friend." His tormented eyes met my feral ones. "Please, Derek, I'm begging you; leave Eva alone."

I pitched my face close to his ear and whispered, "*No.*"

James seethed in protest. "You son of a bitch! Goddamn you to hell. I should have killed you and that whore when I had the chance."

A low, cynical chuckle rumbled in my chest. "Ah, there you are. I knew you were in there. You might put up a front for everyone else and your Evangelina, but I know the type of man you are."

He scoffed with a groan. "What, a ruthless monster... just like you?"

I gritted my teeth, revolted at the thought that I was anything like this spineless fuck.

"Shut up." I pointed the barrel between his eyes. "I'll see you in hell–*Dad*. But before you go, know this: Evangelina is *mine*. Please take your last breath, knowing I won't stop until she's writhing in my arms and screaming my name." He shook his head as I laughed. "Yeah, I'm going to taint and destroy everything you've ever loved. Starting with that sweet piece of ass you care so much about. No other man will ever touch her. I promise you that."

James gnashed his mangled teeth. "You mother—"

Two bullets split his skull, leaving a trail of bone and brain matter splattered against the floor.

I wiped the hot barrel on a cushion and holstered it as I got to my feet. Blowing out a sated breath, I walked to the mantle and snatched Eva's picture.

She would hate me with every fiber of her being. But by then, it would be too late. She'd be too far gone, and I would own her. Entirely and utterly ruin her.

The glass shattered as I smashed the frame against the hard brick, wrenched the photo and tore it in two. James Ford's face fell into the ash as I shoved Eva's half into my front pocket.

With one last sharp glance at the corpse of my sperm donor, I stepped out into the cool night. A starless black sky hung over my head, mirroring the state of my tortured soul. For seventeen years, I had done nothing but fantasize about that moment of retribution, yet his death failed to quell the demons or fill the void in my hollow chest.

Leaning against the rough bark of a tree, I lit a Fuente as a loud explosion rocked the surrounding forest. Wildlife scurried, coming alive as the flames at my back set the world ablaze.

Chapter Two

Evangelina

The needle pierced into my skin. My gaze focused beyond the blood, numb to the pinprick of pain I'd been forced to inflict on myself for the last eighteen years. As if on autopilot, the bloodied strip was already in the meter before I was conscious of my actions. Staring impatiently at the screen, I waited while the timer idled for what seemed to be an eternity.

My Dexcom's reading was within normal range, but I'd woken up in a cold sweat and my heart thundering in my chest. Two hours later, and I still couldn't shake it. This cloying weight of anxiety and the irrational feeling of some impending threat were hanging over my head. Either my meter needed to be calibrated again, or I desperately needed to just chill the fuck out.

A long, calming breath filled my lungs.

I was here. And that was a step in the right direction.

My first full day back at work, and as much as I wanted to hide behind the walls of my home, I knew I needed to keep my mind occupied with all the mundane things necessary to keep me afloat.

Alone with my thoughts and the haunting what-ifs was not a good place to be.

One month.

It had been exactly four weeks since James's brutal murder. The usual petulant tears stung at the back of my eyes, and I inhaled another lungful of air as I fought to keep the horrifying images of his possible last moments at bay. A battle I often lost since it was hard not to blame myself. I was there that night—the last person to see him alive. Helplessness gripped my heart, and regret ate away at my self-worth.

Survivor's guilt was a bitch, and I was three for three.

Pulling out a small compact, I swiped at my tears and scrunched my face before dabbing the small streaks of mascara at the corners of my eyes. My teeth gleamed behind a methodically practiced smile. I'd be damned if I started blubbering in my cubicle on my first day back to work.

I was fine, I repeated to myself. *Everything would be fine.*

On the outside, I was successful. Promoted to detective six months ago. Attractive. Fit. By all appearances, I had my shit together. But inside, sometimes, I felt broken. My life plagued by loss and grief.

Maybe loneliness. I wasn't sure.

The chime of my glucose meter jarred me from my self-deprecating thoughts.

105. Stable.

Huffing out a sigh, I zipped up my kit and shoved it into the top drawer of my desk.

"Eva, this came for you." Sam's voice had me turning in my chair.

"It came here?"

He nodded, his blond curls bouncing as he handed me a business-size manila envelope.

"Doesn't have a return address. And to be honest, I was hesitant to show you without opening it first." My partner's forehead creased as he leaned an elbow on the back panel of my cubicle. "In case it's anything to do with James's case. It's your first day back, and the last thing I want is for something to upset you."

The sound of his name spoken out loud sent a chill to my heart. I bit back the waves of sadness and slipped a finger under the flap, breaking the seal and pulling out a small stack of documents.

"I appreciate the sentiment. But also, thank you for trusting my ability to handle whatever this is."

Black font jumped out against the stark white sheets of paper, and I suddenly felt the need to be alone.

"Sam, I…"

Sam held both hands up, a small smile crooking his lips. "I get it. But if you need anything from me, Eva, please let me know. You don't have to do this alone."

I assented slowly, forcing my lips to curl into a half-hearted smile. "Of course. Thank you."

He flipped his mop of hair and placed a gentle hand on my shoulder before turning to leave.

"Oh, and Sam? Please let me know if you hear anything on Rayne." He nodded. My young informant had been missing for a little over two weeks. Another person I cared about who I felt I'd let down.

"One more thing."

"Yeah?"

"For the love of God, get a haircut."

He tipped his head and laughed. "You know, my wife said the same thing. But I kind of like it." His fingers smoothed through the golden locks.

"Listen to Cat. She's a smart woman."

"I'll consider it," he said with a wink, disappearing around the corner.

I leaned over my desk, shoulders slumped. The deceitful smile

I'd perfected vanished the instant he was out of sight. And without wasting another second, I dove into the pile of papers.

Twenty minutes later, my head was reeling. Each piece of evidence was more unbelievable than the last. James had been a successful surgeon, yet he allegedly had a paper trail of dirty dealings a mile long. Shaking my head in disbelief, I leaned back in my chair and stared hollowly at the white-paneled ceiling.

It couldn't be true.

None of it added up to the man I knew and loved.

Shady business deals. Fraud. A supposed mafia hit.

I couldn't fathom his involvement in that world. I refused.

Tears streamed down my face as I mustered up the courage to keep reading.

Derek Cain. Formerly known as Derek Lyons D.O.B. 11/16/1991
Mother: Sloane M. Lyons
Father: James R. Ford

My heart dropped, breath leaving my body with an audible gasp. I read those words repeatedly, trying to make sense of what they meant.

James had a son.

I'd known him my whole life and loved him like a father. There were pictures of me in his arms just hours after my birth. As far as I knew, he couldn't have children. This had to be a joke, some sick, twisted prank by someone trying to mess with me.

Burying my face in my hands, realization hit me with the force of a freight train. If James were into corrupt business dealings with the mob, what would stop him from having an illegitimate son? Maybe there was a reason Pam left beyond what I'd always been told.

The last month had been one of the hardest of my life since my brother Frankie's death. And now, every layer I uncovered about my beloved godfather's secret life was like a fresh gash into my grieving heart.

I snatched my phone. If anyone knew about his private life and illicit affairs, it would be my dad. They'd been best friends since their residency.

My finger hovered over the call button. Exhaling, I cursed, letting the phone drop with a clang against the wooden desk. This was a conversation that needed to happen in person. Nothing he'd tell me over the phone would relieve these emotions of betrayal. And I prayed my father would be just as blindsided as I was.

I wouldn't assume a damn thing until I knew for sure.

Glancing at my watch, I pushed to my feet. There was just enough time to confront him before his shift.

The front door swung open. My dad's broad smile quickly faded as soon as he took in the sour expression on my face.

"Eva, something wrong?" he asked, ushering me inside and gesturing me into his office. I caught him scanning behind me, worried gaze darting back and forth across the front lawn and driveway. Pricks of awareness niggled up the back of my neck. Ever since I could remember, he kept watch, always cautious of his surroundings. I'd taken it as his way of being a good, protective father. But, somehow, I knew there was more.

How had it never dawned on me before?

"I'm fine," I said, with a little more sharpness than I'd intended. The lines between his eyes deepened as his dark brows drew together, studying my face.

"Eva, you're worrying me. What is it?"

"I'm going to ask you a question. Please, don't lie to me."

He opened his mouth as if to say something, but simply nodded. "You know there are no secrets between us."

I couldn't help the cynical scoff that left my lips, and he narrowed his eyes.

"Did James have a son? Does the name Derek Cain or Lyons mean anything to you?"

In my career field, knowing how to read a person's body language, nervous tells, and even the smallest of twitches was crucial to finding a crack and exploiting it for what it was. The quick rise and fall of my father's chest were subtle, but just enough to notice.

"Eva, I—" His throat bobbed as he swallowed.

"So, it's true? Unbelievable!" I threw my arms up. "You knew. You knew this whole time."

"Understand. It wasn't my secret to tell. James confided in me years ago. He swore me to secrecy, then never mentioned him again."

I pinched the bridge of my nose and exhaled a heavy breath. "And you didn't think to tell me after his death that there's a son out there, the last link to the man who was like a second father to me?" I shook my head indignantly. "Derek's his only son? How could you keep that from me?"

If I were being honest with myself, his omission hadn't come as a complete surprise. Growing up, I never questioned my father's wealth, our privileged upbringing, the lavish vacations, or elite private schools.

He was a doctor, after all.

As I grew, it became apparent our lifestyle was far above a physician's pay grade. But my father was the best man and role model in my life. Turning a blind eye was easier.

"I already told you, Eva, it wasn't my secret to tell. And where did you get this information, anyway?"

I folded my arms over my chest, ignoring his question. "Is there anything else you're keeping from me? Why was James doing business with the Russian mafia?"

My dad schooled his posture, his features hardening. "I know nothing about that."

"Bull! He was like your brother. You knew about his illegitimate son, but somehow you didn't know about his business dealings? You've been investment partners and—"

"Eva, I understand you're emotional, and you have questions about his son. But I won't allow you to accuse me of knowing James's alleged illegal activity, let alone insinuate that I took part in them."

"I didn't say that."

He cradled me by the shoulders. "Look, I have to leave for work in about twenty minutes. The last thing I want to do is argue." I looked away, still not ready to let go of my grudge. "Eva, please. Understand where I'm coming from."

"I just don't like being lied to. And I hate lies of omission just as much. We're all we have—you and me. Mom is gone… and Frankie. I have to know I can trust you."

Emotion clogged my voice, and he pulled me into a hug.

"I promise, *princesa*. No more lies or secrets."

My father's words sounded sincere, but a sinking feeling in my gut told me he still wasn't being entirely honest.

Sighing in defeat, I pushed back the doubts and insecurities and squeezed him tighter. My father was my whole world. I had to trust him.

"You didn't tell me how you came across this information."

"Someone sent it to the precinct anonymously. They had an entire file on James. Sam is running prints for me and trying to trace its origin."

A flash of something gleamed in my father's eyes, but just as quickly, it was gone.

"Eva, I don't like the sound of this. Whoever this person is, they knew to contact you. Knew your place of employment. This doesn't sit right. Should I hire private security again?"

"Absolutely not."

The thought of strangers shadowing my every move, day and night, gave me flashbacks of my college years and the whirlwind affair I'd had with the man hired to keep me safe. He'd done the opposite, shattering my trust in those meant to uphold the law. And nearly my dream of becoming an officer with it.

"Eva," he said, using his *dad* voice.

Patting the Sig at my waist, I reminded him, "I can take care of myself now. End of discussion."

He shot me a look of concern, but let the subject go.

"What will you do with this information? If the Russian Mafia is involved—"

"My job. I'm going to follow any leads that put me one step closer to James's killer. But first, I'm going to visit Derek Cain. Can you believe he's lived right here, in Philly, all this time?"

"I don't think that's a wise idea. He may be James's son, but you know nothing about the man he's become. From what I remember, after his mom died, he went into foster care and—"

"James let that happen?" I pushed away from my father, backing up into a large built-in bookshelf. "I can't believe that. And you knew? Fuck."

The man I knew was a fraud and a liar. How could he have been so heartless?

My dad put both hands on his head, fingers moving over his short gray hair.

"Eva…" he sighed. "I can't justify his actions. And I don't know what else to say, but sometimes it's wiser to leave certain things in the past where they belong. You just never know."

"I can't accept that."

He blew out a weary breath. "Okay, I'm off tomorrow. If you're free, we can meet him together. I don't like the idea of you and him alone. He's a stranger."

"Fine," I lied.

Pulling me to his chest, he dipped his head and dropped a kiss on my forehead. I looked up at him, chin resting over his heart, and forced a smile. If we didn't look so much alike, I'd have doubts about whether or not he contributed half of my DNA. At six foot two, he was nearly an entire foot taller than me. Frankie had taken after him as well. I'd taken after the mother I never got to meet.

"Or I can call in, and we can pick up breakfast. How about it?"

Staring up into his soulful brown eyes, I smiled. "I already ate."

"Of course."

Disappointment cut across his face.

"But it's a date tomorrow."

"Perfect." He smiled and pressed his lips to my forehead again before exiting the office.

Sure, I'd already eaten, but it wasn't why I'd declined my father's invitation. I had plans. As if drawn by a magnetic force, the address I'd scrawled on a sticky note burned a hole in my pocket.

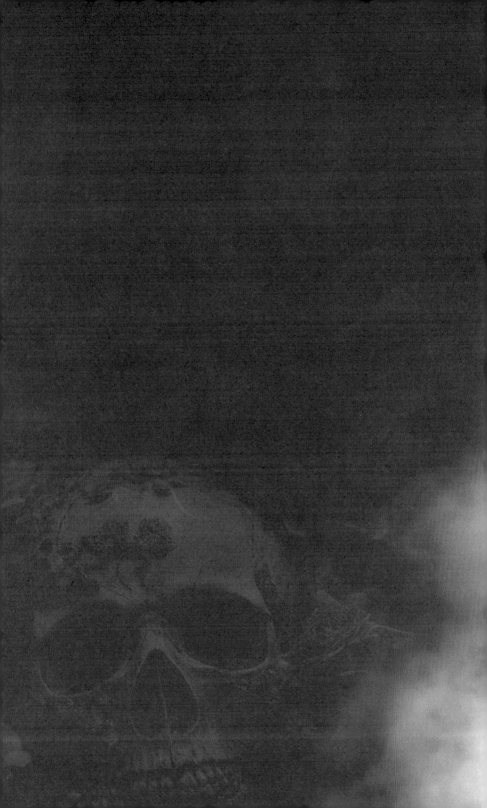

Chapter Three
Evangelina

"Eva, you crazy bitch!"

My cousin's shrill voice pierced through the speaker of my cell as I pulled into Derek Cain's curved driveway. The property was tucked away on the outskirts of Ardmore, a secluded area surrounded by a thick hedge of trees and unmarked roads. No wonder the GPS had me driving in circles before finally leading me down the right path.

I parked the car and peered at the modern home. It was a newer construction, with smooth concrete, sleek lines, and soaring floor-to-ceiling windows making up the exterior.

While there was no mention of a family in the documents I'd received, it was a massive home for just a single man. Despite his time in the system, Derek had apparently done well for himself.

"Eva! Can you hear me?"

"Yeah, I'm here. I just pulled up."

Alexa huffed a breath of relief. "Remind me again why you went there alone."

"I can't wait on my dad, Lex. I just… I have to know. I have to see him."

There was a long stretch of silence before she responded.

"I've said this before, but it's not your fault. You couldn't have prevented what happened, and I thank God every day that you didn't stick around for that. Stop blaming yourself."

She wouldn't understand. No one did. The guilt weighed heavily on my shoulders. Maybe because, deep down, I knew something had been wrong that night. But I'd shrugged it off, placated him, and ultimately left him to die alone and scared.

I would never forgive myself.

"This is his son. It's the only part of him I have left."

"What if he was the one who sent the envelope? Don't you think that's creepy as fuck?"

I rolled my eyes and leaned back on the headrest. "I'll call you as soon as I'm done. You have all the info, just in case."

"You know"—she bit into what sounded like an apple—"this is the perfect way to have some cheap D-list actor play you in one of those murder docs, right?"

A genuine smile spread across my face for the first time in weeks. If there was anyone I could count on to lighten the mood, it was Alexa. "As long as it's you, I know you'll do me justice."

Her spirited laughter followed. "Yeah, well, too bad there's no sizzling affair—oh…" Her voice trailed off, and she gasped. "Oh my God! What if he's hot? What if this is some twisted love story—"

"Bye, Lex!" I stopped her mid-sentence and cut the engine, pushing open the car door.

As I walked toward the front entrance, I stuffed the phone into my bag. My heart was beating so wildly, it felt as if the force of it was swaying me back and forth.

Several calming breaths later, I was up the steps before a slate-gray metal door, gnawing nervously on my bottom lip. Surveillance cameras outfitted nearly every corner of the property, so I was sure he knew of my presence the moment I crossed the opened gate half a mile down the winding drive.

As I lifted a finger, intending to press on the doorbell, the door tore open, and a tall, burly man with a shaved head stood beneath the threshold.

Could this be Derek?

I cleared my throat.

"Hey. I know this might sound a little crazy, but I'm looking for someone," I said as I searched for similarities between him and James. Flashing a wry grin, the man stepped forward, forcing me to inch one step back.

"Yeah? Well, I'm Kiernan, sweetheart." His leering hazel eyes roamed my body, and he cocked a brow when they settled on the gun at my waist.

Everything about this man screamed *sleazeball*. Relief rushed through me at the realization that he wasn't Derek.

"Oh, well, I'm actually looking for someone else."

His stupid grin widened. "No worries, beautiful. I can be whoever you want me to be."

And there it was. My instincts never failed.

Pursing my lips, I shifted my weight away from him. "No, thanks."

"Oh, come on. What's a pretty little thing like you doing all the way out here?" He grabbed my wrist, and my eyes dropped to the intrusive touch around the cuff of my leather jacket.

"Let go." Instinctively, I reached for the handle of my gun.

"What do you think you'll do with that, baby?"

The lust burning behind his eyes ignited a hidden part of me, the one lurking in the darkest recesses of who I was. Memories, sights, and sounds I kept tucked away threatened to resurface and pull me under. But I wasn't that scared, naive girl anymore. And I never would be again.

"Get your fucking hands off me."

The man chuckled wickedly and leaned in closer. "You wouldn't be saying that if you knew what I could do to you with these—Fuck!"

A knee to the dick had also never failed.

He doubled over, grunting and cursing. "You little bitch," he heaved. "Just wait until I—"

"Until you, what?"

A deep, velvety baritone seared me where I stood.

Lifting my gaze beyond the asshole cupping his balls on the ground, I was met with a mountain of a man.

Heat climbed up my body as I drank him in, standing against the door jamb as if he'd been carved from literal stone. With hands in the pockets of his slacks, the black dress shirt he wore pulled taut over every solid peak of his biceps and broad chest.

Jesus.

Black ink, like canvased art, dipped beneath perfectly tailored clothing and up the thick, corded muscles of his neck. But nothing drew my attention like the icy hue of his diamond eyes.

I knew I was staring, but I couldn't bring myself to look away. The ground beneath my feet somehow shifted out of place, even though I hadn't moved.

"I asked you a question, McCall," the man said, never breaking our eye contact.

"That bitch kicked me in the fucking dick! I'll—"

"If I were you, I'd choose my next words wisely."

Kiernan spat near my boots.

"Fuck you, Cain!"

Derek.

Damn you, Alexa. He was hot.

No, not just hot. Derek Cain was the unholy definition of calculated seduction.

Wetting my suddenly parched lips, I watched as he smoothed back the waves of his brown hair and cracked his neck before moving toward us. Errant thoughts of how soft those locks would feel clutched between my fingers warmed the pit of my stomach.

Our eyes remained locked, causing my pulse to thrum faster with every one of his predatory steps.

Relax, Eva.

But fuck me; I was gone, captive to the devilish grin tilting the side of his mouth.

Self-preservation instincts kicked in when Derek was just an arm's length away. And I slowly eased against a metal railing, farther from his heavy and imposing presence.

"I'm sorry, I don't think I heard you right." He dipped down to the sleazeball's level, one hand to the scruff of his neck, the other digging into a pressure point that had the man groaning and doubling over. "What were you saying?"

The officer inside me warred against the woman so utterly taken by this show of dominance, making my core flare as delicious arousal vibrated between my legs.

Derek leaned over the man's ear, his words unintelligible as he dug his thumb deeper into flesh. Kiernan let out one last strangled howl before crawling on hands and knees toward the porch steps. He stumbled to his feet as he reached the paved driveway and disappeared around the west wall of the home.

"Did he hurt you?"

My head snapped back to Derek, and the intensity in his gaze scorched every inch of my skin.

What the fuck was wrong with me?

"No," I said, shaking my head and trying to sound composed. "Is that a friend of yours? Because he's a perverted bastard."

"Kiernan will be dealt with."

The way his jaw immediately tensed led me to believe he hadn't meant to say those words out loud.

Dealt with?

"Meaning, he's no longer an employee of mine," Derek amended, as if reading my thoughts.

He stepped in my direction, and I moved away again, sliding against the banister, hand hovering over my weapon. Even though he'd come to my defense, it didn't mean I could trust him, not after what had just happened.

Derek flashed a row of white teeth and leveled me with a steely glare.

Shivers spiraled down my spine at the feral force reflected in those pools of crystalline blue.

Danger.

He moved with the air and confidence of a man who commanded authority and respect—one accustomed to always getting what he wanted—a walking red flag.

"Hey, I'm sorry about that." He held both hands up, his hard features edging toward amusement. "You're not going to kick me in the dick if I get closer, are you?"

As soon as the words left his mouth, my traitorous gaze strayed to his crotch, where gray slacks highlighted an impressive outline of what the man was working with.

Damn.

He chuckled, and I snapped my eyes to his equally striking face. Thoroughly embarrassed, a flush of heat crept up my cheeks, and I suddenly felt vulnerable against the strange storm of emotions swirling inside me.

"So, what can I do for you?"

That's when I saw it. Pieces of James staring back at me. The way he looked up through his lashes, dark brows pulling together, one hand buried inside his pocket while the other rubbed against his angled jawline. The image was a gut punch.

Maybe my father was right. I shouldn't have come here. Was I even ready for the proverbial Pandora's box I was about to open?

"I can't… I can't do this right now." I hurriedly slipped past him and leaped off the porch, skipping three steps.

"Evangelina."

His tone's sharpness and the way my name rolled so smoothly off his tongue cemented me in place.

Without turning around, I swallowed hard. "You know who I am."

Chapter Four
Derek

Evangelina's shoulders trembled, her body frozen in place when I called her name. Having underestimated her curiosity and attachment to the bastard who had once been my father, I hadn't expected her so soon.

For the last four weeks, I'd watched from a distance and got to know her routine and daily schedule while also giving her time to grieve. The last thing I needed to deal with was tears about the death of that son of a bitch.

There hadn't been much movement at her home besides the occasional food run or delivery. A young woman, who I later learned was a cousin, visited often and was sometimes accompanied by another female. Franco Cruz had been the only male to come and go from the property, which made things easier for me. Tracking down and dealing with unwanted suitors would have been an unnecessary inconvenience.

"Evangelina," I called a second time, my tone gentler.

While I wanted to get this introduction started, I couldn't help admiring the view. Her toned thighs were wrapped in tight jeans, coupled with a fitted brown leather jacket that hit just above her hips.

I'd never been more thankful for a piece of clothing as it gave me a full view of her plump little ass. And while I'd always thought there was nothing sexier than heels on a woman, preferably of the *fuck me* variety, her black combat boots were changing my mind.

She whirled around, confusion and a pinch of anger marring her features.

"How do you know my name?" Her dark eyes flared with fierceness as she demanded answers.

But the truth had no place here. And so, she'd get the story I'd spun a hundred times over in the last four weeks.

"Would you like to come inside?"

"No."

I tipped my head to the angry skies above us; its rage rivaled only by the determined figure of the woman standing in front of me. "You're sure?"

"Answer the damn question," she said, folding her arms across her chest. The movement caused the hem of her jacket to lift, revealing a badge and the handle of a Sig Sauer—a sobering reminder of our circumstances.

"When my father passed, one of his attorneys contacted me. He told me I would inherit some assets and estates."

Evangelina stepped closer, her eyes narrowed and suspicious, and I couldn't help glancing at how her sweet mouth pushed into a slight pout. Carnal thoughts of her kneeling, those red lips wrapped around my cock, had me swallowing a groan.

How James would turn in his grave at the sight of my cum sliding down his beloved goddaughter's throat.

"He left you an inheritance even though the two of you had no contact?" She put a hand over the pressure point between her eyes. "I don't know what to think. He was like a second father. Yet he never mentioned you. Never even hinted at having a son." Squaring her shoulders, she moved closer again. "None of this makes sense. How do I know you're who you say you are?"

"Look at me." We were just a foot apart now. Her head tilted up to meet my eyes, and I caught the fleeting glance she cast at my lips before looking away.

"Sure, you look like him… but—"

"Did I do something, Evangelina?" I interrupted, preying on her emotions and daring to place a gentle hand under her chin. My skin was immediately greeted with a strange electric zing, but I ignored the sensation and lifted her gaze back to mine, mindful of her quick-reacting knees. "Something to upset you?"

She remained quiet for several beats before shaking her head. "How do you know my name?"

The sultry notes in her voice fanned over me, curling around my thoughts, just as sinful as that first day.

How did I know her name?

I'd tasted her name on my tongue and burned it to memory in time with the image of her gorgeous face. Even on days when my plan faltered, when I would vacillate between leaving and never coming back, the need to see this woman, speak to her, taste her just once overtook my thoughts.

I tightened my grip on her chin.

"Your father was one of his investment partners. I just followed the paper trail, and there you were."

As if snapping out of a trance, she swatted my hand away and put a sizable distance between us.

"My *father?* Did *you* send those documents to my job? There are some serious allegations in there. How would you know those things? And where I work. Are they true? Is my father involved?"

Evangelina was oblivious to the world she'd been born into. Franco Cruz might not have had his hands in the criminal underworld the same way as his friend and colleague, Dr. Ford, but the man had a trove of secrets and a closet full of skeletons just as thick.

"No," I lied. She paced back and forth as the first rain droplets hit the ground. "Evangelina? I can answer your questions if you'd like to come inside. The sky's about to break open any minute now."

She stopped and squeezed her eyes closed before speaking.

"Can we go somewhere?" she asked, surprising me and motioning toward her car.

I gave her my most charming smile. "I know a place."

The ride to the café was quiet, only soft rain patters filling the silence. I could have offered to take my car instead of having her drive, but I wasn't ready to be without her presence just yet. Maybe Evangelina hadn't been either, as she hadn't suggested otherwise.

The silent cabin allowed me time to study her.

She drove with her right hand on the steering wheel while the other rested against the door or in her lap. Due to her height, the seat was pushed forward pretty far, and I couldn't help the small chuckle that slipped from my lips.

"What?" she asked curiously, head turning briefly in my direction.

"How tall are you?"

She rolled her eyes. "If you're trying to make a short joke, save yourself the trouble. I've heard them all. And I'll have you know, I like my height."

I put my hands up defensively. "It was just a question."

"Sure, it was."

I leaned my head back and laughed. Fuck, she was adorable.

Getting close to Evangelina was a double-edged sword. As James's only son, gaining her trust would be easy. That alone granted me access to her life. But doing so without distractions and wayward thoughts would prove to be difficult.

That was never more apparent than when I drew a deep breath, inhaling the scent long branded in my memory. It permeated every inch of the small space. Intoxicating as it was addictive. She was sandalwood and smoldering spice, with a touch of floral, maybe roses.

It was exotic.

"Five-foot-three is pretty average," she blurted out. "I get my height from my mother. And I was also a gymnast. You know how they say that rigorous training could stunt growth? But I think that's just a myth."

She kept talking, but all I could process was one word.

"A gymnast?"

Her admission brought forth a plethora of obscene images—my mind now in the goddamn gutter.

"Yeah. A long time ago."

Evangelina's gaze turned distant as if the subject was a sore one. I shouldn't care. I didn't want to. But a small part of me was undeniably intrigued. I filed it away. Maybe it was a tidbit of information that would serve to my advantage later.

"Turn in here," I instructed, pointing to our right, but with eyes solely on her.

She avoided my gaze as she eased into a parking spot. It wasn't until she cut the engine and exhaled a quick breath that she finally turned my way.

"You're staring. And you haven't really answered my question about my dad. You have all this information on my godfather, these crazy accusations. You say you found me through my father, so you must have seen something… or hopefully nothing."

I leaned forward, my elbow on the center console. Our faces were inches apart, yet Evangelina made no effort to move away. She wet her lips, and I had the strangest impulse to lick across the same path.

"I'm staring because I never thought you'd be this goddamn beautiful." The ring of chocolate brown in her eyes thinned. And a pink flush colored her cheeks and across the light dusting of freckles over the bridge of her nose. "As far as I know, your father is exactly who you think he is."

I lied again.

And indeed, not for the last time.

She placed both hands on the wheel and shook her head with a sigh of relief and a hint of a smile on her lips.

The café was bustling with people. Having been open for less than three months, the place had yet to lose its novelty. I walked closely behind Eva as we made our way to a corner booth, brushing my fingers over the small of her back as we moved through the crowd. I'd perfected my death glare over the years, and it usually took no more than one look to have people shifting uncomfortably in the other direction. Today was no different. Only now, I had Evangelina. Never one to be concerned with watching anyone else's back but mine outside of a job, this was new territory.

"Shit!" A clumsy teenager with some ridiculous drink tripped over his own damn feet and tumbled toward her. I righted him by the collar of his shirt, fisting the fabric to keep him steady. "Sorry, man. I slipped," he said with a higher pitch than he probably intended.

"Watch where you're going," I gruffed before releasing him. Eva tossed glances between us until the lanky kid took off. "What?"

"You scared him to death. He's just a kid."

"That *kid* should probably be in school right now. And if it weren't for me, you'd be covered in cream and caramel drizzle." *On second thought.* "Unless that's what you'd prefer?"

Not missing my unintentional double entendre, she looked away quickly, but not before I caught her blushing a second time. And I couldn't help grinning as I followed her toward a booth, satisfied I could affect her the way she had me.

Motioning for her to sit, I slid onto the bench on the opposite side, my back to the wall as always. In my line of work, precaution and paranoia went hand-in-hand, and letting my guard down was never an option.

"This place used to be a garage?" she asked, glancing around and effectively changing the subject. "Impressive."

"Your first time here?"

"No, I'm just pretending." My left eye twitched at her sarcasm. It could have come off as an insult from anyone else, but I couldn't deny that it had the opposite effect. Her defiance seemed to be hot-wired to my dick.

She had a fire to her. And I liked it.

"I'm sorry," she said, leaning back against the cushioned seat. "I'm still hung up on what happened back at your home, and that wasn't even your fault. You must think I'm a bitch."

"Already assured you he'd be dealt with. And I don't think that. This must be a lot to take in. I get it. I've been there." Resting my forearms on the table, hands clasped together, I pinned her with a smoky stare.

And she rewarded me with a smile.

"Yeah, it's been one hell of a month. And honestly, it's still hard to believe you're James's son. How long have you known? And where have you been all this time?"

"I've always known. He knew of me as well, but… our relationship was complicated. I was maybe six the last time I saw him, shortly after my mom died."

She looked away, all traces of her smile gone, and I realized I missed it.

"I'm sorry for what he did. For everything. The fact that he wasn't there. You were just a child and didn't deserve that, Derek."

The moment my name left her lips, something inside me shifted. Before I could register what was happening, Evangelina reached out and took one of my hands in hers. Our eyes snapped up in unison.

It was as if the air charged between us, like volts of electricity produced through the gentle brush of her fingers.

Judging by her slightly parted mouth and stunned expression, she must have felt it too.

I shook it off and tugged my hand away.

I was thinking and reacting with my dick, and I couldn't afford to let her beauty weaken me. I had to maintain control. There wasn't a woman alive capable of breaking me. And Evangelina would be no different. I'd take what I wanted from her, and she'd let me. And that's all she and I would ever be.

"You don't need to apologize on behalf of James. I made peace with his absence a long time ago."

She was still fixed on where our hands had been joined, brows pulled together, her expression suddenly solemn. "I'm sorry I didn't mean to…"

Her voice trailed off, and I reached across the table, touching her on my terms.

"Nothing to apologize for."

I flashed her a smile, thumb running against her soft skin, and her frown quickly shifted, bottom lip trapped between her teeth. I felt the urge to lean over and pull that sweet flesh from its hiding spot.

How pretty would those lips look, bruised, swollen, and mine?

"These are really something," she said, tracing the ink on my hand with the tip of her finger. A slight shiver moved up my spine as she outlined a skull with a halo of roses. "Do they mean something?"

"Yeah, they all do. But you're not here to talk about my tattoos. Ask your questions, Evangelina." Better we move away from the significance behind my ink.

"Eva. Everyone calls me Eva. Evangelina was my grandmother. "I love her, but it's just a mouthful."

"I'm not like everyone else. And it's a beautiful name. It suits you."

She smiled and shook her head, and my eyes were drawn to the soft curve of her neck. Visions of my tongue swiping along its length had my cock thickening under the table as I thought of all the ways I could bend this former gymnast.

Would she taste as good as she smells?

"Derek," she called, breaking me from my thoughts. "Is it true? What's in those documents? Was James really involved in that world?"

I sat back and threw an arm across the back of the booth. "Sometimes those we think we know turn out to be completely different people. I'm sure my mother thought the world of James Ford once upon a time—as did his wife."

Her eyes were downcast, the muscles in her jaw flexing with tension.

"You know, it's almost easier for me to believe those parts of his life, because he's always been ambitious and driven… but to believe he would abandon you. I can't fathom that."

Her admission caught me off guard. She was a cop. And I had just doubled down on the fact that her dear Uncle James was a certified piece of shit, and she was more concerned with his treatment of me.

Interesting.

"You were his only son. His heir. He always talked about being unable to have children with Pam. And he just abandons you and lets you enter the system. That's almost unforgivable."

Eva was shaking; her emotions were so raw. So close to the surface that I expected her to burst into tears. It's what females did. But instead, her eyes pulsed with anger.

She was enraged on my behalf.

My chest tightened with a strange sensation I wasn't quite sure what to do with.

"He was a flawed man—" I started, trying to sound conflicted and sympathetic.

"He was a deadbeat. And a liar."

Well, this was certainly an unexpected turn of events.

Evangelina's car came to a stop at the end of my driveway. She left the engine running and relaxed against her seat, staring vacantly out the windshield. The rain had slowed to a drizzle, and a sheen of moisture lit up her face, remnants of the short walk to the parking lot from the café.

I wondered if she had any idea how positively edible she looked, even wet with rainwater.

"You have a beautiful home," she said, eyes still fixed forward.

The sentiment came off as genuine, not made to feed egos or fill an awkward silence, as Evangelina had grown up wealthy and accustomed to luxuries. And, of course, the love of two father figures while I got fists and the ends of cords and sticks.

"Thank you."

"I'm glad," she said, finally turning to face me, "that you did so well for yourself, despite what you went through."

"There's something to be said about tragedies and how they shape the core of who we are. We either overcome or fall victim to our demons."

Evangelina's gaze darkened for the briefest of seconds before she quickly looked away.

And the game had just leveled up—one where we silently took part in who was the better liar and keeper of secrets.

Peeling back the layers of this woman would be merely half the fun. Consuming her entirely would be the ultimate prize.

"Wise words. And you certainly walk the walk." She leaned across the center console. "But I also can't help thinking how different things could have been between us."

She piqued my interest.

"In what way?"

"We could have been close." A coy smile played on the corners of her lips, and she slipped her hand into mine again. And once again, my skin broke out in tingles. "I just have that feeling. I know it sounds crazy. But we could have grown up like family."

Family?

If she knew the thoughts running through my mind where she was concerned, she would have been hard-pressed to make such a statement.

I'd never had a family outside of Kai. And possibly my mother, though I don't remember much of our time together anymore. That part of my life was nothing more than fleeting memories or perhaps dreams. But maybe her love was the anchor, the one thing that had kept me tethered to the last shred of my humanity all these years.

"No sense in dwelling on things we can't change, Eva. But now, you and I are in control."

A tendril of black hair fell across her cheek, and I had to stop myself from pushing it behind her ear. Instead, I rubbed circles over her knuckles, and her eyes dropped to our joined hands. Looking up from her lashes, she swept her thumb across the hard surface of my ring and nodded in agreement.

"This is a beautiful piece of jewelry. It's a signet ring?"

"Yeah."

She lifted my hand closer to her face, examining the words. "That means blood in Latin."

"It does."

Her eyes were on me now. "I forgot to ask. What do you do?"

It was challenging to focus on her question while her soft hand was still holding mine.

Fuck, I wanted her. I wanted to pull her onto my lap and take what was mine. But this couldn't be rushed. Though I wasn't used to patience in these matters, Evangelina wasn't like the women I kicked out of my penthouse and hotels after sex. I'd never courted anyone before, but something told me she'd be the exception.

"I'm a tactical instructor."

She released my hand and shifted back against her seat.

"You live in a million-dollar home and neighborhood and drive a damn Bentley. That doesn't seem at all suspicious."

I leaned my head against the seat and belted out a laugh. "I thought you were homicide, not FBI."

"I'm a woman of many talents."

Her words sent another jolt to my dick.

"Is that so?" I asked, all humor gone from my voice.

Eva turned to me, the bottom corner of her lip between her teeth again.

"I was talking about the job."

"Of course you were."

She scoffed and squeezed the steering wheel with both hands.

A nervous twitch.

"Eva, I'm not a felon. I own Sloane's Gun and Tactical. And my adoptive father is the CEO of Janus Security, of which I'm also CFO. My GT was a Christmas bonus."

"That was one hell of a bonus."

My face hurt from smiling so much, and I didn't know how I felt about that. "As you said, I've done quite well for myself."

"You have." Her eyes found mine again. "Derek, James was wrong for doing what he did. But you're right; the past doesn't matter. And now that I know you, I want us to be… friends. I want us to get to know each other. If that's okay."

My mouth kicked up into a wider grin. "Of course."

This was almost too easy. Eva handed me her phone.

"You can call and text me whenever." Her shoulders immediately tensed, eyes widening. Perhaps she thought she'd been too forward, yet she was utterly oblivious that she no longer had a choice. She was mine. Better she understood that sooner than later.

I reluctantly exited the car, instantly missing the smell of her perfume.

"Oh, and Evangelina," I said, leaning into the open window. "It's not average." Her eyes narrowed, not following. "Your height. It's not average."

Understanding lit up the corners of her eyes. "Again, with the short jokes, Derek?" Her tone was mirthful and light.

I shook my head. "No. It's just that absolutely *nothing* about you is average."

As she wet her lips, I couldn't help licking my own, as if anticipating a taste.

Soon enough.

She curled that pretty mouth of hers. "Bye, Derek."

Chapter Five

Evangelina

BRYN MAWR, PENNSYLVANIA

I tossed my keys into the ceramic dish by the door, my weapon beside it as I toed off my boots. Any other night I would have stashed them inside the entry table by the front door, but not tonight. I was feeling too fucking high on life to care. Despite how shitty my morning had started, my mood had drastically shifted. News of James's alleged crimes and illegitimate son had been a gut punch, but now, things felt different.

I'd never been one to get caught up on looks, but the man's sex appeal was undeniable. Having been almost a year since my last relationship, I'd never felt such a fast and deep attraction to a man. I wanted to blame Alexa for placing those thoughts in my head before I'd even had a chance to form an unbiased opinion, but I knew it was utter bullshit.

He would have made the same impact. His touch would have sent the same jolts between my thighs. And those damn eyes—I would have found myself lost in them all the same.

I gripped the edge of the kitchen counter and shook my head, a stupid smile plastered on my face. I was in trouble, and I knew it. Derek was definitely flirting, and still, I suggested we be friends, knowing damn well platonic would be a short-lived status between us. I could feel it. Feel what his touch did to my insides and my underwear.

Despite my past—or maybe in spite of it, sexual situations didn't trigger fears or trauma as long as I was in control and sex was on my terms.

My bag vibrated against the marble. I didn't need to look to know it was Lex. She'd called nonstop for the last hour. I felt terrible ignoring her calls, but I needed time to think—about Derek, the allegations against James, and what my father's involvement in all this entailed.

My screen lit up again, highlighting the twenty-five missed calls. All from Alexa.

Finally accepting number twenty-six, I set the device on my counter, far from my ear, because I knew what awaited.

"Evangelina Cruz! I could kill you. How dare you worry me like this? Even if you'd been lying dead in a ditch somewhere, I would have strung you up again!"

"Lex, relax. I'm fine," I assured her, pulling a bottle of water from my fridge. "I was never in any danger. Calm down."

There was no way I was telling her about that asshole Kiernan because I'd never hear the end of it, and I knew it would somehow mar her image of Derek. For some reason, I needed and wanted her approval.

"So you just forgot to text? Bitch. I was *this* close to calling your dad… then Quantico."

That earned a laugh. "Lex, did you forget what I do for a living? Certainly not my first time in an unknown, possibly dangerous situation. And what about Derek automatically makes him a serial killer? You're being crazy."

She blew out a puff of air. "Oh, he's Derek now? And you can't blame me. After the shit you told me James was involved in—"

"Allegedly."

"*Allegedly*. That's all I could think about. Who's to say this Derek guy isn't part of that shady world too? I just have this feeling. You know how I am."

I did. Alexa claimed to be in touch with her spiritual side and was big into astrology, auras, and the whole nine. She was constantly rearranging my chakras, or whatever the hell it was.

"I know. And I'm sorry for making you worry. But you don't have to. Derek was… he was *great*."

There was an uncomfortable silence before Alexa's whistled exhale pierced through the speaker.

"Excuse me? What the fuck was that?"

Chugging the last of my water, I crossed into the living room, her question hanging in the air. When I reached the couch, I plopped onto its soft surface while Lex huffed an exaggerated sigh, impatiently waiting for my response.

Setting the phone on my chest, I feigned innocence. "What was what?"

"That whole breathy *Derek-was-great* thing?"

I couldn't help laughing at her ridiculous imitation of my voice.

"Your imagination."

"Eva, you lying ass hoe! He's hot, isn't he?"

I groaned loudly into a decorative pillow. "Yes!"

The video call icon suddenly lit up my screen. I sat up, unable to suppress the smile etched painfully onto my face.

Lex was in her car.

"Tell me everything! How hot? On a scale of one to fuck him ten ways to Sunday."

"Eat off his abs type hot. Six foot three or four, a mountain of muscle hot."

"Oh, hell. What else?"

"Kissable lips and tattoos covering every inch of him—except his face, of course."

She snorted a laugh. "Hot. And Franco is going to die! But keep going."

"And those too-long lashes men aren't supposed to have. But his eyes, Lex. So bright blue, I swear they look like diamonds."

"And based on where he lives, he's loaded. Damn, Derek sounds like a cocky son of a bitch."

"I won't deny that he knows he's good-looking. But his confidence only enhances his sex appeal that much more. There's more to him, Lex. There's just *something* there that draws me in."

It was clear Derek's past was still very much a part of him. There was a vortex of emotions and experiences reflected in those arctic eyes. Secrets. Mystery. And maybe a little darkness.

That last thought sent a chill up my spine. My years of reading people made me aware of the edge he carried like a second skin. I wanted to delve deeper into his world, past, and everything that made him tick. I was fascinated because, despite my anger and disillusion from the information I learned, my love for James remained unchanged. And Derek was all I had left of him.

Maybe Alexa was right. Maybe meeting him was fate. Was I foolish enough to believe such a thing existed? Especially with the heartaches, trauma, and losses I'd endured?

Probably.

Lex's interrogation lasted another fifteen minutes until the end of her lunch break. She reluctantly hung up, and I remained sprawled over the couch, staring at my white, vaulted ceiling.

As the adrenaline of the day's events wound down, I felt the fog of heavy sleep on my eyelids and made a mental note to text Sam later to call off the fingerprint investigation.

I closed my eyes and exhaled a weary breath, finally coming down from the high of meeting Derek. It was easier to think with my brain now and not my lady parts.

But with rational thought came new concerns. There was one thing I was sure of: James had led a double life all these years, one where he was involved with some of our city's most ruthless criminals. It shook my core to even venture a thought into what all that entailed. How deep were the connections? How dirty were his hands? And how much did my father know? I wasn't naive enough to think that because Derek hadn't found anything, it meant his past was clean.

Maybe I was partly to blame for turning a blind eye to my father's lies and inconsistencies, but perhaps it was time I dug a little deeper. The question was, what would I do with the information if I found it?

I must have unknowingly dozed off on the couch because I was jolted awake by a loud pounding on my front door, coupled with the frantic ringing of the doorbell. Sunlight no longer poured in through the windows.

What the hell?

Adrenaline surged as I jumped to my feet and pulled up the doorbell app on my phone.

Fiery red hair shot out of the hood of a black sweatshirt, her face obscured.

Rayne.

The girl's hair was unmistakable.

My hurried footfalls nearly fell in sync with the rhythm of her wild fists on my door. I ripped it open, and the girl tumbled inside, dropping on hands and knees.

"No… no… no!" she stammered breathlessly, dragging herself across the hardwood.

"Rayne!" She took off running down the long entryway and turned a corner before I could catch up.

My voice was soft as I called out for her again, searching the dark living room for wherever she could have hidden.

At twenty-one years old, Rayne had seen and experienced more things than anyone her age should. She'd been my informant for the last four months, initially arrested for drugs and prostitution. I'd gained her trust, and she'd been a big help in capturing a notorious pimp who'd strangled and murdered five girls over the last two years.

The toes of her white, dirty combat boots stuck out from beside a sofa. Rayne had her knees pulled to her chest, arms around her calves, and her head buried between her legs. Quiet sobs shook her shoulders, and I gave her a moment, rubbing circles on her arm. I suddenly felt like shit. Having been so caught up with personal problems, I'd abandoned her. Didn't even know she was missing until this morning. I should have kept in touch and watched out for her like I'd promised.

"Hey," I whispered. "It's okay." She responded with a slow shake of her head. "Talk to me, Rayne. What's going on? Where have you been?"

The girl hesitated before slowly lifting her gaze. A small gasp escaped my lips when her bruised and bloodied face came into view. Reaching above her head, I flicked on the table lamp, my eyes growing impossibly wider at the sight of her. I gently tilted her chin.

"Who did this?"

Dried blood was smeared under her nose and at the corner of her cracked lips. The white of her right eye was blood red, and the thin ring of green in her irises blurred behind tears before spilling over. Maybe she was strung out on something, and it was the reason for her paranoia.

"Eva, t-they took me. But I got away." She grabbed my shoulders, voice panicked as her eyes darted from side to side. "But they followed me. They're coming!"

Rayne sprung to her feet and peeked through the curtains.

"Coming here? Who?"

I placed my hand on my hip as she continued to pace from window to window, my pulse quickening and thoughts racing. Who the hell had she led to my home?

"They're trying to kill me."

"Rayne, slow down. Who is? And why didn't you call the police?"

I patted my pockets, realizing I must have left my phone by the door.

Fuck.

"Eva, I'm sorry. I didn't know where else to go. But I can't go to the cops."

"Rayne, *I'm* a cop. I can't not report that I saw you and that you're possibly in trouble."

She crawled back into the corner and hugged her legs again while mumbling a string of unintelligible words. Rubbing my temples, I blew a calming breath and slowly knelt in front of her, placing my hand on her knee.

When she recoiled from my touch with a violent jerk, it seemed like a good indicator that she was high. I needed to call Sam.

"Listen, Rayne, I'm going to get my cell, and I'm going to get you help, okay? Please stay put."

She shot forward and grabbed my shoulders again, fingers digging into my skin. "No! Don't go over there, Eva. They're coming, I swear it."

This was the worst I'd seen her since that first day we dragged her half-naked, kicking and screaming out of an alley.

"I promise I'll be fine. Stay here."

Straightening myself out, I gave her one last look before heading to the front door. I must have dropped my phone when she burst through in a fury.

As I approached the dim foyer, the broad silhouette of a man appeared on the other side of the frosted glass. My breath caught, and I stared as he jiggled the doorknob.

Fuck. Fuck. Fuck.

With the alarm system deactivated, my phone lost, and the closest gun in the kitchen, I felt helpless. In the next breath, the man began kicking in my door. I sprinted down the hallway toward the kitchen, but just as I crossed the threshold, another man, this one leaner, stepped out from the mud room.

A wicked grin tipped his mouth as he approached.

"Get the fuck out."

"Shh. No need to get mouthy, sweetheart. We just want the girl."

What were the odds of two assholes calling me by that infuriating moniker on the same damn day? A fresh rush of adrenaline pushed through my veins, and I knew where this was headed. I cursed inwardly at the realization that I hadn't replaced my insulin pump as I'd intended. This ordeal needed to end before the spike I knew was coming caused any problems.

I eased forward, and he gave a throaty command, ordering my arms above my head. Doing as I was told, I lifted my hands toward the ceiling, which caused my shirt to rise about an inch above my navel. His lecherous eyes dropped to my stomach, grin spreading.

"You know, you'd make a great addition to the boss's collection. Turn around," he ordered, twirling his finger.

"Fuck you."

He cocked the gun and pointed it at my head. "I said, turn around."
I pressed my lips into a tight line, glared at him, and spun in a circle.

"Tight ass. Pretty face. Oh, yeah. You'd make a nice pet. We just gotta put that pretty little mouth of yours to better use."

I wanted to crawl out of my skin then, scream and cry, as his words with power and memories with a punch assaulted my senses. One. Two. Three breaths left my body. Techniques I'd learned in therapy when the panic threatened to take over.

The man moved closer and ordered me to kneel. Left with no other option, I complied, biding my time, waiting for him to mess up and get close enough. But it needed to happen before his accomplice became an impossible second problem.

Glass shattered in the adjacent room where I'd left Rayne, and a blood-curdling scream followed, cutting straight to my soul.

Chapter Six

Evangelina

His zipper grated in my mind like nails on a chalkboard. It took me back ten years. Cold concrete. Heavy breathing. Tight hands around my throat, cutting off my air supply. *Pain.*

Two more long sweeps of oxygen into my lungs to settle the demons slowly creeping to the surface. I clenched my fists at my sides, tempering the fury of emotions at war. He wouldn't touch me. I'd make damn sure of it.

I wrenched my eyes open at the sinister laugh in my ear and hard steel to the temple.

"Let's see what that sweet mouth can do."

I bit back bile and locked eyes with him, hoping he'd see my rage and disgust for what he intended.

The only way to help Rayne was to remain calm and gain the upper hand when the opportunity arose. She had stopped screaming, and the silence blanketing the home was terrifying.

"What's your name? We really got a two-for-one deal chasing that little bitch around town. So glad we hung back and let her lead us." He dipped down and dragged his tongue along my cheek before stroking his dick near my face. "Must be fate."

I turned my head away. "You sick bastard."

The words had barely left my mouth when a painful white light exploded behind my tightly clenched eyes. His backhanded slap cracked the side of my face, and the taste of copper spilled over my tongue.

"I'm going to have a lot of fun breaking you," he said, gripping my chin and roughly sliding a calloused thumb against the split in my lip. I swallowed the pain and reared back from his hold.

"Don't touch me." I spat blood on his shoes, and he immediately tangled a fist into my hair. My scalp stung as he tightened his grip so much it felt like he was about to tear out a chunk.

"Bitch! You know how much these cost?"

I made my move the moment he placed his gun on the counter. When my knuckles collided with his dick, he howled and doubled over. Without giving him a second of reprieve, I jumped to my feet and broke the cartilage in his nose with a swift right cross. Blood gushed from his face as he collapsed into a pathetic heap, one hand trying to plug the steady flow of red seeping from between his fingers while the other sandwiched a bruised dick.

"Stay down!" Holding him at gunpoint, my eyes shifted to the corridor that led into the living room. I listened for signs of Rayne and silently prayed she was unharmed. "Don't fucking move."

He wasn't trying to comply. I saw his intentions before he even moved and so I pistol-whipped him unconscious, and he fell face-first onto the tile.

Fuck, I needed a phone.

"Eva!" I raced through the dark at the sound of her shaky voice. When I reached her, Rayne was on her knees by a side table, a bloody shard of glass in one hand. "I-I think I killed him. I cut his throat."

My eyes widened as I followed a thick trail of blood streaking across the floor and toward the foyer. There was so much of it, I half-expected to see a body on the floor when I peered around the corner. Rayne must have severed an artery.

Shit.

Tires suddenly screeched in my driveway before angrily peeling off.

"Come on! We need to get to a phone and ensure they're gone."

She violently shook her head, trying to withdraw from my outstretched hand, but I wasn't about to leave her here again. Not when the potential threats could still be lurking somewhere in my home. I yanked her up and pulled her into an empty kitchen, where we were met with another bloody trail leading into my mud room and out the back door, but there was no perp in sight. The entryway revealed similar findings. Both men had hauled ass, but I knew they'd be back. If not them, others. We weren't safe.

"Help me find my phone. We need to get help."

"No!" She backed up into a wall, letting her body slide to the floor. "You can't. That's how they found me. A fucking dirty cop sold me out!"

I knelt in front of her, confused as hell. "Slow down. What are you talking about? Who sold you out?"

"Dmitry Belov's men knew exactly where to find me. They know I've been feeding you all information." Her voice was thick with emotion. "They told me it was some piece of shit cop. I won't go back, Eva. I won't. And if you call them, I'll leave... but then I'll probably be dead by morning."

Rubbing my hands into my hairline, I tried to digest everything she was saying. What if she was telling the truth? Had Belov paid off one of my colleagues?

I shot to my feet. "Rayne, we have to get out of here. They know you're here, and it's only a matter of time before they return."

"I already told you I won't go to the cops."

I pulled her frail frame off the floor. "Fine, but we need to go. Now. I might know someone who can help."

It was her turn to draw her brows together. "Who?" she asked as I hauled her through my kitchen.

"I'll explain on the way. Just trust me, okay?" I was careful to avoid the pools of blood as we moved through the dark house.

"Grab those keys, and get in the Audi. I'll be right out."

She hesitated for a beat before nodding and disappearing into the mudroom. For a crazy moment, the thought of going to Derek crossed my mind. But it was a lapse in judgment to appease and sway Rayne. Derek was out of the question. I wouldn't involve him. I needed to take her to the precinct, despite her refusal.

My belly wobbled at the thought of Derek, and I shook my head, disgusted with myself for feeling even slight twinges of attraction after being attacked and nearly sexually assaulted just minutes ago.

"Get it together, Eva." I packed my kit and extra supplies and rushed out the door. I'd worry about clothes and underwear later.

Rayne leaned her head against the glass of the passenger side window.

"I'm sorry," she whispered. "I should have never brought those men to your door. I just didn't know where else to go. You're the only person I trust."

I offered a faint smile. "I'm glad you came to me. I told you I'd always be there for you, and I meant it."

In my peripheral, I saw her turn toward me. "Fuck, Eva, you're hurt."

The right side of my face was still throbbing, and my lip stung like a bitch, but she didn't need to know that. "It's just a small cut. Nothing major. Plus, I punched him in the dick. And his wasn't even the first." Two bruised dicks in a day had to be a record of some sort.

I couldn't see, but I sensed she cracked a smile.

There was a brief moment of silence before she exhaled and fidgeted in her seat. It made her look every bit like that scared, emaciated girl from four years ago. While she'd come far from her life on the street, Rayne was still miles from where I thought she'd be. The way I'd hoped back when I was a naive cop who thought I could change the world just by caring. The hard truth was I couldn't save everyone. Sometimes, the demons won.

"Eva, where are we going?" I bit the inside of my mouth, afraid of her reaction to the truth. But I had to tell her. Once I reached the city, she'd know. "Eva?"

"Rayne, you have to understand. I have to report this. It's my job."

She clawed at the door handle until the door popped open. I reached out and fisted her hoodie. "What are you doing?"

"I told you I can't go to the cops. I can't believe you're selling me out too."

She yanked her arm, trying to break my grip, but I held tight, the car swaying as I fought to multitask.

"That's not what I'm doing. I'm trying to help you. Close the goddamn door."

"You're going to get me killed."

Rayne tugged harder, determined to throw herself out of my moving car rather than speak to the police.

Fuck. Fuck.

Decisions.

"Okay. All right. I'll take you somewhere else. Just, please, close the door."

I regretted the words the moment they flew out of my mouth. All the warning bells blared in my mind, knowing deep in my gut that I was making a mistake and going against everything I stood for. But what if she was right? Not only would her life be in danger, so would mine. My dad and Alexa would be defenseless if the threat came to their doorstep. But Derek... He knew his way around guns, security, and self-defense. What other choice did I have?

Was I rationalizing breaking my oath?

I knew the answer but ignored the logic. Guilt tore through me at the thought of the loved ones in my life I could have potentially saved but failed. I couldn't bear the burden of another death on my shoulders.

"Please don't lie to me, Eva. Just let me out here, and you can pretend you never saw me."

I met her watery eyes.

"We're going to see a friend. Someone who can help."

"Can we trust them?"

Trust Derek?

I rolled that question around in my thoughts, not knowing how to answer. After having spent such a short time with him, I couldn't say for sure one way or the other. But something about him, the feelings he stirred, the fire in his eyes.

Derek pushed me off balance, leaving my emotions in a tizzy. And I didn't know whether I wanted to run the other way or wrap myself around him.

No.

That was a lie. I absolutely craved to wrap myself around his hard body.

We pulled into the familiar curved driveway in front of his home. No sooner had I cut the engine, his front door swung open, a large black and brown Doberman at his side.

Of course, he saw us coming.

I put a hand over my abdomen, quieting the flock of birds threatening to take flight as Derek—now dressed in a casual, bicep-hugging, long-sleeved shirt and low-slung jeans—stepped off the front porch. Recognizing my car, a sly smile crested his lips… until I stepped out of the vehicle.

Chapter Seven
Derek

I clenched my teeth, cursing under my breath when she stepped under the glow of floodlights, and I got a good look at her face. Red marks marred her once flawless skin, purpling around the edges. The corner of her lip was swollen, dried blood staining down over the curve of her chin. It was obvious she'd left in a rush without cleaning up.

Five hours.

Only five hours since I'd last laid eyes on her.

What the fuck happened?

We stared at one another, neither blinking nor moving, until she nodded and walked toward the front of her car. I reached her in three long strides, fists tight at my sides.

"Eva," I groaned, tenderly tracing a small welt beneath her right eye.

She flinched under my touch, and another wave of fury rolled through me. I gripped her chin harder than I'd intended, forcing a small whimper from her lips. The sound elicited a flush of heat, and my hold tightened as I tempered my body's visceral reaction to her pain.

As if by instinct, my other hand wrapped around her nape, causing her to briefly close her eyes at the contact. Eva was mine. Mine to mark, wreck, and put back together as I pleased—only mine. And whoever had dared to touch her was as good as dead.

"Who did this?" I growled through my teeth, thumb pushing roughly against her lip, where a bead of fresh blood broke through the damaged skin. Evangelina hissed, sucking in a sharp breath. But before she could protest, I leaned in and swiped my tongue over the red pearl.

Her eyes widened, meeting mine with visible shock.

"Derek... what are you doing?"

I said nothing and simply put more pressure on my thumb, drawing her sweet mouth open just a bit more. Fuck, I wanted to taste her. Throw her over the hood of the car and fuck her until I replaced her pain with pleasure.

There was something to be said about how beautiful she looked under the glow of the stars. The depraved part of me wondered if her tears would gleam just as lovely when they slid down that tender skin and cried out my name.

"I'm going to ask you again. And you're going to answer—Who did this?"

"I-I don't know. They broke in and tried to..." She paused and looked away. "They were after Rayne."

"Who?"

Evangelina broke from my grasp and turned toward her car, motioning for someone in the passenger seat to step out. My eyes narrowed at an obscure figure moving behind the tinted glass. When the door popped open, as irrational as it was, I instinctively placed myself in front of Eva.

A young girl shuffled out from behind the door, shoulders slumped and a black hood over her head, partially covering the top half of her face. Her footsteps were slow and cautious as she approached. And like Evangelina, the girl's face was bruised with spatters of dried blood. However, unlike Evangelina, I didn't give a single fuck.

"What is this?" I asked with a clipped tone, turning to a much more resolute woman than the one from mere seconds ago.

"She's a friend, Derek. And I need your help." Just as I was about to object, the warmth of her hand on my forearm made me pause and listen. "I know you and me... we just met, but I don't know who else to ask."

My mind was reeling, hands buzzing, shaking with the need to spill blood and wreak havoc whenever I looked at Evangelina.

What was more maddening was that she didn't seem concerned about herself in the least. Her only focus was on the girl, which, if I were being honest, resembled more of a stray, beaten dog than a woman of twenty-one years. She was severely underweight, skittish, and withdrawn. Her gaze hadn't deviated from the floor in the half-hour since she'd sat on my sofa.

"You're asking me if she can stay here?"

"I know I've no right to ask, and you can say no, but I just need to think, maybe talk to my partner..."

The girl, Rayne, shot up and wrapped her hand around Eva's arm, holding on with what looked to be a death grip.

"You can't tell anyone, Eva. Please, they'll find me."

"I can't keep this a secret. They broke into my house and assaulted us both. These men need to be held accountable. I have to do my job."

The girl swatted Eva's arm away and pushed to her feet, pointing an accusatory finger near her face. "Fuck! You just don't get it."

My jaw ticked. She was testing my patience. Deimos stood on all fours at the commotion, causing the girl to back up and crawl back into her spot on the couch.

"Rayne, please understand."

"You're the one who doesn't hear me."

Again, she slapped at Evangelina's outstretched hand, and I leaned forward, forearms casually draped over my knee. "Stop." Both women looked my way. "*Don't* raise your voice in my home. And if you even think of lifting another hand to her, I suggest you reconsider." My tone was calm. Even. The implicit threat loud and clear behind each syllable.

Of course, my words were meant for the girl, but my gaze was centered on the only one who mattered. And just like that, Eva and I were locked in another heated stare-down.

"There's a guest room down that hall and a bathroom for you to get cleaned up. Second door on your left," I said, hoping to be rid of the girl for the time being.

Rayne didn't protest or ask a single question. She stormed past me and disappeared down said hall.

Rising to my feet, I extended my hand to Eva. "Let's get you cleaned up too." She stared at it for several moments before placing her smaller hand in mine and letting me lead her toward the main floor staircase, where she came to an abrupt stop.

"Where are we going?"

"The antiseptic and bandages are in my bathroom." That was a half-truth, as there was a first aid kit on the first floor. But what would be the fun in that?

She anxiously eyed the top of the stairs, rolling her lips inward as she seemed to mull over indecision before canting softly with her head and agreeing to follow.

"So, will you finally tell me the names of the men who did this to you?"

She sighed as we reached the second-floor landing. "I would, but I don't know. She's refusing to talk. All I know is they're from the Belov clan. You may not know who—"

"Of course, I know exactly who they are. They were mentioned in James's document, were they not?" She nodded. "Is that the reason you didn't call the cops?"

"Maybe," she whispered, averting her eyes, seemingly withholding something.

We stopped in front of my bedroom door, a slight thrill running through me at the thought of her in my space. Visions of bound wrists and ankles and her limber body bent over the foot of my bed had the seam of my zipper biting into my cock. I stifled a groan and pushed open the bedroom door, motioning for her to enter first. She took tentative steps forward until reaching the middle of the room and turned to face me.

"This is… nice. Immaculate."

A smirk pulled at the edges of my mouth. "For a single man, you mean?"

"Maybe."

The slightest hint of a smile lit up her eyes. That was the second time she'd hit me with that response.

"Come on," I said, letting her insolence slide.

Once we reached the ensuite, I pulled open a cabinet for some ointment, a towel, and gauze. Evangelina slid off her jacket and hung it on a hook before leaning against the sink. The smooth skin on her upper arm had what looked to be reddened fingerprint marks, and I suppressed the familiar waves of anger flaring in my chest because something else caught my eye. Hooking her elbow, I pulled her close, eying a small white device that adhered to the back of her arm.

"What is this?"

"It's a Dexcom. It measures my glucose levels," she said, turning in my arms. I towered over her, and she had to crane her neck to meet my eyes at such a close distance. "I'm type 1."

My thumb brushed her skin beneath the small device.

Evangelina had a chronic illness, and I suddenly felt oddly helpless, an emotion I hadn't experienced since I was a child. What was more disconcerting was that there wasn't anyone I could coerce, hurt, or kill to make her better. That thought process was unnerving, but I shoved it down into the dark place where all my errant musings and human sentiments went to die.

"How long?"

"How long since I've been a diabetic?" I nodded. "Since I was twelve." She took a step back and leaned her body against the sink again. "Crushed my Olympic dreams and my little preteen heart."

"Are you okay?" The question spilled out before I had a chance to stop myself.

She offered me a half-hearted smile. "Yeah, I am. It's been eighteen years. Pain in the ass, sure. But I can't even remember my life before my diagnosis."

I said nothing else and prepared to clean her wound, fully aware she could do it herself. But the need to touch her was a beast with a mind of its own.

Dabbing at her lip with the damp cloth, I lifted her chin, my gaze never wavering from hers. The longer we stared in silence, the more I thought about what she'd just revealed. And the more unnerved I became. I hated the way she made me feel. I hated that I felt anything at all.

"Why did you come here?"

Not expecting the harshness in my tone, she reared back and stammered.

"I told you… I-I didn't know who else—"

"No," I said, voice tight. "Why did you *really* come here? To me? You don't know me. You bring this girl to my doorstep and expect me to just take her in?"

Anger radiated from her pulsing brown eyes. With her lips in a tight line, she wrapped a hand around my wrist and pushed it away from her face. "You know what, you're right. I should have never come here."

It was hard to decipher whether she'd meant now or at all, though I felt it was the latter.

Pity.

As if she would have had a choice.

Evangelina moved past me, cheeks flaming red. Her ire was intoxicating, and I suppressed the grin fighting to the surface as she was so pissed, she'd want to cut off my dick. And I had other plans for her and that part of my anatomy.

Careful not to touch the device on her arm, I tugged her body flush to my chest.

"You haven't answered my question." My tone was softer now. "Why did you come to me, beautiful? Do I make you feel safe?"

She felt so goddamn good in my arms and against my body. Every dip and valley, that sweet, toned ass, and how I eclipsed her petite figure so wholly.

"Answer the question."

She was tense, but made no effort to wriggle free.

"It was a last-minute decision. And you have heavy surveillance. Don't flatter yourself, Cain. Like you said, I don't know you, so there would be no other reason besides convenience."

I dipped my mouth close to her ear, lips brushing the soft skin there, and whispered, "Liar."

Evangelina shuddered, goosebumps scattering across her exposed flesh.

"Derek, why are you fucking with me?" Pushing out of my arms, she backed up against the cabinet, eyes holding no fear. Just a deep curiosity. "If you want us to leave, just say so."

I slipped my hand inside my pockets and grinned. "Yeah, I would very much like your friend to be gone." Evangelina nodded and put a hand on the doorknob. "You, however, should stay."

She stilled, knuckles blanching against the brass handle. "I'm not staying."

"You said it yourself; you could be in danger. Those men could go back to your home to finish what they started. And surely, you don't expect me to babysit the girl, do you?"

Turning back around, Evangelina squared her shoulders. Despite her size, I could tell she had a fire to her. Without grit and a sharp tongue, she would have been hard-pressed to achieve her current status of local badass cop and detective.

Over the last month, I'd extensively researched her life and career, attempting to find weaknesses, scandals, or anything advantageous to use against her. My ace was her father's double life, though that minor detail would be used against the man himself at a later time.

She huffed out a humorless laugh. "I can't stay here."

"Why not?"

"I just can't. Not here, with you." Her eyes darted away from mine, and I drew closer.

"Please, elaborate." Head shaking side to side, she moved for her jacket, but I blocked her path, inching her back and trapping her against the wall, thoroughly enjoying this game of cat and mouse. "Well?"

She put a hand to my chest in either a move to push me away or because her need for contact was just as strong as mine.

"There's just something about you, Derek."

There was a guarded gleam in her eyes, her instincts singing, warning her of the monster lurking on the fringes of my being.

She had to feel it. She had to know I was death incarnate.

The ink on my body was a road map, a graveyard, and an altar to the dead.

It bore the demons of my past, born of tears and despair. And those of ghosts forged in blood and darkness.

And one day, a piece of her, too, would carve my flesh.

Chapter Eight
Evangelina

Despite the pain, I drew my lip between my teeth as warmth settled and throbbed between my legs. He knew exactly what he was doing, and his arrogance was maddening. Not even a full twenty-four hours since we'd first exchanged glances, he was already buried deep beneath my skin. Derek unsettled me in ways I couldn't quite explain. I'd always prided myself on being the woman others weren't expecting me to be. It was a survival mechanism. Yet, all it took was this man with alluring eyes, a cocky grin, and the DNA of a man I so dearly loved to weaken my defenses.

I was still trying to get over the very alarming fact that he'd licked the blood from my lips as if it were nothing. My stomach wobbled at the memory, and I suppressed the shameless part of me that couldn't help but feel turned on by the gesture.

"Can she stay or not?" I asked, gently pushing him back. He complied, and somehow, I knew he wasn't the type of man to cross those lines. Maybe I was blinded because of who he was, but while he towered over me, all brooding, brawn, and muscle, I felt safe in a strange sort of way. Protected. His anger over my state and the indifference he'd shown Rayne hadn't escaped me.

"You didn't answer the question," he said, crossing his thick arms.

"Answer mine first."

He chuckled and leaned against the vanity, looking better than a man had any right to in just a plain white shirt.

"She can stay—one night—as long as you tell me what kind of trouble she's in. And why she dragged you into her mess? But first," he said, picking up the towel from the sink, "let's finish getting you taken care of."

"Fine." The word had barely left my lips, when in one quick swoop, the air rushed out of my lungs as his large hands grasped each side of my torso, lifting me onto the marble counter.

He grabbed the antiseptic, pretending to be occupied with soaking the cloth, but I knew better. The hint of mischief playing on his lips was all the proof I needed.

It had been eight long months since I'd been with a man, so I couldn't blame my sex-deprived inner whore for the extremely naughty images of Derek tossing me around and fucking me against a wall…

I closed my eyes and purged the visions from my thoughts.

Get a hold of yourself, Eva.

"Did I hurt you?" he asked, slowing the tender strokes against my cut.

"I'm just being a baby. I can't believe that bastard slapped me. I should have been quicker, done more."

Derek's features hardened. "You were assaulted in your home. You fought for your life and won. You did enough. Things could have gone very differently."

He reached for the small bandage, but I held his wrist, silently urging his eyes to mine. Our soft breaths were the only sounds surrounding us.

"Thank you for doing this. And to answer your question, coming here… just felt right."

The words came out before I could stop them, and Derek's cocky grin did nothing for the fire heating my face.

"And yet you don't want to stay." Without a chance to respond, his thumb was on my chin, softly stroking the skin there. "That should heal up fine without a bandage." His voice grew hoarse, eyes focused on my mouth. "As long as you stop doing that."

"Stop… doing what?" I asked, a bit too breathy for my pride.

He pulled down on my mouth, releasing my bottom lip from between my teeth where I'd unconsciously trapped it a second time.

"Now, tell me about the girl."

Pain spread through every muscle in my body as I stumbled into my father's kitchen. The automatic coffee drip had just finished brewing a fresh pot, and I felt like I couldn't reach it fast enough.

As I sat at the breakfast bar, the hot liquid sliding down my throat, I waited for my father's footsteps. It was late when I'd gotten to his door last night. Assuming he'd already gone to bed, I hadn't bothered waking him. Since moving out, it wasn't the first time I'd slept in my childhood room. I had a key and sometimes needed his company after a tough shift.

Yet the house was eerily quiet, his bedroom empty. The bed was still undone as if he'd leaped out in a rush. Sure, it was strange since my father was a creature of habit and obsessed with order. But maybe he'd been running late.

Once the aroma of coffee hit, I expected to find him in the kitchen. Again, I was met with his absence.

I tightened my grip around the mug as the pace of my heart

quickened. What if those men had come after my father too?

Bed undone.

Left in a rush.

"No, no, no."

I jumped to my feet, ignoring the slight twinges of pain from my bruises, and raced toward the front door. To my horror, there were droplets of blood on the floor of the foyer, smeared on the doorknob, and dried streaks on the door. It had been too dark, and I had been too tired last night to notice.

"Daddy, no."

The front door swung open just as my heart plummeted to my feet. My dad strolled in, cell phone sandwiched between his ear and shoulder and a black duffel bag in each hand. I nearly collapsed to my knees with relief.

"Eva's here. I'll talk to you later." He slid the phone into the front pocket of his jacket, looking at me with knitted brows and a deep crease between his eyes. "Eva? What the hell happened to you?"

I rushed him, squeezing him tightly.

"I'm fine. But you—I saw the blood. And you weren't here. I didn't know what to think." My voice was waterlogged as I sniveled into his shoulder as if I was a scared kid again, seeking comfort after a nightmare.

The thought of something happening to him was a terrifying one. I wouldn't survive it. Not him too.

"Hey, I'm perfectly fine." He lifted my chin, getting a better look at my battle scars. "But you—Eva, what happened?"

"Perks of the job," I lied. He didn't know I'd left work to visit Derek, and for the next twenty minutes, I let him be a dad and lecture me on the importance of keeping up with self-defense classes, being alert, and looking both ways before crossing the street and all that.

"Enough about me. You weren't home. You left your bed unmade, and you never do that. And what's with the blood? I imagined the worst."

He flashed me a sympathetic smile. "Let's sit down, and I'll explain over coffee."

I let him guide me back into the kitchen, arms still wound around his torso, not trusting myself to not fall into a heap at his feet. My heart still hadn't recovered from the scare.

"I got called into work late last night. One of the on-call physicians couldn't make it, and there was also a staff shortage. I had no idea you'd be coming by, or else I would have given you a heads up."

"Why were you bleeding?"

He held up a bandaged hand I hadn't noticed.

"Bumped into the table by the door on my way out and broke that glass vase you loved so much. The shards broke my fall, of course. But a couple of stitches later, I'm good as new."

I palmed the pressure point between my eyes, trying to push back the headache slowly creeping to the forefront.

"*Papi*, you scared the shit out of me, especially after..."

I couldn't tell him about Rayne and the men from last night.

"Especially after what?"

I sat up straight and locked eyes with my father.

"I met Derek Cain yesterday."

He blinked several times. "You went to see him? By yourself?" I nodded. "Eva, I thought we discussed this. We agreed you wouldn't go alone—Wait, you went to his home?"

"I did."

He threw his arms up and got to his feet. "That was very reckless of you."

Rolling my eyes, I followed him as he shuffled toward the fridge.

"Was it? You don't even know him."

"Neither did you. Hell, you still don't."

"Dad, you forget what I do for a living." That phrase was the broken record of my life.

My father ran a rough hand through his hair, exhaling a deep, frustrated breath.

"You have a partner, Eva. Protocols. You don't just go solo into unknown situations, so don't give me that."

"Dad." I needed to take a seat, my head throbbing even harder. "I'm fine. Derek is…" I hesitated a little too long, trying to find the words to describe the man occupying my every waking thought since I'd met him.

Dad's dark eyes narrowed. "He's *what?*"

"He's great. You should meet him. You have to. He's James's son."

His severe expression softened. "Of course. Look, I trust your judgment. And if you say he's good, then I'm looking forward to meeting him."

It felt good to smile for the first time that morning. The idea of Derek and my dad getting to know each other filled me with an inexplicable fluttering in the pit of my stomach.

"Does he look like James?" he asked, putting an arm around my shoulders.

"Sometimes, when he smiles. And in his eyes." Unexpected tears gathered in my lashes. "It's surreal."

He squeezed me tighter and kissed my temple. "Tell me about him."

I wiped my eyes and nodded. "Okay, give me a few minutes, and I'll meet you in the dining room. I have to grab my kit."

My dad pressed another kiss to the side of my head before heading out of the kitchen.

While I knew there were specific details I'd omit when it came to Derek, I couldn't wait to discuss him with my father. Just as with Alexa, I wanted him to cozy up to the idea of Derek being in our lives. In what capacity, I wasn't sure. Or maybe refused to explore at the moment.

But first, I knew what my growing headache and the parched feeling creeping up my throat meant.

Chapter Nine

Derek

"Twenty minutes late."

Ronan leaned back against the black leather chair, hands clasped over his desk and a smirk cresting the edges of his mouth.

"Something came up."

"Something *came up*?" he repeated, tilting his head in feigned curiosity.

While it sounded like a shit excuse, it was anything but. That girl Eva dragged into my house had barricaded herself in my pantry, of all places. Claimed Deimos was trying to eat her. He very well could have been. And probably should have put her out of her misery.

I rolled my eyes, remembering how ridiculous she'd sounded. It took nearly half an hour to coax the little bitch out without having to tear down the door… or resort to more aggressive tactics. The thought had certainly crossed my mind. But what impression would it have made on Evangelina if I'd gutted her friend in my kitchen?

"This something wouldn't have anything to do with that woman who visited you yesterday, would it?"

My head snapped up in attention, and I narrowed my eyes but

didn't speak, letting him reveal what he knew first. Ronan chuckled a seedy laugh and cocked a brow, playing the same game of chicken.

The only way he'd know about Evangelina would have been through Kiernan—that sack of shit. I'd been so preoccupied with both women that he'd slipped my radar. I didn't like that feeling. It wasn't like me to forget, to not follow through on teaching a lesson when one was warranted.

"So, by your silence, I can only deduce Kiernan was telling the truth, after all."

I returned the fake smile and sat, leaning back and resting an ankle over my knee.

"I wasn't aware having a woman over was against the rules, *Father.*"

His smile wavered for a fraction of a second before sliding back into place. He knew I never called him anything besides Ronan— unless, of course, I was fucking with him. But I didn't give a damn. I decided I didn't like the insinuation in his voice at the mention of Evangelina.

"She was wearing a badge, Derek. And from what he tells me, you were pretty defensive of this woman, were you not?" He paused, again waiting for an explanation I had no intention of giving. "Who is she?"

"You've never cared about the women in my bed; why the interest now?"

He rubbed the graying stubble on his chin and laughed, though his green eyes never left mine, as though meticulously studying every reaction.

"Because if she were just some random whore, you would have said that, and we'd move on from this tedious conversation." Ronan lit a cigar and sat back, motioning toward me with an accusatory glare. "But now you've piqued my interest. And you know there isn't anything I don't know or can't find out."

Clamping down on my teeth, I idly toyed with the signet on my finger, eyes zeroed in on the parchment in front of him.

Our relationship was far from that of father and son. Adopted at fourteen, I'd long forgotten how to form bonds and attachments. He was just another body forced into my hellish life by means beyond my control. Kai and I had made plans to run. We knew how the system worked and what awaited us. Young as we were but streetwise beyond our years, we knew damn well a wealthy man would only take an interest in teenage boys for nefarious reasons.

Interestingly enough, we weren't wrong. But those reasons were far from what we could have imagined. Ronan hadn't just adopted us.

We'd been fucking recruited.

Through the years, he fed the demons he'd seen reflected in our eyes and turned us into depraved monsters with no moral compass. We'd been bred to kill, the fiery tendrils of hell shackling our souls, keeping us chained and bound to this existence and the next.

I knew it was only a matter of time, but I'd take Ronan with me.

Reaching over his desk, I poured myself a glass of scotch, and the usual reel of horrors played through my mind as they seldom did in his presence. One day, just like James, he'd feel the heat of my blade shear through his fucking heart and tear it from his chest. And that was a goddamn promise.

"She's not important," I said, the words surprisingly bitter on my tongue.

"Oh, I know she's not."

Ronan's scrutinizing glare speared through me from behind a haze of smoke. And I briefly toyed with the idea of shoving the goddamn cigar through one of his eye sockets. How loud would he scream until it seared all the way through?

While he had been the man to lift me from despair, to pull me from the clutches of abuse and desolation, he was the worst devil of them all.

His gesture wasn't selfless. The motive clear. He needed Kai and me.

Two unlovable, broken bastards to fulfill a sole purpose. His methods brutal and unhinged.

I was thrown into a world where an oath of blood was the currency of death. A debt collected by entities so obscure, so deeply entrenched into the underworld of the global population that few men had ever been in their presence, let alone knew of their existence. The Six, coined after the original ancient Greek Pantheon, were the ultimate puppeteers of society. The black robes behind the scenes, ruling the masses, doling out punishments—Playing God.

Even Ronan, as powerful as his hand was, was merely another player in the game of stolen souls.

"Your silence speaks volumes. But I know you. Get her out of your system. Fuck that whore, if you must. But be done with her, and get your head back in the game."

He dropped the envelope directly in front of me and pulled an engraved blade from the drawer, running the steel through the flame of a candle. He motioned for my hand, and I obliged, offering my palm as I'd always done. Our eyes locked as he brought the knife to my flesh, piercing the skin. Only this time, the cut was deeper than necessary. I clenched my jaw, pain biting across the wound, but I'd be damned before giving him the reaction he was seeking.

A punishment. This was personal.

But why?

Blood trickled from my now-closed fist onto a metal spoon full of crimson wax pellets. Ronan gripped my wrist with more pressure, pulling me close to his face. "Lies are dangerous, son. Tread carefully."

If there was one thing I knew about the man, he never made an empty threat. And he seemed far too aware, too curious of Evangelina, despite not knowing her identity. Or had he somehow found out? Did he know her ties to Franco?

"If you have something to say, say it," I countered, tugging my hand from his and wrapping it with a handkerchief.

"I suggest getting that taken care of by the good doctor." Again, he held out a hand, and I dropped my ring into the middle of his palm as I attempted to decipher the meaning behind his suggestion. "Though you probably want to give him a few hours. Heard he had a late call last night," he added, lifting his amused gaze and gauging my expression.

Oh, he fucking knew.

"Did he now?"

"Two Russian bastards. One didn't make it."

I narrowed my eyes. "How do you know this?"

He chuckled as he held a metal spoon over the flame. "Kiernan was nursing a possible torsion in his balls, courtesy of your lady friend. You can imagine how much a Bratva asshole will talk with too much happy juice in his system. And what a *small* world. The good doctor received a call while icing a sore dick, and would you know, his lock screen is of a picture of his daughter." He peered at me again, enjoying this charade far too much for my liking. "Imagine poor Kiernan's surprise when he sees the face of the woman who nearly castrated him."

A myriad of emotions passed through me at once. One way or another, Ronan would fuck this up for me, and I wasn't ready to let go of Evangelina just yet.

"Small world indeed."

"As I said, Derek, get your fill of this girl and move on. She's too close. And it will only end badly for her. Then we'd have to contend with Franco. You know the drill."

I did. Civilians and law enforcement who gained knowledge of The Six and the factions they controlled ultimately become names on a contract.

Ronan glanced up once more as he poured the melted wax to the bottom of the parchment, sealing the hit with my signet ring.

"I must say, Evangelina Cruz is an exceptional beauty; I'll give you that. I can understand your—attachment." The wistful tone of his voice set off alarm bells in my mind. And her name on his tongue had my knuckles blanching in a fist. But I said nothing. I'd give him nothing.

With eyes transfixed on the crest branded into the cooling red seal, I became lost in my head and absently read the engraved words like I'd done so many times.

Scrawled across the bottom, below the mark of Ares, were the chains binding my soul to this life until death.

Ligatus Saguine.

Bound by blood.

Chapter Ten

Derek

As I pulled into my driveway, I spotted Evangelina's car as it stopped in front of the steps of my home. She climbed out and turned toward my vehicle, her eyes watching with vested interest as I pushed the door closed and moved toward her.

Eva looked fucking edible. Her long, raven hair tumbled over her shoulders like silk. She was dressed in all black, from her boots and body-hugging leggings to a perfectly tailored pea coat—as if we'd planned to coordinate.

"Where is she?"

There was slight panic in her tone, breaking my perusal of her delectable little figure. She was asking for the girl, and it was all I could do not to roll my eyes.

"Who?" I asked, goading her and reveling in the glacial stare now burning a hole in my face. There was something sexy and primal about that fire that made the specks of gold in her irises pulsate.

"Don't play with me, Derek. Where's Rayne?" She searched beyond me, looking for her in the passenger seat of my car.

"Relax. She's inside. I left her with my brother," I said, waving her off and pulling my phone from the side pocket of my jacket. "He'd let me know if—*fuck.*"

Evangelina's eyes widened as she waited for an explanation. "Fuck? What does that mean? Did something happen?"

"She's gone."

Eva lunged at me, her small hands gripping my lapels. "What the hell do you mean she's gone?"

I held her wrists, aware of nothing else but her closeness, eyes fixed on her lips as I noticed the wound at the corner of her mouth was already looking better. I suddenly felt the urge to nibble, maybe to test just how much.

"Kai said she left a note."

Breaking my hold, she pulled back. "You said you'd watch her. Where the hell did you go? Why did you leave? And who the *fuck* is Kai?"

I stepped around her and made my way to the entrance. As expected, she was hot on my heels.

"Derek!"

Ignoring her pleas, I punched in the code to my door and motioned for her to enter. Evangelina shot me a disdainful look before stepping through the threshold.

Deimos was waiting. Normally suspicious around strangers, he whimpered excitedly, waiting for my command to allow his approach. Once it was given, and surprising me once more, he nuzzled against Eva's hip, licking the hand she extended in his direction before even greeting me.

"Where's your brother? Wait, since when do you have a brother?"

"Come on," I said, leading her to the corridor where Rayne had been staying. I bent over slightly and scratched the back of Deimos's ear. "Traitor. Though I don't blame you."

The door to the guest room was cracked open. Pushing it the rest of the way, I spotted the note atop a white comforter. Eva dashed past me to retrieve the partially folded piece of paper and immediately began reading.

After several moments, she let the sheet slip from her fingers and onto the floor.

"She's gone. Told me not to look for her. I can't believe she took off like this. What was the point of even coming to me?" She crossed her arms. "I'm so stupid," she grumbled with a sigh.

I sat beside her, our shoulders touching. "Let me get this straight. She's the one with the hit out on her head and runs away, putting herself in danger with nowhere to go. Yet you're the stupid one? Care to explain."

Cuffing a lock of hair behind her ear, she sighed another soft breath. "That's not what I meant." Her glassy eyes found my curious ones. "I found Rayne about four years ago. She'd just dropped out of high school, was a runaway, and an addict. The night I arrested her, she had beaten her john with a beer bottle for shorting her. I always wished I could do more for her. Lord knows I tried. She was just one of those faces, those stories that stick with you when you're a cop."

Evangelina wiped the tears trickling from her lashes. I'd been right. The stream of droplets, coupled with the light pink flush across the bridge of her nose, gave her beautiful face an angelic glow.

Angel.

Like her name.

"It's not your responsibility to save her from herself."

"Wouldn't be the first time." She released a humorless laugh. "It's kind of a pattern in my life."

"Evangelina, I'm sure you've helped more people than not."

Her eyes were back on me. And I suddenly wished I could read her thoughts. Could she see the darkness that lived and breathed beneath my painted flesh? Or worse yet, did she only see that frail boy abandoned so many years ago? Would she want to save me too?

Little did she know, there existed no redemption for men like me. Perhaps one day, I would atone for the chaos and bloodshed I'd left behind. But by that time, Evangelina would be just a memory of the past.

"I've never been able to save those I truly care for."

Her voice jarred me back to the moment, and I blinked furiously, processing her words. She couldn't possibly be referring to that son of a bitch, James. The only thing he'd done right was maintain my cover. Otherwise, I would have been forced to dispose of Eva as well, which would have been a goddamn tragedy.

As a response formed in my throat, she took my wrapped hand in hers, noticing the handkerchief for the first time. I'd never needed so much as a bandage to cast my oath, but that asshole Ronan had tried to prove a point.

"What happened to your hand?"

"Deimos gave your friend quite the scare this morning. Ran her into the kitchen and knocked over some plates. It's just a small cut."

Eva turned my hand over where the blood had soaked through the beige fabric.

"And instead of a bandage, you decided that this handkerchief would do? God, you're such a guy." She pushed to her feet and pulled me to follow. "Come on."

"What are you doing?"

"You took care of me yesterday; let me return the favor."

An unfamiliar flutter tickled the inside of my chest as I let her lead me down the hall of my own home. Once we reached the staircase, her intention was to head up to my room like we'd done the night before, but instead, I squeezed her hand and motioned for her to follow me into the kitchen.

She wore a puzzled look until I pulled a first aid kit from the cabinet below the sink.

"I keep this here for my cleaning lady. She cut herself on broken glass once. And I'd rather her take care of things than bleed all over my damn floor."

Eva flashed an amused smile and shook her head as she pulled out a bandage and gauze. "So, was this here last night?"

"Maybe."

"Maybe," she repeated, rolling her lips and hopping onto the barstool, tugging my hand over her lap.

The heat rising from the clothed skin of her thigh scorched the back of my hand, and my imagination drifted to a much darker place.

"Hold still," she said, unwrapping the stained handkerchief while utterly oblivious to her role in my scandalous musings.

Or was she?

The slight tremble of her fingers said otherwise.

"Hurts a little, that's all," I lied, shifting in my seat.

"You don't strike me as someone who flinches from a small hand wound, Derek."

"I'm not."

"Good, because this is going to sting." She tore open a small alcohol pad and pressed it to my skin. "You forgot the antiseptic in your kit here."

Eva's eyes centered on mine as she waited for my reaction, yet the pang was so insignificant it barely registered. I'd be convinced she was enjoying this if I didn't know better. My free hand fell over hers, pushing down and forcing the soaked gauze deeper into broken skin; pain and pleasure coalescing deliciously into one.

"Do you feel that?" she whispered.

We both knew she wasn't talking about the sting of the alcohol. It was how the air crackled between us, electric, drawing us together like two magnetic forces destined to collide.

"I feel everything, Eva. Your hand shaking beneath mine." She averted her gaze. "The heat of your skin," I said, tilting her chin with my finger as I inched closer to her lips.

"I think the pain is making you delirious."

Chuckling against the soft skin of her cheek, I ran the tip of my nose across a dimple, and again, her breath caught. "You could be right… or maybe it's just you."

"Sometimes I have that effect on people," she murmured, pulling away slowly.

Eva was flirting.

"Is that right? Conceited much, Miss Cruz?"

"I could never compete with your ego."

Laughter erupted from deep in my chest, and I suddenly couldn't remember the last time I'd laughed so freely. Even Evangelina's shoulders shook with genuine amusement, a broad smile lighting up her beautiful face.

This was—new.

"Hey," I said, my tone earnest, "your friend, do you have any idea where she could have gone?"

When her features soured into a frown, I immediately regretted bringing up the subject again. With my hand still in her lap, fingers caressing the bandage, she sighed and leaned back into the stool.

"Maybe. I'm not sure. I have a feeling she's not trying to stick around. She seemed terrified."

"As she should be. The Belov family has a reputation for a reason. If they want your friend dead, I'm afraid that will be the likely outcome."

A grave expression moved across her face. "I guess I'm on their hit list now too."

"Bullshit." Her eyes snapped up to meet mine, surprised at my sudden outburst. "No one touches you, Eva."

"They were in my house. Probably know my name..."

My hand flew to the side of her neck, and I pulled her face close. "*No one* touches you. Do you understand?"

Seconds ticked by before she spoke again; the quickened rise and fall of her chest was a telltale sign she was taken aback by my bold declaration. But she needed to know who she belonged to. And no one touched what was mine.

"Say it, angel. I need you to trust me."

Her eyes roved back and forth, searching for an explanation behind my words.

"Okay," she breathed, eyelids fluttering. "For some strange reason, I do."

As I leaned in close to the crest of her ear, the sweet scent of her hair blowing beneath my nose, I whispered, "Good girl."

Evangelina stiffened beneath my touch, a small gasp falling from her lips. Grinning, I pulled away, thoroughly satisfied with her reaction.

"Eva, what are you doing today?" I asked, giving her an out.

"I-I called off work so I can sort things with Rayne, but now that she's no longer here—"

"We'll find her. I'll help you."

I didn't give a single fuck about the girl. She was as good as dead, as far as I was concerned. But this Rayne kid was important to Eva. And for some reason, that mattered to me. I rationalized that the more I won her over, the easier it would be to make her fall.

"Really?"

"I feel a little guilty. She fled under what was supposed to be my watch. Just think of some places she frequents, and I'll take you."

Another beaming smile stretched across her face.

"Sounds like a plan. What about you? I don't want to inconvenience you."

"I'm my own boss." She nodded, content with my answer. "Give me about thirty."

I slipped my hand from hers, but she caught the tips of my fingers at the last second, tugging me back toward her.

"Derek, thank you. For everything."

She scooted forward to the edge of the stool, slowly dropping to the ground, her body pressed against mine, knowing well enough what she was doing to me.

Sporting a goddamn semi, I let her move around me, ignoring the visuals of taking her over the kitchen counter.

Self-restraint was a bitch.

Chapter Eleven
Evangelina

Derek backed into a parking spot across from the Esther C. Transitional Living Center. The small, red brick building sat on the corner of a shady neighborhood, bordered by other run-down homes and businesses. Derek's sleek black Bentley stuck out like a sore thumb and garnered looks from pedestrians, including a group of men hanging out in front of a bodega just off the corner.

"Maybe you should stay here while I run inside. Those guys seem very interested in your car."

"Not happening," he deadpanned, scrolling through messages on his phone, completely unbothered by my observation. He didn't so much as lift his gaze.

"Don't say I didn't warn you when you come out and find four cinder blocks instead of tires."

"You're not going in there alone. End of discussion."

I scoffed. "You do know I'm a cop, right? I've been in worse situations."

He shifted in his seat, locking his unwavering gaze with mine. "I don't give a fuck about those guys or this car. Number one. And two, whatever you do when I'm not around is one thing, but when you're with me, I'm not going to sit by like some pussy while you risk your safety."

Anger flared red-hot in my chest. I'd been underestimated and treated like a breakable damsel my whole life. Always the youngest and smallest in every friend group. Then came my diagnosis. And lastly, my looks. I wasn't naive enough to think being pretty didn't change people's perspective or how they treated me. Working in a field dominated by men reminded me of that every damn day. For whatever reason, Derek's perception of me mattered more than I'd like to admit.

"Eva."

The aggravation I'd felt evaporated the instant my name fell so sweetly from his lips. I didn't know what it was about Derek that obliterated my resolve. Sure, he was nice to look at. But a man's looks had never mattered too much to me. Maybe it was because he was James's son.

My swooning over his protectiveness might set women back fifty years, but I couldn't bring myself to care. It was endearing. He barely knew me, yet he seemed to care far more than he should.

"Fine," I said, trying to sound like I had a choice in the matter.

I'd barely stepped out of the car before the catcalling began. Avoiding eye contact, I rounded the hood, where I met Derek. Never one to feel safer with a man, being in his presence was something entirely different. The group behind me quickly hushed as Derek flashed them a murderous glare, his eyes equal parts ice and scorching fire.

"Come on," he said, tucking me securely under his arm while never taking his eyes off the men, even as we crossed the busy street. His hard body was tensed, like a tightly coiled spring, ready to unfurl at any moment. I wasn't sure what he'd do if the opportunity presented itself, but he seemed confident enough that his stare-down hadn't faltered. Maybe he wasn't aware, but in this neighborhood, staring was the equivalent of challenging someone to a fight.

"Are you trying to get shot?"

"That's not going to happen."

I rolled my eyes. "Oh, so you're bulletproof now?"

"No. I don't need to be. Let's just say I know people."

I'd heard a similar saying, which was always the punchline to some joke. But in Derek's case, I had no doubt he really did know people. Powerful people. It had to be why he was so knowledgeable about the Belov family. Why he trusted his car would remain untouched in a sketchy neighborhood. And why he was unafraid to stare daggers at a group of even shadier men. The thought was a sobering one as I realized I knew nothing of the man my godfather's son had become.

"What's wrong?" His brows furrowed as he pulled open the rickety iron door to the Esther house.

"Nothing. I just hope we get some answers. Maybe she came back here for her stuff."

Derek flashed me a dubious look, but said nothing. Placing his hand on the small of my back, he ushered me inside.

The musty smell of the building was unforgettable. I'd wanted to find a better place for Rayne, but her friend Tori was here, and she insisted on staying. Once I saw how well she was doing, staying clean and off the streets, I felt better about her decision, but clearly, I was fooling myself. Rayne had more demons and vices than I could have ever helped her with.

"What the hell do you want?" The hoarse voice of a woman pulled our attention to the small corridor just before a flight of stairs. Her haggard face, set against shaggy graying hair, looked familiar. Perhaps

I'd seen her during one of my visits, but I couldn't be sure.

"Hi. Have you, by any chance, seen Rayne Johnson?" I took a step forward, though keeping my distance.

The woman eyed me with staunch indignation and folded her arms over her ample chest. "Who's asking?"

"I'm a friend. I need to speak with her. Has she been here recently? Like, in the last four hours?"

She blew a frizzy curl off her forehead and rolled her eyes. "You think you can just waltz in here and get information on our residents? How do I know you're not a cop?" Her dark eyes flicked behind me, where Derek stood in silence, like a sentinel at my back. The woman took a shaky step, bracing herself against the rusty banister.

I felt the heat of him as he moved closer. While I couldn't see him, I could only imagine the feral glower searing a hole through the woman's face.

"Please, if you know anything. I'm trying to help her."

"Eva?"

A soft voice shifted my attention to the top of the staircase.

Tori.

"I-I met up with her," she stammered nervously. "This morning. Rayne called me."

The older lady whipped around; her face pinched into a scowl. "You really gonna rat out your friend? You don't even know this bitch! For all we know—"

"Enough." Derek's voice was calm, yet as sharp as a razor's edge. "Apologize." He moved past me, now face to face with the woman, who was trying desperately to squirm backward, but had run out of room. "Apologize," he demanded a second time.

"W-what?" Her hand clutched onto the railing.

"You're going to apologize for your disrespect. And I won't ask again."

Her eyes ping-ponged between us before she blurted a barely intelligible apology.

Derek placed a hand on the wall above her head, towering over her. Deep down, I knew I should have stopped him. Intimidating people was not how I operated, but damn it, if his defending my honor wasn't sexy as hell.

"Walk away. And if you so much as look her way, breathe in her direction…." He leaned in close to her ear and whispered something I couldn't hear. Whatever he said caused the woman's eyes to widen in shock, and she quickly stumbled past us and out the door.

Derek and I shared a look, and he shrugged his shoulders almost innocently, as if he hadn't just scared the shit out of a stranger.

I'd deal with him later.

"Tori, where did you meet? What did she say?"

The young girl reached the bottom of the stairs and hung her head, long braids falling over her shoulders.

"She was scared and didn't want to come here. So we met at Clover Market."

It would make sense she'd want to meet at a public venue, somewhere she could quickly disappear into a crowd should the need arise. Smart girl.

"Did she say where she was going?"

"She said it was safer not to know details."

"Fuck," I cursed, running a hand over my face.

"Eva." She lowered her voice to a whisper. "Rayne said if you were smart, you'd get out of town before Yuri gets you too. I think she owed that guy money and some favors. But that's all I know."

I put a hand on her shoulder and offered a small smile. "Thank you, Tori. Call me if you learn anything else."

She nodded and glanced briefly at Derek before bolting back up the stairs.

"Let's get out of here." He threaded his fingers through mine and pulled me toward the exit.

The same group of men watched in silence as we crossed the street. He followed me and opened my door to his untouched Bentley before sliding into the driver's side.

"Where to?"

"The market."

"Eva, it's been hours. I doubt she's still there."

I rested my head on the seat and turned to face him. "I know that. But she's close with Carmen, one of the vendors. She must have gone to say her goodbyes. Maybe slipped her some information."

He tipped his chin and pulled into traffic without saying a word.

"What did you say to her?" I asked, breaking the silence.

"Say to who?"

I huffed an exasperated sigh. "Derek, don't play dumb with me. You know exactly what I'm talking about."

His grin was so fucking sexy. I almost wanted to slap it off his face for making me feel this way. Giddy, like a damn teenager. And horny. So incredibly horny.

"You were there. You heard everything I had to say."

"So you didn't threaten her with violence? She just ran off for no reason."

He turned to me as we came to a stop at a red light. While he had a smile on his face, there was something almost sinister in how his eyes burned through me, making the hairs on the back of my neck stand up.

"I won't tolerate anyone disrespecting you. I don't care who they are. And Evangelina," he rasped, reaching over and tipping my chin, thumb caressing the side of my jaw, "I don't make threats."

Instinctively, I knew the conclusion to that statement.

Promises.

He made promises.

A chill raced through my body. Derek was a dangerous man. He exuded authority and walked with a fearlessness I'd never seen in even the bravest men and women I'd worked with throughout the years. It was like he knew he was untouchable. But why? What did it mean? And, more importantly, why did I want to look the other way?

Guilt settled in my stomach as I shamelessly waved off the red flags flashing like neon lights in front of my face. I knew I should ask questions. But I didn't push the subject any further. And let the quiet fill the suddenly awkward void between us.

I watched the city roll by as we drove, now and then stealing glances at the man sitting beside me, studying his handsome profile: the perfectly straight nose, full lips, and sculpted chin. The man was so damn beautiful it almost hurt. Black ink edged his angular jawline and past the nape of his neck, adding to his sex appeal.

Good girl.

Those two words had shaken me, stolen my breath, and turned me on in ways I'd never felt before. I talked myself down from straddling him in his kitchen.

"And yet you claim I have a big ego."

"Oh, I know you do."

"What choice do you leave me?"

I reluctantly ripped my eyes away from him, feeling the climate of our conversation shifting. "I don't follow."

"Well, I'm in a car with an extraordinarily gorgeous woman who can't keep her eyes off me. Can you blame me for feeling like the luckiest son of a bitch alive?"

My cheeks flared with heat, and I bit my lip to keep myself from smiling like a fool.

"You're a smooth talker, Derek Cain."

"No, just telling it like it is. Come on; you know you're stunning, Eva. And I don't lie to women about their looks. I don't have to."

"I bet you don't," I said with an eye roll.

He chuckled lightly and relaxed in his seat, an elbow leaning against the door. "Do I look like a man who needs to sweet-talk women to sleep with them?"

A strange twinge of something clenched in my stomach at the thought of him sleeping with other women.

"Oh, of course not. They just fall at your feet, don't they?"

"Or crawl to them." His voice deepened, and he threw me a sly gaze.

The knot in my belly twisted, and I wanted to die when I felt a rush of wetness between my legs.

I squeezed my thighs together and shifted toward the door, as if he could sense the effect he had on my libido.

"I don't need to know about the women you're involved with, especially the ones on their knees for you."

"I'm not involved with anyone." We stopped at another red light, and his diamond eyes gleamed with menace. "I don't even remember their names."

"Well, that's... *something*." I wanted to feel disgusted by his admission, to use it as a reason to curb my attraction to him, but it only helped fuel it.

Had I no dignity?

"But you on your knees, Evangelina—now, that's something I would never forget."

The air rushed from my lungs, and I nearly broke a fingernail from the death grip I held on the edge of the seat. Naughty visuals took root in my brain and played like an X-rated reel in my head.

"Derek… we're practically cousins."

What the actual fuck did I just say?

Derek laughed outright and shook his head. "We're not related. I don't care how close you were to James."

"No, I-I didn't mean it that way."

I briefly wondered how severe the road rash would be if I jumped out of the car at its current speed.

"Explain yourself then, because I know one thing with absolute goddamn certainty, and it has nothing to do with having an ego."

My heart hammered like a drum in my chest, dreading and anticipating the words he was about to speak.

"And what's that?"

I was convinced he had conspired with the traffic lights because their timing was immaculate. The heat of his gaze seared into the side of my head, silently beckoning for my attention. And so, I gave in, losing myself in those pools of blue.

"You and I would be so damn good together."

Chapter Twelve

Derek

White tents lined the walkway as far as the eye could see. I never understood the lure of being in crowds of people. Strangers walking shoulder to shoulder, bumping into one another. Scents mixing. Personal spaces breached. I wasn't the type of person who trusted others. My brain was hot-wired to be paranoid and suspicious of everyone. Hell, if they knew who I was, they'd run in the opposite direction. It was in my nature, ingrained in me like an innate instinct, to assume every single soul here was as dangerous and calculated as I was. Relaxing wasn't an option, so I meticulously scanned the surrounding area. On higher alert than usual, my hand hovered over the small of Eva's back.

"How do you know she's here today?"

"Carmen is always here. She never misses an opportunity to work. Not when she's the sole guardian of her four grandbabies."

"So, we're looking for an older woman?"

Eva glanced over her shoulder and nodded. "Yeah. Short, pixie cut, and silver streaks. Her daughter... well, let's just say, she's a lot like Rayne."

"That's quite... *unfortunate*."

My attempt at sounding empathetic must have fallen short, coming off as harsh and judgmental. Eva stopped so abruptly that I nearly toppled over her.

Her hardened eyes narrowed at me.

"I won't pretend to know what it's like to struggle with addiction or finances, but I try my best to understand. I've seen the worst and best of society, Derek. And even good people fall on hard times and get caught up in the streets. You should understand that more than anyone."

Evangelina's words stung, though I didn't know if it was because she was calling me out or because I'd upset her. Before yesterday, the only scenario would have been the former. But today, I wasn't so sure, and that thought alone agitated the shit out of me.

"I'm sorry. I didn't mean to come off like some privileged asshole."

The apology felt foreign on my tongue.

Evangelina gifted me a small smile, the sharp lines of her face softening as she waved me off. "Come on. She usually sets up on the south end."

I quickly followed when she pulled into the crowd again. As we continued our trek through the maze of people, many vendors greeted and called her by name.

"You're quite the celebrity here."

"I come here a lot. Sometimes on shift to keep in touch with the community or just to shop and enjoy the scenery."

The crowd thinned the closer we got to the far side of the market, finally allowing me room to walk shoulder-to-shoulder with Eva.

"Maybe I'm being an asshole again, so forgive me. But you don't seem the type to frequent a place like this outside of work."

"And why's that?" she asked, a smirk showcasing the dimple on her right cheek. But she wasn't looking at me. Her eyes were fixed forward, pace steadfast.

"I mean, look at you."

"Look at me," she threw back with a grin. "Is a place like this beneath you, Derek Cain?"

"No, it's just not my thing," I said, pulling my hands out of my jacket pockets, scowl set on a man whose eyes lingered a little too long on her face.

"Not a fan of crowds, or just shopping in general?" she asked, oblivious to the silent exchange of threats and bodily harm.

"Pretty much both."

She pursed her lips, finally twisting to survey me from top to bottom. The weight of her perusal steeled through me and settled southbound.

"Well, you seem to be well-dressed. Who does your shopping, then?"

"Are you asking me if there's a woman in my life who picks out my clothes?"

She shook her head and laughed. "That's a little pretentious, Derek. It's simply a valid follow-up question to your statement."

"Okay, I'll play along." Her laughter was contagious. And, against my better judgment, I decided I wanted to hear more of it. "No, I don't have anyone who shops for me. Said I wasn't a fan, not that I didn't buy my own clothes."

"Fair enough. Well, I'm impressed. You look… really good. Your clothes, I mean."

I'd opened my mouth to say something inappropriate, but Evangelina had already taken off toward a tent tended by an older woman with cropped hair and a bright yellow jacket. They greeted each other with a hug, and the woman, every bit the grandmotherly type, immediately noticed Eva's bruise and cracked lip.

"What happened, *Mija*?" she gasped, tilting her chin to get a better look. Her dark eyes instantly flew to me, and a reproachful look pinched her aged features.

"On the job, Carmen. It's not what you're thinking," Eva said, as if reading her thoughts.

Despite Evangelina's reassurance, the edge in her expression remained in place.

"Carmen, did Rayne come see you today?"

The woman nodded solemnly. "She came by to tell me she'll be gone for a while."

Eva gripped her by the shoulders. "Did she say where she was going?"

"No, but her face was bruised up… kind of like yours. Eva, what's going on?"

Eva blew out a puff of air. "I'd rather you not get involved."

The woman was silent before her features creased in my direction. "And who is he?"

Evangelina turned and met my eyes. "He's… he's a friend, Carmen. And he's helping me find Rayne."

Carmen touched the bruise below Eva's eye. I didn't have to be a mind reader to know what she was thinking. Most people made assumptions about me based on my tattoos, the way I dressed, and the don't-fuck-with-me expression that lived on my face. I was used to it. But I didn't appreciate her scrutiny in front of Eva or the fact that she was whispering into her ear in Spanish. No doubt some warning about me. I wasn't fluent, but I knew enough to understand her advice about making decisions with her head and not by what was between her legs—even though I looked good enough to eat.

Her words. Not mine.

Evangelina's cheeks flushed pink, and she leaned into the taller woman, responding so quickly in Spanish that I couldn't keep up.

Once they said their goodbyes, we'd only walked about five feet before a heavy-set man in a long black coat approached Carmen's tent. He growled her name through clenched teeth and charged forward, trapping the scared woman against a steel post.

Evangelina darted toward them before I could stop her, rounding the small white table and placing herself between Carmen and a soon-to-be-dead man.

"Hey! Leave her alone."

Redirecting his anger, the man pointed a finger just inches from her face, teeth gnashing together.

I clenched my fists as I fantasized about using his severed hand as a chaser for his teeth.

Eva squared her shoulders in what looked like a silent challenge—a dare for him to make his move. Little did she know he'd never get that close.

"What the hell is your problem?"

"Lady, I don't know who the fuck you are, but you better move aside before I move you."

I tightened the strap on my gloves. "You so much as touch her…." I clamped down on my jaw before Eva heard the vile promises clawing up my throat.

The man rolled his eyes my way and cocked a brow, lifting his chin. "This doesn't concern either of you."

I couldn't have agreed more, but the way Eva was positioned protectively in front of Carmen let me know walking away wasn't in her plans.

Fuck.

"Carmen, what's going on? Who is he, and why is he here?"

The woman was too busy sniveling into her sleeve to answer Eva's questions.

"Like I said, none of your business. This is between me and that traitorous bitch."

Eva stepped to him, lifting her face to meet the threat head-on. "I suggest you leave. You're harassing and threatening this woman."

I wasn't privy to whatever history existed between the two. I didn't give a damn either way. My only concern was standing toe-to-toe with a man double her size.

So, this was what they meant about feisty Latinas?

I was oddly turned on.

"What are you? A cop? Surely don't look like a pig to me," he said with a snort.

Placing a hand on her hip, I slid between them, having had enough of how his beady eyes stared her down with a mix of lust and violence. I couldn't afford to kill this man in broad daylight and, worse yet, in front of Eva. There was only so much those bought and paid for by the Order of Six that could be swept under the rug when it came to public slip-ups. And while every fiber of my being wanted to crack his skull open for even breathing in the vicinity of what was mine, there were far too many witnesses for the amount of damage control needed to match my rage.

"I highly suggest you leave."

"And who the fuck are you?"

Eva's hand was on my arm, her fingers squeezing my bicep as the tension pulled my muscles taut.

"Derek, don't."

"Listen to your girl. She's got a sweet mouth on her."

I balled my fist and buried it into his abdomen. He doubled over while grunting and attempting to catch his breath. Leaning close to his ear, I whispered, "Do you know how long it takes a man to die once he's been eviscerated?" He groaned a reply, still unable to speak. "Is that a no?" I gripped him by the collar of his shirt and dragged him to the edge of the tent. His bloodshot eyes were wide, face red and blotchy. "I can assure you that I do."

"Fuck... *you*," he panted.

A lascivious smile crawled across my face. "You got some grit to you. Maybe you'd hold out a little longer."

"This has nothing to do with you, man." His voice was gruff. "I'm just looking for some tweaked-out whore."

Things had just become interesting.

"Rayne?"

He nodded, getting his bearings until suddenly growing silent as his eyes focused on my hand.

"Ares," he whispered, putting his hands up in surrender. "Okay, okay. I'm leaving."

It was then I noticed the ink on his fingers and the back of his hands.

Bratva.

Eva would have recognized him had he been the bastard who'd assaulted her, but there was not a doubt in my mind he knew the names of the men who had.

I fisted his collar. "Listen to me carefully; your life depends on how you answer my next questions." I briefly glanced behind me, ensuring Eva was still tending to Carmen. "Last night, two men followed that girl to a home in Bryn Mawr—I need the name of the one who survived and where I can find him."

"Fuck... I can't, man."

"Oh, but you will."

I reached into the inside pocket of my jacket and pulled out a black wallet. His brows shot up the instant realization hit. Flipping it open, I was greeted with a picture of his family: three kids and a young wife who was wearing entirely too much makeup.

"Would be a damn shame if—"

"Don't you dare. You wouldn't."

I grinned, double row of teeth on show. "I guess the question is, whose life is more important to you?"

He cursed under his breath, but leaned in with the information nonetheless. As the man reached to retrieve the wallet, I snatched it away from his grasp. "You've been very helpful, Vladimir, but I think I'll hold on to this a little longer until you've proved yourself an honest man."

He gritted his teeth together. "No! I gave you what you asked for."

"And you have my word that no harm will come to you or your family if your information pans out."

His nostrils flared, but he knew he had no choice. Comply or die. What he didn't know was that I didn't leave loose ends.

"Derek." Eva's sultry voice cut through my thoughts.

"We're done here. He was just leaving. Isn't that right?"

Vladimir's eyes fell on his wallet as I tucked it back into my breast pocket. He grumbled under his breath and took off, disappearing into the crowd.

"Is he gone for good?"

"He is." My gaze lifted to Carmen, who was now sitting on a wooden stool and dabbing at her eyes.

"He's part of Belov's crew, isn't he? She told me he wanted information on Rayne. Threatened her for it. I told her to press charges and pack up and leave, but of course, she's refusing. I'm going to try to get a unit to keep an eye on her block."

Once Eva helped Carmen calm down, we exited the market. When we reached the parking lot, I leaned against my car, arms folded over my chest. Her gaze met mine, and she offered a warm smile and settled next to me.

"Thank you… for what you did back there. I wouldn't want you to get into an altercation because of me. But…"

"What?" I raised my brow, waiting for the lecture I knew was coming.

"You can't just go around assaulting people or making threats, especially in front of me. It puts me in a tight spot."

"I can't make those types of promises, but I'll try my best. I already told you, I won't stand by and let anyone disrespect you."

The sexy way she bit her lip did things to me. I shifted, and she followed, standing just inches in front of me.

"Do you do that for everyone?"

"No."

She inched closer. "I'm no damsel, Derek."

I pulled her in by the collar of her jacket, our bodies pressed together, while my cock reacted to her proximity.

"I know you can take care of yourself."

"I can."

"Of course, you can." I chuckled, rubbing a gentle thumb over the edge of her healing lip, causing her eyes to flutter. "Where to next?"

She shrugged her shoulders. "I thought of heading into the precinct and reviewing Rayne's file some more. Make sure there isn't anything I'm missing. I also want to compare mug shots, and see if that man is in our system. Did you happen to get his name?"

"No," I lied. Again. "But I can still help." I hated the slight tinge of desperation lacing my tone. Maybe getting far from her at the moment was necessary.

"I won't drag you to my job."

"What? Don't want to be seen with a guy like me?"

"Really?" She gave me an indignant look, and swatted my arm.

I leaned in and used my index finger to slowly trace the contours of her face, the soft slope of her nose, and down her fleshy pink lips.

"Prim and proper Evangelina, in the company of a man with hand and neck tattoos. What would your colleagues say?" I tightened my hold, and slid down the side of my vehicle, so that she was cradled between my legs and nearly eye-level. The warmth of her breath fanned over my lips as hers parted. It would be so easy to kiss her. She was practically begging. And fuck me, did I want to. But I had to play my cards. No matter how goddamn beautiful and captivating she was.

"You can just tell them I'm your cousin. Isn't that what you said?" I teased.

A slow smile moved across her face as she rose onto her toes, feathering her lips over mine, and whispering, "I'll tell them you're my brother."

Ouch!

"Come on. I have to pick up my car," she said, pulling out of my arms and rounding the hood with a smug expression.

"So you really don't want me to tag along? You wound me, angel." I threw my hand over my heart in a show of theatrics.

Eva arched a brow and slid into the car.

There was only one way this was going to end.

Eye on the prize, Derek.

Eye on the prize.

I rapped a knuckle on the car's roof before pulling the door open and climbing inside.

Chapter Thirteen

Derek

Tearing my shirt above my head, I wiped at the sweat and blood splatters rolling down the sides of my face. The cellar was dark, a chill I couldn't quite feel hanging in the air. Hard pants and rolling moans rose from the battered man shackled over a drain. His chains had been slackened so that he was kneeling, slumped forward, and head bowed.

The asshole from the market had followed through on his word and delivered his friend as promised. I only had to wait thirty minutes for the man to step onto his back porch, a cigarette in one hand and Heineken in the other. Being the gentleman I was, I offered the poor bastard a light. To my surprise, he didn't try to run or shout like I thought he would. He simply stared, accepting his fate, as if he knew who I was and that I'd be coming for him.

Blood dripped in a steady stream from some unknown orifice in his face, coating the metal grates below. He spat and coughed, his body jerking with each desperate sweep of air he pulled into his lungs.

I knelt and fisted his blood-caked hair, and he growled in response.

"Just fucking kill me already."

"Oh, that's the plan, Andrey."

Letting his face fall forward, I straightened and dragged my fingers through my scalp. I had long given up trying to avoid getting this asshole's blood spray on me ten minutes into it. Four of his fingers lay by my feet, the first of his punishment, though he owed all ten for touching what was mine.

I didn't make going off script a habit as I'd done with James. But this motherfucker had some skeletons and a rap sheet almost as long as the number of bribes his father had had to make to clear his name. He was young, barely out of high school, and already an errand boy for Belov. Only Andrey wasn't just collecting gambling debts or running kilos; he was also a collector of young girls.

Maybe I was the world's biggest hypocrite. After all, I carried the souls of all the men whose lives I'd stolen like a canvas of fine art on my flesh. But there were limits, boundaries even a sick fuck like me wouldn't cross.

"I just want to have a little fun first." I circled him, and his shoulders stiffened at the uncertainty of my presence at his back. "Tell me, Andy, what made you think you could put your hands on what's mine?"

"Fuck you. I didn't know who that bitch was other than she had the sweetest dick-sucking lips—"

The strangled noise he made when I clutched my hand around his neck was damn near music to my ears.

"She is fucking gorgeous, isn't she, Andy?" I hadn't had the pleasure of feeling her lips slide around my cock yet, but all in due time. "You roughed her pretty face up good, didn't you? Split that little mouth of hers like some limp-dick coward because she would rather die than touch you."

Andrey's eyes were bloodshot, bulging from their sockets the tighter my fist wound around his throat. He was seconds from passing out, and I just couldn't have that. He wouldn't get off so easily. Merely two heaving gasps in, I stuck my blade into his abdomen and twisted the leather handle to the tune of his jerking body. His mouth gaped open in a soundless scream before he keeled over against the chains, writhing in agony.

"You… sick… son of a… bitch," he huffed between heavy pants.

"Two million women in this city, and you just so happen to run into mine. It was fate, you and I."

The middle finger on his left hand was the only one left. He lifted his bloody stump and flipped me the bird, and I couldn't help the roar of laughter that erupted from my throat.

He sure had balls.

For now.

Just as he began a tirade of expletives, a flick of light glittered from a metal table behind my shackled friend. My cell phone vibrated against the surface soon after.

"Here, Andy, hold this for me," I said, plunging another knife under his right ribcage. He tipped his head back and howled, the sound bouncing off the brick walls like the soundtrack to a horror flick.

> **EVANGELINA:** I have an early shift tomorrow, and I was wondering if you wanted to help investigate a tip with me. I found a new contact for Rayne. It's off the books, so it's just me.

Evangelina was seeking my help again.

> **ME:** What time?

> **EVANGELINA:** Pick me up at 4:30. I'm staying at my dad's for the next two days.

Her father's address popped up next.

"Hey… come on, man. I'm dying over here." Andrey's whimpers were low, his breaths shallow, and he no longer held weight on his knees. Slung forward, he was held up by the cutting restraints around his wrists.

"I'm in the middle of something. Let's not be rude."

ME: I'll be there.

EVANGELINA: Thank you.

Those three text dots appeared on the screen, only to disappear and reappear, repeating that pattern three more times. I clutched the phone tighter, anticipation keeping my eyes glued to the bright screen, waiting on whatever she had to say next, and curious as to why she was so unsure. A slight ache on the sides of my face made me realize I'd been grinning like a fucking fool. A realization that made my chest tighten. The same feeling from earlier that day, one I couldn't quite place, washed over me. I didn't like it. I felt strangely… vulnerable.

EVANGELINA: Sleep well, Derek.

All that indecision over those three little words?

ME: You too.

For the past month, while getting all my affairs in order and forging documents on James's behalf, I had also gathered intel on every facet of Evangelina's life. Imagine my surprise when I learned Franco was her father. The poor bastard had been forced, through extortion, of course, to work as the official doctor for Philly's local crime families and beyond, including members of Ares. The haunting revelations hadn't stopped there. Finding out Eva was a homicide detective for Philly's 9th District had me reevaluating my entire plan. The irony was as laughable as it was twisted.

I set the phone down and squeezed my eyes closed, pushing all thoughts of her from my mind and loathing the seeds of doubt sprouting in the impenetrable vault that was my conscience.

Labored groans pulled me from my thoughts.

"Look, man… just let me go. I promise I won't say anything." The way his voice cracked was pathetic. "I never got back to my boss about that night. He would have had my head had he known I fucked up and left a witness."

I pulled up a chair and sat about arm's length in front of him, one ankle resting on my knee. "Now, Andy, what kind of a man would I be if I just let you go? What? You go back to Belov and open your mouth about my girl? I can't have that." I leaned forward. "And how will you explain the loss of all your fingers and your missing dick?"

He looked at me with confusion, eyes in slits, partly due to swelling.

"Fuck. Please don't."

"Don't worry. You won't need it where you're going."

I snatched a cleaver from the table, and he thrashed violently, cursing and screaming for help.

"No one will hear you, so I suggest you conserve your energy," I said, peering at him from behind the blade. "I'm just getting started."

He gurgled out a pained laugh. "You're a real… piece of work, aren't you? Like we're any diff—*Aaahh!*"

"Hold that thought," I said, dragging my blade across his torso before wrenching it free. "Looks like I have a guest."

"Oh…shit." The contents of his abdomen spilled out, hitting the floor with a satisfying squelch.

Our cleanup crew had their work cut out for them.

I watched the tall figure in the live-feed surveillance video, and a smile lifted the corners of my mouth. In all the day's chaos, I'd forgotten Kai was coming by this evening. Using a towel, I wiped at the splatters of blood on my arms and chest before bringing the cloth to my face. "Sit tight, friend."

Andrey began wailing when I stepped away, his cries for help echoing around us until the door slammed shut behind me.

Silence.

I wiped my hands one last time before unlocking and opening the front door.

"Oh. Bad time?" Kai asked, eyes moving from the top of my head to the crimson stains on my fingers.

"Just a little personal business. Come in."

He arched a dark brow and shook his head, a grin finally cracking across his face. "It's always business with you, isn't it?" he said, clapping me on the back.

Kai was my brother in everything but blood. We had come from the same shit foster home, adopted by the same bastard. And ultimately trained into the same type of ruthless monster. However, he was the voice of reason between the two.

"Pour yourself a drink and make yourself at home. I'm going to go get cleaned up."

He already had the decanter of whiskey in hand. "You know me," he said, lifting a cut glass before bringing it to his mouth.

By the time I showered and returned to the main floor of the range, Kai was nowhere to be found. I didn't have to venture a guess as to where he'd gone.

"This doesn't look like *business* to me," he said, his back to the door as he studied Andrey's slumped and motionless body. "He's dead, by the way. But he did mumble something about a 'bitch with a tight ass.' Kai turned to me as he downed the last swig of his drink. "What the fuck was this poor bastard talking about, D? Couldn't be that chick from this morning."

His eyes moved between me and the bloodied corpse, attempting to put the pieces together. There were no secrets between us. We'd been through more shit together than I cared to reminisce about. And we'd saved each other in more ways than I could ever repay him. He's the only person I gave a single fuck about—that thought swirled in my head for a moment, the face of another breaking through my thoughts.

While Kai knew of James's fate, Eva was the one detail I'd left out. But it was time to come clean. After all, he would be in town for a few weeks.

"Damn," he said, drinking from his twice-refilled glass of whiskey. "So, what's your plan? Fuck this girl. Then what?"

Fuck her until I've had my complete fill. Until my cum dripped from every orifice of her body. Until I'd branded her as mine, and she was utterly ruined for any other man. I'd never wanted to sink my cock in a pussy as much as I wanted—no—needed hers.

Then what?

"She's wealthy. Take what I want from her and move on."

"Will she have the same fate as that asshole in the cellar?"

My eyes flashed up at him from behind the glass. "No."

The word flew out of my mouth, cutting and resolute before I could even process its meaning.

Kai's eyes narrowed, a question hanging in the air. But he looked away, a pensive expression etched onto his face. He didn't say anything more, choosing not to vocalize his concerns.

I leaned back and stared into my drink as if the answers to his unspoken questions lay hidden in the amber liquid.

Kai rubbed a hand through his dark hair and huffed a long breath. "So, this Eva woman—she's Franco's daughter. Does he know who you are?"

I lifted the hem of my shirt to a faded scar on my abdomen. "Two years ago, I caught the business end of a blade and he did my sutures. He doesn't know my connection to James… for now."

"You're not planning on meeting him, are you?" He scooted to the edge of the sofa, a severe look on his face. "He's going to put that shit together. He'll know you did it. Then she'll know. Loose ends, D."

"Nobody touches her." My voice came out more like a growl than words.

He put both hands up in his defense.

"You know me, brother. I would never. But word gets around. And Franco isn't going to keep quiet about you sleeping with his daughter. *And* she's a cop? Derek, that's some Armageddon-level shit you're about to jump balls deep into."

Chapter Fourteen
Evangelina

I looked back at my childhood bed. Though hard to see from under the pile of clothes, lavender sheets with white roses still adorned the queen-sized mattress in the center of the room. I twisted my body in front of the mirror for the umpteenth time since my shower an hour ago. For reasons I refused to examine, I'd changed outfits six times, fussed over my hair, and couldn't decide which shoes would still be practical but also give me an inch or two in height.

I finally threw my arms up, realizing how ridiculous I was acting. Since when had I ever gone out of my way to impress a man?

It was just Derek.

I pulled on an oversized knit sweater and let my hair loose, smoothing my fingers through the waves and sighing. *Just Derek*, I repeated in my thoughts—a place where his name, face, and scent had taken up residence for the last two days. I wanted to convince myself that my draw to him was solely due to his connection with James, but I knew better. He made me feel things I hadn't felt in so long.

He'd been so bold. So forward. I could have him if I wanted to. And I did. Fuck, I did.

I just knew he'd be a passionate lover. Those arms, that chest—

why did I have this craving, this need to be ravaged, tossed around, and disrespected in the worst and best ways possible?

My eyes closed of their own volition, and I stifled a moan when I thought of that man between my legs.

"Eva?" my father rasped against the door. His voice, though soft, startled me, and my eyes popped open.

"Come in," I said, leaning close to my vanity as I pretended to retouch a subtle liner around my lips.

His hulking figure walked inside, hands in the pockets of his blue scrubs. I felt his eyes on me and a strange tension radiating from his stance. "You're meeting him again, aren't you?"

I paused to meet his scrutinizing gaze in the mirror. "He'll be here in about twenty minutes. We have plans."

"I don't think that's such a good idea."

I whipped around. "I don't understand. Why?"

"Because you don't know this man, Eva. He can be anybody. Just because he's James's blood doesn't automatically grant him entrance into our family and our lives."

His disdain toward Derek was ridiculous and unfounded. He'd never met him and was already writing him off without giving him a chance. He and James had been so close for many years. None of it made sense.

"So, then get to know him. Give him the benefit of the doubt." I took his hand in mine. "Do you doubt my judgment?"

My father's nostrils flared as he drew a sharp breath. "Of course he's nice to you. All he sees is a beautiful, naive woman, willing to do anything in the name of redemption to shake off the guilt of what happened that night."

His words cut me profoundly, and I felt the sting of tears behind my eyes. Maybe somewhere deep down, I was afraid that what he said was true.

"Wow, that fucking hurts. So, he's only nice to me because he wants to sleep with me?"

My father cupped his hands against my face. They were warm and smelled like his signature aftershave. The same one he'd been using since I was a little girl. It was home. And just like that, my anger dissipated, shifting into sadness.

"That's not what I meant. I just want you to be careful. Guard your heart, Eva. He isn't James."

"Daddy, I know that." I bit back the torrent of emotions threatening to spill over, the grief swelling fresh in my throat. "I'll be fine. And Derek… don't worry about him. He's a good guy," I assured him with a forced smile.

A good guy.

I had to believe that. I wanted to believe it, even though a tiny voice at the back of my mind warned me there were things about Derek that made him different from anyone I'd ever met. Secrets that set off alarms in my heart.

"Am I late?"

Derek moved up my father's porch steps with the gait of a predator. Each movement methodical. Meant to evoke a reaction, to elicit my undivided attention. And fuck did he have it. His smile was wide, tipped to one side, and his eyes seared through mine like he was making it a point to see straight into my soul. I swallowed hard, finding my voice just as he reached the top of the concrete stairs.

Feeling the urge to throw my arms around his neck, I squeezed my hands into fists at my sides instead.

"You're actually ten minutes early."

"So, this is just you giving me curbside service, then. I'm flattered."

I rolled my eyes, unable to repress the smile stretching across my face. "You're not the only one with cameras and security fit for the annual Purge. You and my father have that in common."

My father was a wealthy man. I'd always thought his over-the-top surveillance was paranoid overkill, but I understood it, especially after what happened to James. It only took a millisecond for my thoughts to travel to that night and the never-ending what-ifs that haunted my subconscious.

Derek must have noticed how my shoulders fell and my smile crumbled to a frown. His finger lifted my chin, and I suddenly couldn't remember when we'd gotten so comfortable touching each other.

But I liked it.

"Hey, we're going to find her," he said in that soothing velvet tone that turned my insides into jelly.

I put a hand around his wrist and managed a smile. "You want to come inside?"

Derek's eyes darkened, and his hold on my chin tightened as he leaned closer, minty breath fanning my face.

"Oh, I'd like that, angel," he crooned, thumb feathering against my cheek.

My body was a traitorous whore.

How I squeezed my calf muscles to talk myself out of jumping up and straddling him was downright shameful. The worst part was that he knew how his words and proximity affected me. His smug grin only widened when I put a hand over his chest and averted his gaze.

The day I'd set out to meet Derek Cain, never in my most scandalous dreams had I imagined he'd be so damn attractive, charismatic, and infuriatingly sexy all at once.

"I meant inside… to meet my dad," I said in a breathy voice, stretching my neck so our lips were only inches apart. I could play his game too.

He brought a hand to my hip, gripping my sweater and tugging me toward him.

"Of course you did. What else would you have meant?"

The heady scent of his cologne did strange things to my lady parts. It was crisp, expensive, and oh-so fucking tempting.

"Eva!"

My father's sharp voice startled us both, making me jolt. I whirled around and attempted to distance myself from Derek, but he gripped me tighter and pulled me against his front, hand splayed across my abdomen. As silly as it was, I felt strangely—*protected*.

"Dad… this is Derek." I made no effort to move away from his embrace, even though I knew I should. "This is James's son." The hard planes of Derek's chest tensed at my words.

I'd imagined my dad would be happy to meet his late best friend's estranged son. His only child. But the stony expression on his face screamed the opposite. I'd never seen my father look at anyone the way he glared at Derek.

Hatred?

"I know who he is."

I finally broke Derek's hold, my eyes darting between the two men, narrowed in confusion as they stared one another down. Brown, stormy eyes against amused blue ones. "You… know Derek?"

My father's dark eyes rolled to meet mine, and he shook his head. "No. I meant I knew who he was because you told me he was coming."

Derek stepped from behind me and lifted a hand to greet my father, who hesitated before returning the gesture.

Tension hung thick in the air as the men exchanged false

pleasantries. I was baffled and disappointed, realizing how much I'd wanted them to get along. As I started questioning their strange behavior, my cell vibrated in my pocket. It was a text from Rayne's cousin, Cody, owner of a junkyard across town, where we were supposed to meet.

"Derek, we gotta run. My contact is leaving in thirty. We have just enough time."

"Eva." My dad's voice wavered as he tugged me away from Derek. "You're not going anywhere with him."

"I'm not doing this with you right now. We'll talk later." He tried grabbing my wrist, but I moved out of his grasp. "Later," I repeated, pivoting and walking past a too-smug Derek.

There went those alarm bells again.

Chapter Fifteen

Derek

The drive to the salvage yard was quiet. Eva looked pensive, staring out the windshield almost hypnotically. Now and again, I caught her sneaking glances in my direction, a question or comment brimming her lips, yet she spoke neither. I knew what was bothering her—the tense meeting between Franco and me. There was no mistaking the dawn of awareness that had crossed his face when he saw me and the intimate way in which I'd held his daughter.

"Are you going to talk to me? Or just sit there looking pretty?"

"Derek," she half whined, the sound stirring my cock. I wanted to hear her groan my name again but in a much different circumstance. Preferably with my fist wrapped around that long hair while I was buried balls deep in her pussy.

"I just don't understand him. It's not like him to be so… cold and standoffish. And to you, of all people. He and James were like brothers."

"I'm not offended, angel," I said with a chuckle. "I'm not exactly many people's cup of tea. And frankly, I prefer it that way. Unless it comes to you. Maybe he wasn't a fan of my tattoos."

She turned to me, confusion and intrigue written on her face. "You keep calling me that. Angel."

I pulled into an empty lot right outside our destination, but kept driving until I reached past the end of the lot, until my car was obscured by a thick hedge of trees and shrubs. I cut the engine and shifted in my seat, peering at my watch. Having arrived earlier than expected, I figured we could afford a minute or two.

"You don't like it?"

"I never said that. I'm just… curious. And why are we in the bushes?"

Her lips pushed into a pout.

"Well, first, look where we're at. Chasing leads to a place like this over a girl you barely know. That takes a lot of compassion. And I'm here because I don't know who the fuck this Cody guy is."

"Cody's record is clean. And I've known Rayne for four years. It's called being human, Derek."

She and I had two very different definitions of that concept. There was an obscenely short list of people I'd die and kill over. And by short, I meant one. Kai was the brother I never had, and the shit we'd been through together, the things we'd done and been forced to do, had bound us for life. My eyes flicked toward the woman sitting in my passenger seat. And something about her unraveled my prior statement. She tucked a tendril of hair behind her ear and watched me expectantly, waiting for an answer or possibly a rebuttal, but all I could do was grin.

"There are those who excel at that task and others who fail miserably," I started, ignoring the subject of Cody and Rayne. I didn't care about them. "And which side one lands on is purely objective."

"Is it, though?"

We were treading dangerous waters, and thus a change of subject was in order. I pushed the door open and stepped out of the car, and without question, she followed.

"So, what's the reason your informant couldn't give you this information over the phone or even a goddamn text?"

She pushed away from my car and headed toward the entrance of the building. I fell into stride with her smaller steps and waited impatiently for the answer she was dragging out for no good reason.

"Eva?" I gently tugged on her arm.

"He said he'd only give me what I needed in person. I didn't want to come here alone, so I called you." She looked me up, head to toe. "If anything, one look at you, and he would probably be less inclined to try something."

I threw my hands up. "You knowingly agreed to come here, even though you knew this guy was shady? What if I'd said no?"

"This isn't just about Rayne."

She broke my hold on her arm and began walking again. But I caught her and whirled her around.

"What else is worth risking your safety?"

I wasn't just going to let her walk into dangerous situations willingly, not until I'd had my fill.

"James had ties to Belov. What if he was the one who ordered the hit? Rayne is the key to Yuri and Dmitry." Her eyes became misty. I gritted my teeth, hating that she had such an emotional attachment to that sack of shit, James. "I need to find her. I need her to talk. For her to tell me what she knows."

Releasing her, I folded my arms across my chest.

"Don't you have a whole department that can handle this?"

"Rayne is off the books. We have nothing solid on the Belov brothers that would stick. Trust me; we've tried."

Eva pulled open a rickety gate, and I followed her down a gravel pathway.

"What makes you think that whatever information this girl has would hold up? No offense, Eva; she's an addict and a prostitute."

She cast a sharp glance at me and quickened her steps. "I know that. But maybe… this is for me."

"Stop." My tone was biting, making her halt at the authority behind it. "What did you just say?"

Eva bit her lip, her eyes flickering with what I could only deduce to be fear for just a fraction of a second before she squared her shoulders.

"You wouldn't understand."

"I can't if you don't tell me. What is this? Some revenge plot?" I chuckled humorlessly. "Your little friend tells you what you want to hear, and then, what? You go guns blazing into the Belov estate?" I gave her petite figure a once-over and shook my head. "That's rich."

She clenched her jaw and spun on her heels.

"*Eva.*"

The edge in my voice hadn't worked this time.

"Fuck you," she spat back, continuing her hard steps down the uneven path.

I was a son of a bitch, so there was no surprise that as she stomped off angrily, insulted by my words and insinuations of her capabilities, all I could do was watch her sweet ass and fantasize about how much I wanted to sink my teeth into each cheek and taste her from end to end.

Just as I took off after her, a blacked-out glass door swung open, and a tall, Skeletor-looking motherfucker stepped in front of Eva. She moved back a step, allowing him a wider berth.

"Are you Eva?" he asked with a smile that was a little too happy for my liking.

"I am," she replied as I flanked her.

"I wasn't aware you were arriving with… company."

He dared a glance at my face and forced a smile. I didn't return the gesture. He needed to understand that his life was hanging precariously by a very brittle thread. If I decided I didn't like what he had to say, how he said it, or how he addressed Eva, then he'd be dealt with.

"Rayne is your niece?" Eva asked, ignoring his statement. Skeletor nodded. But then he began to do something that had all my senses on alert. His dark eyes darted back and forth from Eva to the empty lot, as if he was waiting on something. Or rather, someone. Fidgeting nervously with his shirt, he unintentionally lifted the hem, exposing a bloodied undershirt.

A trap.

I lunged forward and grabbed him by his collar. "You have two seconds to start talking. And trust me, you don't want to waste them."

His eyes widened as he sang like a fucking canary. "They made me. I didn't have a choice."

"Made you do what? Talk fast, because I'm running out of patience."

"Derek, what are you doing?" Eva asked, her hand on my arm.

"This man set you up. So there are only two options here: he dies, fast or slow."

A small gasp fell from her lips.

"Talk while you still have your tongue."

"H-he told me that if anyone came asking about Rayne, to let him know. He killed Arnie and Russell to prove his point." Tears ran down his boney face.

I gnashed my teeth, but before I could say a word, the sound of crunching gravel had my head whipping toward the parking lot.

"Eva, find somewhere to hide."

"What? Wait—but what about you?"

"*Now.*"

She didn't hesitate, and I watched her disappear behind a wall of crushed metal. Turning my attention to the asshole in my grasp, I flashed him a wide grin. "Today is your lucky day. Fast, it is."

In one quick motion, I twisted him into my elbow, and the sharp snap of his vertebrae muted the strangled cry he'd readied himself to spill.

After dragging his body under some rusted shrapnel, I took off after Eva as the unfamiliar voices of several men reached my ear.

"Eva," I called in a harsh whisper. "Where are you?"

A small hand appeared through a slim crevice of crushed cars. "Derek, there's a bigger opening on the left side."

We would have to discuss her definition of big once we were out of this shitstorm. Fuck me. The pointed edges of metal caught my skin, but I pushed through, finding myself wedged into a very confined space with Eva pressed up against me.

Maybe this wasn't all bad.

"Derek, what's going on? I called for backup, but a huge wreck is blocking the interstate. I don't know how long it's going to take."

That must have been why those men were late.

"There's a group of men here, probably Belov's guys."

"Derek, if they find us…"

"I'll be dead. But you'll be in a much worse set of circumstances, if you know what I mean."

She shivered against me and rested her head on my chest.

"Shit, shit. This is my fault."

Her anguish prickled places inside me I'd never been aware of.

"Hey, the car is out of sight. For all they know, we never arrived."

Eva's fingers curled around the fabric of my shirt, and she shook her head. "What about Cody? He won't lie for us."

I placed my hands on her hips. "He won't be a problem."

A streak of sunlight lit up a portion of her face. Her irises, usually a dark brown, gleaned bronze against the glow. They were mesmerizing, moving back and forth.

"What does that mean? You weren't serious about what you said back there, were you?"

I couldn't very well tell her I'd snapped the bastard's neck. So I did what I did best when it came to Evangelina.

Lied.

"Of course not. I put him to sleep and hid him behind some shrapnel. He won't be awake any time soon."

She hesitated momentarily, probably digesting my words, before closing her eyes and nodding against my shirt. Her grip on me tightened as she pushed her body forward.

"Sorry. There's a piece of metal at my back."

"You think I'm upset that I have you here? Like this? Because despite what's going on out there, I'm not too torn up about our secret hideaway."

A soft whimper escaped her.

"You're shaking. Do small spaces make you nervous?" My lips were against her hairline, and I grabbed the belt loops of her jeans, dragging her closer, cock hard against her abdomen. I knew she felt the effect she had on me but said nothing, nor did she try to move away.

"No, not really. It's just that you and I—"

I cut her off mid-sentence by sliding my hands down the back of her thighs and hoisting her up to my waist. Eye level now, her brows were raised, shocked by my boldness.

"There's more space for you up here. Doesn't that feel better?"

"How convenient for you," she said in a whisper.

I chuckled, my lips feathering the curve of her neck. "It was a little tight down there for me too."

"I noticed."

Lowering my head to her shoulder, I laughed again, the sound muffled by the fabric of her shirt.

"Just wait," I said, mouth grazing the crest of her ear.

The things I wanted to do to her. Fire burned white-hot in my veins when she hooked her legs around my torso, and my reach shifted up, the globes of her ass in each hand.

Eva leaned into the crook of my neck. "You're going to get tired of holding me." Her breath was warm on my skin.

"Not a chance. I could do this all night, angel." The tip of my nose brushed against hers.

"Is that right?"

"Ask what you really want to know, Eva," I crooned against her skin before brushing up the length of her neck, chin, and bottom lip.

She shuddered and closed her eyes, shaking her head slowly. "I don't know what you're talking about."

"Sure, you do. You want to know how long and how good I can fuck you in this position, don't you?"

Eva murmured my name, but the sound was different than I expected. Her voice wasn't coated in lust for my brazen words. With her fists clutching harder at my shirt and her breaths coming in shallow, rugged pants, it was apparent something else entirely was going on.

Chapter Sixteen
Evangelina

Ten, *nine, eight, seven...*

Breathe. Just breathe. He won't hurt me. It's Derek.

It's just... Derek.

Flashes of *his* face. Hands all over me. The warm, wet feeling of his tongue against my skin. My chest was heavy, the walls caving in. Too small. The space too tight.

Too confined.

I squeezed my eyes shut, beads of sweat rolling down the sides of my face, running parallel to the stream of tears spilling over for that girl in my mind's eye. The one I kept locked away and safe.

That stupid, stupid, naive girl.

"Hey, what's wrong?" Derek's cool hand palmed my forehead, and I recoiled from his touch. "Look at me. What's going on? Why are you breathing like that?"

He sounded flustered and confused. I shook my head at his request and bit down on my lip until the healing wound broke open. The taste of blood filled my mouth, another memory connected to that night.

To *him*.

"Eva, I'm sorry. Maybe I shouldn't have done that—said those things."

"I-it's not you," I stammered out, my voice barely a whisper. "It wasn't you."

Silence blanketed us, and the arm around my bottom tightened, pressing me harder against his body.

"Did someone hurt you, angel?" His voice was strained, spoken between clenched teeth, as if he knew why I panicked. "Tell me. Who?"

Shouts just outside the metal wall caused me to stiffen and drop my head to his shoulder. I needed to pull myself together. If these were Belov's men and they found us, we would be in deep shit. I couldn't afford to have a breakdown. I owed Derek that much for dragging him into this situation for my own selfish reasons.

Six, five, four...

I pitched my mouth close to his ear and circled his neck. "Hold me, and don't move."

Derek nodded, an arm snaking around my torso.

I can do this all night, angel.

A vastly different kind of shudder rippled down my body and into my core, stoking the embers to a fire he'd left burning since the day we met.

"Tell me his name," he demanded in a harsh whisper.

"It was a long time ago, Derek. He doesn't matter."

His fingers dug into me. "It. Matters."

Light from the gaps above us highlighted the icy hue of his eyes. They were mesmerizing, turbulent—the type a girl could get lost in and drown.

"If we make it out of here..."

His lips grazed a spot behind my ear that stole my breath.

"No one will ever touch you."

Those were the last words he said for the next ten minutes, though it felt like hours had passed. In the distance, an engine purred, followed by countless others. Tires screeched and protested against the uneven gravel as the fleet of cars peeled out, and the world went quiet.

Neither of us spoke for another few beats, both on the same wavelength, waiting in case of any stragglers.

"They're gone," he said, and I nodded in agreement.

Placing my hands on his shoulders, I attempted to lower my legs to the ground, but he held firm.

"I'm going to exit first. Make sure it's clear; then I'll come get you."

"The hell you are. I'm the one with the badge here."

"And I've got the dick and balls. You think I'm going just to let you waltz out there while I hide here like a little bitch?"

I narrowed my eyes at him and huffed. "Oh, *let* me?"

"Don't be a brat, Eva."

"Fuck off."

With two fists to his chest, I pushed myself away and slid down his body, backing into the jagged wall. We both eyed the small entrance, and he tilted his head in warning.

"Evangelina."

But he was a second too slow, and I dove out of his reach into a crouched position and crawled out. His massive frame couldn't be as rash, so I had the upper hand. Once free, I scrambled to my feet and drew my weapon, carefully maneuvering through the wreckage. It didn't take long for Derek to flank me, a gun of his own in hand. As a tactical instructor, I was sure he was carrying legally, but I inwardly berated myself because I hadn't even known he was armed. That was negligence on my part as an officer.

We reached the barren lot, greeted only by deep trenches in the dirt left by Belov's men.

Holstering my weapon, I turned to Derek and sighed in relief.

"I'm sorry. I shouldn't have brought you here. That was irresponsible of me. You're a civilian, not my partner. I just—"

"Shut up."

I blinked in quick succession, caught off guard by his words and the venom behind them. "You ever put yourself in danger like this—" His mouth clenched into a tight line. "What if I hadn't been here?"

I released an exasperated breath. "Are you serious? Stop treating me like I haven't been a cop for eight fucking years. Like I'm some weak chick who can't—"

Derek's hands dug into the waistband of my jeans, and he tugged me with so much force I crashed into the solid planes of his front. The impact nearly pushed the air out of my lungs. He gripped my chin and forcibly tilted my face, meeting my wide eyes.

Fuck me, why was I so turned on right now?

"I need you to understand something. You're in my life now. You *won't* be reckless." He brought his lips to my ear and growled. "Mine."

The word rocketed through me like an electric pulse, every inch of me coming alive as the spark settled deep into my center, throbbing, burning. Hot.

"What did you just—"

A thunderous boom and the screeching of metal cut me off. Like a synchronized team, our backs collided, each with our weapon drawn, ready for whatever threat awaited.

"Do you hear that?" I asked, putting a finger up, signaling for him to be quiet.

Derek nodded. "Where is it coming from?"

I shushed him the moment I heard another soft cry.

"A baby?"

Without saying a word, I followed the noise, Derek, on my heels until I reached a pile of twisted metal that had caved in on itself. The shrill cries grew more frantic, and I shoved my Sig into Derek's hand, threw off my jacket, and crouched as I peered into the small opening.

"Eva, what the hell are you doing?"

Clawing dirt and gravel out of the way, I slowly inched inside the crevice.

"You're not going in there, are you? Eva!"

As I got closer to the noise, the ground dipped beneath my body to an opening about two feet wide. "Derek, hold on to my legs. It's coming from this hole in the ground, and I don't want to fall in."

"Fuck this," he growled, yanking me back by the ankles.

But I kicked out of his grip and crawled forward again. "Don't you fucking dare! I'm doing this with or without your help."

Another growl echoed from the shallow tunnel behind me. "You're an exasperating woman, you know that? What if you get hurt? Ever heard of tetanus?"

I couldn't help smiling at the fact he cared so much. It did *things* to me... warm, delicious things to very particular parts of my anatomy.

"Derek, just hold me—*please*."

Should I have felt guilty over the sultry way I begged? Probably. But I didn't. It had gotten the job done, affected him as he said nothing, yet tentatively put a hand over each of my calves, albeit tighter than necessary.

And my skin burned where he touched.

You and I would be so damn good together.

Those words had replayed in my thoughts an obscene number of times. Needless to say, I had reached for my battery-powered boyfriend more than once last night.

"When you pull out a rabid raccoon, don't say I didn't try to warn you."

"Noted," I said dryly, rolling my eyes. Talk about a mood killer.

I lowered myself into the hole and felt around, hoping Derek's raccoon joke wouldn't actually manifest. Soft fur feathered beneath my palm, and I stifled a scream, not wanting to give him the satisfaction of being right.

Not a baby.

I squeezed my eyes closed and felt around, my nerves on edge, when I latched on to its nape and sent a prayer up for a cat or puppy, not a giant rat.

"Oh my God, it's a kitten."

Derek scoffed. "A goddamn cat?"

He yanked me back until I was completely out, the cat cradled against my chest. "You risked stitches and painful shots over a fucking stray cat?" He pulled me into his lap.

Since my hands were occupied with a gray tabby cat, Derek surprised me by tenderly moving hair out of my face. I was pressed against his chest, his mouth close to my ear.

"I thought I told you not to be reckless, angel."

I turned my face, our lips inches apart. God, I wanted to close the distance between us and bite on that fleshy fucking mouth. How would it feel on other parts of my body?

On every part.

"So you would have been the overprotective, big brother type, then?" My voice was low, and calm, waiting for him to take the bait. Neither of us would be stupid enough to deny the chemistry igniting between us. There was nothing brotherly about the hungry way he was staring at my mouth.

"Get up," he demanded, voice tight.

"You're so damn uptight," I replied, letting him pull me to my feet. "I'm fine. Belov's men are gone, and…"

The blood in my veins ran cold when my eyes landed on a lifeless Cody. Derek followed my line of sight and hesitated before turning back to me.

"Looks like Belov's men wanted to keep him quiet."

Chapter Seventeen

Evangelina

"Cody died of a severed spinal cord. At least that's what the preliminary report indicates."

I pushed a black litter box into a corner of the mud room and tucked my cell into my back pocket. Derek was leaning against a shelf, arms crossed over his chest, looking effortlessly edible, despite the day's chaos. Meanwhile, I was a wreck, dirt still caked to the front of my jeans and shirt, and a layer of it sitting uncomfortably beneath my nail beds.

"Did he?" he asked, almost bored.

"Please, don't get too torn up about it or anything."

"I'll try to hold it together," he said, sending a wink my way.

Fucking Derek.

Fucking.

Derek.

God, I'd totally fuck Derek.

It was crazy. Nonsensical. I'd only known the man for three days, but he was on my mind more than not.

"Are you sure you're safe here?"

"Yeah, changed all the locks, reinforced the doors, and updated my security system. If no one has come looking for me yet, then I don't believe they'll be back." I was probably trying to convince myself more than him.

"Maybe you're right," he said. I was surprised he hadn't put up more of an argument.

Dusting my hands on the front of my ruined pants, I walked past him, knowing he'd follow, and stopped at the bottom of my staircase.

"Keep an eye on Diego."

"You named the stray *Diego*?"

I climbed up one step and leaned a hand on the railing. "What? You've never seen Ice Age?"

"No," he deadpanned.

And I immediately wanted to slap myself. Derek had grown up an orphan until well into his teen years. I felt like such an asshole.

"I'm sorry… I shouldn't have asked that. It was insensitive of me."

"Eva. Go upstairs and shower." The power behind his voice shook my core. Heat spread through me slowly, and I splayed my hands against my thighs to keep myself from reaching for him. "And do it before I follow you. *Diego* will be fine."

Fuck.

I rolled my lips inward, my throat suddenly dry. Not trusting my voice, I simply nodded.

I'd only made it three more steps before another shudder skated down my body. "Oh, and Eva? Lock your door."

Turning around was not an option; doing so would only lead to bad decisions and possibly a morning-after pill.

I closed the door to my bedroom and hurriedly crossed the distance to the ensuite. Leaning against the vanity, I sucked in air through my nose and exhaled out of my mouth.

"Get it together, Eva."

Grabbing at the hem of my shirt, I tugged it over my head and tossed it in the hamper. As I turned to face the mirror, I was horrified at the reflection staring back at me. How long had I looked like this? Smeared mascara. Smudged dirt over my brow. I scrunched my nose and smoothed back my hair, convincing myself it had all happened on my way up to the shower.

Lock your door.

The words echoed in my mind, forcing my eyes closed and a soft moan to slither from my clamped lips. Derek was a bold and confident man with a dirty mouth. A shiver moved down my spine at the prospect of his prowess in the bedroom.

I opened my eyes abruptly when the memories of what happened in that junkyard resurfaced. The dire situation, the cramped space, and maybe Derek's dominating nature had triggered the trauma I'd suffered as a dumb college student. I didn't have to say it, but somehow, he knew. Had an idea of why I acted the way that I had. He'd wanted to know his name, and I had a feeling he'd keep pressing. I pushed the thoughts of what he'd do with the information to a dark corner of my mind, along with all the other red flags belonging to Derek Cain.

Through the years, I'd refused to think of him, let alone say his name out loud. And I wasn't ready to either.

I'd lost control. The demons I kept locked away had clawed to the surface. But I couldn't let that happen again with Derek.

Ask what you really want to know, Eva.

Turning on the shower, I let the bathroom fill with steam, and my nipples hardened when the warmth wrapped around my naked body. My eyes fluttered closed, and wetness gathered between my thighs as I imagined him walking through the door and having me however he wanted.

You want to know how long and how good I can fuck you.

Yes, I very much did.

A breathy moan escaped me as my hand traveled south, slowly skimming over my navel and between my legs…

I bit down on my lip and groaned, leaning against the wall as the hot water cascaded over my face. Then I dropped my hand.

Not with him just downstairs. It wouldn't be enough. I needed the real thing, and I was determined to get it. Turning the handle, I quickly dove under the cold spray.

Derek seemed lost in thought, eyes fixated on the pictures on my mantle. But his gaze looked distant, as though he was staring through the frames rather than at them. If he'd noticed my presence, he hadn't said anything or diverted his attention.

"Is this your brother?" he finally asked after countless seconds.

"Yeah, that was Frankie. That was his high school graduation." My stomach grew heavy as the following words left my mouth. "He died two months later. He was murdered." I inhaled a long breath before continuing. "And I was with him when it happened."

Derek finally looked at me, his dark brows furrowed. "You were *with* him?"

I nodded.

There was a time when the wounds of grief were fresh, when I'd cry just thinking his name or remembering his laughter. But Frankie had been gone a long time, and while my heart ached for that crazy, spirited boy I'd loved so much, sometimes I wondered if he was ever here. Had I imagined having a brother for fifteen years? Dad never spoke of him. He took down all his pictures, threw out his belongings, and turned his old room into a storage space. My brother was a ghost—one only alive in my fading memories.

Derek's hand was at my waist, the other tilting my face. The blue in his irises darkened.

"Tell me." He pushed hair behind my ear. "Were you hurt?"

"No," I said, shaking my head. "I ran. He told me to run. I was fifteen… just released after a three-day stint in the hospital. He wanted to cheer me up." Tears welled in my eyes for the first time in years at the thought of Frankie's death. "We were just going for a walk."

Derek's thumb swept the droplets from my cheek. "I'm sorry I asked. I didn't mean for you to get upset."

While his gesture and tone of voice were sweet, his shoulders were tensed. Like he was uncomfortable. I didn't blame him, though. I'd taken him on a wild ride in the last couple of days. And now there I was, blubbering like an idiot.

"I'm sorry. You must think I'm pathetic." Pushing out of his grasp, I walked to the couch and let myself fall, wiping away the last of my tears with the back of my hand. Thank God I'd opted out of wearing mascara.

"I don't think you're pathetic," he said, sitting beside me. "That would have been a rough experience for anyone. And I know a thing or two about childhood trauma."

Whenever I gave thought to the atrocities Derek might have lived through as a child, I felt consumed with guilt. The man who had doted on and loved me endlessly was the same one who'd abandoned his own blood to whatever fate awaited him in a broken system. While our relationship was too new, and Derek had yet to reveal details about his early life, I knew whatever it was, had changed him. Hardened him.

I'd sat across many guilty men, and there was always something about their eyes—windows to the soul and all that. But it was the absence of light.

Of life.

Were they looking at me or through me… just like the frames?

"I'm going to be out of town for the next few days." Derek's voice jarred me from my thoughts. "I have some business to take care of."

"Business?" He cocked an eyebrow at my question. "I'm sorry. You don't owe me an explanation. I'll see you when I see you, I guess."

He leaned in, trapping me against the arm of the sofa and his body.

"Did you already forget what I told you, angel?"

Mine.

How could I forget? I was getting wet just thinking about it.

His eyes were on my lips as he snaked a hand around the small of my back.

"No, but I don't understand," I admitted breathily, hating that my voice seemed to have a mind of its own.

"I know you're still hung up on the search for this girl. But I need you to promise me that you won't do anything stupid while I'm gone."

His words warmed my heart in ways I hadn't felt in so long, but I also couldn't help becoming slightly annoyed.

"Did you forget that I had a whole life and career before we met?"

He let out a short laugh. "Keyword: *before*." Nothing was gentle about how he gripped my cheek and forced our eyes to meet. And the way his dominance was wrecking my underwear had me questioning everything. "I already warned you. You're in my life, and—"

"Yours," I whispered, staring directly into his eyes.

In one quick movement, he grabbed my hips and tossed me onto his lap. With a hand at the nape of my neck, he pulled me down toward his lips, stopping just a breath away. I pushed forward because I needed a taste, but he held me firm, both hands cradling the sides of my face.

"Don't play with me, Derek."

"Don't insult me. I don't play games." His hand moved to my neck and tightened as he ran his mouth along my jaw. "I *will* have you, Eva. All of you."

"Will you? That's pretty ambitious of you, Cain," I said, trying to sound like I wasn't melting into a puddle in his lap.

"I always get what I want."

"I'm not trying to be just another woman in your bed, Derek. That's not what this is."

He chuckled into the skin behind my ear, and my eyes fluttered closed. "I've never had a woman in my bed. Never brought one to my home. I don't share my intimate spaces with easy pussy."

I snapped my eyes open and motioned to remove myself off his lap.

Easy pussy, huh? That arrogant son of a bitch.

Derek's fingers dug into my skin.

"Sit." There was that voice again. The powerful timbre cemented me in place. "We're not done talking."

My hands wrapped around his wrists. "Let me up. I won't sit here while you insult me. I'm not one of your groupies. I'm not easy pussy."

His shit-eating grin was absolutely aggravating.

"If I thought of you that way, I would have bent you over the hood of my Bentley the day you showed up at my door."

My mouth fell open as I attempted to come up with a response, but my thoughts quickly turned on me, conjuring the sinful vision he'd planted in my head. I clamped down on my jaw, sealing in the moan trying to escape.

"Now, tell me what happened back there." His voice was surprisingly tender.

I looked away and shook my head, surprised he'd brought the subject back up so soon. "As I said, it was a long time ago. Someone I thought I could trust betrayed me in the worst way."

"Did he…"

"No, but he wanted to. He tried to. But I don't want to talk about it."

"Eva, I'm just trying to understand. I don't want to repeat what happened today."

I covered my face with my hands and sighed heavily.

"Look, I was just stupid one night and drank too much. I paid for it with lifelong trauma and a stint in the hospital with low glucose levels. Young and dumb."

"Was he a boyfriend? A friend?"

"He's nobody. No one I ever want to think about."

"Angel," he said, frustration lacing his tone, "tell me his name."

I let out a humorless laugh. "That was years ago. What? You're going to find all my childhood bullies and beat them up too? If you are, please start with this little shithead named Trent Almstead. He shoved me off our school playground, and I broke my wrist."

I held up my arm, showing him the faint scars from the surgery I'd had when I was seven. My little gymnast heart had been so torn up because it happened in the middle of the competition season.

He gently pulled my wrist closer to his face, feathering his lips over my scars. Goosebumps broke across my skin under his touch.

"I'll take care of him for you. Break his kneecaps."

"That was in the second grade. I'm sure Trent has matured some since. And I don't want you committing felonies on my behalf."

He scoffed, a knowing smirk on his face. The crazy part was that, somehow, I knew he wasn't entirely joking, and that fact both thrilled and terrified me.

"I don't take lightly to anyone touching or harming what's mine."

There it was again. That word settled deep into the pit of my belly, sending another rush of wetness between my legs. He had to know—had to feel the heat of me over his lap. I was wearing thin leggings, and it was as if every word out of his mouth was hot-wired to my libido.

I gripped his collar. "What makes you think I'm yours, Derek Cain? You barely know me."

"I know enough." His tongue licked along the hollow of my throat. "You're the kind of woman who risks their career and safety over a girl she has no blood ties or obligations to." Wet, hard kisses traveled up my throat. "You save stray, bastard cats from junkyard ditches. True to your namesake."

"Derek… what are you doing?" I moaned, head falling back as he nibbled on my earlobe.

"But you're no angel, are you? I can feel how wet that sweet little cunt is for me. Goddamn, Eva, you're going to soak straight through my pants."

Derek thrust up into me, and another breathy moan slipped past my lips. He leaned in and brushed his mouth over mine, but instead of kissing me, he took my bottom lip between his teeth and tugged gently.

"I'm going to fuck you, Eva. I'm going to taste and savor every damn inch of you. In my bed, in my room—on every goddamn surface of my house."

Shit. I nearly came, right there on his lap, with just his filthy words.

"She's mine," he said, slipping a hand between us, grin widening when his fingers slid across the soaked fabric. "Fuck, yes, she's mine."

The room was suddenly too damn hot. If this man didn't fuck me right here, right now, I was sure to combust.

I leaned forward, willing to risk it all for Derek Cain, but just before our lips could finally come together, the chime of my doorbell was the ice bucket we probably needed.

Chapter Eighteen

Evangelina

Fuck. How had I forgotten?

As I opened the Door app on my phone, I saw two familiar brunettes bouncing up and down excitedly in front of my camera.

"You're expecting guests?"

"I'm so sorry. Tonight completely slipped my mind. It's my cousin and a good friend. Today is the premiere of this new murder mystery show and—"

"You don't get enough of that at work?" he asked jokingly while stroking my face.

I nudged his shoulder. "Don't make fun. It's our thing."

My cousin Alexa's voice blared through the speaker on my phone. "Bitch, open the door! We know you see us." Her coffee-colored eyeball occupied the entire screen.

"Shame," he murmured over my lips.

"Indeed." Feeling a little bold, I snaked my hand over the crotch of his pants, placing it on the rock-hard monster dick beneath it.

"*Oh...*"

He covered my hand, pushing it down onto his erection and

groaning deep in his throat.

"As much as I want you right now, your cousin knows you're home." Derek's fist tangled in my hair, bordering on pain as he pushed me closer to his lips. "When I fuck you, Eva, I'm going to wreck you. Do you hear me? Every part of you belongs to me now. That sweet pussy only gets wet for me." His breath fanned hot over the shell of my ear. "And when that time comes, you'll be on your knees, taking this cock like a good fucking girl."

"Oh… fuck," I breathed, eyes hooded. Completely gone for this man.

No one had ever spoken to me like that. And damn, did I like it.

Fuck you, Alexa.

Was this really happening between us?

Hell, yes.

I felt the heat of a blush creep up my face. "Stay here. I'll introduce you."

"Hey," he called as I made my way out of the living room, "don't introduce me as your cousin." Derek winked, and the reaction in my underwear was immediate.

The girls tackled me as soon as I pulled open the door. It had been a week since we'd seen each other. Alexa and Priya were like the sisters I never had. We were always there for each other through the worst and best of times… but today, I could have certainly taken a raincheck.

"What in the world happened to you?"

Lex gripped my shoulders, her eyes wide and horrified by my bruises. Priya's hand was on my arm, her face just as worried.

"Crazy guy at the precinct," I said, waving them off. "He was a senior, high out of his mind. I'm good. Just another day at work."

I wasn't surprised when Lex shook her head, unconvinced by my explanation. But as she began her tangent, her eyes locked behind me.

"Ladies, this is Derek Cain. He's James's son. Derek, Alexa, and Priya."

Their eyes flitted to me before settling back on Derek.

He greeted them with a nod and a tight smile, his gaze immediately finding mine as he moved to stand by my side. Lex and Priya wore broad smiles and beamed with enthusiasm.

"Damn," I heard my cousin say under her breath as she elbowed me in the rib.

"Well, I'll let you all enjoy your night." Derek's eyes never strayed from mine. "I'll talk to you later."

I nodded, almost closing the gap between our bodies, and tipped my head up as I rose to my toes. "You better—brother," I whispered near his ear with a wink.

"Hmm," he grunted, squeezing my hip.

A shudder rippled through me when his thumb lightly caressed the exposed skin above my waistband. It wasn't until he was out the door that I finally took a much-needed breath.

But that was short-lived. The moment Derek was gone, they pounced, bombarding me with an onslaught of comments and questions.

"*That* is James Ford's son? Oh, girl, you were not lying." Lex looped her arm in mine and dragged me into the living room. "I need all the details! But the most important question is: have you fucked that hot piece of man yet?"

I choked on my spit. "W-what?"

"Have you impaled yourself on Derek Cain's dick?" She punctuated every word.

Priya threw her head back and laughed, letting herself fall onto the couch. "It's a valid question," she said between snorts of laughter.

I pushed my cousin away and shook my head, trying to hide my smile. "Did you forget we just met?"

She rolled her eyes and scoffed. "Did you see the way he was undressing you with his eyes? Right here, in public? For what it's worth, Pri and I weren't even in the room."

"Not even for a second," my friend concurred, still giggling.

"Had I been you, I would have kicked our intrusive asses out and taken Mr. Muscles to bed with a quickness—or the couch, the floor. Wherever."

"If I wasn't married, same! And he looks like he knows some things too. If you know what I mean."

They nodded at each other in unison, complicit smirks lighting up their faces.

There was never a dull moment with these two. Lex and I had been best friends since the womb. Born only three weeks apart, we grew up more like sisters rather than cousins. We were often called *las gemelas*, the twins, as kids, because we looked so much alike.

Though that lasted until about the seventh grade. While Lex got to shop for D-cup bras and hit up all the cool stores at the mall, I was still rocking sports bras, and the Girls' section at Target was my unfortunate go-to. After my diagnosis, though, I quit competitive gymnastics, and things finally started filling out where they were supposed to. With a good four inches on me, Alexa and I might never be *las gemelas* again, but we were and would always be inseparable.

"You got all that from a thirty-second encounter?" I asked, propping my feet on the coffee table.

"You know how I am at reading people." Priya flipped her brown, wavy hair over her shoulder. "That man has secrets. He's wound up pretty tight, sure, but there's something about those mysterious eyes that tell a thousand stories."

Priya and I had been roommates during our freshman year of college. And she and Lex had fallen right into a close friendship the moment I'd introduced them. Solidifying our sisterhood, we'd been dual maids of honor at her wedding three years ago.

"Peel back those layers, girl. And let that man get into those sexually repressed, eight months celibate guts." Alexa chimed in, propping her feet next to mine.

I couldn't hold back my laughter. "Oh my God! Why are you keeping tabs on my sex life? And weren't you insinuating he could possibly be a serial killer?"

"Well, is he?"

I huffed out a breath. "No."

"And does he have a dick where his dick should be?"

I threw a cushion at her face. "You two are worse than men!"

"Eva?" Priya questioned in a bewildered tone. "There's a tiny cat in your living room, and it's staring at me."

I was officially the world's worst pet owner. How had I already forgotten about Diego? I scooped up the little furball and nuzzled him against my neck.

"I saved him from a ditch. Derek helped. Isn't he the cutest?"

Lex backed away from us, one eyebrow quirked. "Well, I'm not a cat person, but it's definitely adorable. You keeping it?"

"So, you and Derek saved this cat, huh? You know what that means?" Priya said, scratching behind Diego's ear. He closed his eyes and purred at her touch.

"I'm afraid to ask what you think it means."

"Well, you two basically adopted this cat together. That makes him your fur baby."

Lex pointed at us. "She's got a point."

"You two are so twisted," I said, chuckling and cradling Diego.

"Look, Eva, if you're not taking that fine ass man to bed, please, let me know. I will gladly step up. After all, we do look alike, no? I mean, except I have a better rack."

"Bitch!" I hurled another cushion at her head, and the three of us broke into peals of laughter. "Hey, I've been told a handful is plenty. Plus, just because I haven't slept with him… *yet*, that doesn't mean I'm not going to."

"I knew it! You little whore. You were practically humping his leg earlier."

I groaned loudly and headed into the kitchen. "I am so done with you!"

Chapter Nineteen

Derek

"What the fuck happened to you?"

Kai was at my front door as I pulled into my drive and climbed out of the car. He looked me up and down, arms across his chest and a cocky grin on his face. I glanced down at my soiled clothing and how one side of my shirt hung over my pants. I was a goddamn mess.

"Do I want to know?"

Tossing my jacket over one shoulder, I shrugged as I pushed open the door. "Snapped some asshole's neck and had a little run-in with Belov's crew while dumpster diving with a hot detective. You know, nothing too crazy."

Kai followed me inside, bellowing a laugh. "Your day sounds a hell of a lot more interesting than mine."

We moved into the kitchen, and I pulled out a bottle of Weller, setting two glasses on the counter with a loud clang. I slid a drink toward Kai and lifted my own with a nod before knocking back a sip.

"I thought you had that job out in Seattle." I glanced at my watch. "No way you came and went so fast."

Kai savored the amber liquid in his mouth, shaking his head and swallowing. "Trash took itself out. Guy turned himself into a street stain this morning. Jumped 200ft out of the City Centre building. Made my day a whole lot smoother and gave me time to catch up with Leni."

Needing to take the edge off, I poured myself another drink, brow cocked at his statement. "You and Helena again?"

"No, not like that. We have our fun, but we know what this is." He eyed me curiously. "How's the princess?"

I looked at him from behind my glass and chuckled. "What do you really want to know?"

Kai shrugged his shoulders and sat back on the barstool. "Ronan was asking questions. Something about you getting close to this girl bothers him. He didn't say as much, but it was obvious. Says you're letting pussy—his words, not mine—knock you off your game. Making you messy."

"Fuck him," I growled, squeezing the glass between my fingers.

My gratitude for what he'd saved Kai and me from only extended so far. Through the years, he'd proved his motives and where his loyalties lay. He didn't give a damn about either of us in any way that mattered. Neither did his whore of a wife.

"Well, you can tell him that in person, brother, because he warned me he'd stop by."

Speak of the fucking devil himself. No sooner had the words left Kai's mouth, my doorbell rang, and his image popped up on the screen of my cell phone.

"Fuck me. He brought Maeve with him too."

I cut across my living room and into the foyer, Deimos on my heels. Glancing at my screen one more time, I hoped they'd left or burst into flames.

The left side of Ronan's mouth twitched as he regarded me with disgust. Always one to take pride in my appearance, I was sure I saw him double-take at my disheveled look. Maeve simply offered a flirtatious grin, as usual.

"Derek, darling, you get into some kind of scuffle? Look at you!"

Maeve was the type of adoptive mother whose duties ended with signing the legal docs. I probably could have counted on one hand the times we'd been in the same room with her those first few years. Shortly after my seventeenth birthday, something about how her eyes lingered too long and how she'd lick her lips and blush around me made me uncomfortable. I didn't know it then, but she wasn't trying to be a mother figure. She was attempting to be a woman in my life.

One drunken night, she stumbled into my room, naked and panting like a whore in heat, proposing I let her teach me how to tame a woman as she dropped to her knees and grabbed my cock.

Ronan beat her bloody when I'd dragged her ass back into their quarters by her hair.

"Something I should know, Derek?" His voice was threatening yet calm as he walked to my bar and poured himself a drink. "You look like hell."

"No." My voice was sure, betraying no emotion.

"He's right, Der; you need me to run you a bath?" Maeve's hands reached for the collar of my halfway unbuttoned shirt, but I caught her wrists, eyes lancing through her in a warning. "Don't."

"Wait in the car," Ronan ordered, slamming the whiskey decanter on the bar.

Used to her harsh but lavish life beside Ronan Cain, Maeve simply scoffed, patting my chest before I could stop her.

"One of these days, Derek. You'll see," she purred with a wink.

I gripped her elbow and leaned close to her ear. "The only thing I want from you is to know what your screams sound like when I gut you like a fish."

Another humorless chuckle fell from her lips. "Don't threaten me with a good time, darling." She blew a kiss and strode out the door.

"You're going to tell me what you've been up to? The clean-up team had quite the mess to take care of this morning, none other than one of Belov's men. Are you trying to start a war? And over pussy, no less."

I gritted my teeth as he watched, waiting for a reaction. Always waiting for me to fuck up.

"We have access to more whores and wet cunts than we know what to do with, yet you're out here defending the honor of some woman you barely know."

He took a long swig of his drink, eyes still fixed on me. Visions of breaking that glass over his head and shoving the shards down his throat raged in my thoughts. It was just one of the many creative ways I'd fantasized about taking his life. Hell, I'd spilled my own father's blood, split his fucking skull in two, and went home and slept like the dead while his brain matter was still painted on the front of my shirt. Killing Ronan would be no different. It would bring me immense satisfaction, yet I knew I couldn't. As the head of Ares, he was untouchable.

"That's not what happened."

Ronan leaned both hands on the marble counter. "Don't play me for a fool, Derek. Andrey Smirnoff was the same son of bitch at the infirmary with Kiernan." He leveled me with a poignant stare. "What? You were teaching him a lesson? Staking your claim on that tight little ass, huh?"

"Enough."

Ronan's grin spread wide as he lifted the glass in front of him, an accusatory finger pointed at me. "I let you go off the books with your little revenge plot against that bottom feeder, Ford. Hell, I don't care if you cut the dicks off every bastard in this city." He lowered the glass onto a side table, eyes steeling me in place. "But *not* Belov's men. Is that understood?"

I tilted my head and studied him. How easy would it be to make him disappear? To tear out that black heart of his as he watched. The sharp steel tucked inside my pants suddenly felt heavy. Hot. Begging for me to reach for it.

"I see that look in your eyes, Derek. It's the same one I saw all those years ago. The reason I knew you were exactly what I was looking for." He moved closer until we were just a foot apart and at eye level.

I couldn't deny there was a part of me that felt indebted to this fucker. And maybe it was the reason I'd learned to control my rage when he challenged me.

The day he walked into that run-down group home all those years ago, that house of horrors and perversion, he'd saved me.

Saved us.

"I promised you'd never be on your knees for another man again, didn't I?" His voice was a hard rasp near my ear. And I clenched my teeth, a growl rattling in my chest at his words and the visuals they evoked.

Those tortured memories dwelled in the darkest recesses of my mind.

"And I let you have your revenge. Gave you the skills, the power to make that son of a bitch cower at your feet before you took his head."

I squeezed my eyes closed, conjuring the face of a long-dead piece of shit named Robert. The smell of his blood, his wails, the pathetic way he begged for his life and clamored for mercy—a courtesy he never afforded me while he severed my last tether to innocence.

"Don't forget who made you the man you are. Gave you all this—Turned you into a god." Ronan clapped my neck. "Tomorrow, you'll be in Marseilles. My people there will hook you up with all the top-shelf European pussy you could ever need to flush this one insignificant woman from your system."

Chapter Twenty

Derek

Evangelina: How was your day? I'm wrapping up paperwork on a case and grabbing coffee with Sam.

I wasn't the jealous type. Never had to be. But something about Eva enjoying another man's company rubbed me in all the wrong ways, especially when it had been just over a week since I'd last seen her. Meanwhile, that asshole Sam had probably been like her goddamn shadow for hours on end—day after day.

Fuck him.

ME: Good. In bed. Flight is in five hours. Are you at our coffee spot?

EVANGELINA: I didn't know we had a coffee spot.

I pictured her dimpled grin and felt the pull of a smile at the corner of my own mouth.

EVANGELINA: I'm at a cute little outdoor shop on 8th Street. You'd like it.

ME: You'll have to take me when I get back.

EVANGELINA: It's a date.

EVANGELINA: Goodnight, Derek. Have a safe flight <3

Since the day I'd told her I would fuck her over every surface of my home—which I had full intentions of doing—things had been strange between us. Our text conversations were kept light and always to the point. She wasn't cold or distant, but… guarded. I convinced myself it was because she was still broken over her missing friend. But there was an odd feeling in my chest. Heaviness. A longing I'd never felt before. And it wasn't until two days ago that I realized what it was. The foreign sensation surprised me, sending an icy chill through my body.

I missed her.

I fucking missed her.

Her smell. The smoky sound of her voice. The way her pouty upper lip curled up when she smiled.

Fuck me. When had I ever noticed or cared about those things in women? All I needed was a pretty face and a wet cunt.

Simple.

But why did I crave more?

The French whores who'd thrown themselves at my cock checked those boxes, but for the first time, I wasn't interested.

None of them were Eva.

I stuffed my hands in my pockets as I turned the corner on a busy street near downtown Philly. Once she came into view, I came to a full stop. The weight in my chest was gone. She was exactly where she said she'd be and looking every bit as gorgeous as when I left. I'd wanted to surprise her, though I didn't understand why, and finished the job in Paris sooner than planned before jumping on the first flight out of France. And while jet lag was a bitch, I couldn't wait another day to see her, so I raced through rush-hour traffic the moment she'd given me her location. Now, there I was, behind a tree, watching her like some creepy fuck.

Her partner spent a lot of his time with his face glued to his phone or fixed on whatever he was penning into a notebook, even as they engaged in conversation. While I was happy their relationship was strictly professional, I was also baffled by his disinterest. Evangelina was fucking stunning, even with her hair pulled up into a messy bun at the top of her head. I'd never tire of looking at her. Though I supposed I was glad I didn't have to be the reason she mourned another person in her life.

I'd never regret killing that bastard, James, though the thought of her hatred filled my chest with angst.

Wasn't that the point?

It was—is.

Maybe Ronan had been right. I just needed to purge her from my system. Her pussy was no different. I'd have my fun and move the fuck on.

Evangelina slid her chair back and pushed to her feet, heading toward a coffee truck and giving me the perfect opportunity to approach. I took a few moments to admire the sweet curve of her ass and toned little thighs in those black leggings and signature combat boots.

The scent of her perfume assailed my senses and heated the blood in my veins. I wanted nothing more than to pick her up, take her back home, and burn the whole fucking house to the ground.

Patience. I had to control myself, or else I'd follow through with my intrusive thoughts and pluck her right off this sidewalk.

Eva stiffened at the feel of my presence at her back. I ran my lips along the soft skin at her nape, and her hand shot to the holstered gun at her waist. But I quickly covered it with mine.

"Not the welcome back greeting I was expecting." She released an audible gasp. "There it is. Miss me, angel?"

She spun around in my arms. "Derek? You sneaky bastard! Why didn't you tell me you were back?"

Her arms came up around my neck in a hug, and I pulled her close, nuzzling into her hair and drinking her in.

"Thought it would be a fun little surprise."

Her pretty features softened. "It is."

She looked past me and shook her head at who I could only assume was her partner. By the time I turned around, he was closing up the side of his jacket where he'd tucked that pussy Glock 26.

Eva introduced us, and I put on my good guy act—as much as my pride would allow. He seemed uneasy, eyes unsettled, ping-ponging between the two of us. And I caught him glancing at my tattoos. Exactly as I'd predicted. While my suit was probably worth more than his whole wardrobe, and my net worth more than he'd ever see in his lifetime, he'd turn his nose up at me.

And here I almost tolerated Sam.

"Eva, how about I take this home and finish up the notes? Give you two some time to catch up or whatever."

Maybe he wasn't half bad.

"Sure. If you don't mind?"

He gave her a smile that didn't quite reach his beady eyes before turning to me and putting on his best performance of loyal partner.

Gathering his belongings, he gave Eva one last nod as he climbed into a white sedan.

"Why didn't you just tell me you were back stateside? What if I'd left before you got here?"

"Well, I know where to find you, don't I?"

A smile crested her pretty lips, and she closed the gap between us, hands on my chest.

"You missed me or something, Cain?"

A loud rumble in my stomach beat me to an answer. Eva's eyes widened with amusement, and she chuckled.

"Sorry. Haven't had dinner yet. My flight got in two hours ago."

She grabbed my hand while slinging a black bag over her shoulder. "There's this cute little Mediterranean spot up the street."

The thought of being cooped up in another enclosed space was not appealing. A 22-hour flight tended to fill the confined space quota for one day or ten. Even the short drive here had me nearly crawling out of my skin.

"I think I prefer the fresh air."

Her face lit up with the brightest smile I'd ever seen on her.

"I know a place!"

A ten-minute walk had us in front of a street vendor, the name Big D's Footlongs painted red on the side of the white truck.

I side-eyed her as she strung me along. "Street food? Big D's?"

"Oh, come on, it's a clever name. And don't tell me you're above food trucks."

"Call me crazy, but I'm not a fan of food poisoning."

She laughed outright and hauled me closer to the counter by my wrist.

"It's certainly no Michelin star, but close enough," she said, throwing me a wink.

"Close enough, she says."

Another joyful laugh filled the air, and I couldn't help smiling at her happiness. It was contagious.

"Trust me. Ian makes the best dogs this side of Philly."

I dug my heels into the pavement, and we came to a stop. "Ian, is it?" Eva playfully rolled her eyes. "I can't remember the last time I had a… hotdog. And it's probably attached to a memory I'd much rather forget."

Her mouth parted slightly, guilt pinching her features. "Derek, I'm so sorry. I didn't even think—"

Sliding an arm around her waist, I put a finger to her lips. "It's okay. I'll eat the damn hotdog." She made a motion to protest, but I shook my head and leaned in close. "As long as you eat one for me too."

My finger was still pressed against her lips when she brushed them lightly and nodded, eyes on mine.

This woman didn't even have to try, and she already had my dick hard and aching to be inside her. Sliding her fingers through mine, she pulled me toward a large cardboard menu with an endless list of toppings and unhealthy entrées.

As a kid, I was lucky to get a cold hot dog, let alone bread. But the amount of variation in front of me had my eyes wide and, maybe, just a little bit, my mouth watering.

We sat with our dinner on a nearby bench, far enough away from the sidewalk that we had privacy. I held a small tray piled high with toppings and fixings while Eva had one breadless dog wrapped in aluminum foil.

"Not that hungry?"

"It's not that. I just have to watch my carbs."

Eva was so beautiful, so full of life, that it was easy to forget her illness.

"How was your trip?" she asked, carefully unwrapping the food over her thighs.

"It was just business. Nothing special. I'm glad to be back."

She let out an incredulous laugh. "You're happy to be back here? In Philly, over France? I don't believe that for a second."

I eyed the mountain of toppings on my lap, trying to figure out how the hell I was going to dig in without looking like I needed a bib.

"I don't understand what you mean. This is home, isn't it?"

"Anything's better than here. Some of my best summers were spent in the French Riviera and Marseilles." Her eyes slid in my direction, and she shrugged her shoulders. "The sights, the city of love and all that? I'm sure those French girls were swooning over your tattoos and unapproachable, brooding face."

Nearly choking on a bite of hotdog—which was surprisingly quite good—I swallowed audibly, washing down the remnants with water. "For one, this face is very approachable." She belted out an exaggerated laugh. "And two, I don't give a damn about those French girls. Look at me, angel." I reached for her, tipping her face to me. She was serious now, gaze drifting between my eyes and lips. "I'm exactly where I want to be."

The smile she gifted me made my chest tight. And another loud swallow echoed in my throat. I suddenly felt the urge to put a hand over my heart and grip my shirt.

Was I having a fucking heart attack?

"I'm glad you're back too. But you have something on the corner of your mouth." She giggled.

"Oh, fuck."

Eva beat me to the rough sheet of sandpaper they tried to pass off as a napkin and gently wiped the corner of my mouth.

"It's just ketchup." Her soft touch was warm, heating my skin where her fingers lay on my forearm, the fire bleeding through the fabric of my jacket.

A lightheaded feeling forced my eyes closed, and I drew a breath.

Was I coming down with something?

"So what's the verdict? How's your hotdog?"

"It's good," I said, blinking away the haze. "Better than I remember. And it's cooked, so that's a plus." Her smile instantly vanished, pulling mine with it. "What's the matter?"

"Can I... ask you something?"

The seriousness of her tone and the hesitancy in her voice made the direction of her questioning clear.

I nodded.

"What was it like for you? Growing up?"

"You mean, growing up in foster care where not one person in the world gave a damn about me? Pretty fucking shitty."

She dropped her eyes, shaking her head. "I'm so sorry. I wish I'd known. I would have—"

"Would have, what?" I lifted her face again, but she refused to look me in the eyes. "You were just a kid yourself, Eva." A tear beaded at the corner of her lashes, and I leaned in and pressed my lips to the droplet, whispering into her skin, "None of that was your fault."

Not her fault.

Fuck.

"You didn't deserve that." Her voice cracked. "He could have given you the world, Derek. Instead, he just left you... abandoned you."

"Eva," I murmured, cradling her face, "why are you crying?"

Emotion burned inside my throat, and I swallowed back the painful lump. I couldn't recall the last time I'd felt the sting of tears in my eyes or the weight of anguish on my chest. My body had probably forgotten how to cry. Hell, I'd cried a lifetime of tears as a child and simply thought my well had run dry decades ago.

She latched onto my shirt. Our food, long forgotten, had fallen to the pavement.

"Whatever you went through, whatever happened to you, I know it changed you." Leaning her forehead on my chin, she sniveled and exhaled a long, shaky breath. "I can see it in your eyes. You carry so much pain."

"That was a long time ago." I kissed her hairline. "You're crying for me, angel? Why?" She peered up at me through the fringe of her lashes. "*Why?*" I pressed, needing to hear her say something. Anything. For her to tell me, she gave a damn.

Why? I asked myself... Did *I* give a damn?

My breath hitched.

No.

Fuck.

Fuck.

Fuck.

And it all suddenly made sense. But it couldn't. This—*we* couldn't be.

I couldn't.

Swiping at her tears with my thumbs, it was like the pieces of my life suddenly fell into place when I realized I'd give anything at that moment so I'd never see her cry again.

Shit.

"Because it matters. You matter... to me," she said, jarring me from my stupor.

My ability to speak faltered, leaving me utterly speechless as she watched me, waiting for a response. Met with silence, the light in her eyes dimmed, and she looked away and sat back against the iron bench.

What did she expect from me?

I wasn't the man she thought I was. Evangelina had no idea who I truly was. The depravity and chaos I was capable of. She'd never understand my past and the darkness lurking within me. And most importantly, she could never fathom nor forgive the horrific things I'd done.

Whatever this was, whatever bewitching spell she had cast on me couldn't be. Falling for her was never the plan. She was supposed to be mine to ruin. To make that bastard roll in his grave. She was...

Fuck.

She was beautiful.

Light.

I hadn't realized when she'd gotten off the bench, but she was picking up the lost hotdogs from the ground and tossing them into a trash bin. God, did she have to be so goddamn virtuous? And when the hell had that particular trait ever mattered to me?

I needed to clear my head. To get away from her.

"Eva, did you drive here?"

She nodded slowly. Her red-rimmed eyes were narrowed, sad. I'd disappointed her with my indifference.

"Yeah, my car's back by the coffee spot."

"I'll walk you. I just—I..."

Was I fucking stammering?

"Derek," she said, throwing her bag over her shoulder, "is there something wrong?”

"No. Why?”

"It's just that, one moment, you're—I don't know. But now you're… acting differently.”

I shoved my hands into my pockets and started down the sidewalk. The mask firmly back in place, and my feelings locked away where they belonged.

"You brought up a sore subject. That's all.”

I stopped when I couldn't feel the warmth of her presence close by. I turned to find her still standing by the bench, staring at me with those beautiful brown eyes. They were pleading for something I couldn't give her.

If I cut her from my life, it would save us both from the inevitable fallout later.

"I didn't mean to upset you. If I'd known—”

"So drop it.” My tone was harsh, causing her to rear back as if I'd hit her.

She clutched the strap of her bag and shook her head indignantly. "I don't understand you.”

"Of course you don't, princess. We come from two different worlds.”

"Princess?” She rolled her eyes and started down the sidewalk. "Don't bother walking me to my car,” Eva clipped as she moved past me.

"Eva?” She stopped, but didn't turn around. This was a defining moment. I had to kill whatever fire, whatever forbidden emotion this was brewing between us. Fucking her was one thing. But feelings—I didn't do feelings. I didn't know how to feel. "I don't need you to understand, nor do I want your sympathy. And you can keep your tears. They mean nothing and won't change a damn thing."

Her shoulders stiffened for the briefest moment before she took off down the street and around the corner without another word. And while I warred with every fiber of my being to go after her and apologize, I remained in place, fists clenched at my sides.

This was the way things had to be.

But if that was true, why was there another sentiment overpowering my every thought?

Mine.

Chapter Twenty One
Evangelina

9th PRECINCT, PHILADELPHIA

I swayed back and forth in my chair, only half focused on the file in front of me, feeling wired, even though I'd had a shit night. In just a few minutes, Yuri Belov would be sitting in front of me. The underboss of the Belov crime family and the last person in contact with James. This interrogation was a long time coming. Blood whirred in my ears at the anticipation of being in his presence, the man possibly responsible for James's death. From what we'd uncovered in the past week, we knew he owed Yuri money stemming from a deal that had gone sideways. And I could only speculate Belov might have felt double-crossed. It seemed like a plausible motive.

Unfortunately, I couldn't interrogate him on any of those findings—some bullshit about a conflict of interest and circumstantial evidence.

My cell buzzed against my desk, and I hated the quick fluttering inside my belly when Derek's name lit up my screen. It had been nearly a week, six days, to be exact—not that I was counting—since I'd seen or spoken to him. I hated that I missed him. I hated even more that

I'd thought about him nonstop, even though he'd acted like a dick. Derek was such an enigma. One moment, he was so charismatic and sweet, then the next, it was like something else entirely came over him.

I silenced the phone and clasped my hands together to keep them under control, tearing my eyes from the tempting device and trying to occupy myself with the notes in Yuri's file.

DEREK: Angel, can you talk?

The audacity of him to think he could just text out of the blue and use nicknames after being rude and ghosting me for a week.

I tapped my nails on the desk, contemplating if I should reply. And what would I even say?

Damn it.

Picking up my cell, I pushed the call back button before I could regret it and sat back in my chair, waiting for him to say his piece… but mostly craving to hear his voice.

I was weak. Sue me.

"Derek."

"Eva. I know you're at work, so I don't want to keep you. I just want to apologize for being a dick."

I nodded as if he could see me. "Yes, you were."

He chuckled low on the other end. "That wasn't my intention. My past is—"

"I get it. I won't bring it up again. Anything else?" My tone was curt, meant to sting, but I died a bit inside when I was met with his silence. Treating him this way felt wrong and unnatural.

Especially after coming so hard last night with his name on my lips.

"I'm sorry, angel. I'll let you get back to work."

That's it?

"Wait…"

Shit.

"What is it?"

Sam poked his head into my cubicle before I could answer. Maybe it was divine intervention because Lord knew I was about to sound much too desperate.

I looked down at my watch. "Nothing. Listen, I'm about to go into an interrogation with Belov and…"

"Did you say Belov?" he asked, his voice sounding strangled.

"Yes, but I can't really get into details—"

"Evangelina." I heard him exhale into the receiver.

"What is it?"

"Just… be careful."

I let out a cynical laugh. As attracted as I was to Derek, I couldn't deny the pricks of agitation nipping up the back of my neck because I knew the reason behind his unwarranted concern when I mentioned Belov. I'd worked my ass off to make detective. I wasn't a rookie or some weak chick who couldn't hold her own. Having stared down the worst of society was what I did almost daily. It was my job. And I was damn good at it too.

"I'll talk to you later, Derek."

Before he could utter a response, I ended the call. Having met three weeks ago, I shouldn't feel the heaviness settling in my heart, this dark cloud hanging thick over my head.

Sam's brows knitted together when he studied my face more closely.

"Cruz, something wrong?"

"No, men are just stupid," I said, swatting him with my file as I walked past him.

He put a hand over his heart in a show of theatrics and cried, "Ouch! And here I thought I was different."

"Nope. You're all the same."

"Oh, come on, Eva!" he said and laughed with his hands on his hips.

I reached room 2B. Yuri was leaning back against his chair, looking like he didn't have a single care in the world. The sight was infuriating, knowing he was probably just going to get off like he'd done every time. Power and money were enough to sway an often biased system, and the Belov family was in abundance of both. I wanted nothing more than to nail his ass to the wall. If he wasn't going to go down for murdering James, then we had to get him on the Southside junkyard murders. We had his plates, an eyewitness, and a shitty video. He didn't need to know the footage was crap. He just needed to think we had something concrete.

Derek and I had no idea he'd also been there.

Of course, I wouldn't. I was too busy wrapped around his hard body to care.

I shook those thoughts from my mind and steadied myself, putting my game face on.

"Yuri Belov." I locked eyes with him as I strolled into the small room.

"*Nakonets-to poyavilos' chto-to krasivoye, krome etogo urodlivogo ublyudka,*" he said, a lecherous grin on his face. *(Finally, something pretty to look at other than this ugly bastard.)*

Placing his file and both palms on the table, I challenged his leering gaze.

"*Kak naschet togo, chtoby vy porezali der'mo i davayte pristupim k delu.*" (*How about you cut the shit and let's get down to business.*)

I leaned forward a little more, my breasts pushing against the front seam of my blouse. While it contradicted everything I stood for, I wasn't above using my God-given assets for a bit of sway if it meant he was put away for good.

Belov's grin pulled wider as he straightened, interest piqued. "Ah, you know my language, do you? *Krasivaya latinoamerikanka, umeyushchaya govorit' po-russki? YA ochen' vpechatlen.*" (*A beautiful Latina who speaks Russian. I'm impressed.*)

His lawyer sat beside him and nudged his elbow. The prematurely balding attorney was sweating, looking just as spineless.

"As I said, let's cut the bullshit. You know why you're here."

"Do I? Your men come into my business and say they want to talk to me. And I'm a good guy." His accent was heavy. "So, here I am, Miss—"

"Detective. Detective Cruz."

"Of course. *Detective Cruz.* And how can I help you?"

I pushed off the table and paced with calculated steps. The heat from his stare burned at my back. With the corner of my eye, I watched him widen his knees and adjust himself. Bile quickly rose up my throat, and I swallowed it down, trying to mask my disgust.

"What can you tell me about the murders at Cody's Salvage Yard on the Southside?"

"Never heard of this Cody person," he said, not even looking me in the face or trying to hide his ogling.

"That's funny, CCTV says differently. Your face, your plates." His slimeball lawyer opened his mouth to speak, but Belov put a hand up, shutting him down. "An eyewitness."

"*Fignya*! Bullshit!"

I pulled a still photo from his file. The image had been enhanced to make his face clearer and more recognizable.

"Don't say anymore, Mr. Belov," his lawyer warned.

"One of the victims also had your DNA under his nailbed." The preliminary results hadn't come back yet. But from the footage, one of Cody's employees had left a gnarly gash on his right forearm. "Can you roll up your sleeve for me?"

"*Nyet*. It's not me. You've made a mistake."

"That's fine," I said, leaning both hands back on the table. "We have search warrants being processed as we speak. For both of your businesses and your home."

His face flushed red, and he pounded a fist against the metal surface before going off into a Russian tirade. He called me a whore and said I'd be better off on my knees sucking his dick than pretending to be a cop. The insults didn't faze me in the least. Unfortunately, I was used to the sexual innuendos, the sleazy looks, and lewd offers. I'd heard and seen it all.

"Mr. Belov, calm down," the other man cautioned as he stood.

Yuri was in a rage. He shoved his lawyer, making him stumble backward. I signaled for backup into the two-way mirror as Belov seemed to be spiraling out of control.

In a sudden flash of movement, the Mafia underboss pulled a blade from between his belt and grabbed me, pressing it to the side of my neck. Sam and six more officers barreled into the room, their weapons drawn.

"I'll kill this bitch! Put your guns on the floor and let me go."

"Yuri," I said, my voice breaking, "please, don't do this. Put the knife down." Tears streamed down my cheeks, wetting his arm. I made eye contact with my partner, sending a subtle wink his way.

Of course, I was scared shitless. The man was unhinged, but I had to play it up. Play the part he expected from me to buy some time.

He cackled close to my ear, whispering in Russian how he wished to fold me over the table and fuck me while I begged for my life.

Having had enough of his shit, I executed the maneuver I'd practiced dozens of times for a knife-to-the-throat scenario. I gripped his hands and pulled in a downward motion as I tucked my body into his and under his arm. Caught off guard, his reaction time was slow at first, but just as I tried to slip away, he attempted to twist the blade and stab me. I was ready for him, though. Using his own momentum against him, I pushed his knife-wielding hand into the side of his abdomen, plunging the blade beneath his ribs. Yuri howled in pain and fell to his knees.

Several officers dogpiled him while Sam pulled me into the hallway.

"Cruz, you're hurt. Sit down. Paramedics are on the way."

I shook my head, fighting against his attempts to put me in a chair.

"You did *not* call an ambulance. Sam, I'm fine."

"No, you're not."

My protests died on my lips when I finally registered a warm trickle sliding down my neck. Sam pressed a small towel against my wound.

"He cut you. It doesn't look too deep, but it's better to take precautions. How are you feeling?"

Fuck. I hadn't even felt that asshole cut me, which meant I was high as a kite on adrenaline. I knew the spike was coming. Maybe it was the stress of it all still fresh and hanging over my head that made me feel like it was creeping. Either way, I needed my kit. To make matters worse, I hadn't replaced my pump this morning. I needed a bolus of insulin and the mental preparation to deal with the next several hours.

Chapter Twenty Two

Derek

Having broken a handful of traffic laws, my car skidded to a halt in the driveway of Evangelina's home. News had leaked of an assault on an officer at the 9th precinct. When my texts had gone unanswered and my calls straight to voicemail, I jumped in my car and raced over. The need to see her, to know she was all right, was frighteningly overwhelming. I charged up the steps, taking them two at a time, and curled my fists, resisting the urge to pound on the door.

Stabbing at the doorbell instead, I waited for what seemed like a fucking lifetime until the sound of the locks pulled a sigh of relief from my lungs.

"Derek?" Her voice was hoarse, eyes squinting against the bright porch lights.

She'd been asleep. But she was okay and in one piece.

"What are you doing here?"

I reached for her and said nothing, tucking her into my arms, chin resting on the top of her head as emotions I didn't know what to do with gathered in my throat.

"Hey," she whispered, tenderly putting her hand over my chest, as if sensing the storm brewing inside me, "I'm okay. It was mostly superficial."

I didn't let her speak another word. Reaching down, I scooped her up and cradled her body. Eva's brown eyes locked on mine, and neither of us said another word as I cut across the long entry hallway to the living room.

Unbelievable. Eva was trying to comfort *me*.

Yet I'd been the asshole, and she was the one who was hurt.

"I called you. When I heard what happened and you didn't answer, I didn't know what to think."

Her eyes narrowed ever so slightly as she regarded me curiously before answering. "I'm sorry. When I got home, I fell asleep. I wasn't feeling too well and—"

I dropped my forehead to hers.

"I'm sorry," I whispered, unable to remember the last time I'd sincerely apologized to anyone. "I'm sorry for what I said and for acting like an asshole."

Though my apology was sincere, I wasn't here solely for her feelings. I was here for mine too. Letting her walk away that night wasn't just to spare her pain but rather to save myself. I was a ruthless son of a bitch. Letting her go to avoid breaking her when she found out the monster I truly was should have been a good enough reason to stay gone. But I'd never been a righteous man a day in my life. I was far too selfish, too depraved, and obsessed to let her go. I needed a taste, all of her, until I'd had my fill.

I told her I would have her, and I had every intention of following through on that promise.

Eva was already mine.

"You were a jerk," she said, placing a hand over my cheek, and I leaned into her touch.

"I won't deny that I am a certified dick. But you already knew that."

She cracked a smile.

"I won't argue that. But you can put me down now."

"Is that what you want?" I asked, running my mouth along her jaw. "I've told you before. I can hold you like this as long as it takes."

"Don't let go," she murmured against my cheek.

Pressing her closer, I lowered our bodies onto the sofa.

Diego watched us intently from his perch on the arm of a recliner. For whatever reason, I felt the need to greet the little bastard, so I acknowledged him with a nod. His yellow eyes gleamed as he looked on, tilting his head.

Eva was staring again, waiting for something. Maybe a deeper explanation, waiting for an answer I wasn't prepared to give her. Mostly because I didn't know who the fuck I was when I was with her. Her touch, her closeness, lit up everything inside me. Even my dick was hard beneath her, making me feel like an inconsiderate jackass.

"What happened today?"

She sighed and rested her head on my shoulder.

"When Yuri knew we had him, he just lost it. Assaulted his lawyer and pulled a knife on me."

"How the hell did he sneak a knife into a police interrogation room?" I gritted my teeth and swallowed hard, talking down the demons, lusting for revenge.

"Mistakes were made. And those involved are being disciplined."

"Their fuck up could have cost you your life. That's not something to take lightly. What if he'd cut you deeper? Were you in there alone?"

Evangelina straightened on my lap, a serious look on her face. "Do you know how many times I've stepped into that room alone? I don't need a man to protect me, Derek. I handled myself and did exactly what I was trained to do."

There was an edge to her tone, probably residual anger from how our phone call ended earlier that day. If she thought I was underestimating her, she was dead wrong. I was wholly aware of the fire that lived inside her.

She motioned to lift herself off my lap, but I gripped her hips in place.

"Hey, whatever you're assuming I meant earlier on the phone, that's not the case at all."

"Look, I'm used to people thinking I belong pushing papers behind some desk or in a different field altogether. But you're the last person I want thinking those things about me."

I held her face.

"I don't have many people in my life I give a damn about. You, angel—I told you once before. You're in my life now. You're important to me. I was just worried."

Evangelina's hands snaked up my chest. "Is that why you left tire treads in my driveway… because you were worried about me?"

My eyes moved to her lips, and she smiled. "I would have kicked the damn door down if you'd made me wait one more second."

"Oh, you were destruction-of-property type of worried?"

Her fingers crawled up the front of my shirt, curling around my collar.

"For you, yeah." That earned me a smile, but instead of returning the gesture, my expression turned serious. "Eva, if something happens or you ever feel sick, I want you to call me. No matter the time." Another smile hitched the corners of her mouth. "An adrenaline rush like you had today can spike your glucose levels, right? Is that why you're feeling sick?" I asked, thumb pushing on her bottom lip as they parted in surprise.

"How did you know that?"

I shrugged my shoulders, not wanting to make a big deal out of my research. "I've been reading some stuff."

"God, *Derek*." Her tone was low and breathy.

Evangelina hoisted a leg over and sat on my pelvis, thick little thighs straddling my lap.

It was at that moment I registered what she was wearing. Skin-tight black shorts as tiny as underwear peeked out from under an oversized, white t-shirt. The collar was stretched out, hanging off a bare shoulder, and she wasn't wearing a bra.

A groan rattled in my chest at the sight of her pert nipples jutting through the thin fabric as she ground her ass against the shaft of my rock-hard cock. I stilled her hips, fingers digging into her skin. "Angel, if you keep doing that."

"*Quédate conmigo*," she whispered, lips brushing up my neck.

Stay with her.

"I'll stay for as long as you need me to… but if you keep that up…." I squeezed her hips harder, stilling her once more. "Eva," I warned.

"Oh, I'm just Eva now?" More kisses up my jaw.

"Baby, you got me losing my head over here." She smiled against my skin, thoroughly enjoying this game of seduction.

"I recall you saying you were going to fuck me over every surface and have me on my knees, Derek Cain."

The tip of her tongue swiped my earlobe.

Fuck.

"You're not feeling well, and I won't make things worse." I pitched my voice low, mouth brushing over the shell of her ear. "No matter how badly I want to bend you over this goddamn couch."

She cursed under her breath and arched her back, the seam of her ass pushing against my dick. "You won't hurt me." Her sweet little tongue was mesmerizing as it swept across her bottom lip.

"There's nothing gentle about the things I want to do to you." I pulled her face close as I licked the same path hers had taken seconds before. "I already warned you." Sliding a hand under her t-shirt, I caressed the underside of her breast. "I'll tear you apart, angel. Piece by piece. Inch by delicious inch."

Her eyes were hooded as my thumb rubbed circles over the stiff peak of her nipple.

"Do it," she whispered.

"Eva," I cautioned again, squeezing it between my fingers, causing her to whimper.

Since when had I cared about anyone but myself? I was convinced I'd officially lost my damn mind. A gorgeous and very willing woman wanted me to fuck her until she was wrecked, and I was rejecting her, afraid I'd hurt her.

Evangelina gripped my belt buckle and leaned forward, nipping at the pulse point on my neck.

"It's 10 p.m., Derek. Why are you still in a damn suit?" The heat of her breath against my flesh had me thrusting my cock against her ass, the friction forcing a groan from my throat.

I knew I couldn't have her like this. And I hated that I even cared since I'd never given a shit. As long as I got off, that's all that mattered. Kai would never let me live this down if he ever found out.

Things were different with her. Always fucking different. But I was done trying to overanalyze my feelings. She and I would have our fun and walk away as unscathed as we could.

"You're always in your head, Derek."

Looking onto her eyes, it was difficult to focus on anything else but her warm little cunt grinding against my dick.

So I gripped her wrists, and she was on her back in one fluid movement, arms trapped above her head.

Eva's eyes flew open and remained wide. Only when I felt the resistance against my hold did I remember what she'd told me about her past.

"It's just me. You can trust me." I didn't know if I was trying to convince her or myself.

She closed her eyes and mouthed something I couldn't understand before opening them and nodding slowly.

"I know."

I grinned as I used my knee to push her thighs open and settle between them.

"I'm dying to know what you taste like."

"Find out."

Chuckling over her lips, I said, "My girl is so fucking needy."

"Your girl?"

My grip on her wrists tightened, and I thrust against her. Eva was tempting my non-existent self-restraint.

"You're mine. You've been mine from the moment I saw you. How many times do I have to remind you?"

"I don't want you to remind me. I want you to show me." She lifted her head off the couch and slid her tongue vertically across my lips. "So, what the fuck are you waiting for?"

My mouth crashed into hers without another second of hesitation, and I got my first real taste of Evangelina. She tasted like fucking heaven—and fresh mint, and I smiled against her lips, understanding why it had taken her so long to answer the door.

Kissing her harder, I swallowed all her little whimpers and moans, my tongue snaking inside her mouth and sliding against hers.

"So goddamn perfect," I growled, trailing tongue and teeth down the column of her throat.

Moving to her chest, I sucked on the tip of one breast while cupping and kneading the other. She moaned and arched her back, offering more of herself to me. The brown imprint of her nipple was visible through the wet fabric, and I couldn't help the low growl that rumbled through my teeth. She was so fucking sexy. All I wanted was to bury my cock inside her.

Evangelina fought against my hold, and I released her wrists, my hand sliding down until it was around her throat.

"Angel, you let me take care of you." As I applied pressure, she hissed in pain when my fingers grazed her bandage. I immediately released her and sat back on my knees. "Fuck. I'm sorry."

She leaned on her elbows, a perplexed look on her face. "I'm fine. You didn't hurt me."

Shooting to my feet, I ran a rough hand through my hair. She was lying, for my sake. I didn't know what was more unnerving, the fact that I was so bent out of shape for hurting her or that I was denying myself sex for fear of the same outcome.

I straightened out my jacket.

"It's late—"

"Stop it. I'm not made of glass." She stood and put a hand on my forearm. "Hey, I'm *fine*."

"We can't do this right now."

"We're adults, Derek. We can do whatever we want. You want it. I want it. What's the problem?"

As she folded her arms across her chest, disappointment etched onto her face.

"I'm no good for you." Tugging her to me gently, I ran a thumb against her swollen bottom lip, wiping away all the traces of our passion.

"What are you talking about?" Her voice was a whisper.

Our gazes focused on one another, her wary eyes searching mine for answers. Everything inside me screamed that I should run and never return. But like the masochistic fuck I was, I knew I wouldn't.

And for the first time since I was a vulnerable child, I felt powerless at the mercy of this woman.

I pulled her closer.

"Do you have a guest room?"

"A guest room?"

"Or I can leave."

"Do you usually turn down women who all but throw themselves at you? God, I'm so stupid. I thought—"

I grabbed her hand and pressed it against the still-hard length of my dick. "You thought what? That I don't want to fuck you? Oh, I'm going to fuck you, angel. Fuck that defiance right out of you."

Her breathing accelerated. "What's stopping you, then?"

"Where's your guest room, Evangelina?" I asked, my tone rough by her ear.

Eva put a hand on my chest and pushed away from me. Before I registered what she was doing, she wrenched her shirt over her head and tossed it on the couch. My hungry eyes instantly dropped to her gorgeous breasts. They were perfection. Just big enough for me to hold and worship, peaked with light brown nipples, begging to be sucked. Journeying down the subtle curve of her waist, lined with defined muscle, my mouth watered.

A small white device adhered to the skin just above the waistband of her shorts.

She'd felt sick today. As much as I wanted her, I wouldn't have her like this.

"You can take the guest room down the hall, past the kitchen. The attached bathroom has extra toiletries. Goodnight, Derek."

Her tone was cold. I caught her wrist as she walked past me, but Evangelina refused to turn around, remaining rooted in place and silent. Maybe her stubbornness was a point in my favor, because I was sure if she saw the amused grin stretching across my face, she'd cut off my dick.

"What?" Again, with the curt response.

With the back of my hand, I caressed the smooth skin of her back. Goosebumps broke over every inch of her. I wanted to turn her toward me, indulge my eyes with her tight little nipples. I clenched my jaw. I wasn't a fan of this newfound moral compass.

"Goodnight, angel."

She scoffed and sauntered to a side table next to the recliner, pulling out a fucking hot pink dildo before sprinting up the stairs.

Oh, she was wicked.

Chapter Twenty Three
Evangelina

"You're unusually quiet." Lex eyed me suspiciously from the passenger seat.

"What do you mean?"

"Exactly what I said. Don't play dumb with me, Eva. I know when something's bothering you. Now, tell me, what's wrong?"

Hiding anything from Alexa was pointless. We had always been in tune with one another since childhood. Any stretch of uncomfortable silence between us was a red flag. The only reason she never found out about my fight with Derek was that I'd kept myself buried at work and on the Belov case while still searching for leads on Rayne's whereabouts.

I sighed, releasing a long, defeated breath.

"I feel like you already know what I'm about to say."

She nodded, her lips pursed. "Yes, but go on."

I rolled to a stop as the traffic light turned red and shifted to face her. "He spent the night at my house a couple of days ago."

Lex squealed and shoved my shoulder so hard it made my head whip sideways, nearly hitting the glass.

"Bitch! And you didn't tell me?"

"Lex, relax. I don't need a concussion."

She smoothed back her short black hair and clasped her hands together as excitement lit up her face. "Sorry. I can't believe you didn't say anything."

"There really isn't anything to tell." As the cars in front of me accelerated, my attention was back on the road.

From my peripheral, I saw her scrunch her face in confusion. "Nothing to tell, as in, he sucked in bed—which would be quite the tragedy, by the way—or nothing, as in, there was no naked humping?"

"Option B."

Lex laughed incredulously. "Okay. I get it. You just met. Gotta make him work for it. But why the sleepover, then? Seems like an unnecessary temptation."

My cousin listened intently as I relayed the story of how Derek had raced to my house after Yuri's attack. Alexa's grin widened at the mention of how he'd carried me to my living room and the shameless swooning that followed. Never one to tone down the theatrics, with a hand over her heart, she feigned fainting at the revelation of Derek's diabetes research. As the recipient of endless gifts, notes, flowers, and an unbelievable amount of unwanted marriage proposals, strangely enough, Derek taking time to learn about my diagnosis was the sweetest gesture any man had ever done.

"So, you gave him the green light to turn you inside out, and he refused?"

"Pretty much."

"Well, is he gay?"

"Lex! He's not. He's very interested."

Alexa whistled out a breath. "Eva, you're fucking smoking hot. You're telling me you had your tits on show, practically begging this man to fuck you within an inch of your life, and he turned you down?

Listen, either he's playing for the other team, or his little teammate ain't playing at all—if you know what I mean."

I couldn't hold back my laughter. No matter the circumstance, I could always count on Lex to cheer me up. "Trust me, that's not the problem."

"So, there *is* a problem?" she asked, brows raised.

"No... I don't know. He's just always... thinking. One moment, I swear he's about to eat me alive." I turned to her and licked my lips. "God, and I would just open up and let him." Gripping the steering wheel, I grimaced. "Then other times, he's so... hesitant. Like he can't decide what he wants."

The morning after he'd spent the night, I woke up to an empty house and a note on my kitchen counter. A damn note. He'd slipped out early, wished me a good day, and promised to return my extra key the next time we saw each other. Feelings of shame and regret made my stomach heavy. The sting of his rejection was still fresh, no matter how many times I tried to convince myself he was just being a gentleman.

But I didn't want a gentleman.

He'd left me so goddamn wet that night. Teasing him with that dildo, a birthday gift from Lex, no less, had only backfired because his resolve was fucking unbreakable, and I was too pissed to take care of the problem myself. The same couldn't be said for two days that followed. Derek's name had slithered from my lips more times than I was proud of.

Fuck, I needed to get laid.

Darkness shrouded my cabin as I pulled into the parking garage of Alexa's condo.

"Hey, look at me and listen carefully," she demanded, a no-bullshit expression on her face. "That man wants you, okay? Whatever his reasons are for keeping you at a distance right now has nothing to do with you, Eva. You're a goddamn goddess—mostly because you look like me," she said with a wink, and I snorted a laugh. "You're a badass female detective. You check all the boxes, girl. And the way he was looking at you and *only* you when Pri and I met him—Damn." Lex shook her head and fanned herself.

Reaching over, I pulled her into a tight hug. "Thanks, sis."

"Of course. And I'd invite you up, but my boy toy will be here in under two hours, and I have places to wax and get situated before then."

I chuckled and pressed a kiss to her cheek. "Go get laid, Sasquatch. And thanks for always being my sounding board. Love you, *pendeja*."

Lex blew me a kiss. "Love you always, babe."

She closed my car door and waved one last time before making her way to the silver elevator doors at the end of the walkway. I waited until she was safely on the lift before pulling away. As I turned the engine, a message popped up on my screen. Snatching the phone faster than my pride would admit, my shoulders deflated when I saw Sam's name instead of Derek's.

Since when had I ever sulked over a man?

> **SAM:** Belov is willing to speak and drop some names.
> Can you be at Einstein Medical within the hour? Says
> he'll only talk to printsessa voinov. Meaning you.

The Warrior Princess?

> **ME:** Yeah. I'll be there.

I popped open my glove box—one magazine and a Glock. There wasn't enough time to run back home and restock, so I had to make do. The chances of needing more rounds were slim at best, but I couldn't shake the paranoia crawling up my back. We'd let our guard down with Belov before, and things took a wildly dark turn in a matter of seconds. Unreasonably suspicious or not, I knew being overly prepared was better than being caught with my pants down…

Damn, if that last thought hadn't made me spiral into one's of Derek.

Okay, at this point, I crossed into the territory of being pathetic.

My phone's pulsing vibrations from between my thighs jolted me from my seat.

Speak of the devil himself.

"Hey!" I said, trying to sound as composed and carefree as possible.

"Angel." My insides melted into horny puddles of goo every time he used that nickname. "Are you busy tonight?"

Of course, he'd want to hang out when I had to work. Derek knew Thursdays were my days off, but neither of us had counted on Belov developing a conscience.

"Unfortunately, yes. I have to go…" I paused. Mentioning that asshole's name would only lead to twenty-one questions and concerns from Derek. In the name of avoiding becoming annoyed, I opted not to go into details. "Last minute call into work. It could take most of the evening."

"I could swing by and bring you dinner?"

He wasn't going to make this easy, was he?

"I won't be at the precinct. My suspect is at Einstein."

There was silence on the other end.

"Medical?"

"Yeah." I huffed out a sigh. "Belov, Derek. He allegedly has some information he's willing to give up." Derek didn't need to know that Yuri specifically asked for me.

"All right," he said moments later. "When can I see you, Eva?

I had some last-minute things I had to take care of as well. So, I apologize for my absence these last two days. And I fucking miss you."

I leaned back and closed my eyes, the pit of my stomach bursting into flames.

To hell with Yuri Belov…

I ran a hand down my face.

No, I had a job to do. Job first, dick later.

"We can still have dinner together, if you'd like. It's my father's hospital too. Maybe you two can talk things out."

I heard him scoff on the other end.

"It's fine. I know this is a big deal for you, and I'd rather not be a distraction." Before I could object, he cut me off. "If you're up for it, call me when you're done. No matter the time."

"Oh, another sleepover?"

He laughed. "No batteries needed this time."

"Promises, promises, Derek. You left me a note like some peace offering after I'd practically shoved my vagina in your face. Doesn't exactly make a girl feel confident. And I don't care how this makes me sound, but men don't reject me."

"That's not how that went down, and I assure you that when you shove your pussy in my face, you won't have a single goddamn doubt about where we stand."

My whole body shuddered, and I gripped the wheel with one hand until my knuckles turned white.

"I'll see you tonight, then," I murmured, eyes fluttering closed again.

"Angel…" He trailed off into another stretch of maddening silence, as if he'd decided against whatever he was about to say. "Take care."

I hadn't realized I was holding my breath until the call ended.

And it was a good thing I didn't need prep time like Lex.

The heels of my boots clicked against the freshly waxed vinyl tile of the hospital's forensic unit. Two officers and one armed security guard manned Belov's room. I stopped at the nurses' station to introduce myself and get a quick update on the man's condition. He was two days out of surgery for a lacerated liver. Under any other circumstance, I would have felt remorseful, but Yuri Belov was scum. The blood on his hands, direct or indirect, was probably miles thick.

"Evangelina?"

I lifted my gaze to the familiar, feminine voice on the other side of the wide desk. Helena Adamos, the hospital's clinical psychologist, greeted me with a riveting smile. I'd met her seven years ago when I was just a fresh-faced rookie. She and my dad developed a close friendship through the years, and I often wondered if he'd taken to her so quickly because she was the same age Frankie would have been if he'd been alive. There was a time when I toyed with the idea of my dad having romantic feelings for the young doctor. It wouldn't have been too far-fetched. Leni, as everyone called her, was insanely beautiful. She was the daughter of a wealthy Greek financier whose mother was said to have been from a village in the Philippines.

"Hey, Leni!"

"Here for Belov?" I nodded. "Ah, so you're the *Warrior Princess* he's been going on about."

"Really?"

Leni rounded the desk until she was in front of me, a manila folder in her hand. I couldn't help but stare as she approached, tall and regal, like she was working a runway. Her caramel hair was pulled back into a sleek bun.

"He's been talking and behaving a little erratically, so they called me in to evaluate his mental competency. Only two days post-op, he really should be resting, but he's insistent on talking to you." She flipped through some notes, shaking her head as she pulled two sheets and handed them to me.

"I guess knifing a man and sending him into emergency surgery is a turn-on these days."

A grin crooked the side of her mouth. "My kind of woman."

Before I could ask what she'd meant, not taking Leni for the violent type, the elevator down the hall dinged and slid open. Sam held two cups of coffee as he walked toward us.

My brows pulled together as I studied his tight expression and tensed body language.

"Sam?" I said, touching Leni's wrist and grabbing her attention. As soon as her eyes fell on him, her shoulders stiffened, head sweeping the unit in what looked like a strangely calculated motion.

"Eva, are you armed?"

My focus never left Sam as I nodded. His eyes were wide and panicked, blue irises blurred behind a wall of tears.

Something was wrong. Those pinpricks from earlier now stabbed at every fight-or-flight instinct I possessed. Reaching into my waistband, I unholstered my gun, ordering the young nurse at the counter to hide under her desk.

"Leni, take cover. Get back there with her."

"Eva, I think we're about to have company."

"Leni. Now!"

Why wasn't she moving?

A sharp whizzing flew across the side of my head, disheveling strands of hair as it blew past. In the following seconds, another suppressed pop exploded against medical equipment at my back.

Gunshots.

I made a run for Sam, but Leni fisted the back of my jacket and pulled me back.

"Eva, no! It's Belov's men. We have to run, or we're dead."

Heavy gunfire erupted around us, drowning out her voice in a sea of chaos. One of the officers keeping Yuri's room guarded dropped while the other and a guard ducked for cover before returning fire.

Shit. Shit. Shit.

"We can't leave… Sam…" The words died in my throat as I watched in horror as his knees hit the floor.

With eyes half-mast, rivulets of blood poured from a bullet wound on the side of his head.

"No!"

Leni dragged me to the floor. Once we were behind the desk, tears slid down my cheeks. For Sam, the other officer, and the nurse who lay dead on the floor beside me. Leni and I made eye contact, shaking our heads in disbelief.

"It was a trap," I whispered. "We have to get out of here, Len. Do you know how to make it off this floor?"

A barrage of bullets exploded over our heads as automatic weapons came into play.

She pointed to the far side of the room. "The vent. They're strategists and most likely blocked off the elevators and stairwells."

I swiped harshly at the last drops of tears and inhaled a sharp, resolute breath. "Go, Leni. I'll cover you."

Well aware that the chances of making it out alive were slim, I sent a quick prayer up for my father. Thoughts of the devastation my death would cause strangled the air from my lungs. It killed me to know he'd be alone—first my mom, then Frankie, his best friend, and now… me. I was thankful he'd decided to go home instead of taking on a double shift like he'd planned.

Leni rolled up the pant legs of her medical scrubs. Strapped to each calf was a Glock 17. Before I could even register what I was seeing, the woman, who seconds ago was just a civilian, pulled up her shirt, revealing a tactical belt around her abdomen. She tossed me two magazines without batting an eye, as if all of this was perfectly normal.

"No time for explanations. Let's go."

With that said, she was gone, and I was on my feet, raining hellfire down the slim hallway. By the time I reached the vent, Leni had popped it open. Eying her with an edge of suspicion, I motioned for her to crawl in first.

Twists and turns took us far enough from the gunfire that they were mere echoes in the distance. Leni came to a stop and leaned her head against the metal. Closing her eyes, she blew out a heavy breath. As she turned to face me, she froze, the barrel of my gun pointed between her eyes.

"Leni, I need you to talk to me right now because what the fuck just happened? Who are you?"

"Put the gun down, Eva. You know who I am. And if I wanted to hurt you, you'd be back there with Nurse Callahan."

"*If* you wanted to hurt me?"

"Yes, of which I have no desire. But I will defend myself if it comes down to who leaves this tunnel alive and who doesn't."

Had I been transported to the twilight zone?

The once-friendly clinical psychologist and good friend of my father just threatened to kill me if the stakes came down to it.

"You're armed to the teeth. I could have you arrested for unauthorized possession of a firearm and ammunition in a hospital."

"But you won't."

Her voice held an undercurrent of danger. The threat was loud in the hard glare behind her eyes. But I wasn't one to back down from a challenge. I clenched my jaw, the weapon still trained on Helena Adamos—or whoever the fuck she was.

"Don't fuck with me, Leni. This is not the time."

"You're right. It's not. First, we need to get the hell out of here. Then, you and I can talk."

Her phone vibrated in her hand. Throwing one last cautionary glance my way, she opened the message.

"We need to get to the south exit. Calvary is waiting."

"That's two floors down."

"Right," she said, peering through the slits overlooking a utility room. "The stairwell should be down the hall from this room."

Silence reigned between us as she waited for my decision. I was never one to deal in chance and let my guard down, but my gut instinct was to trust her. I swallowed hard and exhaled, lowering my weapon.

"Fuck. Okay, let's do this." Sliding off my jacket, I wiped the sweat trickling down my forehead. "We don't know what we're going to run into. In case we get ambushed, if there's a chance for you to make a run for it—"

She put a hand on my arm, features softening. "We're both getting out of here, Eva."

I nodded once, suddenly realizing she'd been right. I wouldn't arrest her.

We slinked into the empty utility room, darkness our temporary cover. The small, rectangular glass on the door didn't give much of an angle to view potential threats in the hallway, so we had to go in blind. Impossible as it was to avoid the high-pitched creak, I managed to crack the door without alerting the three armed men at the end of the unit.

"Leni," I whispered, "I don't know how well of a shot you are, but we're outgunned. Make every hit count." Bile rose in my throat at the words I was about to speak. Taking a life, even when necessary, was never something a good officer wanted to do. There were protocols in place. But these men, they weren't here to negotiate. They were here for blood. My blood. "Kill shots."

The whisper of a grin played on the corners of Leni's lips, as if she'd been waiting for the green light to do exactly that. The stark realization was like a gut punch. This wasn't her first time in a life-or-death situation. She was too cool, too confident, with a sureness that only came with experience. The fluidity of her movements and her calm demeanor hinted at one thing: Leni was a professional.

The question was—*of what*?

"Ready when you are," she said, cautiously peering around the doorframe. "I'll get the one on the right. You take out the two on the left."

"Watch for civilians," I warned, kneeling below Leni's line of fire.

A bead of sweat broke away from the tip of my nose as the back of a tall man's head centered within my sights. Two shots pierced the air, hitting their mark with precision. The third just a heartbeat later. We took off running, stopping shoulders to the wall at the end of the corridor. Dropping to my knees again, I peeked around the corner, only to be met with a hail of bullets. The wall opposite us exploded as the high-powered lead violently tore through its surface.

Leni put a hand on my shoulder, and a litany of unspoken words drifted between us. We were resigned to whatever fate awaited, but if dying was the plan, we'd go out fighting and take as many of these assholes with us as possible. The moment their gunfire ceased, we were ready.

Four more bodies dropped, and we raced toward the stairwell. Without an instant to recoup, more of Belov's men charged up the stairs.

Two by two, they fell.

Leni peered over the railing. "These fuckers don't stop coming!"

"How many?" I asked, dropping my empty mag and reloading.

"Looks like six."

A commotion of voices and shuffling echoed from the levels above us. "We're going to get pinched if we don't keep moving."

She picked up an AK from one of the dead perps and handed it to me. "Then let's take the fight to them."

"Let's, because I'm ready to go the fuck home."

Leni's excitement was unabashed this time, splitting her pretty face with a bloodthirsty grin.

"I knew I liked you."

Belov's men lay splayed across the cold concrete stairs. One more door, and we'd be in the clear. Leni cracked it open, not expecting a fist to the side of her face, and she fell unconscious.

"Put it down, sweetheart," said a deep, accented voice from behind, his gun pressed to the back of my head. "Pakhan never said you looked like this. What a nice surprise."

He disarmed and pinned me to the wall, his large body pushing against my ass. Hot, vile breath fanned over my face as he chuckled close to my ear. The man was easily over six and a half feet tall. His massive height was only second to his girth. My stomach lurched when I felt his dick harden on my back.

"Fuck you!"

"If you insist."

"Nikolai!" the other man chided. "Our orders were to kill the bitch."

He violently turned me toward him, lecherous green eyes burning with apathetic cruelty. "Yes, but he never said we couldn't have a little fun first."

Chapter Twenty Four

Derek

Everything in front of me was a blur. I was on autopilot, tearing mercilessly through flesh with the edge of my blade and the heat of my HK. There was only one thought in my mind. One objective. Reaching her.

Saving her.

The moment Kai's grave look connected with mine, I knew the message he'd received involved Evangelina. She and Helena were under fire by Belov's men and had taken shelter in the ventilation system of Einstein. I blamed myself. I should have taken care of that sack of shit the moment he'd touched her the first time. But I was trying to be level-headed and not bring war down on Ares.

Fuck every single one of them. For Eva, I'd go to war with the whole goddamn world.

The flame of a bullet scorched my skin as it grazed the top of my left shoulder. Clenching my jaw, I turned to find a familiar face. His mangled, silver-capped sneer twisted even wider as he raised his weapon, thinking he'd gotten the jump on me, but Kai was faster. Lead to the temple.

"There's a body, D."

Fear snared my heart as I neared the slim form of a woman on the floor. Streaks of brown in her hair brought a fresh wave of relief, and I exhaled the residual tension and pushed forward. I knew Kai would deal with Helena. The soft rising movements of her chest suggested she was alive. Alive, but not conscious and, therefore, would be no help in locating the woman I had come for.

The only one who mattered.

That's when I heard her voice, muffled by the commotion and distance between us, but it was unmistakable.

I threw open the metal door, and Evangelina was standing over the body of a large man, a bloody knife in her hand. She startled at the noise and turned to me in a panic. The gun she'd been holding out of view was pointed center mass in my direction. Through the haze of chaos and shadows, she hesitated just long enough to register my face before pulling the trigger. But there was a second of indecision. A flash of mistrust in her eyes as they narrowed on my weapon. I couldn't deny the tinge of hurt her suspicion caused, but I understood it.

"Angel." A shuddering gasp fell from her lips as we ran into each other's arms.

"Derek! What are you doing here? How did you know?"

"I came for you," I said, resting my forehead against hers. She was trembling, and I framed her face, wiping away spatters of blood with my thumb. "Are you hurt?"

She shook her head. "It's not my blood. He tried to…"

Red rage edged my vision as it fell on the corpse of the man who'd tried to take advantage of her.

"He got what he deserved," I said through gritted teeth. Pride and relief swelled in my chest at what she'd done. I wanted to take her home and sink my dick inside her. "That's my girl."

She took care of fucking business and got herself out.

The loud creak of a door saw us both drawing our guns. Kai put a hand up as he crossed the threshold, Helena under his other arm. She was awake, though looking dazed and weak.

Evangelina's heated gaze met mine as the four of us shared the same space. It was as if I could see the wheels in her mind spinning, fueled by endless questions whose answers she couldn't even begin to comprehend.

Answers I could never reveal. Not if it meant losing her.

"You're… the calvary? How do you know Leni? And who's that?" she asked, motioning to Kai.

"No, we're not. PPD has this place surrounded." I tipped her head gently. "Angel, you and Helena have to walk out that door. I'll see you out until it's safe."

"Wait, what about you?"

"Kai and I have our own exit plan."

Her fingers curled tightly around the sleeves of my jacket. "Derek, no. Please, come with me."

"I'll meet you outside." My lips brushed over her hairline as I leaned in. "I'm going to keep you safe. I promise."

Watching her walk into that parking lot without me felt wrong, that vulnerable feeling hitting me again in full force.

The lot was dimly lit, but the flashing red and blue lights flickering around the corner eased my worries. Helena looked back, her eyes narrowed and questioning, attempting to decipher Evangelina and me.

She and I had crossed few words over the years beyond business. We'd been on partnered assignments less than a handful of times. Never speaking more than necessary. She was skilled, beautiful, and deadly. Her beauty had struck Kai, and the two had engaged in a very short fling, remaining close friends once it was over.

"Let's go," Kai said, clapping my back.

I cast one last glance at the corner where Eva had gone out of sight.

Nearly two hours had elapsed since finding Evangelina. Kai and I stayed behind the police barricade, playing the part of concerned citizens as we waited for the endless questioning and statements to come to an end. Helena was the first to be released. Again, her curious gaze swept over me. Motioning with her chin, she walked beyond us to a more private location.

I leaned against the brick of a storefront, waiting on the barrage of questions I knew were coming. She lowered the ice pack from the wound on her right eye, a steely glare piercing me where I stood.

"What are you doing with Franco's daughter?"

"None of your business."

"Do you understand the implications this could bring down on all of us? Tell me, does Franco know you're fucking around with Eva?"

I exhaled a harsh breath and pushed off the wall. "What makes you think I give a damn one way or the other?"

"That's exactly it. You don't give a shit about anyone but yourself. Evangelina, she doesn't deserve your cruelty. She's too good for you."

"I know."

"Stay away from her before she gets caught up in your shit, Derek."

I enclosed on Helena, a move that didn't rattle her in the least. Not that I was surprised. She had only one weakness, and it was on full show. In our line of work, there was no room for feelings. They fucked with instinct and reaction time. But Helena was different. It was as if she had a switch she could turn off and on at will. I'd seen her mow down a room full of men with a swing in her hip and a grin. Some had nicknamed her Harley for that very reason. Only her weapon of choice had been an AK instead of a wooden bat. Within the hour of that massacre, she volunteered at her hospital's fundraiser.

"I hate to disappoint you—actually, I don't care."

Her laugh was as cold and humorless as the daggers in her eyes. "You're a real son of a bitch," she snapped, rising to her full height.

At 5'6", while taller than Eva, I stood over her, an arch in my brow. "I'm glad you're aware."

"That's enough." Kai had broken his silence. With a hand on my chest, he shoved me back. "Come on, brother. If it wasn't for Leni, neither of us would know shit. Show some damn gratitude. She helped your girl."

Helena scoffed from behind us.

"His girl, huh? And *we* helped each other." A cunning grin crawled across her face. "Cain, you go ahead. But just know, if you fuck with her, she's the kind of woman who will not hesitate to put her foot up your ass. And something tells me you'd let her." She shook her head and chuckled with a twisted sort of amusement. "Never thought I'd see the day Derek Cain would be pussy-whipped."

I opened my mouth to sear her with a response, but a low whistle from Kai had my attention elsewhere. Evangelina's presence triggered a series of visceral reactions. The blood in my veins flowed a little faster, settling in my cock. The edges of my lips tilted into an irrepressible smile. And one word echoed in my mind like a mantra: *Mine.*

The joy at the sight of her was short-lived. Two steps behind was a taller, older man. His thick eyebrows were pulled together, eyes blazing. His gaze moved to each of our faces, ultimately settling on Helena's and softening into a smile. After pulling her into a tight hug,

Franco waited for our cover story for his daughter's sake.

This should be interesting.

Eva put her arms around me, resting her head against my chest. I didn't need to look up to know Franco was watching. I felt his scathing glare and heard the heavy breaths when I returned Eva's embrace.

"I'm not quite done, but I had to see you, make sure you were okay," she whispered into my shirt. "Give me about thirty more minutes."

Every instinct pulled me to follow her across the dark lot, but I knew Franco and I had some business to settle. Always on the same wavelength, Kai nodded and followed the two women.

"I don't know what sick game you're playing here, but stay the hell away from my daughter." Franco stepped forward, hands on his hips. "Why are you pretending to be James's son?"

As much as I wanted to admit how much I loathed carrying half of that asshole's DNA, it wouldn't be wise to reveal my hatred.

"How about we bypass the bullshit. I am who I say I am." I cocked a grin. "But I have pictures of my mother, if you need proof. I'm sure you've heard the stories about her from your good friend, James."

Franco surveyed his surroundings before leaning in closer. "I don't care who you are. I know *what* you are, and that's more than enough. I won't say it again; stay away from my daughter."

"Franco Cruz, are you threatening me?" His lips pressed into a straight line, and he took a step back, his bravado wavering. "Listen, this is what's going to happen. You're going to convince Evangelina to stay with me—"

"The hell I am!"

"Your daughter has a bounty on her head, courtesy of Philly's most notorious crime family. Who do you think is going to keep her safe? Some shit officer sitting in a car outside her house? You?"

He raked both hands through his scalp and paced. "Why do you care so much? You're just like them. Why would I trust you, of all people, with my daughter's life?"

"Because I would never hurt her."

Franco's jaw twitched as he shook his head from side to side. "The moment I knew it was you, I did my research. I asked my questions, and your reputation doesn't exactly evoke trust or confidence. You're the worst of the worst. No different than those bodies in there. If you think that's the kind of man I want in my daughter's life, you're dead wrong." He turned his back, moving toward the lot. "Stay away from her. I'm her father, and I will protect her."

"Like you did when you got her a personal bodyguard." He froze. "Adrian Walker ring any bells, Franco?"

"Fuck you, Cain," he spat, still facing away from me, shoulders trembling.

I chuckled darkly. "Don't worry. I took care of that problem too. I think I still have that bastard's blood underneath my nails."

Franco bowed his head. "May God forgive you."

"I'm not looking for forgiveness."

"You're a sick son of a bitch."

"Maybe." I gritted my teeth, patience running thin. "But this sick son of bitch is the only one willing to do whatever it takes to keep Eva safe. And let's not be hypocritical. You know what Leni is."

He whirled around. "I can't protect my daughter from one enemy just to send her into the arms of an even bigger devil."

"But you will."

His cheeks flushed red, and he pointed an accusatory finger in my direction. "If you touch her…"

"I already told you I won't hurt her."

"No. You know exactly what I mean. You think I missed the way you look at her? The way she clings to you. And don't give me the bullshit that you feel anything for her. She's beautiful, smart, rich— You won't make a whore out of my daughter."

There were many things I could say to get under his skin, but out of respect for Eva, I ignored his statement and leaned back against the brick building, shoving both hands into my pockets. "You have Ares at your disposal. Use it."

"If keeping her safe means using Ares, then she can stay with Leni."

Fuck this.

His permission and approval meant nothing. I'd be damned if I left Eva's safety in anyone else's hands but mine. Not even Leni's.

"Where are you going?" he asked as I moved past him and across the street.

"To get what belongs to me."

Chapter Twenty Five
Derek

"Sit."

Evangelina pushed on my chest until the backs of my knees touched the wooden chair. I let my body fall and she positioned herself between my thighs. A wave of warmth coursed through me at having her so close. The sliver of exposed skin above the waistband of her jeans called to me, beckoning to be touched. I bit back the impulse. She'd been through too much tonight and needed comfort, not my advances. Her eyes glistened with emotion, but the mask she held remained firm.

"I'm fine."

"Derek, you were shot."

"Barely a graze."

She rolled her eyes, dabbing a gauze pad with alcohol. "Stop being so damn stubborn, and let me help you. It's the least I can do."

Reaching out, I gently took her wrists in my hands. "You don't owe me anything. Do you hear me? Not a damn thing."

Evangelina shook her head. "That's not true. You risked your life to help me." Her brown eyes darkened. "And it was a very, very stupid thing to do. Why would you put yourself in harm's way like that? You could have been killed!"

"What did you expect me to do?" I said, shrugging my shoulders. "Just sit by and wait?"

"Yeah, exactly that. You're not a cop, Derek. And you're not Bruce Wayne or immortal. You're a civilian. And this," she said, pointing at my shoulder, "could have been much worse."

She was wholly unaware of the lengths I was willing to go to, the people I'd kill without so much as a second thought if it meant she was safe. The day I'd set eyes on Evangelina, something inside me shifted out of place. Out of balance. The fabric of my very existence had been unraveled. The code I lived by. All of it, in shambles. She'd turned my world upside down and inside out.

Eva agreed to stay with me, even if her conditions meant it was only for a few days. I knew she had questions. Explaining away what Helena, Kai, and I had done would be virtually impossible. But I was up for the task. Lying to her felt wrong now, but my options were slim. Losing her wasn't one of them.

"But I'm fine."

"I'll be the judge of that," she said, dripping more alcohol onto the pad.

"That looks personal."

She managed a small laugh. "You just hold still. My dad taught me a few things."

As she pulled at my shirt's collar, the fabric's stretch wouldn't give enough. I yanked it over my head, careful not to tear at the sensitive skin.

"Is that better?"

She wet her lips and stepped back, eyes roving my upper body. A smile crept across my face at her appraisal, and I leaned back in my chair. "Thought this would give you better access."

"It does," she said in a breathy tone. "There's just so much—ink." With her free hand, she ran her fingers down my chest. "Every inch of you. What do they all mean?"

I instinctively closed my eyes at her touch, and my cock jumped against the seam of my pants.

"Angel." I caught her hands. "Put the damn pad on my shoulder."

Pain was necessary. I needed to feel the burn of the alcohol. An even trade for the flames caressing my skin with each brush of her fingertips. Everywhere she touched was on fire. I gripped the edges of the chair, willing myself not to act on impulse as I fought the urge to throw her back on top of the table. Goddamn. This woman.

Evangelina hesitated, lip pulled between her teeth, before she pressed the cool gauze to my wound. I clenched my jaw, and a loud groan resonated in my throat.

"Sorry."

"It's fine. Just a little burn. Nothing I haven't felt before."

Her focus shifted from me to beyond my shoulder. She was quiet. Pensive. Eyes squinting ever so slightly.

"How do you know Helena? How are you both so... skilled?" Full attention back on me, her gaze was penetrating, demanding answers. "Derek, she had a tactical belt underneath her scrubs. Two Glocks—And you…" She leaned back against the table, as if gauging my reaction. "You went in guns blazing into a shootout with Russian mobsters." Palming her temple, she shook her head and pushed off the table, pacing back and forth. "I can't even believe I'm saying that out loud. Who are you? *What* are you?"

She was too close, teetering on the precipice of a truth that would rip her from me.

"Eva, you know who I am. I own Sloane's. I'm a tactical instructor. It's what I do. And Helena is a long-time client of Kai's."

"Your adopted brother."

I nodded. "That's right."

She broke off again, heading into the living room. Hand on her hip, one on her forehead. Incoherent ramblings exploded from her lips, mirroring her frantic movements.

I grabbed her by the wrist, turning her to me. "What is it?"

"You can't do that again. You just can't."

"I had to."

"No!" Her sharp voice echoed off the vaulted ceilings. "No," she said in a whisper. "I lied today. I broke my oath, and I lied for you. I lied for Helena. What am I even doing?"

She buried her face in her hands.

"Angel, come here." I pulled her to my chest. She was crying, trembling in my arms. Emotions I couldn't place or knew what to do with pummeled me mercilessly, settling in the pit of my stomach. "I'm sorry. I didn't mean for you to have to do that."

"Derek, you could have died." She tilted her head to look at me. "I've lost so much. People I love and care about. And I just found you."

My thumb wiped at the tears sliding down her cheeks as I held her face. "I'm not going anywhere. And I'm not that easy to kill," I said with a wink.

Evangelina rolled her eyes and sighed. "Nothing about this is funny."

"Hey, worrying about me is pointless. This is about you. Yuri is dead, but you still have a target over your head. How do you think that makes me feel?"

Spanish expletives spouted from her pretty lips. And as inappropriate a thought as it was, all I wanted to do was kiss her.

"That son of a bitch, Belov. He really tried to have me killed, didn't he?" Fresh tears filled her eyes. "Oh, God, and Sam..."

She rested her forehead on my chest and cried.

The shower stopped running over an hour ago. I hung back, listening outside my bedroom door, ensuring she didn't need me. As much as I wanted to be in her company, I knew she needed space and time to clear her mind.

I'd given up being surprised by my actions and the kind of shit that mattered to me now.

Leaning against the door, I tipped my head back, closing my eyes. *Who are you?*

Those three words were on repeat in my thoughts. The truth was, I had no fucking clue. She made me feel so much. Made me act outside myself.

As naive, broken children, Kai and I looked out for each other against assholes with ill intentions. While it hadn't always worked, we survived. But even through the darkest moments, I'd never consoled him like I had Evangelina. She was in my arms until the last tear had fallen.

I clenched and unclenched my fists as I tempered my emotions. There would be time for blood later. I'd get my revenge, even if it meant obliterating the entire Belov lineage.

The door opened behind me, and I stumbled a step before catching myself. Eva was wearing one of my shirts. The white garment was massive on her petite frame, almost reaching her knees. Bare legs were adorned with my black dress socks, pulled to mid-calf.

"I know. I look ridiculous."

"You look… a lot of things, but ridiculous isn't one of them."

She leaned a shoulder against the doorframe and pushed a strand of dampened hair behind her ear. "We didn't exactly think this through. I don't even have underwear."

I bit the inside of my lip and gripped the frame above her head so hard it felt like it would splinter in my grasp. Eva looked up through her thick lashes.

"What? You didn't expect me to wear yours, did you? And every pair of pants I tried on fell to my ankles."

I reached for her, hands on her hips, slowly gliding up the hem of her top as if to confirm she was bare underneath. Only my eyes never left hers. Fingers feathered along sheer skin, digging into the supple flesh of her ass.

"Derek," she whispered, closing her eyes and shuddering under my touch.

I dipped my head, lips brushing up the side of her face, scenting my body wash on her skin. She was wearing my shirt, had bathed in my scent, would soon be wrapped in my sheets, and even had on my goddamn socks.

I'd never been more envious of inanimate objects than I was at that moment.

I needed to remedy that.

It was as if the universe had conspired against me, karma for being a depraved fuck, since again we found ourselves alone, but with circumstances that would prevent me from taking her the way I wanted to.

That didn't mean I couldn't make her feel good.

"Ready for bed?" My mouth settled against her cool forehead, lips running along the smooth skin as the heady scent of her called to me. I lifted her into my arms, and she wrapped her legs around my waist. The heat from her thighs scorched me, marking my hips in a raging fire.

"I know it's been a shit night, but I want to make you feel good. Can I do that?" She nodded, lips parted, but said nothing. "Get on your knees," I said as I set her on the bed. My hands needed to touch her, and I indulged in rubbing down her beautiful ass as she turned away. The look she tossed over her shoulder nearly did me in.

I climbed in behind her, pulling her close so that she was tightly pressed against my cock. Kissing the back of her ear, I slid my hands beneath the shirt. There was nothing sexier than her soft moans as I nipped at her neck and rolled her nipples between my fingers.

"I told you I've been dying to taste you. But I know I'll lose control, and that's not what I want for you right now," I said, smoothing my hands up and down the length of her magnificent body. Light touches drew goosebumps over her flesh, then longer, drawn-out strokes until my fingers moved past the trimmed hair of her pelvis leading to what I was looking for.

She opened for me as I slid two fingers down the seam of her soaking wet pussy.

"Fuck," she whispered when I massaged her clit in slow, deliberate circles until her head fell back onto my shoulder with a groan.

"Already so fucking wet for me, baby. She knows who she belongs to." Eva clutched at the sheets as my fingers dipped inside while my other hand journeyed back up her flat stomach, taking a handful of her breast and squeezing.

Fuck me, was she tight and so damn wet, my cock leaked with the desperate need to be inside her. I closed my eyes, warring with the man who wanted to tear her apart, devour her, bite, spank, and even spit on this goddamn pussy to mark it as mine.

Growling into her neck, I used my thumb to pinch and put more pressure on her clit, reveling in the whimpers fluttering from her lips.

"Feel it, angel. Feel how fucking wet I make your cunt," I said, stroking her faster. Harder. Her thighs trembled, head lolling from side to side as she reached for herself, following my motions. When her hips bucked against mine, the delicious friction nearly caused me to thrust into her.

"Oh… fuck, Derek," she cried, turning her head and biting at my throat as she dipped a finger, both of us inside her at the very same time.

"Give me a taste, baby," I demanded, squeezing her again between my thumb and forefinger.

Eva jolted slightly, but did as she was told and slid her slick fingers into my mouth. My eyes closed as the taste of her tempted every goddamn ounce of self-restraint left in my body. She was so fucking good, so damn sweet—I'd just found my newest addiction.

"Angel, I want you to ride my fingers like a fucking good girl. Show me how you want to be fucked. How you'll come all over my dick." I kissed up her neck. "Then you can watch me lick every single drop of you."

Pushing two more fingers inside, I stretched her, causing her to hiss as she rocked her hips in tandem with my movements. Every twist of her shoulders and flex of her spine, every moan and exquisite grind pressed me closer to the edge of losing control.

"Yes… so good," she murmured, grinding her ass against my aching cock.

I needed to be inside her almost as much as I needed my next breath, but I knew I'd take her too hard and fast. Her bruises were still fresh, and her wounds, physical and emotional, still healing.

Goddamnit, what had she done to me?

"Eva… you keep that up…"

The last thing I wanted was to bust in my fucking pants. I lifted up onto my knees and pushed her forward. The sight of her pussy glistening and swollen, open for me, had me on the verge of doing just that. Fuck, she was perfect. I brought my hand up and cracked her once, then twice between the legs. Gasping loudly, she clawed at the sheets, but I held her hips and spanked her clit again until my name was a sweet mantra flowing from her lips. She bucked and came so hard that she collapsed face-first into the sheets, the fabric muffling her whimpers.

So much for being gentle.

I stood up and paced, needing to walk off the strain in my pants. The sight of Eva, completely shattered by my hand, made me want to fold her over the side of the bed and fuck her until my cum dripped from every orifice of her body.

I briefly contemplated another shower. One cold as ice, but I returned to the bed instead, where Eva lay on her side, her breaths slowing as she lifted her hooded gaze to my face.

"Derek… that was—"

She sucked a sharp breath when I leaned forward and slid my tongue up her inner thigh, lapping at the wetness until reaching her slit and growling as I gripped her ass cheeks so hard her skin blanched beneath my fingers.

"Shit."

I tore myself away, knowing I was on the verge of taking her completely. Restraining myself when I was so close to everything I wanted, from what was mine and only mine, was the hardest thing I'd ever done. I wasn't the type of man who thought of others before himself. But there I was, at her mercy.

I climbed back into bed and lifted my chin, beckoning her to me.

"Derek," she whispered, crawling toward me and looking like a goddamn goddess. I knew what her intention was as she reached for my dick, but I grabbed her wrist and tugged her to my chest instead.

"Go to bed, angel. Get some sleep," I said, clearing my throat and kissing her forehead.

Evangelina remained quiet and blew air against my neck, sending shivers down my spine and a zap straight to my aching balls.

"How are you feeling? And I'm not talking about what just happened," I said, skimming over the pod on her arm with a light touch.

"I'm okay."

Her phone was already docked on the nightstand beside me. "Your cell, it'll alert us if something is off?"

She nodded with a slight yawn. "It will. Goodnight, Derek."

"Goodnight."

It didn't take long for the arm over my abdomen to slacken and her quiet breaths to slow. Staring up at the white ceiling, one arm behind my head, still sporting a semi, and this beautiful, sated woman tucked securely on the other, I came to a stark realization.

I was officially fucked.

Chapter Twenty Six

Evangelina

I looked like utter shit.

But I couldn't bring myself to care. I was too fucking high on what happened last night to dwell on trivial things such as my appearance.

Smoothing my fingers through my hair, still wet from a shower, I stared at my reflection in the mirror. Despite the bandage on my neck, the bruises, and the small dark circles beneath my eyes, something was different. A glow, maybe. My body's reaction to the explosive orgasm Derek had brought me to with just his skilled fingers and hand. I wondered what I'd look like once I was properly fucked.

He was already gone by the time I'd woken up, though he hadn't left a note this time or a text.

Memories of the night before, the siege at the hospital, that large man attempting to assault me—all of it—slammed into me at once, as did the nightmares that followed. There were moments I'd cried out in my sleep, waves of grief heavy on my heart, but Derek's soothing arms were there as he kissed my temple and whispered words of comfort until the fog of sleep pulled me back under.

I'd wanted to question his involvement further, but everything he'd said made sense.

Hadn't it?

He was fiercely protective of me and was a tactical instructor like his brother Kai. And Helena…

Helena was armed like she was part of the very mafia trying to kill us.

Fuck. It was so much easier to believe what he'd said.

That man was doing things to me, slowly burying himself inside my heart. His sweet gestures, the hunger in his eyes. Part of me knew he held secrets and trauma from his past. Red flags I knew I shouldn't ignore. But damn it all.

Couldn't I just be reckless for once?

A knock at the door saw me pulling on one of Derek's shirts.

Panties be damned.

As I jogged across the spacious bedroom, the door creaked open, and Philly's cutest kitten trotted in.

"Diego!" I scooped him into my arms, nuzzling his cold little nose. "How in the world did you get here?"

"He hitched a ride." My head snapped up at the unexpected sound of Derek's voice. He crossed the threshold, a rolling suitcase in each hand. "Your cousin offered to keep him, but I thought you might miss the little bastard."

"You spoke to Alexa?"

He nodded, slinging the bags over the bench at the foot of his massive bed. "I did."

I set Diego on the floor and approached him. "For the sake of not asking twenty-one questions, please explain."

Derek suddenly tugged me toward him, nearly sweeping me off the shaggy rug below my feet.

"Come here." His mouth slanted over mine, kissing me soft and slow. I melted into him, tongue snaking out to glide against his.

"I called her." Teeth nipped at my bottom lip as one hand journeyed up my back, tangling into my hair. "Last night." He squeezed my ass, crushing me into his hard body. "Told her to pack your stuff." His fist tightened against my scalp, tugging my head back so he could run his mouth down the column of my throat.

I held his shoulders, nails digging into flesh. "You do these things for me," I whispered, head tipped back. "Why are you so good to me, Derek?" Soft moans slithered off my tongue as hard, open-mouthed kisses trailed up behind my ear, making me squirm.

He pushed my head forward instead of answering my question, and his warm lips were over mine again.

"I'm sorry I left without saying anything. You were asleep, and I didn't want to wake you."

"It's okay," I squeaked as his lips now stroked over my hairline.

"How are you feeling?"

Derek's hand moved between our bodies, and he smiled, no doubt pleased by my lack of intrusive underwear. Two fingers slid against my clit, and I whimpered, forehead falling on his chest.

"Good." My voice was barely a murmur.

"This pussy of yours is always wet for me, isn't it?" he asked, groaning into my ear.

I rolled my bottom lip between my teeth as his fingers ran languid strokes, splitting me open.

"Maybe," I said, feeling playful.

Derek stilled and gripped my chin, tilting my head. Our eyes met, and his darkening gaze held a glint of mischief.

"There's something I need you to understand." He slipped his hand from between my thighs and traced wet fingers along the contours of my lips. "*This* is mine."

He gently pushed two digits past the seam of my mouth, and the taste of my essence spilled over my tongue, pulling a low moan from my throat. I lapped at the wetness before taking him to the knuckles. Tension ticked in his jaw as he watched. With a tight hold on my face, he rasped, "She only gets wet for me. Is that understood?"

Derek was unlike any other man I'd been with in the past. I never knew how fucking turned on I would feel to be owned and dominated. The thought had always been a terrifying one. But damn, if I didn't long to be his in any way he wanted to take me.

Savoring the last drop, I slowly withdrew him from my mouth and nodded. He leaned in and licked across my bottom lip.

"*Angel.*" His voice was a low, husky groan demanding an answer.

"Yours, Derek. Only for you."

I pulled him down by the collar of his shirt. His mouth covered mine, sealing my words with a heated frenzy of teeth and tongue. "You taste so *fucking* good. All I thought about this morning was feasting on your pussy. I need to have you."

He reached down, a hand on each ass cheek, and hoisted me onto his waist.

My legs wrapped around him, nails scraping the back of his scalp.

With a growl, he rounded the bed and tossed me onto the mattress with such force that I bounced twice. But before I could gather my bearings, he hauled me to the edge by my ankles, spreading me open. His hungry eyes were laser-focused between my legs.

"Like what you see?" I asked, shedding my inhibitions as I let my thighs fall farther apart. It didn't matter that we hadn't known each other long. I trusted this man to take care of me, just as he'd done since the day we met.

Derek shook his head and dropped to his knees. "Prettiest fucking pussy I've ever seen."

Sliding his arms under each thigh, he hooked them around my hips and dragged me closer to his face. The tip of his nose caressed my skin as it moved at an agonizing pace toward my sex. Sweet anticipation caused my legs to tremble around his head, even before the first touch.

I reached for my shirt.

"Don't. Leave it."

"Leave it?"

He answered with a single nod. "I want to focus on this needy little cunt of yours."

Heat settled low in my belly, stealing my breath. With my head thrown back, I mewled as his thumb moved up my slit, forcing my back to arch off the mattress when the flat of his tongue trailed the same path a heartbeat later.

"*Shit*," I whined as he licked me from end to end, flicking my clit before suctioning it into his mouth. Pleasure bloomed in my core, drawing another strangled cry from my lips.

"Fuck, angel. You have no idea what it took for me to be good last night. From the moment I saw you," he said, between long, slow laps, driving me to the fringes of madness, "I've been dying to know what you taste like." He dipped his head, tongue plunging inside me. "And I just knew you'd be *fucking* delicious, Evangelina. I could die here."

Throwing my legs over his shoulders, he dragged me impossibly closer. My whole body shuddered as he continued drinking me down, worshiping every soaking inch as if he was a man starved. The sounds rising from between my thighs were absolutely filthy.

"*Fuck... Yes...*" I fisted his hair and thrust my hips, seeking more friction. "*Oh...*" Another whimper fell from my lips when he slipped two fingers inside, curling them and causing me to jolt off the bed.

My thighs closed around him, the pressure almost too much, but he pushed them open, eyes locked on mine as he shook his head.

"Open up that pretty pussy for me. I'm not done yet." His face glistened, and I watched with hooded eyes as his tongue snaked out. "I knew it would be even better from the tap." Gripping my hips roughly, he pulled me back to his mouth.

I grabbed a small pillow and bit down, crying out his name as I pressed it against my face.

"No!" His voice was sharp as he ripped the cushion from my hands, launching it across the room. "I need to hear you. You won't deny me what's mine." My fingers clutched the sheets, chest heaving as I attempted to swallow before nodding. "I said I need to hear you."

"Whatever you want. Just don't stop!"

He chuckled darkly, pressing a kiss to the wet, trembling skin on my inner thigh. Before I could process another thought, Derek grabbed my hips and flipped me over, pulling me to my knees. I felt so vulnerable and exposed, but I fucking loved every second.

There was a time I thought I'd never enjoy foreplay and sex this way with a man, not after my experience. And while there are still moments of hesitation, of slight insecurities, I trusted him.

Closing my eyes, I buried my face in the soft white sheets as he licked his way inside me. The scent of his cologne clung to the fabric, hitting my nose like a pheromone, and a new rush of wetness dripped over his tongue.

"Evangelina… *so good*. So damn good." He squeezed my ass and bit down.

Tears gathered in my eyes as I danced on that precipice between sweet punishment and feral pleasure.

"Say it." His fingers were inside me again. "Say you're mine."

"Fuck, fuck…"

Two more calculated strokes were all it took to tip me over the edge. And I fell hard with his name like strangled cries flowing from my lips. This only seemed to fuel his hunger as his hold on me tightened, mouth ravenous. He lapped and sucked at every drop. I tried to crawl away, the sensations overwhelming and painful, but the voracity of his lashes intensified.

"Derek… *please*…" I begged, clawing at the sheets. "Too much..."

"You're mine and I decide when you've had enough." He bit my other ass cheek, marking my flesh before nursing it with a tender kiss. "Say it. Tell me who you belong to." His tongue ran along my swollen pussy, flicking my sensitive clit until I was too weak to remain propped on my knees.

Collapsing onto my belly, I grabbed at the blanket, my voice ragged. "*Yours!* I'm yours… always yours."

It took several minutes for my breaths to slow as I lay motionless, too damn worn out to move. Derek climbed over me, bunching up my shirt and trailing his lips along the column of my back. The contact sent tingles throughout my body, lighting up every nerve ending, as if I wasn't still trying to recover from a soul-shattering orgasm.

I slid my arms out of the oversized top, letting him pull it off the rest of the way.

"We gave Diego quite the show," he said, sweeping hair off my shoulder and kissing the dampened skin there. I laughed, lacking the strength to look for my corrupted cat. "Might as well give him the grand finale."

Derek's cock pushed against my ass.

"I don't think he'll mind." When I turned onto my back, his eyes dropped to my breasts. "Derek," I purred, reaching between us and wrapping a hand around his dick. "Let me return the favor."

He grinned, sliding his mouth over mine. The taste of me on his lips had me moaning and stroking him harder.

I tore at the buttons on his collar—

The chime of a doorbell echoed around us. We froze. After the ordeal with Belov, I couldn't help but feel the pangs of anxiety ricocheting up my body and rooting themselves inside my heart. He must have sensed my anguish because his gentle hand cupped my face.

"You're safe with me. You know that, right?"

"I-I do. I just…"

"Angel, you're safe." His gaze was penetrating, an absolute conviction in his voice. "And it's probably Kai. Either way, no one gets in here unless I want them to. Understand?"

"Yeah."

He kissed my forehead and dashed off the bed and into the bathroom.

I grasped at the sheets, bunching them to my face and squealing into the fabric. Fuck, that was amazing. The best I'd ever had. I'd have to both thank and kill the woman who'd taught him those skills.

After slinking to the floor on wobbly legs, I scanned the room, looking for Diego. He was under a chair by one of the long windows, licking at his paw.

"Sorry, you had to see that, little guy." He stopped to glance at me before continuing his tongue bath.

Fuck. Tongue bath, indeed.

Derek must have been on the phone, his voice filtering from the other side of the door. The casual tone reinforced my confidence in his assurances about my safety.

Since when had I ever needed a man to feel safe?

I slid open the zipper of my bag and pulled out an outfit. As much as I enjoyed naked time with Derek, I was glad to have my things. Flutters tickled my chest at the thought of his gesture. The way he'd reached out to Lex, so I'd have everything I needed.

Moments later, he exited the bathroom, washed up and wearing a new suit.

This man and his damn suits.

A warm smile tipped his lips the moment his eyes found mine.

"Get dressed. Kai is downstairs."

I'd started to walk past him, and Derek looped an arm behind my back.

He dipped his head to kiss me, slow and gentle, our tongues gliding together in a sensual rhythm.

"I'm sorry we didn't get to finish what we started," I said over his mouth.

He hauled me closer, his dick hard against my abdomen. "Not your fault. And we'll pick up where we left off when I get back. You owe me two orgasms."

His little joke would have been funny, but my brain could only focus on what he'd said before that.

"What?" I pulled away, eyebrows knitted together. "When you get back? What do you mean? Where are you going? What about—"

"Hey." He took hold of my chin, staring into my panic-stricken eyes. "I have some business to take care of out of town. Kai is going to stay here. Watch you while I'm gone."

Annoyance clawed up my back, replacing the fear from seconds ago. I hated he was talking about me as if I needed a babysitter. But I was mostly aggravated with myself, because I realized the thought of him leaving put me on edge.

"I don't know Kai. I get that he's your brother, but you didn't even discuss this with me."

"There isn't anyone else I trust more to keep you safe."

I moved away from him, hugging myself as I stared hollowly out the window.

"I can just go back home, Derek. I don't want to be an inconvenience to anyone. And I can't just hide out here forever. Plus, my colleagues are working Belov and his men as we speak…"

Derek inched closer, trapping me against the glass, an arm on each side and a grave expression cutting across his face.

"You're not leaving."

I raised my chin in defiance. "I should be out there doing my job, not trapped in here with a damn babysitter."

He huffed out a sharp breath. "What don't you understand? You're a walking target. You think I'm going to just let you be out and about without protection?"

"*Let* me?"

"You know what I mean. Why are you being so stubborn?"

Pushing his arm, I slipped from his grasp. "You don't understand. And you're leaving, anyway," I bit back, aware I was acting childish.

He hooked my elbow as I made a move for the bathroom. "It's only two days. And my brother—"

"I'm afraid, okay?" I blurted out, the sting of tears pricking at my eyes. "I hate feeling this way. It's not who I am. But please, Derek… stay." I held the collar of his shirt, feeling all kinds of pathetic, but I didn't care.

Derek's gaze was stormy, tormented like he was grappling with the decision. He reached for the back of my neck on the wingtips of a deep sigh and pulled me to him.

"I promise this is important. I wouldn't leave if I didn't trust Kai with my life." He paused, the ice in his eyes piercing through me. "And that's exactly what I'm doing."

Chapter Twenty Seven

Derek

The chill of the metal railing bled through my leather gloves. I leaned on my elbows, breath billowing into the frigid night air as I looked down over the city, still buzzing with life below. Most of Central Park was bathed in shadows, save for rows of lights outlining the winding walkways. The city view was magnificent from this altitude, and the urge to share such a beautiful and rare sense of peace with Evangelina was damn near overwhelming. One day, when things settled down, I'd bring her here…

Fuck you, Derek. What have you gone and done?

I'd set a trap, lured her, and ended up falling headfirst into my own scheme. Now, there I was, wanting to share experiences and moments in life I never thought meant anything. But with her by my side, life was different. Cliché as it goddamn was, everything had new meaning. I wouldn't deny that.

She's not meant to stay, a petulant voice in the back of my head whispered the sobering reminder. Our time together had an expiration date. She didn't belong in my world.

"Mr. Cain," a soft, feminine voice called from behind me.

She had a heavy accent, and when I turned, her full-figured frame rested against the door jamb. Golden curls framed her rounded face and delicate features. The woman was conventionally pretty, though much younger looking than I anticipated.

"Amalia Montesinos."

Tipping her head with a nod, she pushed away from the door, green eyes cautiously watching my every move. "How was your trip?"

"How about we get right down to business?" My voice held a hard edge, and she faltered for a fraction of a second before regaining her composure.

I flexed my shoulders, gripping her by the neck and shoving her body against the railing—my gun against her temple. The stories I'd heard about Amalia seemed to contradict that of the woman in my grasp. Amalia didn't hesitate. She was ruthless, fearless—and she didn't fucking flinch.

"Who the fuck are you?"

Fingernails clawed at my hand, desperate for air. I squeezed an ounce tighter, and her face shifted to a bright red. "You have two seconds to tell me who you are before I blow your fucking brain all over Madison Blvd."

"Tell me, Mr. Cain, how exactly would she be able to give you what you ask while you're choking the breath from her at the same time?"

The business end of my HK was now pointed at the unfamiliar presence on the terrace. A more petite woman with long hair so black it looked blue under the moon's glow. She was slender, her body encased in an all-black, skin-tight outfit. Her walk, calculated and leonine, exuded the confidence the one in my grasp had lacked.

"I suggest you lower your weapon," she said, raising a perfectly arched brow. My eyes dropped to my chest, where I was dotted with a handful of red rifle spots.

"What fucking game are you playing here?"

"Please, let Sofía go. My aunt won't be too happy if we go back to *México* without her." Her accented voice held an implicit warning, dark eyes fixed on mine.

The larger woman had stopped flailing, her body limp against the railing. I let her fall on the cold concrete and stepped toward Amalia.

The *real* Amalia Montesinos.

"Explain," I said, holstering my gun.

Amalia lifted her gaze to the surrounding buildings, and with a single nod, the glare of the rifle sights was instantly gone—a testament to the power she commanded.

"I had to know you were the real deal, Cain. I don't do business with posers and wannabe bad guys with small dicks and no brains."

She sauntered past me, licking her lips as she sized me up with a leering grin. "Hm, you don't seem to have either of those problems."

Amalia was an extraordinarily beautiful woman. Two months ago, I would have indulged in her company, but there was only one woman whose touch I craved.

"So, tell me, Mr. Cain, what exactly brings you here? Helena tells me, you want to take down a Russian crime family. That's quite the ambition."

"Something like that."

"Surely, a man with your skill and resources doesn't need my help to execute such a plan, no?"

Metal scraped against the concrete as she pulled out a chair and sat, crossing her legs and casually leaning back.

"This doesn't involve Ares. It's personal."

The door slid open, and a young woman with features similar to that of the unconscious Sofia strode toward us with a bottle of cognac and two glasses.

"Please, sit. Have a drink and tell me more about this *personal* problem of yours."

I snatched a glance at our surroundings before taking a seat. The reputation of *Las Mercenarias* preceded them. Not one to let my guard down, I refused the offered drink and pierced her with a glare. "That's my business. You get your money, and I get what I want: Dimitry Belov's head on a fucking slab."

Amalia took a swig of her drink and set the glass down with a laugh. "Well, that certainly sounds personal. Let me guess. This revenge plot involves… a woman?"

I clenched my teeth. "Do we have a deal or not?" She didn't need to know the details. My trust only stretched so far, and I'd never chance Evangelina's life.

"Seems I've hit the nail on the head." Another wicked chuckle fell from her painted-red lips. "Ah, crimes of passion are one of my favorites. There's nothing more romantic than a man defending his woman's honor in blood."

She got to her feet and rounded my chair. All my instincts flared to life the moment Amalia stood at my back. I moved my hand over the blade inside my jacket.

"Relax, Cain," she murmured, breath fanning over my ear. "No blood will be spilled here tonight." The back of her finger slowly slid down the side of my neck. "Unless… you're into that sort of thing?"

I caught her wrist, and within a heartbeat, my body lit up with the lasers of red scopes.

Amalia put her free hand up, waving off my death. "A loyal man. You just keep impressing me, Cain. She is one lucky woman."

Chapter Twenty Eight
Evangelina

Sweat droplets rolled down the curve of my cleavage and into my black sports bra. I set the weights on the floor and remained on the bench. My muscles were humming, tight from the intense, hour-long workout. Cold water splashed down the back of my throat, and I couldn't help the exaggerated sigh that followed.

Derek's home gym was impressive. It was easy to see how he maintained such a delicious, muscular figure. I lay back on the long, cushioned bench and closed my eyes as the memories of his tongue, his touch, and the command he held over my body ignited a different type of burn.

"Hey." Kai's knuckles rapped against the door. Stepping inside, he leaned an arm against the bar of an apparatus. "I'm about to order lunch. Do you want anything? And please say yes. I'm under strict orders to make sure you eat."

"Are you now?" I asked with a sarcastic tone, sitting up as I wiped the sweat from my forehead and slung the white towel over my shoulder. "Derek's orders?"

He put his hands up defensively. "He means well. He worries about you."

"A little too much, I see. Listen, I've been doing this for a long time. I don't need—"

"I get that. It's just…" he paused, as though debating whether to continue speaking, "Derek isn't the kind of man who worries about other people. His circle is extremely small. Take that how you want."

Kai had soulful eyes, almost as bright blue as Derek's. He was handsome, with well-defined muscles like his brother, only leaner. His deep tan suggested he was of mixed heritage, though I couldn't venture a guess. Unlike Derek, whose expressions and body language were the kind most avoided, there was something about Kai that drew people in. But just like his brother, there lived an edge in those pools of blue.

An hour later, we sat at the breakfast bar. I stabbed at my chicken salad while Kai finished off a cheesesteak.

"He's okay, you know."

Had my sulking been that obvious?

I flashed him a half smile. "I know. He said he was on an important business trip. I shouldn't be worried."

"But you are."

I nodded. "I feel like whatever he's doing involves me somehow, and not in a good way."

Kai leaned back in his chair. "Look, Eva…"

"I know he's your brother. And you don't owe me any loyalty, but I care about him a lot. I don't want him to do anything stupid because of what happened."

"Eva, Derek is exactly where he said he would be. Trust me when I tell you that."

He chose his words carefully, and the ones he wasn't saying were loud and clear. But there was no cracking Kai. His loyalty to Derek was unshakable.

Could I really fault him for that?

It's not like I would betray Lex for someone I'd just met, either. But damn, if it wasn't maddening. And as much as I wanted to trust Derek with the truth behind his whereabouts, I couldn't shake the feeling of paranoia.

"Eva!"

The moment I opened the front door, Alexa's arms were around my neck, nearly choking off my air supply. "I'm so sorry I couldn't come sooner. I had some meetings I couldn't get out of—Are you okay?"

Her words were frantic as she gripped my shoulders. "Lex, I'm fine. I saw your messages."

"*Tío* Franco called and told me what happened. And I saw it on the news… and then *Derek* called for help with your stuff. He said I could see you. Are you sure you're all right?"

I pulled her into a tight hug, quieting her frenzied words. "I am. Promise."

"Someone tried to murder you, babes. A group of someones. It's okay to not be okay." Emotion filled her words, and she squeezed me tighter.

"I know," I said, my voice on the verge of breaking too.

We held each other for what seemed like hours. And the hug was exactly what I needed—familiar arms and support. But I refused to fall apart again. I needed to be strong for the chaos that awaited me beyond the walls of this house. Strong for Sam, my team, and myself.

A throat cleared behind us. I introduced them, and Kai nodded his greeting—a tighter smile than usual on his face.

"Derek said it was fine."

"You didn't look before you opened the door." There was a bite to his tone he'd never used with me.

"She sent me a text. I knew who it was."

"Anyone could have taken her phone, hacked it, could have followed her. Your cousin's instructions were simple. She was to contact my number first." His eyes flickered to Alexa, then back to me.

Anger flared inside me. "I'm not a prisoner here. She's like my sister."

"That's not the point. You're welcome to see and speak to whomever you want. But your safety is my priority at the moment. And blindly opening the door was foolish."

I straightened my stance and stepped in front of him. Instantly feeling silly since I had to extend my neck to meet his cold gaze fully. He was a couple of inches taller than Derek, and that was saying something.

"I'm not helpless, Kai."

He'd started to speak, but Lex intervened. "It's fine, Eva. He's right. Your safety is what's important here, and I didn't follow through with the plan."

I took a moment to compose my anger, reminding myself that Kai was here when he didn't need to be. That Derek cared about my well-being. But alarm bells still sounded off in my head. What made these two so protective, knowledgeable, and calculated about my safety?

I looped my arm through Alexa's and pulled her into the living room.

"Okay, but hear me out. That man is sexy as fuck."

"*Lex.*"

We plopped down onto the sofa. "What? Just because you're hung up on the other Cain brother doesn't mean you're blind." She craned her neck to look down the hallway, then leaned in close. "The way his voice went all low and authoritative. *Damn*. I wanted to get down on my knees and beg for forgiveness."

I mushed her face away from mine, unable to stifle my laughter. "You are a lost cause."

"But is he single?"

"You're not! What happened to your guy from Brooklyn?"

She clucked her teeth and sat back against the cushion. "Ancient history."

"Ancient history two days ago?"

"You know how it is. Gotta kiss a shitload of toads to find my prince." She motioned around us with one hand. "Not everyone can be as lucky as you."

Thoughts of Derek killed all the humor of the moment. Alexa noticed the mood shift and grabbed my hand. "Hey, you sure you're all right?"

I forced a smile. "Physically, yes. But the last twenty-four hours have been... *something*."

The doorbell chimed, and my hopes soared for a fraction of a second, but that optimism deflated just as fast. Derek wouldn't ring his own door.

"You expecting company?" Alexa's brow creased with concern as she got to her feet and took a protective stance in front of me. The gesture warmed my heart.

"Not that I know of."

Kai's voice and that of another male filtered in from the front of the home. The neutrality of their tone set our worries at ease. Lex fell back onto the couch, but I remained standing, waiting for our unexpected guest.

A tall, silver-haired man crossed into the living room. Kai, one step behind. The older male was lean, though the fabric of a tailored gray suit hugged his broad shoulders and the curvature of muscled biceps. He moved with sure steps and the swagger of a man who was used to giving orders and commanding respect. He reminded me a lot of Derek.

The moment his emerald-green eyes centered on me, his cocky, bearded grin widened.

"Evangelina Cruz!" he almost sing-songed with excitement, as if we were old friends meeting after a long stretch apart.

Not waiting for Kai's formal introduction, he sauntered forward, taking my hand. "I'm so very pleased to meet you finally."

Narrowing my eyes, I examined him. There was something strangely familiar about his face, but I couldn't place it. "I'm sorry. Do I know you?"

He looked back at Kai and cocked his head before returning his attention to me. "My apologies. I assumed my sons had told you about me."

Sons?

"You're Ronan Cain," I said while simultaneously attempting to reclaim my hand, but his hold on it only tightened.

"That's me."

Derek and Kai's adoptive father.

Alexa reached for Ronan's hand, leaving him no option but to release mine. My cousin's greeting was curt, the tension radiating from her body palpable. A smile that hadn't reached her eyes faded when she turned around, tugging me with her.

"I'm sure the two of you have plenty to catch up on. We'll get out of your hair," Lex said hurriedly as she walked us toward the staircase.

"If you don't mind"—his voice dropped two octaves, the smile gone from his face—"I'd love for you to stay."

I pulled back against Alexa's grip, my feet rooted in place by the undercurrent of authority lacing his tone.

The older Cain rubbed his beard with one hand while the other rested inside his pant pocket. The man's stance took me back to the day I'd met Derek. "Promise I won't keep her long—Miss?"

"Alexa Cruz. Eva's sister. And if *you* don't mind, *we* have a lot of catching up to do."

"Alexa? Like that little device? Cute."

Lex crossed her arms over her chest. The moment she took in a lungful of air, I knew I had to intervene.

"It's fine. Just wait for me here." My hand on her shoulder served to settle her ire momentarily.

She whirled me around. "Eva, you're really trying to be alone with this guy? He gives me a bad vibe." Her angry whisper wasn't as quiet as she thought—or maybe that was the intention.

"Lex, he's Derek's father. I'll be fine."

What did I have to fear? Derek had hinted their relationship was one of mutual respect, not affection. And if Kai had no reservations about letting the man inside, even after our little spat over Alexa, then I had no reason to be wary. I cared too much about Derek not to attempt a relationship with the man who'd pulled him out of foster care.

"I'll meet you back here in a few minutes." As if on cue, Diego pranced down the steps. "Take care of Diego for me. His food is in the kitchen pantry."

Alexa pursed her lips and didn't say another word, her harsh glare set behind me.

Ronan and I walked side by side down the hall to an office den just off the front foyer. He motioned me inside with one arm, promptly following and leaning against a thick mahogany desk.

Shelves of books lined the small space. I pulled one out, curious about Derek's reading preferences.

The Art of War.

"My son, always so serious."

I slid the book back into its spot and rested my hands on the back of a sleek office chair. "He is," I said, giving him a small smile. "Was he always that way?"

Ronan chuckled. "Always. But that's part of what makes him unique. He takes his time. Scrutinizes every little detail. Has a good eye for things—and clearly good taste," he added with an eyebrow raised and a smirk playing on his lips.

I chose to ignore his compliment and the glint of what looked like lust in his eyes. Averting my gaze, I caught sight of the ring on his finger. It was identical to Derek and Kai's.

"He left yesterday afternoon. I'm surprised he never mentioned you coming to visit."

"It was a last-minute decision. Though I'm sure he's been informed. He and Kai are extremely close."

I pulled the chair back and sat, crossing my legs, and his eyes flickered down for the briefest of seconds. I didn't want to read too much into it as it could have been just a natural reaction, but coupled with his previous comment, I suddenly felt slightly uncomfortable.

"You adopted them together. That was very selfless of you and your wife."

"Maeve and I always knew we wanted to have children. But having our own just wasn't in the cards. However, over the years, we gave a home to many young boys and girls in need."

I simply nodded. Sleazy or not, what they'd done for all those kids was truly an amazing gesture of love. Though a part of me worried about the young girls in his care, irrational as it was. Maybe I was jumping to conclusions in the worst way. I was an adult woman. He was a man. It was unfair to assume he was anything but fatherly to the underprivileged girls in his care.

"You sure have grown, Eva."

That comment had my full attention. "Excuse me?"

He moved closer and reached out to grab my left wrist. My eyes followed his movements as if in slow motion, and I didn't make a single effort to stop him. Turning my hand over, he used a finger to trace the faint vertical scar of the surgery I'd had as a child.

"Your father Franco and I go way back. Before Derek." The rhythm of my heart accelerated. "I ran into him one day at the grocery store. You were with him, a bright pink cast on your arm."

I stared beyond Ronan, the images of that morning returning to me like a movie reel.

"I was seven," I said, still focused on the memories inside my mind.

"And missing a couple of teeth. You were quite chatty and just about the cutest damn thing I'd ever seen. I went home that night and told my wife I was ready to adopt. To be a father to an adorable little girl just like you. And that's exactly what we did."

Setting my arm down, his eyes were like a magnetic force, drawing me to lose myself in them, in the images of that stranger from so many years ago. I remembered being intrigued by the tall man in a navy-colored suit, but the memories that struck me the most were of my father. In hindsight, I could see how his reaction to Ronan wasn't normal. The way he pulled me close, placing himself between us while exchanging awkward pleasantries. The slight tremor of his hands as he continuously tried to keep me out of sight and prevent me from talking.

"I knew you looked familiar. But how do you know my father? He's never—*I've* never seen you since that day."

"I always knew you'd turn out to be beautiful," he said, ignoring my questions. "Small world, isn't it?"

His phone vibrated from somewhere inside his jacket. As Ronan read the name lighting up the screen, out of my view, his jaw twitched, but he composed his features in the next breath.

"It was so nice to see you again, Eva. Now that you and my son are friends, I hope to see more of you. And maybe I'll pass by and catch up with Franco."

He was dismissing me.

"Yes. You'll have to tell me more about you and my dad."

A Cheshire Cat grin spread across his face. "Of course."

His gaze burned at my back as I exited the office. Alexa's intuition about Ronan had been spot on.

Chapter Twenty Nine

Derek

One of Kai's legs hung over the side of the couch while Diego was curled on a cushion above his head. Both asleep. I searched for signs of Evangelina, but the house was dark and quiet. It was just past midnight, so I could only assume she'd gone to bed. Everything inside me was itching to find her, but I needed to be prepared. Have my story straight.

"Hey. Wake up." Kai stirred, then sat upright in a flash, the barrel of a Glock pointed at my face.

"Shit, D. I'm sorry. I wasn't expecting you." He cursed under his breath, setting the weapon on the coffee table and rubbing rough hands over his eyes.

I wouldn't have batted an eye at the gun in my face—wouldn't have been the first or last—but what if it had been Eva? Kai read the tension on my face and put both hands up in his defense.

"Fuck, Derek. I said I was sorry. You snuck up on me while I was asleep. What'd you expect?"

I rubbed my knuckles over the pressure point between my eyes. "Where is she?"

"Probably in bed. I'd be exhausted too after the day she had."

"What happened? What did he say to her?"

Kai regarded me with confusion. "Ronan?"

When I received Kai's text that our adoptive father had dropped by and was speaking to Eva in private, I damn near jumped on the next flight back to Philly.

"Who else would I be talking about?"

My brother stretched and leaned back against the cushion, a hand over a still-sleeping Diego.

"This is one cool cat. He's been hanging with me all day. You should see how he bosses Deimos around."

I clenched my fists. "Are you purposely fucking with me? I've had a very stressful forty-eight hours. I don't give a damn about your day with Eva's cat." I leaned in and lowered my voice. "What went down between her and Ronan?"

"Come on. Don't you think I would have told you if something serious happened?"

I was simultaneously relieved and frustrated by my brother's unhurried communication.

"Okay, so what did you mean?"

"Alexa. Her cousin." He whistled out a puff of air and shook his head. "That broad can talk. She's fine as hell, but goddamn."

The night I'd reached out to her and told her what had happened at the hospital, the woman began spouting off at rapid-fire speed, switching between English and Spanish like she was possessed. I barely got a word in before she was racing across her apartment, demanding to see Evangelina.

He put a hand on my shoulder. "She'll be happy to see you." His expression suddenly shifted. A crease formed between his brows as he leaned forward, head hung low, and clasped his hands together. "Derek, I hope you know what you're doing here. This woman. You're in deeper than you thought... maybe deeper than you know."

I couldn't deny his claim. Similar thoughts had been consuming my mind since I parted for New York. I'd just made a deal with the proverbial devil to orchestrate a massacre of the Belov family in the name of seeking revenge on behalf of Evangelina. Consequences be damned.

"How was your meeting with Amalia? When do we go knocking down some doors? And is she as vicious as the rumors make her out to be?"

I stood up, the need to see my girl with my own eyes now overwhelming. "Aside from the part where her people almost killed me? Twice. It went as planned. I paid her half of what we discussed, and the other half will be collected later at her discretion."

Kai rose, arms raised at his sides, his face twisted with confusion. "What the fuck does that mean?" I was already halfway up the staircase. "D, why do I feel like this will come back to bite us in the ass?"

Without answering, I kept pace toward my bedroom, assuming Eva was asleep, until I heard the faint whooshing sounds of water from deep inside the room.

She was in the shower.

My dick's reaction to that news was instant, straining against the front of my pants. I pushed open the door, confirming she was indeed in the ensuite and not asleep. The bed was undisturbed, still made since what I could only deduce to be some time that morning. One of her bags was open on the bench, the clothes in disarray as if she were frantically searching for a particular item. I made a mental note to question her about it later, knowing I'd set out to get her anything she needed if that were the case.

Damn, Derek, this woman's got you all kinds of bent out of shape?

I slid off my jacket and tossed it on the bed, not wanting to waste another second. I'd had a taste of her, and I'd been longing for another ever since.

As I neared the door, her voice poured over me in smooth velvet waves. She was singing, calling to me, drawing me in like a goddamn Siren, leading me to ruin.

Chapter Thirty

Derek

Steam billowed from the bathroom when I opened the door. My eyes immediately fell on her naked silhouette behind the fogged glass. Her hands were tangled in her hair as she stood under the spray of hot water, suds running delicious rivulets down the curves of her body.

The door clicked behind me, startling her just enough to make her gasp until her anxious gaze found mine.

"It's just me, angel."

"You're back," she whispered.

"Don't stop. Sing for me, baby."

Eva tipped her head back, the lyrics flowing out of her like poetry. Her hands were back in her hair as she rinsed out the shampoo. Only now, there was a slight sway in her hips, a cunning smile on her face, and her fingers moved at a slower, more calculated pace. I gripped the edge of the vanity, fighting back the urge to rip open that door and take what was mine.

"You have no idea how fucking beautiful you are." I worked the buttons of my shirt, pulling it out of my pants before kicking my shoes against the door. The sudden thud forced her eyes open, her voice trailing off.

"Thought I said not to stop."

Her tongue swept across her bottom lip, drawing in the water droplets streaming down her face. She closed her eyes as the song curled around me again. My pants dropped to my ankles, and I quickly pulled at the waistband of my boxer briefs, freeing my aching cock and stroking from root to crown.

"Did you miss me?" Without missing a beat, she nodded. "I missed the hell out of you, angel."

Evangelina rewarded me with a sexy side-eye and a dimpled grin. "All I could think about was how fucking good you tasted and how I couldn't wait to have you again."

"Derek…" She bit down on her lip.

"Don't stop." My voice was tight. She placed both hands on the tile in front of her, soft notes flowing from her lips. "Did you touch her while I was gone?" She nodded again, her head down, and I could only imagine the beautiful flush of her cheeks as she made that admission. "Show me."

There was a moment of hesitation when her heady gaze met mine before her hand slid over her flat stomach and down to the perfectly trimmed V of her pelvis. She dipped two fingers in her pussy, her strokes long and measured.

"Were you thinking of me while you were touching that wet cunt of yours?" I asked. Her voice faltered, breath catching as she nodded. "Were you imagining my tongue, angel? Devouring every inch of you?" Her nods turned languorous as she rode her fingers faster. "Keep fucking singing."

"Derek, I—I can't…" she panted, dropping to her knees as soft moans rose from her throat.

When Evangelina's other hand moved over her breast, thumb and forefinger tweaking a hardened nipple, I nearly lost it. I fisted my dick and swallowed a groan.

"That's my fucking girl. Show me how badly you want this cock inside you." The song was long forgotten, her breaths and moans louder, hips moving in time with her hand. "Look at me, baby. Look at what you do to me. How fucking hard I am for you."

"Oh... *fuck*, Derek!" she cried as she pushed two fingers inside and fell back on her legs, no longer able to hold her weight on trembling thighs.

She was so close.

"Don't you fucking come."

Eva tossed a pleading look over her shoulder, bottom lip tucked tightly between her teeth. Unable to stand another second without touching her, I threw open the glass door. Sprays of hot water tumbled over my body as I stood under the showerhead.

Smoothing both hands around my hips, she grabbed my ass. As she looked up at me, blinking away water, she ran her tongue along the underside of my erection, flicking the tip.

I cursed, tipping my head back at the wicked sensation.

But as much as I wanted to feel the heat of her pretty mouth wrapped around my dick, the craving for her taste was overpowering.

I tangled my fingers into her wet hair, tugging her head back. "Not yet, angel. I need you first."

Bending at the knee, I dipped my head, crushing my lips to hers and sucking her tongue into my mouth.

The hours away from Eva had felt like a lifetime. I wasn't sure when, how, or why things had changed, but there was no going back. I'd never missed anyone, never craved their companionship, not even Kai. She wasn't special, wasn't any different than other beautiful women I'd come across and fucked in the past.

But she was *everything*.

With a hand on each side of her ribcage, I lifted her to a standing position and kissed my way up the side of her neck. I used my teeth to pull her lip from its favorite hiding spot before devouring them again.

"God, I missed you," I rasped over her mouth before biting at the swollen flesh.

"I missed you too." Droplets of water rolled down her face and into her mouth. I licked across, lapping up the liquid. Whimpering, she shuddered against me. "What have you done to me, Derek?"

"Nothing yet. But I'm about to." My hand snaked up her slick body and curled around her neck. Using my thumb, I tilted her chin. "I'm going to fuck you, Evangelina. I'm going to ruin you the way you've ruined me completely." My grip on her throat tightened, forehead pressed against hers. "You're mine. Always mine. Do you understand that?"

"I do," she whispered. "I'm yours, Derek. Please…"

I chuckled wickedly against her ear. "Please, what? What do you want, beautiful? Because all I want to do right now is drop to my knees and tongue fuck you until I get my fill."

She bit back a moan. "Let me—"

A growl rolled off my tongue when her hand fisted my dick. She pumped me twice before I caught her wrist and stilled her movements.

Goddamn.

"Not yet." I pushed her against the tile and nipped at her skin as I journeyed south. My mouth suctioned a tight nipple, and she hissed, eyes rolling to the back of her head. When my knees hit the shower floor, I pressed a kiss to her slit. "Lean on the wall."

Grabbing a thigh, I threw a leg over my shoulder and buried my face in her pussy.

Fuck, I missed this.

Sliding my tongue along the slickness of her opening, I circled her clit, and she shuddered above me, fingers twisted in my hair.

"Yes... God, yes!" she cried, thrusting against my face.

I hoisted her other thigh over my shoulder, deepening the contact as I fucking licked her clean.

"I'll never get enough of you," I growled over her clit. The sweet little noises she made were music to my black soul. I'd do anything to make her sing for me the way she was. To pull those sounds from her every day of my fucking life.

My cock throbbed painfully with every moan and every whimper that fell from her lips. I needed to be inside her. She broke apart in my mouth when I squeezed that swollen clit between my teeth. Her cries echoed around us as she writhed on my tongue.

Evangelina tried to squirm away from me, but I held her firm, my hands digging into the flesh of her ass. She tasted too damn good, and I wanted everything she had to give.

I guided her body down to the tile, her sharp breaths slowing as she came down from the high of her orgasm. She leaned forward on her hands and knees and kissed me, tongue circling the edges of my lips.

"You didn't tell me you'd be back tonight. I was expecting you tomorrow."

Grabbing a fistful of her wet hair, I tugged her closer, kissing the side of her cheeks. "I wanted to surprise you. Needed to see you."

She climbed into my lap, wrapping her legs around my waist. The warmth of her pussy against my abdomen made my dick ache with the need to be buried to the fucking hilt.

"It's a pleasant surprise."

"Hold on to me," I said, getting to my feet.

I briefly remembered the first time I saw Evangelina and how I envisioned this very scenario. Her glorious naked body against mine, legs wrapped around me.

As exhilarating as those thoughts were, they threatened to take me to a dark place I didn't care to visit any longer. A moment in time when she was once the object of my revenge and the woman I had set out to destroy.

How things had changed.

I knew I didn't deserve her. That our time would come to an end sooner rather than later. We were doomed from the very beginning.

I must have been in a daze when I felt her hands on my face, eyes brimming with concern.

"Derek, what's the matter?"

One look at her was enough to dispel my worries and the uncertainty of whatever fate awaited us.

Damn it all to hell.

I tossed her on the bed and straddled her body, seizing her wrist. "Just thinking…" I said, kissing her palm before reaching over and pinning both arms above her head. "How I can't wait to fucking wreck you, angel."

My tongue dragged along her collarbone, licking up the droplets still dotting her skin. She moaned, eyes closing as her back arched off the bed, offering herself to me. I trailed down between her breasts, hard teeth across her skin, reddening her flesh and marking her as mine.

Every piece of this woman tasted like heaven. It was the closest I would ever get to that elusive paradise I was never meant to touch.

"Please," she pleaded, wrapping her legs around my back. I suckled one nipple before kissing my way to the other. "Fuck me, Derek."

I grinned against her skin, suctioning an erect little bud before releasing it with a pop. Climbing off the bed, I pulled open the top drawer on my nightstand for a condom, tearing the wrapper with my teeth.

Eva propped herself on her elbows, mouth slightly parted as I rolled the latex over the hard length of my erection. Her eyes were transfixed on my cock, and I watched with a laugh as she squeezed her thighs together.

"Like what you see?"

She gave a slow nod, a hint of worry in her eyes as she took in my size.

I gripped an ankle and tugged her roughly toward the edge of the bed, a leg on each side of me. "Remember what I told you. You're going to take this cock like a good girl." I ran my thumb along her slit, pushing on her clit, and she moaned and arched her back.

"Now, turn around."

Eva wet her lips, intending to do as she was told, but I was an impatient son of a bitch. My fingers dug into her hips, and I flipped her over and hauled her ass to me.

"Goddamn, angel. Look at you, cunt dripping like a little slut." I suppressed a growl, fisting my cock at the sight of her bare and open, swollen and so fucking wet for me.

The bed dipped when I knelt behind her, hand smoothing over her ass and the sexy curve of her back. I pushed her chest into the mattress.

"Just like that. Keep that ass up for me." My finger trailed up and down her slit, causing her hips to push back and soft whimpers to flutter from her lips.

"You just can't wait to get fucked, can you?"

"You're a bastard; you know that?"

"I do. And don't you ever forget it." She hissed when I pushed two fingers inside her, hooking them forward and making her legs tremble. When she mewled under my touch, it only spurred me on. "I told you I was no good for you. But it's too late now," I said, giving my dick long, hard strokes. "You're mine now, Evangelina. You hear me?"

"Yours," she whined as my teeth closed around her plump ass.

"No going back."

"No going back," she repeated breathlessly.

"Look at me," I said, my tone sharp.

Evangelina tossed a heated gaze over her shoulder, pushing herself up on her hands as her eyes followed my hand, and grinned when I sucked my fingers dry. My new obsession.

Gripping her hips, I lined my cock at her entrance, and she arched, easing back into me. A hard slap to the ass had her stilling her movements and stifling a hiss.

"This is all me. Understood?"

"Yeah," she breathed, clenching her fists around the sheets.

"Good girl."

Without wasting another second, I pushed inside her, and the heat of her tight walls squeezed around my dick so damn good.

Eva tensed, groaning beneath me as I buried my cock inch by inch, letting her adjust until I bottomed out.

"Fuck, Angel."

Her pussy was so wet, so fucking tight, that I had to take a moment and draw in a sharp breath, or this would end far sooner than either of us anticipated. I leaned forward and ran my tongue up the middle of her back.

Her skin was damp and salty-sweet.

I pulled back before surging into her again, burying myself to the hilt.

"Eva… so good."

She rocked into me, meeting my pace, thrust for devastating

thrust. Throwing my head back, my eyes closed of their own accord as I climbed to paradise. The realization of how utterly fucked we were dawned on me at that moment. This was it. We were too far gone. And I didn't give a single fuck. It didn't matter what awaited me on the other side of this proverbial shitstorm. As long as I was with this woman, nothing else mattered. I would die here. Die for her. Kill for her.

Anything for her.

I leaned forward, biting her shoulder, while my hand snaked around her pelvis, strumming her clit.

"Yes… Baby, so good," she cried, smothering her face in the sheets.

Curling a fist into her wet hair, I yanked her head up and away from the mattress. "Don't you fucking hide from me. I told you I need to hear you."

My strokes intensified, and I drove into her with delicious cruelty. Evangelina's body jolted forward, incessant moans spilling from her lips with each thrust. The sheets bunched around her blanched knuckles as she fought to stay upright.

"Oh… God, don't stop."

I leaned close to her ear, her little body dominated, eclipsed by mine. "No, not God. Derek."

My fingers found her swollen clit again, and I pinched it. "Fuck… fuck," she sobbed, biting into one of her wrists.

Her whole body trembled, and the walls of her sex constricted around my cock.

"So close, angel. Let go and come for me." Evangelina's cries built to a crescendo. "I want to feel you come all over my cock. I want you to show me how good I fuck you, baby."

She shook her head from side to side, eyes squeezed shut while cursing in Spanish. I laughed darkly at her defiance and gripped her ass cheek, hooking my thumb and putting pressure over her tight rim. "I want this too." I leaned over and spit until she was coated, and I pushed inside.

"*Oh…*" she whimpered, biting at the sheets.

Another hard pinch to her swollen clit as I pushed deeper. Harder. Filling her so fucking completely. Two more unforgiving thrusts and Evangelina cried out, writhing beneath me.

"That's it. That's my fucking girl." I gripped her hips with bruising force. The pressure in my balls coiled each time the waves of her release clamped down on my dick. "You come only for me, angel."

I rammed her body, my ball sack slapping against her thighs. Faster. As I pulled her back into me, her hands no longer grasping the comforter, I whispered, "Remember who you belong to." I cupped her breasts, my thrusts slowing as I held her tight, branding her flesh with the imprint of my fingers. "Say it."

"Derek. I'm yours."

One. Two. Three hard strokes.

I snapped inside her.

"*Fuck.*" Loud grunts rumbled past my clenched teeth and into the crook of her neck as I bucked into her. Rope after rope of my seed pumping out of my cock.

Chapter Thirty One

Evangelina

Derek's toned bare ass was all I could look at as he made his way into the bathroom to dispose of the condom. I'd lost track of what time it was, but that was the third one of the night.

Every inch of his body was covered in dark ink, and I never knew how attractive that could be until now. Closing my eyes, I let out a low squeal as I focused on all the parts of me that still hummed with the memory of his touch. I'd never given control over to a man as I had with Derek. Never knew how thrilling and, frankly, how fucking hot it could be. I lay on the bed, feeling utterly boneless, the sting of bruises biting at different parts of my body.

He climbed in beside me and slid under the thick comforter. I was still sprawled on my stomach, head resting over my arms, too damn worn out to move or keep my eyes open any longer. The fire of his gaze warmed my skin, sending goosebumps cascading across my flesh. I shivered, and the smile permanently etched on my face grew wider.

"Are you cold?" he asked. I shook my head, not trusting my voice just yet. The back of his hand caressed my bare shoulder, then down my arm. "Talk to me, angel."

My eyes fluttered open at his softened tone. And I lost myself in those eyes, the same ones that had captivated me from the very first day.

"I just…" I croaked as I propped myself on my elbows. "I've never…" I shook my head, trying to clear the high. "You called me a slut." I laughed. "And I fucking loved it."

Derek pulled the sheet from my body and feathered his fingers down the curve of my ass. "In here, you're mine to fuck and bend, tear apart, and put back together. Only mine."

Leaning in close, I hovered over his lips. "Then I never want to leave," I whispered as he pulled me into a slow kiss by the back of the neck. His tongue licked the roof of my mouth, and I moaned into his, feeling my ravaged pussy throbbing for more of him.

Would I survive another around?

I wasn't sure, but I was more than willing to make the sacrifice.

"Angel," he said, arm circling my waist and tugging me to his chest. Our legs intertwined, and I lay my head over his shoulder, waiting for him to continue. "Ronan." His body tensed beneath me as he spoke. "He didn't say or do anything that made you uncomfortable, did he?"

How could I put our exchange into words? There wasn't anything concrete one way or the other. Maybe it was just in my head, planted there by Alexa's disapproval. But I knew better. His presence was unnerving, as if he knew things about my life, about me, that I wasn't even aware of. Worst of all, he seemed to enjoy having the upper hand.

"Eva." His voice was suddenly tight, his grip on me like a vise.

"He knew who I was. I'd met him. Years ago, Derek. When I was still a little girl, only I didn't remember until that moment." Derek remained quiet, and I lifted my head to look at him. His eyes were set on the ceiling, the tension on his face causing his jaw to twitch. "You didn't tell me you had a sister."

Derek's eyes snapped to mine. "He told you about Athena?"

"Athena?"

"He doesn't talk about her to anyone. Not even Kai and me. I'm curious what his motives were behind revealing that to you."

It was as if I could see the wheels in his head turning. His dark brows pulled together, a crease between them as he digested that information.

"Where is she?"

"What else did he say?" he asked, ignoring my question.

"Not much else—Derek, what happened to her?"

He sat up, clutching me by the shoulders. "Athena has been gone a long time."

"I'm so sorry. I didn't—"

"She's just gone. We don't know where she is or what happened to her. But I don't want to talk about that right now. I just need to know you're okay. Ronan can be an asshole. And if he so much as—"

"No, I'm fine," I assured him, arching my neck and brushing my lips against the stubble on his face.

He held the side of my neck and pulled me down to his waiting mouth. There wasn't any heat behind our kiss. There was something else. Something softer, more profound. I cupped his cheek and brushed my lips back and forth over his as flutters rose from my belly, settling in my chest.

The arm he curled around my waist tightened, and he sighed into my hair.

So much of Derek was a mystery. And I often wondered how deep his scars truly went. How big of a role had his adoptive father played in the man he'd become? And was Ronan Cain the reason Athena had gone missing?

"What are you thinking about?"

"How I forgot to ask about your trip?"

The reason behind his leaving town still didn't sit right.

"It was nothing special. Just business."

I sat up, pangs of doubt nudging at my insecurities. "It just seemed so abrupt, especially after what happened."

Derek sat up too, blue eyes searing me with their intensity. "Evangelina, I wouldn't have left you if it wasn't absolutely necessary."

"That's what I don't understand. On the one hand, you wave it off as just business, but then you say things like that, look at me like that, and it makes me feel like there's something more. Something you're not telling me."

He swallowed hard, seemingly uncomfortable with my accusation, and moved off the bed, pulling a t-shirt over his head. "I still have obligations, angel. Clients. Prior commitments that I can't just blow off at the drop of a hat."

My eyes cast downward, suddenly feeling like an immature brat. "I'm sorry. I shouldn't assume you're lying. That's rude of me."

"Come here." Derek looped an arm behind my back and hauled me toward him, crushing my body to his chest. "I would drop everything for you."

The pit of my stomach plummeted, like the sensation one feels during a free fall. "Derek," I murmured into his ear, my voice suddenly shaky as he scented up the side of my throat and squeezed me just an ounce tighter. The way my breasts were pressed against his hard body caused a fresh flush of moisture to drip from between my thighs.

"Mmm?"

"I want you to fuck me and call me your little slut again."

I felt him grin against my neck. "I'm going to take you to the shower, angel. And I'm going to fuck that naughty mouth of yours until you cry and choke on my cock." He squeezed my ass until I locked my ankles behind his back. "Then I'm going to fuck you against the tile. And you're going to come for me again."

Fuck. Yes.

Chapter Thirty Two

Evangelina

The elevator doors closed behind us. A tall, dark-haired man was standing in the far-right corner, face in his phone. While he hadn't so much as acknowledged our presence, I couldn't help my reaction upon seeing him. Gripping Derek's arm a little tighter, I moved closer to his body. The sights and smells of the building only added to my paranoia, since the last time I was here, I was being shot at and nearly assaulted. My breath sped up, my pulse drumming, reverberating in my ears and overpowering the droning of the cables as we went up.

"Hey." Derek's gentle voice eased me back off the ledge of a panic attack. "I told you you're safe with me."

He must have sensed my nerves taking a nose-dive, though the way my grip was probably leaving fingerprints on the skin of his forearm, it wouldn't be hard to guess. I was spiraling. He pulled me to his chest, lips brushing my forehead.

The ding of the elevator caused me to jump in his arms. "Eva, look at me."

I shook my head, the inside of my eyelids burning as tears gathered. The stranger's footfalls echoed on the floor as he exited the small space, leaving us alone.

"He's gone."

Derek's large hands framed my face.

"I'm sorry," I whispered, lifting my eyes to his. "I don't know what's wrong with me. This isn't me. God, I'm so pathetic."

He shushed me, pushing hair away from my face and tucking it behind my ear. "Don't say that. You had the fucking mafia trying to kill you." The cords of his neck strained as he spoke. "You fought your way out… back to me. And you killed a man twice your size who was trying to kill you. That's far from pathetic. It's fucking badass," he added with a grin.

I couldn't help smiling at his use of that word.

"If you're not ready to be here, we can always come back another time."

I shook my head. "No, I have to. Sam may not make it. And I could never live with myself if I didn't come see him because I was being a coward. I'm done hiding, Derek. I have to do this."

Sam was still unconscious and on life support. The fact he survived a gunshot wound to the head was a miracle in itself. Four days had passed since we came under attack. And I felt guilty enough having waited this long to visit. But working up the courage to step inside the hospital again was nothing short of daunting. The only reason I'd made it this far was because of Derek. He assured me I was safe with him, and I believed that with every fiber of my being. I'd never felt more protected, more cared for than when I was with this man.

Once the elevator doors slid open again, Derek twined his fingers through mine as we moved into a brightly lit corridor. The unit was quiet except for the clicking of keyboards and medical machinery beeping, buzzing, or rolling around us. Nervous energy zinged inside my chest, causing my heart to pump faster. But I bit back the fear trying to take me under. I wouldn't let them win.

I looked to Derek, but his focus was solely on our surroundings, every room, and even the nurses' station. Every single soul on that floor was on his radar.

This side of Derek intrigued me and, if I were being honest, made me question everything. While I knew he was a tactical instructor by day, like Helena, something in the overly confident way he moved and scrutinized every detail screamed of something more.

"I can stay outside, if you'd like," he said as we reached Sam's room in the ICU.

Two guards were standing watch, their eyes flicking to us as we approached.

"I.D.?" A shorter, burly male with light-colored sideburns stuck out his hand, barring us from moving farther. His tone was terse, and his stance impassive.

"Detective Cruz," the female guard said, a hand on her partner's forearm.

I nodded, and without another word, she motioned us inside. Derek sent the male guard one of his infamous death glares, causing the man to shrink back, which allowed us more space than necessary as we entered Sam's dark hospital room.

"Oh, Sam." My voice broke as I rushed to his side.

His head was bandaged, and he had so many tubes. Sam was a marine vet who'd always taken care of himself and followed a strict gym regimen. Seeing him lying there, looking so frail and helpless, knowing he'd likely never be the same, tore at my heart.

"I'm so sorry this happened to you." Tears slid down my cheeks as I clasped his hand in mine. "It was supposed to be me, not you."

Derek's hand fell on my shoulder. "Don't you fucking say that." There was a bite to his tone.

"They were trying to get to me. He didn't deserve this."

"And you did?" His eyes were narrowed into slits.

"No, but—"

Derek whirled me around, rough hands on my shoulders. "Listen to me—fuck him! If the whole goddamn hospital had to burn to the ground with everyone inside in exchange for your safety, then I call that a good day."

A small gasp escaped me at his revelation. "*Derek*," I breathed, unable to believe his complete lack of empathy.

His darkened eyes flickered like the embers of a fire.

I was appalled by his words, but I was also incredibly turned on and so shamelessly and hopelessly attracted to this enigma of a man. No one had ever been so passionate about my well-being. I squeezed my thighs together, suppressing the licks of desire threatening to make me abandon my scruples and lever up to kiss him.

"Eva?" The frail female voice called my name from the door. Sam's wife, Catherine, appeared just as fragile as she sounded. Dark circles marred the skin beneath her eyes, partially hidden behind tendrils of hair that had fallen out of the messy bun at the top of her head.

I threw my arms around her shaking form as choked sobs fled her lips. "Cat, I'm so sorry. I should have been here sooner."

She swiped at her tears with the sleeve of her brown cardigan. "I heard what you went through. I understand. How are you?"

"I'm good. What are the doctors saying?"

My partner's wife informed me that Sam was still in critical condition, but showing minor improvement. The swelling in his brain was stable; that was all they could hope for.

She exhaled heavily, her gaze briefly shifting to the corner of the room, where Derek was leaning against the wall. I turned to look at his stoic expression, his eyes connecting with mine.

"Cat, this is my—Derek. This is Derek."

Despite the hours we'd spent burning the sheets, the sweet gestures, the afterglow moments of affection, neither had discussed the title defining who or what we were to one another. There was an awkward pause as Catherine took in my tall, serious companion. She didn't know James, so explaining their estranged relationship would only make things more uncomfortable.

Derek gave her a stern nod, then quickly turned his gaze back to the door. His stance seemed to tense in response to whatever had drawn his attention.

I instinctively gravitated to Derek's side, my pulse quickening, fearing the worst, until my father's tight smile greeted me as he stood in the doorway.

I rushed to him, big arms scooping me into a solid hug.

"I thought we agreed for you not to come here until things settled down."

"I had to see Sam. I can't hide forever."

My father's attention was set beyond me. On Derek. "How are you? Is he treating you right?"

If he only knew exactly how *good* Derek was treating me. Heat rose up my neck, reaching my cheeks. I prayed the dim room worked in my favor and hid the blush I knew was coloring my face.

"Derek has been a perfect gentleman."

He and my father were in a staring match. I still couldn't comprehend the animosity that existed between the two. Not the reaction I expected when he met his best friend's only son.

"Can we talk?"

Derek's question was directed at my father. Seconds ticked by before he answered, and he did so with a raise of his chin.

"I'll be right outside." His curled forefinger lifted my chin, mouth brushing my hairline. Conscious that my father was standing merely two feet from us, and with his earlier comment hanging in the air, I pulled back from his touch, even though my skin felt an instant coldness in its absence.

"Okay," I said, turning toward Catherine and Sam. Derek's arm slid behind my back and crushed me to his chest, lips dragging over my ear.

"I don't give a damn who's watching. Don't ever forget who you belong to, Eva." He leaned in closer. "Or else I'll have to put you over my knee when we get back home."

Was that deliciously sinful threat supposed to make me want to behave? I raised my face, and his mouth moved over mine. Our kiss was short, but it still managed to leave me breathless.

"Good girl," he whispered against my lips.

Chapter Thirty Three

Derek

"Are you sleeping with my daughter?"

I leaned an elbow against the vacant nurses' station and regarded Franco's wild eyes and flared nostrils. He knew the answer to that question long before it was asked.

"I won't violate Evangelina's privacy. It's quite disrespectful, don't you think?"

Franco lifted both hands toward me, as though he were about to grasp at the collar of my shirt but curled them into a fist at the last second.

Smart man.

"You son of a bitch. You take advantage of your position. Of her vulnerability!"

"Might I remind you that Eva is a grown woman, free to do as she pleases… and *who* she pleases."

"If you lay one finger—"

"I assure you I've done more than that, and she enjoyed every second of it. But it's frankly none of your goddamn business."

The enraged man's fist came down on the wooden desk with so much force, I was surprised when it didn't splinter.

"Does Ronan know?"

I scoffed. "What you or Ronan think of my relationship with Evangelina is irrelevant."

He shook his head and ran a hand down his beard. "Why wait until James's death to show your face? I know damn well you knew where he lived before his murder. Yet you wait until after he's gone to show up. To get close to my daughter."

"Something you wanna get off your chest, old man?"

I raised a brow, daring him to make the accusation dancing on his tongue. But he stepped back, clenching a fist on the counter.

With softened features, he said, "She's the only family I have left. Please, just let her be."

It wasn't the first time I'd heard a man grovel on Evangelina's behalf.

"I didn't ask you out here to pick a fight. But I do need a favor."

It was his turn to chuckle incredulously. "What makes you think I'd pay you any favors?"

"Because it's not for me. It's for a common interest. This is about her safety."

I started explaining my plan until a discrepancy near the hospital room grabbed my attention.

Something was off.

I charged at the fucker from earlier, resisting the urge to pin him against the wall by his neck. "Where's your partner?" His eyes widened, his mouth opening and closing like a damn goldfish. "Where did she go?"

"She headed toward the east stairwell. She had to take a phone call. Said she'd be right back."

My fingers itched to bash his head against the wall for his incompetence. "Your orders were clear," I seethed, slamming my fist on the hard surface instead.

Franco was already behind me when I turned around. "Watch her. Lock the door, and don't let her out of your sight."

"What's happening?"

"I don't know, but neither of those guards is to leave their post. One has gone missing, and you're the only one I trust right now with her life. There's a Glock and ammo taped to the bottom of her partner's bed. You empty your mag at anything that tries to come through this door."

"And what if it's you?" His words held the undertone of a threat.

A grin tipped the corner of my mouth. "Then you better not miss."

He studied me, tilting his head to the side, curiosity brimming in his dark eyes. "You actually care for my daughter?"

I turned my back on him, his question hanging in the air.

"Don't make it obvious. She's still nervous about what happened," I said, headed for the stairwell.

A white metal door came into view, where a woman's voice could be heard on the other side. I leaned against the cold surface, a hand on the leather of my blade.

"I've called you a dozen times and left messages," she said in a loud, angry whisper. "It's her. She's here."

Betrayal.

"Of course, I'm sure. Evangelina Cruz, right?" There was a pause. "What do you mean, you can't risk it? What about the money you promised?" The bitch had sealed her fate. It had been a while since I'd had a female mark. "I want my fucking money. You said to let you know when she shows up, and that's exactly what I did," she shouted, slapping a hand on the door.

I peered up and noticed a surveillance camera at the corners of the hallway. I couldn't risk gutting this bitch in the stairwell, so a little home visit was in order.

Social media was an interesting place. It had taken less than thirty minutes to figure out all the relevant information I needed without accessing more resources. Leslie R. Almonte. Twenty-eight years old. Divorced. Bar and club hopping every third Saturday of the month. As a cop, one would think she'd know better than to post her entire life online like a sweet little crumb trail. I was sure she regretted informing her followers about her plans to pick up Chinese take-out after her late-night shift.

I rested an ankle over my knee as I waited for her to wake. After all, what fun would this be if she was unconscious?

The young woman was shackled at the wrists, chains hanging low, allowing her body to rest on bent knees. Bleached blonde hair pooled on the tiled floor in front of her as her head lobbed forward.

I didn't particularly enjoy taking the life of females, but there wasn't an ounce of sympathy for the woman before me. Once she intended to harm Eva, she'd become just another stain on these hands of stolen souls.

A splash of ice water saw her snapping awake, arms yanking on her restraints as panic set in. She threw her head back, eyes wide and frantic, attempting to see through the strands still sticking to her dampened skin. I let her scream and thrash for several moments before volts of electricity pulled a hard gasp from her throat and forced her body into a silent, trembling heap.

"Screaming is futile. These walls are soundproof, and we're a good fifteen feet underground." I leaned forward and clasped my hands together. "So, I suggest you conserve your energy."

"W—who are you? What do you want with me?"

Her chest was heaving as she attempted to catch her breath.

"What do I want? With you, Officer Almonte? Nothing. Nothing but to watch you die the way you intended for her."

Her eyes narrowed as she studied my face through the shadows, brows shooting up to her hairline upon making the connection.

"Oh, God… I didn't have a choice. They threatened me!"

I got to my feet and rounded her naked form. "Did they now?"

"Yes! They told me they'd kill me if I didn't keep them informed. I swear that's the truth."

She probably wasn't lying, but her demands for payment and follow-through had sealed her fate.

I pulled at the lever, adjusting the slack on the chains to position her arms above her body. Crouching, I grabbed a fistful of hair and lifted her head. "Who contacted you?"

Tears streaked her dirtied cheek. "I don't… know."

My grip tightened. "Wrong answer." The heat of my blade sliced a vertical line down the left side of her face. She cried out and thrashed. "I'm going to ask again. *Who* gave you those orders?"

"Please! I'm telling you the truth." Another gash. Blood poured from her wounds, mixing with her tears. "Why… are you doing this? You're a sick fuck."

I chuckled close to her mangled face. "I'm glad you're aware of what I am. Silly expectations only prolong your suffering."

Her eyes flew wide with terror. "Who are you? Please, let me go."

"Now, you know I can't do that, Leslie. And who *I* am is irrelevant." I let her head fall forward, and I straightened, pulling at the lever until the chains were taut and she balanced on the tips of her toes. "You tried to hurt someone I care about. You betrayed your colleagues' trust. And for what, Leslie? How much was the bounty?

Tell me, what is Evangelina's life worth to you?"

Leslie's eyes shifted wildly upon hearing Eva's name. Her body tensed against the restraints. "Fuck her!"

Ah, just when I was feeling the tiniest sliver of empathy.

Oh, well.

"Hit a sore spot, have I?"

"You're willing to torture and kill me? For *her*?"

"Yes."

She didn't want to know the depraved things I was willing to do for Evangelina.

The woman swallowed hard, a cynical laugh sputtering past her lips as she spat the blood falling in a steady stream down her face.

She was brave; I'd give her that. Or stupid.

They always got stupid when faced with their own mortality.

"I had seniority. But of course, she fucked her way to the top."

"Is that so?" I said, folding my arms across my chest. "Let me guess; she was promoted to detective over you?"

Leslie hissed in pain, face contorting when a thick tendril of hair caught on her wound. "You men are all the same. Pretty face, tight ass, and nothing else matters. What? You're fucking her too?"

I pressed the side of my blade to her chin, lifting her face. "She's goddamn perfect, isn't she?"

Leslie looked deeply into my eyes and recoiled. Had she seen what awaited?

Fresh tears slid down her cheeks.

"Please, I'm sorry. I'll do whatever you want. Anything." She puffed out her chest, bare tits jostling suggestively. But I couldn't be any less interested.

"There is *one* thing," I said, bringing my face closer.

"Please, anything," she begged between heavy pants.

My lips neared her ear, and I whispered, "Die."

I plunged my knife into her side and twisted. She fought not to scream, pain leaving her body by way of grunts and rolling moans.

"I'll need you to deliver a message for me." Another gush of blood poured at my feet as the blade moved in and out of her a second time. "I'm sending Dmitry Belov a gift. Your head in a box." She gurgled her words, trails of red running down her body. "What was that, Leslie?"

"W-why?"

I tilted her chin.

"Easy. Touch or threaten what's mine, and you die." She tipped her head back and belted out a blood-curdling scream. Her vocal cords were the obvious next choice.

The life drained from her body, and Leslie slumped forward, blood running down the grates by her feet.

Chapter Thirty Four

Derek

Gravel crunched under the tires of Kai's SUV as he rolled into the parking lot. I saw Evangelina's silhouette behind his darkened windshield, cell phone to her ear. We made eye contact from behind the glass, and a smile stretched across her pretty face. I'd left early that morning while she was still asleep to deal with Leslie, and it had taken everything to drag me away. Naked as the day she was born and curled against my side.

Visions of a future when waking up to her were the norm cycled through my mind, like the clips of a cliché romance movie. But I dispelled those thoughts as quickly as they had manifested. My only job was to enjoy the hell out of today and for however long she was in my life.

"Hey," she said, arms circling my neck as she rose to her toes for a kiss. "I was cold this morning."

My eyes lifted to catch Kai's wry grin as he rolled down his window, acknowledging me with a nod before pulling off down the street.

"I'm sorry. I forgot to mention this morning's building inspection."

And the lies continued.

I held her face, my thumb caressing the soft skin of her cheek. "You have no idea how hard it was to leave."

She gripped the collar of my jacket and levered up to rub the tip of her nose against my chin. "And why's that?"

I dipped my mouth to meet hers, kissing and gently nibbling on the soft flesh. "Because it was too damn cold."

Eva playfully swatted my shoulder. "Oh, not because you had an incredibly hot woman in your bed? Naked, sore?" Her lips were at the hollow of my neck. "The taste of you still on my tongue?"

I crushed her to me, the front of my pants painfully tight.

"There's no one here for another three hours, angel. I think a little redemption is in order."

By the time we made it inside the building, Evangelina's playful demeanor had shifted. She stared at the screen of her cell, perfectly arched brows creased together.

"What is it?"

"One of our officers has been missing for three days. She was one of Sam's guards. They just listed her as a missing person after performing a well-check."

"Oh," I said. "That's unfortunate."

Her bloodless corpse had been removed from my property just this morning.

I tugged Eva to my chest, my thumb smoothing out the stress lines on her beautiful face. She needn't worry herself over some bitch who'd made the mistake of cutting a deal with the devil in exchange for a payday.

Leslie failed to understand that I was the worst one of them all.

"I hope they locate her soon."

Tears welled in her eyes, every drop dissolving the once impenetrable barrier encasing my heart.

"I can't help thinking this has something to do with Belov. It's too much of a coincidence. She was on duty for Sam. And if that's the case, how many more people have to die before—"

"All of them. Every single last one. If it means keeping you safe."

She stared at me, a myriad of emotions flashing in the dark depths of her eyes. Blinking away tears, Evangelina took a deep breath and placed a hand on my chest. "That's not what I want."

I wanted to tell her that I was working on a resolution. Working with others to ensure those responsible for her attack would pay with their lives.

Dmitry Belov was mine.

"Come on," she said with renewed strength, pulling at my wrists. "I need to relieve some fucking stress before I explode."

"What are you in the mood for? I asked as we approached the counter. "Long or short range?"

She regarded the row of weapons, eyes settling on the rifles section. "How about that one?" she said, pointing at a sleek McMillan TAC-338.

"Good choice."

"And you?"

I pulled out a black CheyTac M200 rifle. "Grab the ammo, angel. Let's go play."

A smile crested her lips as she slid the glass case open and loaded the boxes inside a basket, the stress of the day momentarily forgotten. Evangelina hip-checked me as she passed by, turning and walking backward toward the range as I followed. My cock twitched at the sight of those skin-tight black leggings, and I licked my lips in sweet anticipation. I would have her today; of that, I had no doubt.

"So, how often do you practice? Or is your expertise mostly in the business side of things?" She turned and pushed open the heavy door.

I cocked a grin, setting both rifles in the stall to our right. "What do you think?"

She seemed to lose herself briefly inside her head, eyes gazing beyond me and unblinking. "I think you're about to impress me," she said, her attention back on my face as she leaned against the steel divider, a sexy smile in place.

"It's my one goal in life. To know I'm the one who put that smile on your face."

Evangelina slipped her brown leather jacket from her shoulders and tossed it to a far corner of the room. The outline of her black bra beneath the thin white fabric of her shirt sent an electric pulse to my dick.

Her eyebrow quirked as she eyed the bulge in my pants.

"It's so easy with you, Derek."

I put my hands up defensively. "Hey, I can't help it. Have you seen your ass?"

She laughed and swatted my shoulder. "That's not what I meant. I was talking about how easy it is to forget all the shit hanging over my head. This thing with Belov. My grief. Rayne. All of it."

I grabbed the back of her neck and slanted my mouth over hers, claiming it roughly as she leaned into me, molding herself against my chest.

This woman. God, this woman. There was no doubt in my mind.

She was mine.

Made for me.

Born to ruin me.

When this was over, when she no longer belonged to me, nothing would be left of the man I used to be. Of the life I lived before she walked into it that godforsaken night.

"You're up first," I said, brushing my lips over hers, her mouth lush and swollen.

With eyes still closed, she nodded slowly and leaned in for one last kiss before grabbing her rifle and propping it on the table. I watched with rapt attention as she readied the weapon and slipped on the ear guards and goggles. Her lithe little body bent forward, eyes narrowed on the gun sights as she aimed down the target line.

One. Two. Three. Four shots rang out.

The way her ass flexed tempted all my primal instincts. And like the depraved son of a bitch I was, my eyes never left her backside to check her progress on the target.

Eva kept firing, oblivious to my proximity as I came up behind her. When she removed her finger from the trigger, I slid my hands down her waist, settling on her hips. She tensed for just a fraction of a second until my nose nuzzled into her hair, lips against her neck, as she removed the protective gear and let it fall at her feet.

"Angel, you keep teasing me with that sweet ass, and I'm going to bend you over this table and take what's mine."

Eva moaned and dropped her head back on my shoulder as my lips trailed rough kisses behind her ear.

"Here, Derek?"

I pulled her flush against me, my erection like a rod between us. "No one here but us. This is my place. I told you before that no one gets in unless I want them to."

Her hand snaked into my hair. "So then, what are you waiting for, Derek Cain? Take what's yours."

I chuckled into her ear before nipping the shell, and she hissed at the slight sting, but I gave her no time to dwell on the sensation as I had much more to inflict.

"Hold on to the edge," I instructed, pushing her forward so she was bent against the table.

Our size difference would make the task tricky, but I'd make it work. Hooking the waistband of her pants, I pulled them down her legs, then licked my way up her body, teeth catching the back of her thighs, making her jerk.

"Easy, angel, I'm just getting started."

She glanced over her shoulder, lips parted into a tempting little bow, just begging to be filled by my cock.

"Don't go easy on me."

"You know that's not in my nature," I said, smoothing my hands over her ass cheeks. "Not with you."

As I started to unbutton my pants, I realized I didn't have condoms with me, and I hesitated, cursing under my breath.

"Are you going to fuck me, or are you waiting on a special invite?"

My hand came down hard on one of her ass cheeks, leaving a partial print. It was her turn to curse, looking back at me with a satisfied smirk.

"I'd love nothing more than to watch my cum drip down your legs, angel. But this is your call," I said against her ear while smoothing the reddened skin with a gentle massaging motion.

"Do it," she breathed as my hand trailed down over her clit, paying it the same homage.

I tugged her ass closer to the edge and wasted no time plunging inside.

Holy fuck.

Her pussy was always so goddamn tight, so warm like it had been tailor-made for my dick.

"Fuck, baby. You've ruined me," I growled, sinking deeper. "Look at us—how perfectly we fit together."

I surged into her, and each time felt more glorious than the last. Being inside her like this, without a barrier, feeling her tighten around me with every thrust, my name on her lips, was like a goddamn revelation.

"You ruined me too. So fucking gone for you."

Eva came as I drove into her so hard the stall shook around us. She rode out her orgasm, her greedy little cunt still meeting my thrusts.

"You've made a mess of my cock, baby. I should make you clean it up—lick every last drop so I can fuck you and do it all over again."

Eva turned around, giving me a sexy grin, as she wet her lips and fell to her knees. "Well, we can't have that, can we?" she said, taking my ruined dick in her hand, eyes on mine as she slid her tongue up my shaft before taking me into her mouth.

"Fuck," I groaned, my hands in her hair as she sucked and licked me clean from root to tip. "You taste fucking good, don't you, baby?"

She smiled up at me, my dick popping out of her mouth and bouncing off the tip of her nose. We laughed as I pulled her to her feet and tossed her back onto the small table, tearing off the leggings still bunched at her ankles. Gripping both of her knees, I pushed them open.

"You know, a little warning next time. I would have stretched for you."

"I got you," I said, wickedly pushing one of her legs higher, closer to her upper body, while the other curled around my waist.

Eva sucked in a sharp breath, biting at the corner of her lip as I stretched her to the limit.

"That's it. Open up for me, angel. Your pussy is so goddamn beautiful."

I lined myself at her entrance and sank inside with a grunt, letting go of her leg and throwing my head back as she tightened around me.

"Derek... I—" She shook her head and pulled me down by the neck, smothering whatever she meant to say with a frantic kiss.

My arms rounded the back of her waist, and without missing a beat, I scooped her up, pushing her against the stall.

I made a quick mental note to stabilize the damn things. They were shaking a bit too much for my liking and probably wouldn't withstand another one of these sessions.

"Come for me again, angel."

"You're getting tired already, Derek?" she panted playfully into my ear. "Thought you said you could do this all night."

I snorted a laugh. "Should have told you I could do this one-handed."

Her eyes twitched, confused by my words, until one of my hands was wrapped around her throat. She moaned and closed her eyes as my hold tightened.

"Close that pretty mouth and do as you're told."

I felt my release coiling in my balls. The muscles in my arms strained and flexed as I pushed into her time and time again, her breasts bouncing against me until she broke.

"That's my good fucking girl."

The way she contracted around my cock, so damn good, sent me over the edge. My hand was still around her throat as I spilled inside of her.

"Fuck… fuck, Eva," I growled, knowing I was squeezing to the point of bruising.

She whimpered, face pink, and bit down on my shoulder as I released her and dropped to my knees, unable to hold my weight any longer. I was too fucking spent.

I leaned against her, her back on the stall, careful not to crush her.

"I stand corrected," she murmured between heavy breaths and peppered kisses along my jaw.

"I'm insulted you doubted me. Clearly, you're begging me to

redden the other side of that—*Oh, fuck!*"

Eva's pussy walls bit down on my dick, stealing my breath as a delicious electric current jutted into my balls. She laughed outright and squeezed me a second time. I groaned, doubling over into her as she continued to be amused at my agony… sweet fucking hell.

The thought of throwing her over my lap and spanking her until she cried and orgasmed crossed my mind until my cell chimed with a notification letting me know someone was at the front door. We wouldn't have been able to hear the knocking from inside the station room.

"Who is it?"

"Someone who needs to go fuck off. I'm not done with you yet."

With a loud grunt, I circled Eva's body and pushed to my feet, already half-cocked inside her. I sat her on the stall table and snatched my phone to see who the fuck needed a new hole to breathe from.

Shit.

Ronan.

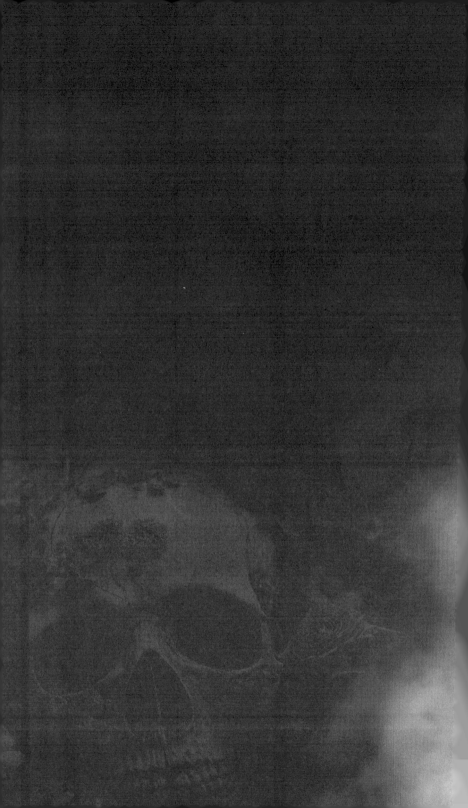

Chapter Thirty Five
Evangelina

"Derek, where's my thong?"

He was pulling on his pants, his back to me, and shrugged his shoulders. The ringing from his phone became incessant, so rather than waste more time searching for underwear, I reached for my leggings and decided to make a run for the bathroom and get cleaned up.

Derek hooked my elbow as I passed him and rested his forehead on mine.

"Take my keys."

"Why? What's going on?"

"It's just better this way. I don't…" He hesitated, as if not wanting to say the words he'd intended. "I don't know how much I trust him around you."

I framed his face, forcing our eyes to meet. "What does that mean?"

I'd never told him how uncomfortable his father had made me feel. No one wanted to hear those things about their parents. And the last thing I needed was to be the reason for a rift in their relationship.

"Because he is who he is, Eva. And I can't be responsible for my actions or keep a level head if he does something to provoke me."

There it was, brimming to the surface and gleaming in his eyes. That darkness lurking inside Derek. Maybe I was flawed, broken to the red flags in people I cared about. My whole life, I made excuses for my father and explained away his inconsistencies and lies. Rationalized that whatever it was couldn't be that bad because… I loved him.

Absurd as that logic was.

"Okay," I said, choosing not to question his request. "Did you want me to pick up lunch?"

He put a hand on my neck, his thumb smoothing along my chin. "No, go straight home. I'll place an order."

The chimes suddenly ceased, only to resume by way of a loud ringtone from Derek's pocket.

"Dramatic fuck."

"Maybe it's an emergency."

"I doubt it." His hands settled on my backside and squeezed, pinning me to him. "Promise me you'll go straight home. You know the code."

"Please don't do that. I don't want to feel like I'm trapped."

"Eva, there are dangerous people out there who are looking to harm you. Until that threat has been neutralized, we need to take precautions."

I rolled my eyes and nodded. "I know. I just hate feeling so damn helpless."

Derek rested his forehead on my shoulder; his small gestures of affection warmed my heart and other places on my body, adding to the stickiness between my thighs.

"Let me deal with this here, and I'll be home. Told you I'm not done with you just yet," he growled into my neck.

"Oh? And what should I be anticipating?"

Brushing his lips along my throat, Derek inhaled and said, "You, on your knees, angel. And that pretty mouth around my cock, finishing the job wearing nothing but this new necklace."

My core flared white-hot at his dirty words as I ran my tongue along the contours of my lips and feathered my fingers around my throat. My mouth was suddenly watering. That particular deed had never been a favorite of mine. It was always more of an obligation. Reciprocating the favor. But with Derek, it was different.

Everything with him was different.

"Don't keep me waiting too long," I said, tipping up onto my toes. What was meant to be a sweet goodbye peck quickly turned into a heated kiss as our tongues battled for dominance.

He scooped me onto his hips, and the friction between my thighs forced a moan to slither from my throat and into his mouth.

"Derek," I panted. "Ronan is about to break down that door."

"Fuck him," he said, now suckling the base of my neck.

I chuckled as I tipped my head back, fingernails on his scalp. "Later, baby." I gently pulled on his hair so that he could look at me. "And you better put me down before I ruin your shirt. My thong is in your pocket."

"Busted." He laughed, kissing me one last time before setting me on the floor.

Ronan's sharp voice echoed from the main room down the hall as I dressed in the bathroom sans underwear.

As expected, he was angry. Derek was not the type of man to hold his tongue for anyone, but he also wasn't the type to lose his cool, so it didn't shock me when he didn't take the bait.

I padded to the front entrance, debating briefly whether to intervene, but decided against it. It wasn't my place.

The chill of the wind blew through my clothes, biting into my skin as I ran toward Derek's car and climbed inside.

He'd told me to go straight home, and while I knew I should, I needed to see my father. As I came upon the intersection, I turned toward my childhood home.

Derek would understand.

As I pulled into my father's driveway, he was backing out of his garage. I'd caught him just in time.

We exited our vehicles almost simultaneously, but where I was wearing a smile on my face, his features were creased with anger.

"Evangelina!" It was the tone he'd used on me as a child when I'd get into trouble. "I have called you all morning. No answer. I've left messages, texts—I spoke to Alexa, and after damn near threatening her life, she caved and gave me that man's address."

Fuck.

I'd left my phone on 'do not disturb,' which was unfortunate because I'd probably missed Lex's calls and warning messages about my dad being two minutes away from contacting the FBI.

"Dad, I'm fine."

"Save it, Eva. You're being reckless and irresponsible." His nostrils flared as he paced in front of me. But he wasn't being fair. My hands were tied. What more did he want from me?

"How could you say that? After everything I've been through. I'm doing the best I can right now."

My father's eyes narrowed into judgmental slits. "Are you?"

"What is that supposed to mean? Of course I am."

He folded his arms across his chest and scoffed. "You're not fooling anyone, least of all me. I know you. And you look like you rolled out of bed or clearly out of someone else's bed."

My cheeks flamed red-hot at his accusation, or rather the audacity to comment about a subject that was none of his business.

"How dare you? I'm not a child. Who I sleep with is none of your concern."

He shook his head, face twisted into one of disgust.

"Already, huh?"

"I am *not* having this conversation with you. I'm sorry I even came here." I turned to leave, but my father caught my arm and pulled me back.

"Like hell you are! You have no idea who he is—" He clamped down on his jaw and sucked in a sharp breath.

"Let me go." My voice cracked, and tears blurred the vision of my father's rage. I couldn't remember the last time I'd seen him so angry. I didn't want to fight; I just needed to leave. "Please."

"I can smell him all over you." His eyes suddenly widened. "Look at your neck! He did that to you?"

"It's not what you think."

"So you're his whore now? Have you no goddamn self-respect?"

My mouth parted, and pain ripped through my chest at the venom behind his words. As I tried to respond, another voice filled the void of my silence.

"You have approximately until your next breath to get your hands off her. And I won't ask twice."

We both whipped toward the end of the drive, where Derek was now stalking toward us. We'd been so caught up that neither one of us heard Kai's car approaching.

Derek's face was a stone-cold mask of pure, murderous rage. And it was directed at my father.

Heart hammering in my chest, I looked at him, silently pleading for him to release my arm.

"This conversation isn't over," he said between gritted teeth while sweeping an icy glare in Derek's direction. "And you and I need to talk."

But Derek acted as though no one else existed in that driveway besides him and me. His expression was a mixture of relief tinged with anger. By the time I looked back, my dad was already gone.

"Are you okay?"

"Of course."

"Not of course. You're crying. Did he hurt you?"

"What? Of course not. He's pissed right now, but he'd never hurt me, Derek."

Derek hauled me against his chest. "No one puts their hands on you. No one. Not even your father." He held my face. "I heard what he said, and he won't disrespect you again." Kissing my forehead, he whispered over my skin, "I told you to go home, angel."

"My father is not a threat." Derek opened the passenger door, and I climbed inside as he waited on my answer. "You did tell me to head home, but I couldn't do that. And this is my father we're talking about. I'm not some prisoner."

"I never said you were."

"But you threatened my dad, Derek. You can't do that."

"He grabbed you and disrespected you. I won't allow that."

Fuck. Why am I so turned on right now?

I rested my head against the seat as Derek sat beside me.

"I understand maybe you have this hero complex, but I—"

Derek twisted in his seat, eyes searing through me. "I'm no hero, Eva." He leaned in and grabbed the nape of my neck. "I'm something else entirely. Nothing and no one else matters to me. I'd bathe the whole goddamn world in blood for you."

Chapter Thirty Six

Derek

"I'm going back to work tomorrow."

Eva placed her phone on the side table and climbed on the couch beside me. Even in an oversized t-shirt and sweatpants, she looked good enough to eat. And while I'd certainly had my share before breakfast and twice after lunch, I would never get enough.

"Come here," I growled, pulling her into my lap and slipping my hands beneath her shirt and up her back. No bra.

Perfect.

"Derek, did you hear what I said?" She pulled back when I tried to kiss her. "Derek, tomorrow. I'm going back."

I fisted the back of her hair, tugging just enough to get her to shut up and let me stick my tongue in her mouth. Eva obliged with a sigh, her hands on my chest. But just when I grabbed two handfuls of her ass, she bit down hard on my bottom lip.

Little hellion.

"That's okay. We can get into a little blood play if that's what you want."

"You're avoiding the subject," she said, trying to suppress a smile.

"Of you trying to put yourself in danger? Damn right I am."

"I have a job to do. I've been holed up here for two weeks. My father refuses to speak to me. Rayne is still missing. James's case has no leads. Sam is still in the ICU." She tried to climb off my lap, but I held her hips firmly. Exactly where she belonged. Straddling me while the warmth of her pussy sheathed my cock.

"All of that can wait. I need more time, angel."

She studied me, eyes narrowing. "More time for what? I can't pretend the outside world and all its problems don't exist. I have a job to do. And newsflash, Derek," she said, laying her head on my shoulder, "it's not the first time someone has threatened to kill me."

Her words were like a stake to the heart. The thought of someone hurting her sent my demons into a frenzy.

I held her tighter.

"But it will be the last."

"Baby, I have to do this. And I'm not asking for your permission or approval. I'm letting you know what's going to happen."

I shifted sideways, taking her with me until I was on top.

"I won't stop you, Eva. But I'll make sure you're safe. And I have a condition."

She shook her head. "Of course you do. But I'll hear you out."

As if she had a choice.

"You stay here with me," I said, trailing slow kisses down her neck. "In my bed. In my house."

Eva's fingers curled into my hair. "For how long?"

For how long?

Forever.

Forever.

I rolled that word around in my thoughts. The implication of what it meant. The weight and sincerity behind it and all it carried.

My chest was swollen. Overflowing with emotions for her that I didn't understand. Feelings that were foreign to me, lost in the void of a time I was too young to remember. I knew my mother loved me. And that I had reciprocated those feelings. But even that seemed... inadequate.

"Derek," she whispered, her soft hand on my cheek, bringing me back to the present. I looked down into her brown eyes, and my chest constricted.

"I have something for you."

"Yeah? But clearly not an answer to my question."

"Don't be a brat, angel." I pressed a kiss to the hollow of her throat. "Or I'll have to punish you."

"Mmm," she moaned. "Sounds like a good time."

My dick roared to life, and I thrust against the apex of her thighs. "Just give me five minutes," I said, raging against the need to sink inside her.

I peeled myself from her body and reached into the side table drawer, pulling out a black velvet box. Eva watched me curiously as she straightened into a sitting position.

"What is it?"

"The way this works is I give this to you; you open it and find out what's inside."

She leaned forward with a small laugh, outstretching her hand. "Well, then, give me my damn present already."

"Double the punishment. Don't make me change your nickname."

Eva took the squared box and brushed her lips over mine. "Don't ever stop calling me angel."

I held her face and kissed her. "Never."

"Never sounds like a pretty long time."

"Open your gift."

Our eyes were locked for several beats, unspoken words drifting between us before she popped open the small box. Her face lit up as she reached inside and pulled out a diamond-embedded bracelet.

"Derek, it's gorgeous."

She held up the white gold medical bracelet, the diamonds on the small plate catching the light and reflecting in the pools of her eyes.

"Do you like it?"

"Of course I do," she said, running her finger over the jewel-encrusted cross.

"Turn it over."

As she read, her smile widened, and she looked at me from beneath her lashes, shaking her head. "You're my emergency contact?"

"Absolutely. I want to ensure I'm there for you when you need me. In case… something happens. I don't want to find out hours later like last time." I tugged her back into my lap and cradled her against me. "I already told you. You're mine, Eva," I said, pushing a lock of hair behind her ear and chuckling in disbelief. "What have you done to me?"

She reached up and caressed my lips with the pad of her fingers. "What have I done, Derek?"

"You've turned me into a damn fool."

She laughed as I kissed every one of her fingers.

"How so?"

"Well, for one, I've never given anyone a gift in my life."

"Never?"

I shook my head. "Never. But you, Eva, I'd give you the whole world. Just ask, and it's yours."

She threw one leg over my thighs so that she sat astride my lap, hands on either side of me, holding the back of the sofa.

"I don't want the world, baby. I just want you."

My hands were on her hips, pushing her pelvis into my erection.

"You have me," I said, holding the back of her head and pulling her in for a kiss.

"The bracelet is beautiful. It's the most thoughtful gift anyone has given me."

Eva flashed me a devilish grin as she grabbed the hem of her shirt, pulling the white tee up over her head. My eyes dropped to the captivating sight of her breasts. Wasting no time, I tore mine off too, and leaned in, taking a pebbled nipple into my mouth, my hands splayed across her back. She felt so fucking perfect in my arms and my mouth. I licked across to the other breast and was gifted the sounds of her soft mewls with each long pull.

I wasn't sure the exact moment she'd reached for my forgotten glass of whiskey, but when I looked up, she had a small ice cube trapped between her teeth. And as if reading each other's thoughts, I tugged her by the back of the neck, opened up, and let her drop the cube into my mouth.

Eva chased the piece of ice with a flick of her tongue over my parted lips.

"I need these off?" Her hands were on the waistband of my pants.

"What do you want, angel? I need to hear you say it." I gripped her wrists.

"Always looking to have your ego stroked."

"That's not what I want stroked right now," I said, brushing my index finger across the seam of her mouth. Her sweet little tongue grazed the tip until she allowed me entrance. "Is this what you want?"

Her eyes were hooded as she nodded, taking me deeper while also working the belt and zipper of my pants. Lifting my hips, I slid them down to my ankles.

I'd had Evangelina in every way humanely possible, but I'd never tire of watching her take me into her mouth.

"Get on your knees," I said, stroking myself.

She dropped to the floor, a smirk on her face. My fist was in her hair, and I tipped her head back. "Show me how pretty those lips look wrapped around my cock." Eva swiped her tongue over the bead of precum at my tip, but I tugged her back and reached for my glass. As I knocked back a swig of the drink, I took another cube in my mouth and held her chin. "Open up for me, baby." She did as she was told, and I let the melting cube drip from my mouth into hers.

Eva sucked on the ice until it was mostly dissolved before she fisted the root of my cock, and used her cold tongue to lick an icy trail up my shaft.

"Fuck." A chill rocketed up my spine, and my hold on her hair tightened. She drew circles around my crown before taking me fully into her mouth. When the heat of my skin met her cool tongue, the sensation coalesced into a delicious union of fire and ice. I tipped my head back as she sucked me off, head bobbing back and forth in time with the tight strokes of her hand.

"Fuck, Eva… so damn good."

She looked up at me, mischief written on her face, and hollowed out her cheeks, taking every inch of me as far as it would go.

"Look at you taking my cock like a good fucking girl." Tears gathered at the corners of her lashes. "That's it," I groaned, holding her head as I pushed deeper, hitting the back of her throat until her cheeks flamed bright red. "Fuck, baby. You look so goddamn beautiful choking on my cock."

Eva smiled up at me and continued working my dick like she hadn't been five seconds from passing out, a hand squeezing and kneading my balls. Fucking goddess. That's what she looked like, on her knees for me, worshiping my cock like it was her last meal.

My head fell back against the couch, squeezing my eyelids closed as the pressure in my balls had me clutching her hair and guiding her faster and harder. "So… good." My voice was strangled as I bucked into her, fucking that sweet mouth until I came. Ribbons of my cum spilled over her tongue as I continued to push in and out of her, riding out my release until she milked me for everything I had.

"Don't you fucking swallow. I want to see me in your mouth." Between rugged pants, I gripped her chin and held her mouth open. "Look at you, my greedy little slut. Do you want to swallow?"

Her hands squeezed my thighs as she nodded, causing some to drip from the corner of her mouth.

"Do it."

As my cum slid down her throat, I leaned forward and kissed her, tasting myself on her tongue.

Fuck. The things I would do for this woman.

Eva used her thumb to scoop the dripping cum from her chin, and slipped it into her mouth before standing between my legs. Letting her shorts and panties drop, she climbed into my lap.

"You need to give me a minute, angel." I laughed, kissing her roughly again.

"Okay, a minute," she crooned into my ear. Her voice alone was enough to stir my dick to life. And when she began to grind her leaking pussy against it, the reaction was instant.

My hands were on her hips as she slid over my cock. Nothing would ever compare to the warmth of her wrapped so tightly around me. To the way her breasts bounced up and down as I fucked her harder, faster, hitting that spot that made her scream my name and cuss in Spanish. When she broke apart in my arms, and the little noises I pulled from her lips as she came down from the high of her release. The afterglow on her beautiful face, that sated smile she saved only for me. And fuck me, that pretty pussy I'd branded as mine in all the ways that mattered.

No.

At that moment, I decided I would never give her up. She was mine. Mine to keep. To worship.

To love.

Only mine.

And I'd be damned if I ever let her go. I would find a way to be the man she needed and deserved.

No matter the cost.

She lay quietly against my chest, our naked bodies sprawled on the shaggy living room rug. I stroked her back and watched as goosebumps scattered over her smooth skin.

"Everything is going to be okay."

She lifted her curious gaze to mine, chin on my chest. We held eye contact for several moments before she sighed and placed her head back on my chest. "I hope you're right."

"I am. You trust me to keep you safe, angel?"

"I do."

I'd planned on having Franco take her out of town when Amalia's crew arrived, but the man was ten shades of pissed off, even days later. The marks on her neck were enough to send him into a rage. He'd sent Eva messages about how I'd turned her into a whore.

As long as she was mine, that was a bonus. My chest shook with amusement as I thought of all the ways I'd fucked Eva tonight. Franco would have me skinned alive.

"Not that I'm complaining, but I'm full to the brim with you, Derek."

I lifted my head and looked down her line of sight, where my cock was hard and standing at attention.

"Fuck, Eva, that's sexy as hell."

Hugging her tightly, I sat up, sweeping her off her feet and throwing her body over my shoulder. She laughed as I slapped her toned ass and ran up the stairs to fill her up some more.

Chapter Thirty Seven

Derek

L ead.

The soles of my shoes felt like they were made of goddamn lead. Every step was more challenging than the last. But each represented my freedom and opened up a life I never thought existed for me. At least, that's what I wanted to believe. But I knew better. I wasn't dumb enough to think Ronan would cut me loose with a parting gift and well wishes for a better future.

No.

He'd find some way to fuck me over. Like death, that was the only truth I was sure of.

I squeezed my fists, and the stitches of my leather gloves protested when I thought of him possibly using Eva as leverage to keep me bound to this life. I'd butcher him alive if he even thought of harming her.

In five days, Amalia's crew would be here. I'd hate to have another debt hanging over my head, but I was willing to negotiate a deal with her. A pound of flesh for whatever price she deemed worthy of taking the life of the head of Ares.

I knocked twice and pushed the door open without waiting on a response. The bastard barely flinched. Most likely saw me approaching on surveillance. Even then, he hadn't the decency to cover what was happening behind his desk.

He had a fist full of blond hair, his head tipped back against his chair, and his mouth parted.

Fuck me.

What was worse was that it wasn't the first time I'd caught him fucking some whore, whether it was Maeve or even while she was in the other room—most times fully aware. His infidelity never bothered her. And strangely enough, I never batted an eyelash. As a man, I understood his need to get off in whichever pussy was willing, then move on.

My views were a little different now.

"Get out," he said to the woman on her knees.

She did as she was told, wiping her mouth and buttoning her blouse as she stood. I recognized her as one of the staff. Didn't know her name or care to remember, but she knew who I was in relation to Ronan.

"See you tomorrow, Mr. Cain." Her voice was purposely breathy and painfully forced. She strode past me. "Hello, Mr.—"

I snatched her by the wrist before her hand could reach my chest, careful not to make contact with any part of her that would have been touching Ronan.

"I'm assuming you need these hands?" My grip on her tightened. "You ever try to touch me again, and I assure you you'll regret it."

"I-I'm sorry," she stammered.

I released her and wiped my hand against the front of my jacket.

"Derek!" he called with feigned enthusiasm. "To what do I owe the pleasure of your visit on this fine morning?"

"Cut the bullshit. I'm here to talk about my contract."

"Straight to business." The insidious smirk on his face caused me to grit my teeth. "Sit down," he said, leaning back, a cigar in his mouth.

"I'll stand."

"Always so damn serious." He took a puff and let the smoke billow from his mouth. "We're here to talk about that sweet little piece of ass, Evangelina, am I right?"

Red hazed my vision. My HK hot on my hip. Fuck. I wanted to end his miserable existence.

"*Easy*, Derek." He let out a laugh and held his hands up in mock defense. "Just calling it like it is. But you already know that, don't you? What I wouldn't give…"

"Don't fucking provoke me. Don't say her name. Don't even think about her." I gripped the top of the chair in front of me. "Leave her out of this conversation. And I won't repeat myself."

He waved me off with another cynical chuckle and got to his feet, rounding the desk. My hands twitched, begging to rip him apart.

"Your threats don't affect me, Derek. I made you. Gave you the whole goddamn world. And you want to throw it all away for a—" I balled my fist and clenched my jaw, ready to be reckless. "For… a woman? Because that's what you came here to discuss, isn't it?"

He walked behind me, my reflexes on high alert, but I refused to react. To give him what he wanted.

"I've given you eighteen years of loyal service. I want out."

"Oh, Derek," he said, "You think that by rescinding your service for Ares, you cleanse your soul of all the blood you've spilled? That you'd become a new man? Then what? A husband?" He doubled over with laughter, and I put a shaky hand on my gun. As he returned to his desk, Ronan gave me a suspicious side-eye. "Wait, don't tell me— you want to be a father too?"

"Fuck you!" I spat, pulling my gun, the barrel trained on him.

He placed his cigar in a dish and held his arms at his side. "Do what you gotta do, Derek. But if you think you're walking out of this building in one piece after shooting me, you press your luck. You'll be sealing your fate, as well as hers."

I shook my head and aimed. "You threaten her, and I'll feed you your fucking dick."

"Don't be so hasty. I never said I wouldn't consider your request."

I arched a brow with curiosity. "You have fifteen seconds to explain yourself."

"You know the rules, Derek. There's always a price to pay. The oath isn't broken on a contract of words. Blood seals your fate in Ares, as sure it will grant your freedom. The question is, what are you willing to sacrifice—for *her*?"

"Everything."

"Well, I'll be goddamned." He laughed. "Didn't even hesitate. That must be one hell of a pussy." I lowered my gun to center mass, the tension in my jaw almost painful. "Calm down, kid. Just jokes."

"It's not a request. Name your fucking price, and we're done here."

Ronan picked up his cigar and took a puff, eyes on me through the haze of smoke.

"You're a cold-blooded bastard. You think I'm going to make this easy? Some random sack of shit that you wouldn't even bat an eye for? Oh, no."

My blood ran cold, anticipating the heavy price of my freedom. There was only one other person I'd kill and die for, and he knew exactly how to twist the knife.

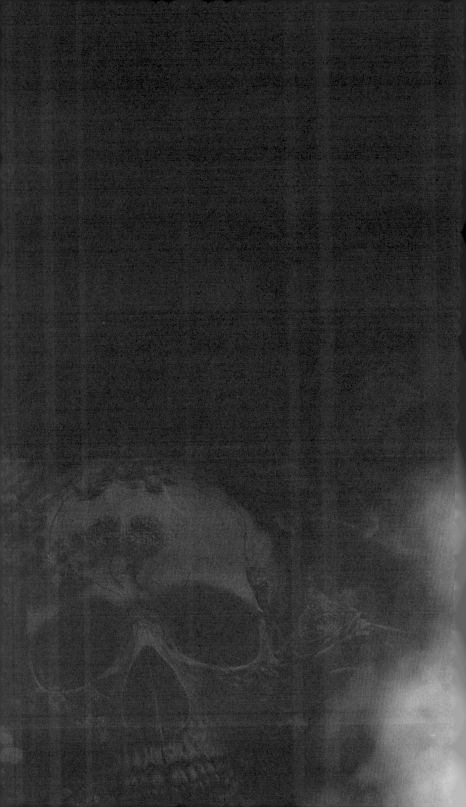

Chapter Thirty Eight
Evangelina

I threw my damp hair over my shoulder as I reached for a water bottle. Leaning against the open door of the fridge, a smile spread across my face. Today had been a good one. Sam was showing more signs of improvement. And my first day back to work had proved to be just as rewarding. I'd received an email from Rayne, where she told me she was staying in Boston with her great-aunt and assured me she was doing well. Best of all, charges were likely to be filed against Dmitry for his role in the siege at the hospital. Getting those charges to stick would be the hard part, but I was determined not to get discouraged by the probability of him using his money and status to get off.

As I closed the refrigerator door, the sight of Derek nearly made me jump out of my skin.

"Fuck, baby, you scared the—"

The air rushed out of my lungs as his arms came around me. He buried his face into the crook of my neck, squeezing almost too much for me to expand my chest. "Derek," I panted, drawing a breath of air. "Too tight."

He loosened just enough for me to take in a lungful. I tried to open up some distance between us, but he was too strong, too determined to hold me.

Something was wrong.

"Derek, what is it? Did something happen?" He was silent, shaking his head against my shoulder. "Hey, look at me. Talk to me."

His grip on me tightened again as he exhaled a heavy, shaky breath. Cold shivers ran up my spine. I'd never seen him like this, on the verge of some emotional breakdown. My chest felt heavy with anguish and helplessness. It physically hurt me to know he was in pain, and I couldn't help him.

Not when he wouldn't speak.

As I started to call his name, he lifted me up and rested his forehead on mine as I circled his abdomen with my legs.

"What happened?" I framed his face gently with both hands. "Derek, you're not alone anymore. I'm here. Let me help you."

Silence.

His eyes were closed, and his breathing was steady and calm. There were no signs of tears in his lashes or tension on his perfect face. He almost looked like he was sleeping.

"Derek, you're scaring me."

With those words, he finally opened his eyes, blue orbs staring straight into mine. He shifted us and pushed my body against the cold steel of the fridge, burying his face into the side of my neck again, only this time his lips suckled my skin as they moved up toward my ear. I squirmed under his touch, flames of arousal igniting in my belly.

"Derek," I breathed, closing my eyes as he trailed kisses along my jaw. "I need to know you're okay. Please, talk to me."

A growl rumbled into my neck as he pushed me harder against the fridge. I knew I should stop him, that all I had to do was ask, and he'd comply. There wasn't a shred of doubt in my mind. But something inside me also knew he needed me this way. Needed my affection and my passion, and I was willing to give him that and more.

"I'm yours."

Another groan echoed into my chest as he kissed with more frenzy, biting and nipping at my skin. My fingers smoothed into his hair, and I tilted my head back as delicious jolts of desire rocketed through my body.

Derek suddenly tore me away and dropped me on the kitchen counter. Wasting no time, he pulled my cami over my head and tossed it. His mouth was on my breast in the next second. Long pulls had me moaning and thrusting my hips into his torso, seeking friction and relief from the fire swelling inside. I fisted his hair, his name falling from my lips as he alternated, suckling and squeezing.

"I'll always be here for you," I murmured as he moved down my abdomen. "Always."

His mouth was between my legs, tongue licking up the dampened cloth. He inhaled a deep breath and growled into my sex, biting at the scant fabric.

Derek was never one to shy from words in the bedroom. He always had this way of making me feel so damn sexy, so feral. And I loved every second of being his, of being taken by him in any way he wanted me.

As I closed my eyes, the sound of ripped cloth pierced the air, and his mouth was on me in the next second, rendering me speechless. He licked and sucked, drinking from me as if it were the last time. That fleeting thought caused an ache to lance through my chest for a moment until his skilled tongue diverted my thoughts.

"Fuck," I moaned, clutching his hair between my fingers as he pushed his face deeper, gripping my hips with a force that was sure to leave bruises. "Fuck, fuck... Derek." Strangled screams fled my lips as his fingers pushed inside me, curling and stroking until my body arched off the marble.

My orgasm crashed into me, and I cried out his name over and over as tears spilled from the corners of my eyes. I tried to close my thighs and move from his voracious lashes, but he groaned and pushed them open, pulling me back to his mouth.

"It's too much," I whimpered, trying to squirm away. But he only tightened his hold while his other hand grabbed my ass. His index finger moved up my slit and inside me before trailing back, smearing my cum and pushing against the rim of tight muscles.

"Oh, fuck," I cried when it thrust forward.

My reaction only spurred him on as he sucked on my clit with more enthusiasm.

He didn't need to say the words. I knew what his actions meant.

I was his.

In every way, I belonged to him.

That thought alone pushed me to the edge, my legs widening for him as another orgasm crested. His finger moved in time with his tongue, and I banged on the counter with my fists, coming undone in his mouth.

"Baby… please…" I didn't know what I was pleading for.

Was it for him to stop?

To feel him fill me completely?

I shuddered as I fell back to earth, my breaths heavy.

The reprieve was short-lived because he took hold of my hips and flipped me over. Hard teeth bit at my flesh, and I hissed as the pain only elevated the euphoria of the moment.

His tongue licked up each cheek, then along my slit as I clawed at the hard surface. But there was no leverage. My feet hung off the edge.

I was at the mercy of his sweet torture.

Looking over my shoulder, I whispered, "I'm yours."

He moved up my body and peppered kisses along my back.

Derek slid the head of his cock over my seam and against my sensitive clit, though I wasn't sure when he'd removed his pants and underwear. Soft whimpers fluttered from my throat as he hauled my hips to the edge of the counter and thrust inside. The walls of my pussy stretched around him as he filled me, pumping into me mercilessly. I bit back the twinges of pain as he took me hard and fast before flipping me over and surging to the hilt with deep, powerful strokes.

"Derek… Oh, fuck!"

He threw both my legs over his shoulders and fucked me like he'd never get another chance.

And despite how good he felt taking me with such delicious brutality, I couldn't get out of my head. Couldn't shake the feeling that something was wrong.

His thumb was on my clit, drawing circles and putting pressure until he brought me back to the moment, his name on my lips, as I felt myself climbing toward another orgasm. He pinched me between his fingers, and it was all it took. Derek came shortly after, fingers digging into my thighs as he grunted and groaned loudly until every drop was spent.

After several moments, he pulled me into a sitting position and stood between my legs. I wiped away the sweat dotting his forehead and held his face, forcing our eyes to meet.

"Talk to me," I pleaded. "Are you okay?"

Derek nodded and kissed my hairline, lingering over my skin.

"Everything is going to be fine," he finally said. "I promise."

"Do you want to talk about it?"

"I fought with Ronan. It's nothing to worry about."

"You're sure?" I asked, placing a short kiss on his lips.

His arms wound around me tighter. I'd never felt more loved, more protected than I did at that moment. Whatever was troubling him, we'd get through it together. That's when I realized there wasn't anywhere else I wanted to be than in his arms, like this, for always.

"Derek." My voice was hushed as I caressed his cheek, and he put his hand over mine, kissing my palm as he waited to hear what I had to say. "I think… I think I love you."

Derek's eyes darkened, and he squeezed my hand against his face. "Eva…"

"You don't have to say it back. That's not what I expect. I just felt like you needed to know."

I'd be lying if I said his silence hadn't stung. At the same time, I didn't expect him to reciprocate. I'd hoped he would, but I knew, despite his silence, he cared. The way he held me, made love to me, the things he said. This couldn't just be one-sided.

He leaned in and kissed the tip of my nose, forehead, and lips. Even though I didn't have his words, I had his affection, his love. For now, it would do.

"Have you eaten?" he asked, and I nodded. "Good, because I want to show you what you mean to me. And I want to take my time."

The pit of my stomach ignited with anticipation, and I bit down on my lip. "Show me," I urged before running my tongue along the seam of his perfect mouth.

Mine.

He was mine.

Chapter Thirty Nine
Evangelina

I picked up Derek's note, having lost count of the times I'd read it. He hadn't called or sent a text. He'd left a handwritten note. It was his thing. His writing was shit, like a typical man, but it was the principle. I'd committed every word to memory, especially his parting phrase.

> Make sure you're naked and wet for me, angel.
> I'll be home soon.
> Love,
> Derek

Love.

It wasn't just a standard phrase. He wouldn't have written it had he not meant the sentiment behind it.

My face hurt from the obscene amount of smiling I'd been doing since arriving home. Initially, I was disappointed he wasn't here. I missed him. Wanted him. We'd burned the sheets well into the morning hours last night, rutting like damn animals. It was primal. Passionate. Derek didn't need to say those three words. He showed me his heart with every kiss and caress and the endless times my name danced off his tongue as he came inside me.

I unclipped my badge and gun and set them on the dresser, swooning like a schoolgirl as heat crept up my neck.

In love.

I was in love.

Fuck, it felt so good. To love and be loved so thoroughly. Who knew? Who knew I'd fall for the man whose father had been such an important figure in my life?

Putting a hand over the medical bracelet, I sighed audibly like some lovestruck fool. The gift was one of the most thoughtful gestures I'd ever received. He knew I wasn't impressed by flashy or expensive gifts, and while the price tag was indeed a hefty one, the sentiment behind it was one I'd cherish forever.

I slid my jacket off my shoulders and closed my eyes as thoughts of Derek sent warm tingles between my legs.

Grabbing the hem of my shirt, I started humming my favorite love song, when the clicking sound of the knob caused me to pause and smile broadly.

Derek.

I ripped my shirt off and whirled around, but his name died in my throat when I was met with another man's face.

"Ronan? What the hell are you doing here?" I scrambled to get my blouse back over my body and glared until intrusive thoughts began to manifest. "Did something happen to Derek?" Fear paralyzed my heart. Why else would Ronan be here? I moved toward him, attempting but failing to control my breath. "Please tell me he's okay."

Ronan was serious. Eyes narrowed and impassive. I tried desperately to read him, but he was giving nothing, and I feared the worst. "Ronan, what happened?"

"What happened, you ask? If anyone knows the answer to that question, it's you."

Something was off. He wasn't making any sense, and his voice was cruel. Cold. He looked at me as if I was something insignificant to be crushed under his shoe. A striking contrast to when his eyes lit with lust the first time we'd met.

"I—I don't understand." I took a cautious step back, unsure of his intentions. "Where's Derek?"

"Killing his brother—for you."

My heart faltered.

"What did you just say?"

He moved closer, and my hand fell on the gun I'd placed on the dresser. His eyes slid to my weapon, and the most insidious smile I'd ever seen crawled across his face.

"You know, for a so-called detective, you sure are good at missing those brightly colored red flags."

"What are you talking about?"

He chuckled wickedly. "Oh, Eva, so beautiful yet so goddamn stupid."

I swallowed hard as I attempted to compose my nerves.

Red flags.

Was he right?

He took two more steps, and I drew my weapon. "Don't come any closer."

"You won't shoot me because you want answers. You want to know what the fuck I'm talking about and who exactly is the monster you've been sleeping with."

I shook my head. "Stop. Stop with the fucking cryptic comments and just say what you came here to say."

"As you wish." He leaned against the bedpost, arms folded over his chest. "You think him finding you was some coincidence? Quite the contrary."

I played back to those moments when we'd first met, how he knew my name and place of work. But he found them in the files. It's what he'd said. And I believed him.

I had to.

Ronan pushed off the post and approached again. And again, I aimed my weapon at his torso.

"Let me ask you a question, Evangelina. You're supposed to be good at instincts and intuition… well, except when the likes of my son blinds you."

"Stop fucking with me."

"The night your godfather was murdered, did you know he was there?"

My throat tightened. "Who?"

"Let's not play dumb. You know who," he taunted.

"No, you're lying," I said, shaking my head in disbelief.

He ate the space between us, but I was too entangled in my memories, numb to my surroundings apart from the crushing words spewing from his mouth.

"Am I?" he asked, circling me. "Tell me, dear, you ever get that feeling? The one where the hairs at the back of your neck stand up. When you feel eyes on you, and the weight of a presence you can't see." His breath fanned over the side of my face. "Did you feel him, Eva? Did you feel him that night? Watching? Waiting? And let's be honest, probably debating whether he'd have to kill you too."

Ronan was in front of me now, but he was just a distorted figure behind the tears flooding my eyes.

"No." My voice was barely a whisper, the devastating truth tearing into my heart. "No!" I yelled, shoving him away. "He wouldn't. He'd never—you're lying."

I wiped roughly at the droplets sliding down my face.

And he grinned, thoroughly amused by my anguish, as he cocked his head and rubbed at the short beard on his chin. "Well, then, there's only one way to find out. Follow me."

"Like hell I will." Ronan Cain's devilish laugh made me want to scream. He really was enjoying this, the bastard. "Why are you telling me this?"

"Purely selfish reasons, my dear," he said with a wink. "Derek thinks he can just leave, as if I haven't invested years in him. He's one of the best. Never misses a mark."

The question was hanging on my tongue, burning it. But I didn't want to hear his answer. I didn't want to know anymore.

"However, James—well, that one was personal."

Pain.

"Please, stop," I begged, throat clogged with emotion.

Ronan shrugged his shoulders and eyed me one last time before walking toward the closet, turning back to me as he reached the entrance. "Your choice, Eva. Choose to live in darkness or, as they say, let the truth set you free."

I closed my eyes and hung my head, tears diving off the tip of my nose. This wasn't happening. I loved him.

I loved him.

He wouldn't.

He couldn't.

But I had to know.

I took off behind Ronan. When I reached the doorway, a trap door had opened in the middle of the closet, beneath the large dresser where Derek stored his accessories.

"Fuck you. I'm not going down there, especially not with you."

Pulling out my phone, I dialed Derek's number.

"You're so hung up on my son's cock that you refuse to see the truth."

"Eva? Can you hear me?" Derek's voice called for me on the other end of the open line.

"I have a meeting in about twenty minutes, so I won't be sticking around. But you're free to continue wearing that blindfold."

Derek's voice was frantic now. Had he heard his father?

My finger hovered over the end call button as Ronan walked away.

"Oh, and Eva," he said with menace, "Don't forget to ask Franco how long he's known about Derek. If we're dusting out the old closet, we might as well get all the skeletons—including one named Frankie."

An audible gasp leaped from my lips, and I pushed the button and tore down the stairs until I reached a room with my mouth gaping open in shock. Rows upon rows of rifles, handguns, automatic weapons, endless ammo, knives, hatchets, and even fucking throwing stars.

The logical side of my brain knew this wasn't just the stash of a weapon enthusiast. This was something else. Something darker, more sinister. But the stupid woman, blinded by love, tried to take over.

He's a tactical instructor. He owns a gun range. Maybe this was where he kept inventory.

Maybe...

The excuses I'd conjured disintegrated when I spotted a small photo collage on a shelf by the damn stars.

My phone vibrated as I clutched it between my fingers like a lifeline. Derek was calling and texting nonstop. I opened the line and moved toward the photos as he called for me. Tears slipped down my face, sliding past the seam of my lips as my throat tightened, making the act of breathing difficult.

"Eva!" he called, his voice desperate. "Angel, please, say something."

I shook my head and suppressed a sob when I saw myself in every photo.

Sitting in my shop.

Having lunch with Sam.

The parking lot of my gym.

My fucking front porch.

Clutching at my chest, I set the phone down when my eyes fell on a smaller photo. A wrinkled one, ripped in half. I knew this picture. It wasn't one he'd snapped. This was from James's mantle—the only one in existence. I thought it had been lost that night, along with everything else.

"No..." I breathed. "No, no, no..."

My heart splintered, and my knees buckled, but I held the edge of the table and let my head fall forward as a sob finally broke.

"Eva, baby... *please*," he begged. "Answer me. Let me explain."

I snatched the phone from the table, chucked it across the room, and watched it shatter...

Like me.

Chapter Forty

Derek

I couldn't remember climbing out of my car or taking the stairs to my room. My thoughts were only on Evangelina, racing, frantic. She knew. I wasn't exactly sure what she knew, but I'd heard what he said.

I clenched my jaw and snarled Ronan's name. His time had come, but I'd deal with him later.

Bursting into the room, I expected to find Eva on the bed, the floor, or in the bathroom, but I was met with emptiness and deafening silence. My heart slumped as I redialed her number, but as the voicemail message began to play, I noticed the dresser in the closet had shifted.

Fuck.

There wasn't any time to feel, rationalize or devise a diatribe of excuses. I needed to get to her, to see her.

The room was only illuminated by the backlights on each shelf. I scanned the space and saw her curled-up figure sitting in a corner.

"Angel," I said, flipping the light switch and moving toward her.

"Don't!" Her voice was sharp as a razor's edge, and she'd pulled a gun from her lap and pointed it at me.

"Eva, I—"

"I remember this day," she said in an eerily calm tone, holding a photo in her hand. "He was the keynote speaker, and since he and Pam had already separated, he asked me to go instead. It was a great night." A frail smile pulled at her lips as she recalled the memory. "We took this picture after dinner, and he put it on his mantle the next day and promised to make me a copy. But he never did." Her eyes snapped up to mine.

Black streaks of makeup carved her cheeks, and her red-rimmed eyes lanced through me as she got to her feet, the weapon still on me.

"This photo was still on his mantle the day he died. I know it was. I saw it. How is it that you have it?"

"Listen—"

"Shut up!" she yelled, dropping the photo and steadying her grip. "I've been racked with guilt, so much fucking guilt about what happened that night. I blamed myself for not picking up on his distress cues—You were there, weren't you? *Why?*"

"Angel…"

"Don't call me that. Don't you ever call me that." Her voice was strangled, her lips trembling, and I only wanted to hold her.

Fuck.

"You killed him? You killed your own father."

"He was never a father to me."

She let out a loud shriek. "You're a murderer, Derek. A fucking psychopath. Is that what all this is?" she asked, motioning around the room. "*Never misses a mark.* Is that what you do? Kill people?"

"It's more complicated than that."

A humorless laugh left her throat. "Complicated? There's nothing complicated about the fact that you kill people for a living. The fact that you killed your own father, a man I loved as if he was…"

Her chest shuddered as a sob robbed her words. She lowered the gun and slumped forward, crying with her head bowed and her dark hair falling around her like a curtain, obscuring her beautiful face.

"You can hate me, Eva. Hate what I did. Hate who I am, but don't you dare shed a tear for that son of a bitch. You have no idea of the man he truly was and everything he was involved in."

I dared to place a hand on her shoulder, but she ripped away from my touch.

"Who the fuck are you to judge anyone's morality?"

"I don't claim to be a saint. But I don't hide my demons either like he did."

She scoffed and shook her head.

"Oh, really? Why did you seek me out? Why were you following me?" she asked, pointing at the pictures on the shelf. "Was any of this real, Derek?" Her voice was broken again, and her pain was like a gash to the heart.

With a hand over my chest, I fisted my shirt. "I didn't plan this, Eva. I didn't mean to—"

"You absolute bastard."

"Please, let me explain." I tried to reach out, but she recoiled, raising her weapon again.

"Don't fucking touch me."

I loathed the way she was looking at me. In some ways, I preferred her hatred over the fear reflected in her eyes. She was staring at me like everyone else, and I couldn't stand it. Not from her.

"You can yell, scream, hate me, Eva, but don't be afraid of me. I'm a monster. I know that. I've killed in cold blood, and I won't deny that. But you, I would never hurt you."

She squeezed her eyes closed and cried, the gun dropping to her feet. I moved in and cradled her face. "Baby, I'd never hurt you.

Please, believe that."

Her hands wound tightly around my wrists, and her eyes flew open.

"You're wrong," she said in a whisper. "No one has ever hurt me more than you. You fucking broke me, Derek."

"No."

"It all makes sense now." Eva pulled my hands from her face. "God, I'm so fucking stupid." I tried to reach for her again, but she slapped my hand away. "I told you I loved you, and you couldn't say it back. And now I know why. This was all some plot to fuck me over, wasn't it?"

She stepped toward me, hatred burning in her eyes.

"Eva, you don't understand."

"You're a son of a bitch." Her hand connected with the side of my face with a force I wasn't expecting. My cheek was aflame, my skin pulsing. "How you must have laughed at me. You and your brother."

"That's not true, and you know that."

"You fucked me like some whore, degraded me, and probably laughed behind my back while my dumb ass fell in love with you. God, I hate you!"

Her fists came down on my chest, the force of her blows biting, but I let her hit me. I deserved to feel all the pain I'd caused her.

"Eva, stop," I finally said, grabbing her wrists. She didn't fight me anymore and crumbled to the floor.

"What am I supposed to do with all of this?" she cried, fingers clutching her heart. "What do I do with everything I know?" A scream rippled from her throat. "You fucked me in so many ways, Derek."

I knelt beside her. "Do whatever you feel is right. But please let me speak."

"No," she said, shaking her head and jumping to her feet. "I don't want to hear any more of your bullshit—your lies. I never want to see or hear from you again."

I caught her elbow before she could run through the door and pulled her into me, her back flush against my chest. My lips were on her neck, and she melted into me, letting me kiss her.

"Angel, please, don't leave. I wish things were different. I wish I were the man you deserve. Let me make this right. Please."

"You know what I wish, Derek?" She turned around in my arms, watery eyes meeting mine. "I wish you would have killed me that night too."

I clenched my teeth. "Don't you fucking say that."

"What's the difference? At least it would have been quick. And not like this."

My hold on her loosened as the blades of a thousand serrated knives cut deep into my heart. I let her walk away, and she stopped beneath the threshold but didn't turn around. A glimmer of hope bubbled inside me, but as swiftly as it bloomed, it crashed and burned when the vitriol behind her words choked the very life from me.

"If I ever see you again, if you ever come looking for me, I'll have you arrested for murder... or kill you myself."

Chapter Forty One

Derek

"Derek, stop!"

Kai's hurried steps closed in on me. It didn't matter. He wouldn't stop me. Nobody would until I had Ronan's head. Not only had he destroyed my relationship with Eva, but he'd also put a target on her head for revealing himself and me in the process. My girl hated me, and she could potentially be in danger. I wouldn't let that stand. I'd make him pay in the most painful ways imaginable.

"Come on, brother, think this through," he said, gripping my arm.

I shook off his touch and cut through the parking lot, but he grabbed me again.

"Kai, you're not going to stop me. I'm going to rip him apart with my bare fucking hands."

He pushed me by the shoulders, slamming me against the back of a truck. "The only thing you're going to do is get yourself fucking killed. You won't walk out of there, and neither will I because there's no way in hell I'll let you do this alone."

"The fuck you will."

"Try and stop me," he challenged.

I shook my head and closed my eyes, the heat of tears stinging behind my eyelids, the pain in my chest still raw, stealing my breath. The agony of losing her, of knowing she hated me, was a unique form of torture I'd never experienced. Not even the atrocities of my childhood compared. I'd live those horrors a thousand times if it meant I could unsee the hatred and sadness in her eyes.

It didn't matter that I always knew this would be our end. That she never belonged in my world, that she was too good for the darkness that lived inside me. But I was a selfish son of a bitch, and intended to keep her at any cost.

My gaze fell on Kai, and the guilt of what I'd planned caused my stomach to lurch.

"I don't deserve your loyalty." My voice broke. Shit.

"Bullshit, D. We're fucking brothers. Before Eva, it was just you and me. And now, I'd do anything for her too, because you love her."

I loved her.

I fucking loved her.

And I needed her back.

"Kai," I said, swallowing the knot in my throat. "I told him I wanted out. Told him I was done with Ares."

"I figured that much. Explains why he pulled this." He clapped the side of my face, his eyes alight with compassion. "We have to go about this differently."

"No," I said, shoving him back. "You don't get it. He forced my hand. Said I had to kill you to buy my freedom." Kai's eyes narrowed as he waited for me to continue, knowing full well where this was going. "I'm so fucking sorry, brother."

I slid down the side of the truck, falling to a pathetic heap on the ground. Kai crouched in front of me, a hand on my shoulder as he exhaled.

"Derek, I get it. I would have come back and haunted your ass, but I get it. Eva must mean a lot to you. Look at you. You look like shit."

I let out an unamused laugh, relieved he didn't want to put a bullet between my eyes.

"I wasn't going to go through with it. I was thinking maybe you could hide out for a while. Go back with Amalia's clan until I dealt with Ronan."

"Fuck, D, I'm glad you got my life figured out for me," he joked halfheartedly. "But I'm not leaving. We're going to take care of this asshole together. Then work on getting Eva. Plus, I heard that chick Amalia is certifiable. Not exactly my first choice to go on the lam."

Kai was the only other person who knew and understood me on a level no one could ever comprehend. One I'd wanted to reach with Eva.

Despite the fallout between us, I was grateful that he also knew me enough not to ask why I was still recruiting *Las Mercinarias*. No matter what awaited us in the future, I'd always be there for her. And if her happiness was in the arms of another man… well, fuck that. I'd kill every motherfucker who would dare to breathe within five feet of her.

Kai kicked the door open and shot the two men on Ronan's right while I took out the two on his left—one of them being that bastard Kiernan.

"What the—"

He tried to reach for the gun he kept in the top drawer, but he wasn't fast enough.

"I suggest you freeze."

Ronan's jaw twitched before it slid into a grin as he stared down the barrel of two guns. "So this is how you two repay me for the life I've given you?"

"Shut up," I snarled, coming around and slamming his head against the wooden desk. "I should kill you right here. Cut you open and let you die the slow, painful death you deserve."

"But you won't."

"Don't fucking tempt me. I'm out of my head right now, and the only reason you're still alive is Kai. I won't implicate him in my fucked-up business, but you know me well. Sometimes the blood just calls to me, and yours is fucking singing right now."

I pushed the hot titanium of my silencer into his temple, searing his skin.

"So what's your plan, Derek?" he asked in that frustratingly calm voice of his.

"You're going to leave Philly, leave the country—I don't give a fuck where you go, but I suggest hiding in the deepest, darkest hole you can find."

He laughed outright. "What makes you think you have the power to make me do a damn thing? That little cunt of yours sure gave you some balls, didn't she? Shame she—*Aahh!*" I couldn't suppress the urge to stab my blade through his hand and into the mahogany desk. His cries were just as pathetic as he was.

"You're not the only one with eyes and ears around here. Let's just say Zeus is going to receive a very interesting email with photos, audio, and video of you and his wife in various compromising positions. And a detailed audit of where his 10.8 million dollars ended up."

Ronan growled, holding his trapped hand as blood pooled over the desk. "Bullshit. If you had all that on me, you'd kill me yourself."

"I'd much rather watch it all play out." I leaned in close to his ear. "And when I get that green light, I'm going to hunt you down." Twisting the knife, I reveled in his howls of pain. "Find you, and make you choke on your own dick."

Chapter Forty Two
Evangelina

Ten, *nine, eight, seven…*
I held my legs tighter, forehead resting on my knees as the disastrous revelations from two days ago played on repeat in my thoughts. I'd cried for most of the night once I'd gotten home, but I still managed to drag my ass out of bed for work. Having missed so many days already, there was no way I would call in. I did my best with makeup to cover the puffiness around my eyes and sucked it up, convincing myself I'd have plenty of time to break down later. And I was grateful my new partner knew better than to ask personal questions.

Fresh tears rolled down my bare thighs as the face I tried to purge unsuccessfully from my mind appeared front and center. His smile, those eyes… God, the way it felt to be in his arms. I released a small sob and wiped my eyes against my forearm.

It was a lie. All of it.

I was nothing more than a pawn to him. A cruel plot of revenge for a man who was no longer alive. Couldn't he have just let it go? Left me alone?

My phone vibrated for the umpteenth time. It was new, so I had no idea how Derek had gotten my number so fast. The thought was terrifying and further solidified how dangerous and unpredictable he was. "Leave me the fuck alone!" I swatted it off the couch and across the living room. Diego, who had been napping close by, was startled and took off up the stairs.

Derek and my father had both been calling nonstop. The former would never hear my voice again, and I wasn't in the right headspace to hear anything my father had to say. I couldn't handle any more painful truths.

Loud pounding on the door caused me to jump.

"Eva! I know you're home. Please, open the door."

I screamed into a decorative pillow.

My father's voice boomed from outside again. Maybe if I ignored him, he'd go away.

"Eva, I'm off tomorrow, so that means I can stand here all night. Your choice."

Coming to terms with the fact that he wouldn't let up, I shuffled to the front door and ripped it open.

"What?" I bit out, refusing to look him in the eyes.

"I get that you're upset, but you will not disrespect me."

"I'm not a child. Respect me by leaving, by understanding why I don't want to see or speak to you right now."

On my drive home from Derek's house, I'd called my dad and left him a detailed voice message, where I informed him not to contact me in the near future because he was a fucking liar.

"Eva, I tried to warn you. You refused to listen. Now, look."

I pinched the bridge of my nose as tears welled beneath my lashes.

"I need you to leave. Throwing in my face how much of a fool I was doesn't help. You're hurting me. Please, go. And you're just as much to blame here." I opened my eyes and glared at him. "I'm really,

really trying not to think about all the ways you've deceived me. And everything I don't know about you because I can't take anymore."

My voice broke, and I put my arms around myself and cried.

"Eva, please let me help you."

I shook my head. "You can't help me. No one can." Looking away from him, I exhaled a shuddering breath. "You're just as bad as he is. Maybe worse, because we're family, and you betrayed me. Lied to my face every single fucking day."

He stepped forward and put a hand on my shoulder. "*Princesa*, I can't leave you like this. Please, let me stay. Let me explain."

I recoiled from his touch. "No! I want you to leave. Now. If you don't leave, I will."

My father hung his head as he swiped at his eyes with both hands. "I'm so sorry. I should have told you. Should have told you about Frankie."

I turned my back and covered my ears like a child. "No, please stop."

"Eva." His voice was strained. He swallowed hard and continued to speak, despite my protests. "One night, shortly before you were born, I accidentally witnessed something I shouldn't have. I begged for my life, offered them money—they were going to kill me until I offered something of use. Myself. My expertise."

I leaned on the wall to steady myself, but I didn't turn to face him.

"They forced me. I had no choice. I tried to leave. Years later, I was determined to…" I'd never heard or seen my father cry, not even when Frankie died. But I was too numb and broken to care. "To teach me a lesson, to keep me compliant, they murdered him. Told me you were next."

"Mom?"

"I've never lied about your mother. She died giving you life, and that's the God's honest truth."

He touched my shoulder. "Please go," I whispered.

"You have to understand. I didn't have a choice. The world is not what you think it is, Eva. Derek is a testament to that."

I bit down on my lip and swallowed the sob tearing my throat. "Go."

My father didn't say another word and slipped out the door.

While a part of me hurt to see him upset, I didn't care. And I wouldn't care for a long time.

Six, five, four...

Leaning against the door, I let myself slide to the floor as sobs racked my body. It hurt. Everything hurt. It hurt to breathe, knowing Derek used me. But it hurt even more, knowing that despite his betrayal, I still loved him. I clawed at my chest, seeking relief from the pain and weight of his lies. I didn't know what to do with all of those emotions. It was as if the more I cried, the bigger my grief and longing for him swelled.

"So stupid. So fucking stupid."

A soft knock at the door made me pause. I shot to my feet and tore it open.

"I thought I told you to..." The words died on my tongue when instead of my father, it was Derek staring back at me. I'd never seen him so... disheveled. The hair on his head and face was a mess, and he was wearing sweatpants and a wrinkled t-shirt. He looked as if he'd just rolled out of bed.

God, I hated that I wanted to jump in his arms and say to hell with everything... but I couldn't be that pathetic. I had a shred of dignity left beneath the shards of my shattered heart, and I refused to let him take any more of me than he already had.

"I thought I told you I never wanted to see you again. That I'd—"

Derek rushed me, sweeping my feet off the floor as his mouth crushed mine. He kissed me with desperation, his tongue seeking entrance, and for a second, I wanted to give in. Every cell in my body was humming as if it recognized precisely who it belonged to…

Fuck.

No.

I pushed him away and punched at his chest.

"No! Stop. Get your fucking hands off me, and get out of my house."

"Eva, please… I can't. I need you. Please."

I backed up, putting a sizable distance between us. "It's over, Derek. Why are you here? You don't have to keep this charade going."

He moved forward, but I raised my hand, causing him to halt.

"Charade? You think I'd be here if you meant nothing to me?" He clutched the sides of his hair before raking back the unruly strands. "Fuck, Eva, you gotta know that's bullshit."

"I don't know anything, because everything was a lie. Everyone. You, my dad, Helena—Everyone!" His eyes narrowed. "Yeah, you think I'm too stupid to put those pieces together. She's like you, isn't she? And Kai? Ronan."

"I told you it's complicated."

"My God, Derek. You don't get it. Even if I did believe what we had was genuine, what would it matter?"

He reached me in two long strides, hands at the side of my neck. My eyes closed instinctively as I let myself lean into his touch.

"It's all that matters," he murmured close to my lips.

I put a hand on his chest and shoved him back. "No." My bottom lip wobbled as I breathed out the words, trying to hold myself together. "We were doomed from the start. I put people like you away for a living. And you're not even anything like those people, Derek—you're worse. You go against everything I stand for. I was just stupid for not being able to see it sooner. For refusing to see what's been in front of my eyes this whole time."

"Eva, don't do this. Please. I've never given a damn about anyone. You came along, and you changed something inside me."

His anguish pricked at my skin, fighting to penetrate my shield. But I took in a lungful of air and braced myself for the next question.

"Have you killed anyone while we've been together? And please don't lie to me."

He averted his eyes; it was all I needed to know.

"You are the same monster you were before I met you. And that's all you'll ever be. It doesn't matter that I love you," I said through tears and sniffles.

"Baby, we're so good together. You and I."

I shook my head as another sob tore through me. "You can't say it, can you? Even now."

He cupped my face again. "It's not that I don't—"

"You don't know how to love."

Derek rested his forehead on my mine. "Angel, I'll spend the rest of my life showing you what I feel for you is real. Just give me a chance."

My shoulders trembled, and I squeezed my lips together to keep the sobs at bay. "Get out."

"Eva?"

Three, two, one…

"I already told you. Nothing else matters because I'll *never* forgive everything you've done."

Chapter Forty Three

Evangelina

"Eva, come on. I've been waiting two hours. You're dressed, and you look half alive. Let's go."

Lex dragged me across the driveway by my wrist. I'd fought her the last two days, but today, having no fight left, I'd let her win and even pick out my outfit. She swung open the car door and shoved me inside, slamming it closed before running around the hood of the car and climbing inside as fast as she could.

"You think I'm going to run off or something?"

"In case you change your mind." She shrugged as she pulled into the street. "Now, the only way you'll get out of our outing is if you're willing to risk road rash on that pretty face."

I'd felt numb these days. The prospect of pain, of feeling something other than this void in my heart, seemed almost enticing.

"Where are we going?"

"First lunch. I know you know better than to not take care of yourself, especially over some asshole who doesn't deserve you. You don't get the luxury of wallowing in depression while starving or binging like the rest of us."

Leaning my head on the glass, I scoffed. "You have no idea how hard it's been having to force myself to eat without an appetite."

"Oh, babes, I'm so sorry. I wish I could kick him in the dick for you, and you know I would too."

I offered her a slow smile. "I do. Thank you for this."

She waved me off. "No need to thank me. You're my sister, Ev. I don't know what he did to break you so deeply, but I will help you get over him, okay?"

My eyes filled with tears, and I looked away, absently watching the world go by as people went about their lives while I was stuck in this endless vortex of sadness and betrayal. There was no end in sight. It was as if Derek was embedded beneath my skin and part of my bloodstream. Everything held reminders of him, even Diego.

"Hey, no crying allowed in my car. You'll ruin my leather."

A sob and a humorless laugh broke from my lips as I wiped under my eyes.

"I'm trying here, Lex."

The crushing pressure in my throat gave way to more sobs, and I bowed my head, using my hair to hide my face and the pain and despair I knew she'd see there.

Alexa pulled into a parking lot and threw the car in park before quickly enveloping me in a tight hug. Our bodies shuddered as I cried into her shoulder for a good ten minutes, and she let me, rubbing soothing circles across my back.

"Okay," she said, pushing hair out of my face. "Now that we got that out, let's take deep breaths and relax."

She wiped beneath her eyes with the back of her finger and fanned her face.

"I'm sorry," I said in a hushed tone. "You must think I'm pathetic. He's just a guy, right?"

"Look, you're already bumming, so don't make me slap some sense into you on top of that." She pulled me into another hug, and I lay my head on her shoulder. "Of course I don't think you're pathetic. Your heart is broken, Ev. Been there, done that. But you're going to grieve that loss, pick yourself up and move on because you're Evangelina *fucking* Cruz, and he's the biggest idiot in Philly for losing you."

She wouldn't be saying those things if she knew I was upset over a serial murderer and the man who had tortured and killed James.

"I wish it were that simple. I just… I don't know what to do with all of this." I gestured to my heart. "I love him, Lex. I love him so fucking much that it physically hurts."

"Oh, Eva," she whispered, cradling my trembling face.

"I hate him just as much too."

"Good. Channel that and push out everything else. He doesn't deserve any more of your tears. You're a fucking goddess, okay."

I laughed through the tears and threw my arms around her. "Let's go. I am a little hungry all of a sudden."

"Perfect!"

Alexa kissed my forehead and stepped out of the car. As I grabbed my bag, I heard male voices and Lex addressing them, but her tone was higher pitched than usual, distressed. No sooner had I held the door handle, my cousin's body slammed against the car's side so violently that it rocked from side to side. Before I could process what was happening, two loud cracks and a man in all black stood over her, beating her with his fists.

No, no. Shit.

I pulled my gun and jumped out of the car.

"Stop! Get away from her."

It was all I got to say before hard steel pushed against the back of my head.

"Put it down," a thickly accented voice commanded near my ear.

"And if you try anything at all, he will shove his gun in that dirty mouth of hers. Is that what you want?"

Dmitry Belov.

I shook my head slowly. "Why are you doing this?"

"Oh, I'm just here to collect what's mine. And you know that saying, if you want something done, do it yourself and all that? Well, here I am."

One of his henchmen grabbed the gun from my hands, and Dmitry quickly pushed me against the car, his body flush against my back.

"So you're the little angel of death responsible for my brother's murder. You know, I saw your pictures and knew you were beautiful, but I see now they did you no justice."

The tip of his nose grazed my shoulder while his other hand smoothed up my torso and under my breast.

"I was going to give you to my cousin, but no, *kroshka (baby).* You're mine."

He flicked my nipple with his thumb and inhaled into my neck.

"Don't you fucking touch me." I tried to push him back, but he shoved me harder against the glass.

"Oh, Evangelina, I fully intend to *fucking touch you* as you say, and then maybe teach that insolent little mouth of yours its proper place."

He fisted the back of my hair, and I hissed in pain as he dragged me around the hood of the car. I would have fought back with everything I had, but my thoughts were on Lex. He'd threatened her life if I didn't cooperate. As he pushed me past the driver's side, I caught sight of her still body slumped against the car, face obscured by bloodied hair.

"Lex!" I cried out for her, extending my arms, even if it were useless.

Dmitry hauled me by the waist and threw me inside a black van. I knocked my elbow on a metal latch, the pain lancing through me and ripping a scream from my now raw throat.

"Dispose of her," he ordered, motioning toward Alexa before climbing beside me.

"No, you son of a bitch!" I got one clean right hook to the side of his face before pain exploded behind my eyes, and I lost consciousness.

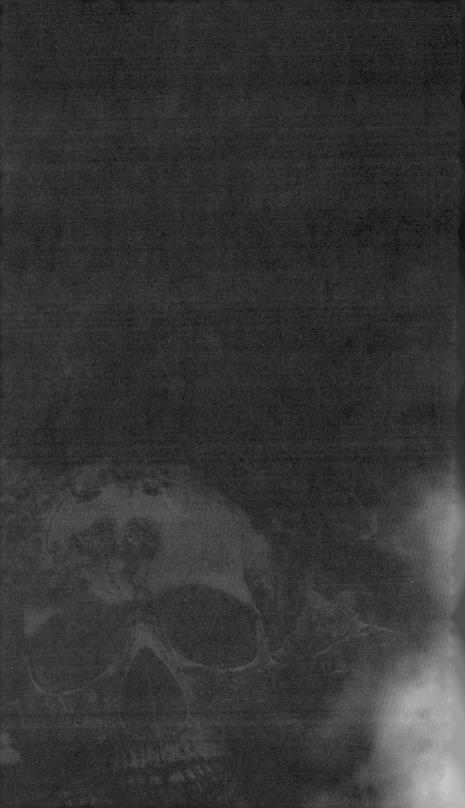

Chapter Forty Four

Derek

I slammed my glass of whiskey on the counter, shattering the damn thing. Droplets of blood mixed with the liquid, but I felt nothing. Pain was a welcome change to the numbness—four days without her.

Four fucking days.

Might as well have been an eternity. I wasn't sure what I did with my life, how I lived day to day before I knew her. She'd become such an integral part of who I was that without her, I was lost.

But it wouldn't remain like this. Eva was mine. She was made for me, and I'd find a way to get her back, even if it killed me.

"Don't look at me like that," I told Deimos as he watched me from his mat on the floor. "You liked her too, huh, boy? Never seen you take to someone so fast." His ears pulled back as if he knew what I was saying. "She's something special, isn't she?"

He stood and huffed beside me, signaling that he wanted to be taken out. As I placed my hand on his head, an unknown number flashed on the screen of my phone. I silenced the call, slipped it into my pocket, and stepped off the stool to grab a leash. I'd barely reached the back door before my cell vibrated again.

The same number.

I never answered unknown numbers, especially now that I was in a fucking shit-ass mood, but something was nagging me, an instinct niggling the back of my neck.

"Come on," I called for Deimos, and he followed me to the porch. I leaned on the banister as he searched endlessly for the best spot to take a piss as I dialed the unknown number.

"Derek!" The voice on the other end was frantic. "Derek, is that you? Please. Please. You have to help."

They repeated the exact phrase three more times. I didn't recognize the woman's voice through the sobbing.

"Who the fuck are you? What do you want?"

"Derek, it's me, Alexa." My heart sank to my feet. "They… they took her—Eva. He thought he killed me… but he missed."

I straightened, trying to find my voice, trying to string the words together, to comprehend what the fuck she was saying. Someone took her. Eva. My girl.

"You have to help her, Derek. She doesn't have her insulin. It's been five hours."

A growl rippled off my tongue.

Five fucking hours.

I tore through my house, Deimos following, as I ran upstairs, taking the steps two at a time.

"Why did you wait so long to tell me? Who took her?"

"We were ambushed. They fucked me up. I woke up in the hospital. And Eva is just gone." She was speaking a mile a minute. I set the phone on speaker, so I'd have use of both hands. "I told the cops it was that Russian piece of shit. But they won't do anything without going through proper fucking channels. And you know she doesn't have long. She needs her insulin." There was a pause on the other end as I continued to pack duffel bags full of equipment. "I know you can help, Derek. I know what you are."

I froze, waiting for her to elaborate.

"I heard my Uncle Franco talking to that Leni woman the other day. I hate you right now for hurting Eva, and you deserve a kick in the dick, but I need you to pull whatever resources you have out of your ass and find her before it's too late. You owe her that much."

I hung up the phone and pounded the table with both fists. My breaths were fast, and all I could think about was Eva in the hands of that son of a bitch. He was dead. Everyone he loved was dead. His family. His friends. The whole goddamn bratva.

I snatched the phone. It rang twice, and a familiar voice greeted me on the other line.

"Derek Cain."

"Amalia."

Kai and I pulled up to a red brick building on the corner of a lonely street. Neither of us had said a word on the drive. He looked at me as I threw the car into park and nodded.

"Ready, brother."

I returned the gesture; my jaw set tight. "All of them."

A smirk tipped the edge of his mouth. "You don't have to tell me twice."

I climbed out, pulled a large duffel bag from the back seat, and slung it over my shoulder. Kai did the same.

We charged up a short porch. Not in the mood for bullshit, I kicked the door open in two hits. As pieces of wood went flying, two men scrambled into the foyer with their guns drawn, but not fast enough. Kai dropped them, and I moved toward a sack of shit trying to run into another room. I cornered him inside a small bathroom and pulled out my blade.

"Please," he begged like the cowardly bastard he was. "I have a wife and kids. Please."

"I don't give a fuck about your wife or your goddamn kids. You're going to die in this bathroom. How quick and how painless depends on how you answer my questions."

He sat on the toilet with his hands raised in front of him, still uselessly pleading for his miserable life.

"I'll tell you anything."

I gripped the front of his shirt. "Where is she?" I growled through clenched teeth.

"Where is who?"

My knife plunged into the top of his right thigh. He howled in pain, and I put a hand around his throat, snuffing out his pathetic cries. There would be no mercy. Even if he had no involvement or knew of his boss's plans, he'd die just the same.

Guilty by fucking association.

"I'm going to ask you one more time before I cut off your dick and shove it up your ass. Where is she?"

"Please," he croaked out as I loosened my grip enough for him to speak. "I don't know who you're talking about. Is this about Dmitry?"

"Still wrong answer."

"Oh, fuck!" As I twisted the knife, flaying his quad muscle, he screeched like a pig at slaughter.

Drips of piss hit the floor in time with the blood from his wound.

"He took something of mine, and I'm going to get it back, even if I have to go through every single one of you motherfuckers." I pushed down on his mangled thigh, and his eyes rolled to the back of his head. Fisting his hair, I tipped his head back and shoved the knife beneath his chin and into his skull. His body slumped over and hit the floor with a thud.

I ran my hands across the top of my head, blood caking my forehead and hair, and growled in frustration, having gotten nothing from this bastard.

"Derek, come check this out."

I met Kai at the bottom of the main floor stairs, where a young boy was sitting with his head buried in his knees, shoulders shuddering. He couldn't have been more than seven or eight years old. I narrowed my eyes as he looked up at me, tears running down his face. I'd vowed to end the Belov lineage and anyone associated with him, but something about this boy pulled on the last shred of my humanity. Maybe because I'd been a frail and orphaned child, the fear in his blue eyes reminded me of a time when I'd felt just as small and helpless.

"Is there anyone else in this house?"

I attempted to soften my voice somewhat, but he flinched at my words and crumpled into himself, quietly sobbing.

"Cleared the rest of the house. It was just a woman upstairs." Kai knelt beside the boy. "Piece of shit tried to shield herself behind the kid."

I grabbed the boy by the scruff of his neck and walked him to the door. He didn't fight me or resist.

"Are you looking for the girl with the long hair?" he murmured between sniffles.

I froze and roughly tipped his chin. "You've seen her? She was here?"

He shook his head. "Not here. At Papa's place on Belmont Street."

"How is she? Is she okay?"

His eyes were downcast, and he shrugged his shoulders. "I think she was sleeping... and bleeding."

I punched the wall, splitting the sheetrock while yelling obscenities.

"Are you sure?" I asked, throttling his shoulders. "How long ago?"

"I don't know. It was after school..." He flashed a sheepish look and turned away from me. "She didn't have any clothes on," he confessed in a whisper.

I tore out of the house and tossed my bag into the trunk. Kai followed, the boy jogging behind him.

"Get somewhere safe. Far from here, you hear me? I'm serious, kid," he said, gripping his arm and shoving him forward. "This shit is about to blow."

I didn't look back to see where he ran off to; I didn't give a damn. Wherever he went, he'd find his way. Just like Kai and I had. Or not.

My thoughts were reserved solely for Eva, and the hell I was about to rain down on Dmitry Belov. As we rounded the corner, a loud explosion rocked the night air for the third time that evening. And it sure as fuck wouldn't be the last. I'd find her, even if I had to burn the whole goddamn city to the ground.

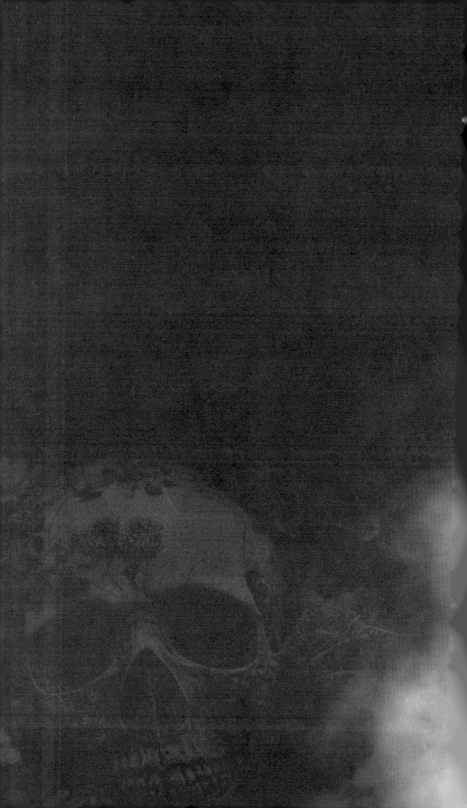

Chapter Forty Five

Evangelina

"Fuck."

My head was throbbing, the pain radiating through my face and neck. I didn't have time to dwell on the physical discomfort as the memories of what happened crashed into me with the force of a freight train. Darkness shrouded my vision, and I quickly realized there was a foul-smelling cloth tied tightly around my eyes. Horror sent my heart racing when I couldn't bring my arms to my face. They were bound above my head, my wrists raw from the pressure.

"No, oh my God... no."

I was naked on a mattress, the cold air from what I could only assume to be an open window mercilessly biting my skin. Cars passed by, voices, all oblivious to the nightmare unfolding in this dingy room. It smelled like urine and other bodily fluids. My stomach lurched at the thought of what it was used for.

Of what awaited me too.

If I screamed, it would bring attention to the fact I was awake. If I remained silent, they'd still come for me eventually.

Tears welled in my eyes, spilling over, only to be soaked up by the cloth.

I cursed and suppressed the fiery sobs burning my throat.

How could this happen? How would I escape?

If Lex was dead, that meant no one was coming for me. A strangled cry broke from my lips at the thought of Alexa murdered in some parking lot... because of me.

My cries filled the space, my stomach twisting at my horrifying reality.

"This can't be happening," I croaked into the darkness, words breaking, overcome with the thoughts of everyone I loved, even Derek. I told him I'd kill him out of anger, but I knew I'd never be able to hurt him, despite the pain he'd caused me. I loved him, and even if I had more time, I knew my heart could never belong to anyone else.

I wished I had more time to make things right with my father. A part of me knew he'd accepted his life, the lies and deceit out of coercion, and did his best to keep me safe, untainted from the world that had him shackled to violence.

"Are you done?"

I froze. The voice was low and filled with morbid amusement.

Had he been there this whole time? Bile rose to my throat, feeling violated in more ways than just my state of undress. He'd watched me break and grieve. The sick son of a bitch probably enjoyed every second of that.

"It's about time you're up."

I felt the heat of his gaze on me, roaming my naked body. His shoes made the floorboards creak as he moved through the room and slammed the window shut. The soles of his shoes were loud on the surface of the floor. As he neared, I felt his looming presence directly beside me.

"I didn't mean to strike you, *kroshka*. Forgive me. I just lost my temper, that's all." The back of his hand feathered down my abdomen, and I stiffened under his touch. "I know you're not used to this, and I'd love to tell you that you'll learn and bend under my direction as they all do. But you're different, aren't you?" he said, putting pressure on my hip. "You have a medical condition that would take too much effort to keep up with. So, I'll enjoy you while I can."

His calloused fingers dipped between my thighs.

"Don't fucking touch me." I tried to close my legs, to crawl out of my body as I yanked on the restraints and thrashed wildly in the bed, but it was no use. I was at his mercy. He'd touch and take everything he wanted. My chest suddenly felt heavy and constricting, making it difficult to breathe.

Ten, nine, eight…

"Relax, Evangelina. I'll make you feel good, I promise."

He lifted the cloth from my eyes, but I refused to look at him, squeezing my lids shut as tears spilled and pooled inside my ears.

"Come on, *kroshka*, let me see those eyes," he said, gripping my face so hard my teeth cut into the inside of my mouth. "There you are," he crooned close to my face as I blinked furiously, trying to disperse the moisture and adjust my vision to the room's brightness.

"W-why are you doing this?" I asked, swallowing back the taste of copper.

"You're like a three-for-one deal. I settled a debt, I'll avenge my brother, and I'll get to have my fun. Pity, it won't be for much longer."

My eyes fell to my bare abdomen where my insulin pump used to be. They'd removed it, and I had no idea how long ago and no fucking clue what my levels were. Shit. It was hard to gauge anything or feel any symptoms of distress. Adrenaline was pumping through me, and I was fucked. Completely and utterly fucked.

A fresh wave of tears crested in my eyes, and I fought hard to keep them from spilling. I hated that he'd see me so weak, frail, and helpless.

The mattress dipped when he sat, his mouth grazing over my collarbone. "You are beautiful, Evangelina." He pressed the flat of his tongue to my skin and licked his way just below my chin. "You better keep those eyes open because the last thing I want you to see is how good I fuck you and that mouth of yours."

Dmitry cupped my breast and took the other into his mouth, trapping my nipple painfully between his teeth before lapping at it with his tongue.

My whole body trembled as I forced my mind to escape, to hide somewhere he couldn't hurt me.

Seven, six, five…

Fighting him wasn't an option. I stared at a stain in one of the ceiling panels above me, its shape resembling a tiny paw, and I thought of Diego. The day I found him and how Derek helped me save him.

Derek.

I'd always felt protected by his side, as if nothing could hurt me. It was ironic how the one person I thought would always be there ended up being the biggest heartbreak of my life. I missed him on a visceral level. And despite his betrayal, I knew he'd never let this happen. A smile ghosted over my lips at the thought of what he'd do to Dmitry when he found out. It was a thought that both scared and thrilled me.

I bit down hard and suppressed a painful groan as his rough fingers pushed inside me.

"No… please, stop." My pleas went unanswered as he continued his assault.

"Such a pretty pussy. Mind if I have a taste?"

"Fuck you! Don't you fucking do it," I cried out as he positioned himself between my legs, running his tongue up my inner thigh. I screamed louder and thrashed more violently the closer he got. "Four, three, two, one!"

As if on cue, the rapid fire of guns rang out from what sounded like the floor beneath us. We froze, waiting to confirm what we'd just heard.

Again. More shots.

His eyes widened, and he cussed, jumping from the bed as he quickly zipped and buttoned his pants.

"Help me! I'm up here!"

His hand was over my mouth in a fraction of a second. "Don't you fucking say a word." Dmitry removed his hand slowly, and the moment I was free, I yelled again. This time, he backhanded me with a loud crack.

"You're going to die," I told him, spitting blood in his face.

"You first, bitch."

My mouth gaped open when he put his hands around my throat and squeezed so hard I thought my head was about to pop off.

Black spots peppered my vision as he slowly faded. His face was replaced by Derek's, and I felt myself smiling in my thoughts.

Get him, baby.

Just as I felt weightlessness taking over, a loud thud jarred my eyes open, and oxygen rushed into my lungs when I drew in a gasping breath.

In two quick movements, my arms and legs were free, and a woman I'd never seen before was standing above me.

A smirk curved her deep red lips.

"So, you're the lucky woman? Not bad," she said, casting a glance over my body. "I didn't anticipate you to be naked, but you're going to have to just roll with it. You can pull it off."

A hail of bullets rang out from the hallway. "Come on, princess," she said, handing me a gun she'd pulled from a holster inside her jacket.

"It's Eva."

Damn nicknames.

Bullets tore through the walls, hitting just behind my head. The woman shot up and unloaded her mag toward the gunfire before throwing a chair into the window and climbing on the sill.

I leaped off the bed and followed, cutting the soles of my feet with the glass, but I sucked up the pain and climbed out behind her. There was a flat landing just below the window, making it easy to descend to the ground.

"Run west. There's a black van half a mile down that road. My girls are waiting."

She didn't wait for a response before intending to run back toward the warehouse.

"Wait," I said, grabbing her elbow. "Are you here with Derek? Is he in there?"

"I was paid to get the job finished. Finding you was just a bonus."

I grabbed at my hair in frustration as the gunfire from inside the warehouse was endless. If Derek was in there, he could be dead or dying. I couldn't let that happen.

"Answer the damn question."

"I like you, princess," she said with a grin. "Yes, he is. But you're not going in there, especially like that."

I gritted my teeth. "I know my way around a fucking gun. I can do this. And the only way you're going to stop me is by killing me."

She arched a perfect brow and pursed her lips. "You two are definitely made for each other. Both so fucking stupid." Tossing me an extra mag and pushing a gun to my chest, she chuckled. "I don't know where you plan on stashing that, princess—"

"Eva."

"*Eva*. Just don't get yourself killed."

I hooked her arm again. "Who are you?"

"Amalia. *La mercinaria*."

Chapter Forty Six

Derek

I wrenched my blade from the man's throat with a groan, blood spraying back into my face before plunging it repeatedly into the jagged wound until he was no longer moving.

Blood dripped from my lashes and the strands of hair hanging over my forehead. The air was thick with the smell of iron. Carnage abounded. Each one deserving of a brutal death for touching what was mine. But I had yet to find her, and until I did, they'd all die begging for mercy, my face the hell they sought to be freed from.

"Derek! This way." Kai stood beneath a narrow doorway. One moment, he was flagging me over. The next, he had his gun trained in my direction. Two shots rang above my head, and a body dropped behind me.

"Cain, you're just going to sit there finger painting or what? Amalia and some of her girls were clearing the second floor," Helena said as she breezed by and into the stairwell. "Let's go get Eva. I have an early morning patient and need my eight hours."

Kai and I followed close behind, spilling onto a dark landing where five of Belov's men were posted up. We ducked behind a wall as gunfire tore off pieces of the flimsy wood.

"When they reload, cover me." I'd barely gotten the words out when the men yelled as bullets riddled their bodies.

Amalia's crew had snuck up from behind and neutralized the threat.

A tall woman with shoulder-length hair stepped over a body and addressed me with a grin. "Amalia has your girl."

My chest suddenly expanded as if it were the first time I could breathe since I found out she had been taken... or maybe, since the night she told me she'd never forgive me.

"Where is she?"

The woman shrugged her shoulders. "We lost contact with her twenty minutes ago."

I clenched my jaw. "And *him?*"

"No sign of boss man."

As if I'd conjured him from the pits of hell, there he was, slumped against an adjacent doorway, holding the side of his torso while blood pooled at his feet.

In one swift motion, they all raised their weapons.

"NO!" My voice echoed within the walls of that space, and eight pairs of eyes turned to look at me with curious expressions. "He's mine."

"Derek, I know what you want, but just put a bullet through that fucker's face, and let's get Eva."

I shook Kai's touch from my shoulder as I stalked toward Dmitry, holstering my gun and pulling my knife. "He doesn't deserve a quick death. That's too easy. Find Eva and get her out of here and to a hospital."

Leni and the other women took off without another word. Kai remained and placed a hand on my chest, holding me in place.

"Let me help you."

"No, I got this. Get my girl, Kai. Get her out of here."

I wasn't sure when he left as all my attention was set on Dmitry, who flashed me a grin and disappeared into the dark room.

"Why does it feel like you know exactly who I am? And why I'm here?"

My guard was on high alert as I crossed into the dimly lit space. He sat at the edge of a small bed, the mattress stained to all hell. There was a sheared rope attached to the iron headboard and rope on the floor at the foot of the bed. Just steps away was a broken window and bloody shattered glass. And it hit me. Eva had been kept in here and tied down to that bed like a prisoner—like a goddamn animal.

My fucking girl.

I saw red and gritted my teeth, squeezing the hilt of my knife as the urge to tear his head from his body with my bare hands had them trembling.

"I know who you are, Cain. And I must admit, I'm absolutely envious of you. What I would give for a more thorough taste of that sweet little cunt."

A growl rippled past my clenched teeth as I lunged for him, burying my blade deep inside his abdomen. He sputtered blood between choked laughs, and I twisted the steel as it tore up the tender muscle.

Dmitry leaned forward, hissing near my ear. "She was so tight for me." He howled as I plunged it again over the same gaping hole.

"Die."

Another strangled laugh spluttered from his bloodied lips. His breaths were fast and shallow as he clung to my shirt. "You... first."

Pain ripped through my side as warm liquid spilled down my legs. The leather hilt of a knife protruded from just below my ribcage. He pummeled me with a right hook to the stomach, and I stumbled back, falling on my ass. Taking advantage of my shocked state, he lunged forward and pushed the blade deeper.

"Fuck…"

"Doesn't feel so good, does it?" He pushed harder, and I arched my neck, groaning in pain. "We'll continue this little spat in hell, Cain."

Dmitry yanked the knife out of my body and held it over his head. I growled and clenched my teeth, bracing myself for more pain.

But it never came. A single shot tore through the air and into the middle of his forehead. He slumped over me, and I cursed as the dead weight put an insufferable amount of pressure on my wound.

My eyelids were suddenly heavy.

"Derek!"

That voice.

Angel.

I knew I couldn't be dead. Not if she was here with me. She knelt beside me, pushed him off, and held my face. I noticed she was wearing Kai's shirt.

"Derek. Oh my God. There's so much blood. You're covered in it."

I chuckled between groans. "It's not mine. I did a lot of bad things, baby. But I needed to find you… And look, you found me."

"Shut up," she cried, putting pressure on my wound, forcing a loud grunt, and I punched the floor. "Save your energy, Derek. It's pouring out of you, and I don't know how to stop it." She screamed for help, then set her beautiful eyes back on me again. A smile crept across my mouth as I looked at her and touched her cheek.

"So fucking beautiful, angel." She leaned into my palm, her tears trickling down my skin. "It's okay; you're safe now. Don't cry. Can't fucking stand to see you cry."

She shook her head and sobbed, gripping my wrist. "I'm not

crying for myself, Derek. I can't lose you, and I feel like you're leaving me. Please, hold on."

"You're crying for me?"

Eva shushed me, but I felt my breath grow heavier, the weight of my body settling near my back as if I was falling through the floorboards. I couldn't die without telling her how much I fucking loved her.

"Hey, I'm not going anywhere… but if I do, you should know I love you. I love you so goddamn much. I didn't even know I could feel this way about anyone. You have to know that. All of it was real."

She bowed her head and cried, holding on to me fiercely. "Derek, please… stop."

"No, I have to get this out." I sucked in an agonizing breath, but before I could say another word, a multitude of voices filled the room.

And I lost her.

"Eva," I called, but she never answered.

My eyelids were too damn heavy, and I couldn't focus on any one person or object as they lifted and moved me from one space to the next, everything moving past in a blur.

"Keep pressure on it."

Kai.

I couldn't see him, but I knew his hand was gripping mine. "Fuck, brother, you messed up your good shirt, huh?"

I laughed weakly around a groan.

"You will help him!" Eva's frantic voice filled the car's cabin. "I don't give a damn how you feel. I love him, Daddy. Please, I'm fucking begging you!"

Franco was on the line. I wouldn't blame him for refusing to help. Hell, I wouldn't blame him if he finished the job himself. I'd broken her heart and shattered her trust. The fact that she was even here, worried about my well-being, served as a shred of solace that I hadn't damaged her beyond repair.

Or maybe I had.

I must have lost consciousness because I didn't remember being transported from the car to a cot in one of Franco's patient rooms. It was dark, with just the low light from a nearby lamp. Running a hand down my torso, I realized I was no longer dressed in my own clothes. I'd been outfitted in a pale blue gown. My left hand was also bandaged around my palm and two fingers.

"You're awake."

Her voice had this way of moving through me and curling itself around my heart. My tensed muscles instantly relaxed when I looked into her eyes. She forced a smile, and my stomach dropped as I waited for my world to fall apart again. For her to tell me that it would be the last time I'd see her because she was only here out of pity.

Eva uncurled herself from the leather-bound loveseat and took tentative steps in my direction, misty eyes never wavering from mine. She sat at the foot of the small cot, the lamp's glow highlighting her features. I swallowed the pain radiating through my body as I attempted to shift into a sitting position. Anger coiled inside me upon seeing the bruises, the blown blood vessels in her eyes, and the purpling around a busted lip.

"What did they do to you?"

She shook her head, her mouth pulled into another fake smile. "I'm fine. And there's no use being upset. They're all dead."

She didn't have to say it. The accusation written between the lines was clear as day. They're dead because I'd been at the helm. I'd orchestrated the massacre of an entire clan without a single fuck given or an ounce of remorse. But couldn't she see I'd done it for her?

Always for her.

Despite it all, she still hated the man in front of her. Yet I'd do it again without a second thought. Every drop of blood spilled was worth her life. And they all needed to pay.

Even if she wouldn't have me.

"You don't have to stay."

Her head snapped up.

"You want me to leave?"

"Isn't that what you want? Look, I know I'm not exactly your favorite person right now. And a part of me feels responsible for what happened to you. I'm so sorry, Eva."

She looked away and scoffed.

"You're so stupid, Derek Cain." I narrowed my eyes, confused by her words. "So fucking stupid."

"Care to elaborate?" I said with a painful chuckle.

She stood up and sat beside me. "To say I've been through hell and back would be the understatement of the century. Derek, I was beaten" —she gripped the sheets— "violated and kidnapped, all after having my heart broken and learning the world as I knew it was all just a lie. Like I've been asleep this whole time while everyone around me was in on the secret." Her hand slowly settled over mine, fingers feathering over the ink of my index finger. "Do you think I'd be here if I didn't want to be?"

My heart thundered in my chest. She *wanted* to be here. I sat up and held her face with my bandaged hand, hope soaring in my chest.

"Angel, what I said back there is true. I love you, woman. And I'm sorry for everything I put you through."

Tears rolled down her face as she rested her forehead on mine. "I love you too, Derek. But—"

No, no, no.

"Eva, please."

"I can't, Derek. I just can't," she whispered, shaking her head.

"But you just said…"

Eva tugged my hand from her face.

"My love for you is one thing. It's not a switch I can turn on and off. Trust me, I wish I could." She pushed to her feet. "You and I come from different worlds. I can't imagine you just walking away from something like that. You know you can't," she sobbed, wiping at her tears. "And I don't even want to know the price if you could. I couldn't live with myself if—"

"Don't you do that. That's not your burden to bear because I'd do anything and everything to have you. I'd make this whole goddamn world burn for you, Eva."

She turned around and cried. "No, Derek… please, just stop."

I clenched my fist, needing to punch something out of frustration and impotence. Nothing would sway her because, ultimately, I wasn't the man she deserved. I didn't know how to be anyone else. There was no redemption for men like me. I lived my life toeing the line between hell and the one on this plane of existence. I couldn't fault her for wanting to run.

"Go, Eva." She froze. "It's okay."

"Derek…"

"I'll see you around."

Eva didn't look back. A part of me wanted her to run out of the room before I scooped her up and never let her go, but this was a necessary evil.

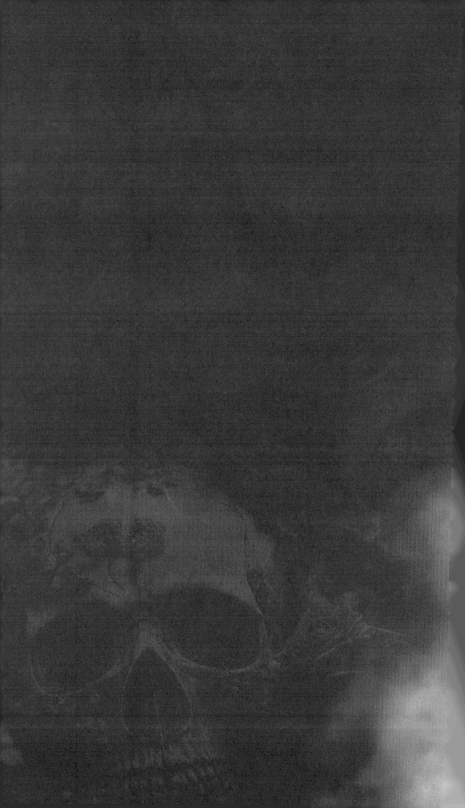

Chapter Forty Seven

Evangelina

The food on my plate was getting cold as I pushed it around with a fork like a toddler. I hadn't had much of an appetite for the last few weeks, but as Lex always said, I didn't have the luxury to skip meals. I peered down the aisle of the small cafe—my favorite one to frequent for obvious, pathetic reasons—to see whether my cousin was on her way back from using the restroom. Just the thought of putting any of this food into my mouth made me want to vomit.

I'd been feeling that way for a while, and was horrified when I realized the possibility of pregnancy, then devastated after half a dozen negative tests confirmed I indeed was not having Derek's baby. It was a strange roller coaster ride of emotions.

I hadn't seen him in a little over a month, but it was as if I felt him nearby. The heat of his presence, the charge in the air that crackled between us. And maybe he was close by, keeping an eye on me. I'd like to think that was true and not the alternative where he'd moved on and forgot about what we had—selfish as it was. I tried to convince myself he deserved happiness, though his life was so complicated that the notion was ridiculous. And did I really want him to fall for another woman?

The logical part of me knew what that answer should be, but the hopelessly-in-love woman, whose favorite color happened to be red, knew better. Derek had ruined me for any other man. How would I ever give myself to someone else when he owned every piece of my heart forever? But I couldn't look past who he was and what he'd done, even though there were days when my resolve faltered. I still held on to the hope that I'd wake up one day without the longing, the endless search for the missing half of my soul.

"Hey, babes, just got a call, and I gotta run to the office. You want me to drop you off?"

I shook my head as I took a swig of water. "I'll call for a ride. I don't want you to go out of your way."

Lex clucked her tongue and rolled her eyes. "You know what, Evangelina? I won't even entertain that comment."

I leaned in the booth and laughed, unable to recall the last time Lex had addressed me by my full name.

"I'll see you later at Dad's for dinner."

"I'll be there," she threw back from the door.

Lex was my buffer where my father and I were concerned. We were on much better, albeit rocky terms these days, but I forgave him and would always love him dearly—I could never forget the years of deception, his involvement with the criminal underworld, and how it had cost Frankie's life.

"Beautiful bracelet."

I jumped in my seat, startled by the waitress's voice as she gathered Alexa's empty dishes.

"Oh, thank you."

I absently slid the piece of jewelry back and forth across my wrist, the light catching the diamonds in such a mesmerizing way. I hadn't worn it since the day I found out the truth about Derek, and I'd only slipped it on this morning because Diego decided to use my other one as a chew toy.

The gorgeous piece was a reminder of what was and could have been.

I blew out a long, resigned breath, my eyes being pulled to the window, where a tall figure dressed in all-black tailored clothing stood at the end of the street. Tossing some cash on the table, I darted out of the cafe without thinking. It had been a month. What would I even say? Were we supposed to hug? It was an odd question regarding a man who had bent me over and fucked me senseless in ways that still sent shivers of phantom pleasure down my spine.

Maybe it was my nerves and trepidation, but I suddenly felt light-headed. Filling my lungs with oxygen, I pushed forward and snaked through the bustling street. A couple of weeks before summer, all of Philly came out in droves. Annoyance clawed up my back as an older woman shoved in front of me, looking back as if I was the one who needed to watch where she was going. Her cold eyes scrutinized me, and I didn't know what to make of her brazen perusal. The world wasn't the same place I knew a little over a month ago. As far as I was concerned, she could have been some CIA operative.

I averted her gaze and finally reached the man I'd seen from the cafe, placing a hand on his forearm and causing him to twist in my direction.

But something else was happening simultaneously. Black specks dotted my vision, and my knees gave out.

"Miss?" he said, reaching for me as I fell.

Not angel or Eva, but a cold and detached "miss" from a stranger. "Are you all right?"

Why was I so utterly disappointed and—sad?

"No," I muttered weakly, the cloud of tears stealing the last of my vision before the world turned black.

My mind was in a haze, plunged into darkness with the scents of unknown surroundings. I clutched at rigid sheets, the smell sterile and cold, but I was surprisingly warm. When I opened my eyes, I realized I was in a hospital room, and the moments just before losing consciousness hit me all at once. I'd felt light-headed, a cold sweat coating my forehead. But mostly, I'd felt empty and heartbroken. And completely aggravated with myself for being disappointed that the man I'd pursued wasn't Derek.

Wasn't that what I wanted?

I collapsed on the street and woke up in a hospital bed, and my first thoughts revolved around a man I could never be with—a murderer. Flipping over onto my back, I covered my face with both hands and sighed.

"Sleep well?"

My body stiffened as that voice poured over me like smooth honey. Eyes wide under the cover of my hands, I almost couldn't bring myself to remove them, unsure of what I'd do when I saw him.

"Derek, what are you doing here?" I said, slowly lowering my arms.

"Hi." His smile was disarming, and I had to clutch the sheets to keep myself from jumping into his arms as my heart raced, screaming for me to claim what was mine. Instead, I remained a mask of calm and indifference, and I hated myself for it.

"Hi," I threw back at him stupidly. "Now, answer my question."

He stood and moved toward me, and my breath hitched as I took in the sight of him. There was nothing left of the broken man I'd last seen a month ago. That cocky and intimidating man I'd met that first day was the one standing before me.

He's a killer, Eva.

It was the mantra on repeat in my thoughts.

"Don't you think the better question is what you are doing here?"

"I fainted. I was walking on the sidewalk... and I thought I saw—I felt dizzy."

Looking away from him, I glanced down at my hands, the diamond bracelet jumping out like a beacon. "My bracelet. That's why you're here."

"I didn't think you still wore it."

"I don't. I mean, I didn't. Today was just a coincidence."

He chuckled and leaned in close.

"A coincidence? Eva, what are the odds that you experience a low that sends you to the hospital on the day you decide to put on that bracelet?"

I couldn't help watching his lips as he spoke. God, it had been so long. I missed his touch, his kisses... making love to him. I was weak. I knew it. But he and I could never be. I was a homicide detective, for fuck's sake. How could I turn a blind eye to the lives he'd taken and the ones he'd eventually take? I couldn't be that person and live like the biggest hypocrite. Putting away bad guys by day while sleeping with a hitman by night.

"Thank you for coming and making sure I'm good, but—"

His thumb and forefinger lifted my chin, and I drowned in the sea of his eyes, raging like the ocean during a storm.

"I didn't just come here to make sure you're okay. I came here to let you know, to remind you, Evangelina, who you fucking belong to." My heart thundered in my chest, core flaring to life. Words escaped me. "I don't want you to say anything. But I was away for weeks, taking steps and trying to make things right. Trying to be the man you deserve because you deserve the world, angel." His thumb caressed my cheek, and I closed my eyes briefly, basking in the moment. "But I can't promise that anything will be different tomorrow, in a month, or even a year. It won't be an easy road. But I'll eventually gain my freedom from that life and, in return, your love."

I shook my head. "Things aren't that simple, Derek. It's not about whether or not I love you. You know the answer to that."

He smiled and ran the back of his hand along my cheek. "I'm a patient man—most times," he added with a wink, "and I'm willing to wait as long as it takes."

Derek framed my face with both hands and kissed the tip of my nose.

"Don't ever scare me like this again. Why aren't you taking care of yourself? Your nurse said you were severely dehydrated. What have you eaten today?"

A feeling between annoyance and shame crawled up my neck.

"It's not something I can control all the time."

"I know," he whispered, brushing his lips over mine.

God, I wanted to close the small distance and relish in the taste of him, but as I closed my eyes and cupped his hands, I felt cold metal press beneath my palm.

His ring.

I opened my eyes and lowered our joined hands, staring at the dark piece of jewelry. He'd told me once it was an heirloom, a family crest, but the pieces were slowly falling into place. *Bound by blood*. His signet ring symbolized his alliance and oath to the organization he'd been bound to. The piece was a stark reminder of what he was and all he'd done.

Maybe James hadn't been a model citizen, but he also hadn't deserved such a cruel death at the hands of his own son.

Releasing Derek's hands, I looked away and hugged my body as I fought with everything I had not to cry again.

He was silent for what seemed hours, the tension between us thick and nearly suffocating.

"You know, Eva, I can't change who I've been or wash away the sins of my past. I just want an opportunity to love you."

I knew that if I looked at him, I would either sob like a child or jump into his arms. And I wanted neither. My emotions were much too raw and too vulnerable for sound decision-making. As much as I wanted him to stay, I also needed him to leave.

"Mine," he growled into my ear.

The cot dipped when he shifted his weight to kiss my temple. And without another word, he was gone.

Again.

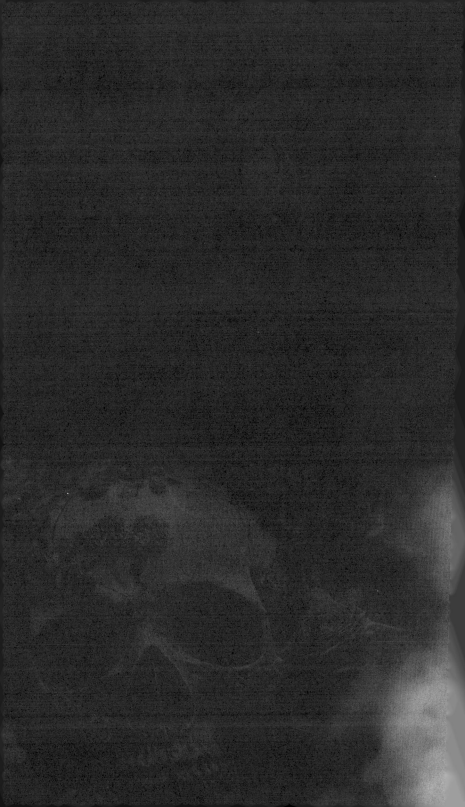

Chapter Forty Eight

Evangelina

Diego was curled up beside me on the chaise sofa, tail flicking from side to side as his little ears perked up whenever the rain outside strengthened, or the wind picked up. I scratched the top of his head, and he purred, rubbing it affectionately against my thigh as I ended my phone call with Catherine. While Sam would never be the man or officer he once was, he was alive and alert.

My eyes drifted out the window for probably the hundredth time in thirty minutes. But Derek was late and most likely not coming, especially not with this torrential downpour.

For the last two weeks, since I'd been on leave, he hadn't missed a day. Every morning, he hand-delivered a full day's worth of meals. His note had said he'd hired a renowned chef to cook the meals in his home since he knew I was too stubborn to accept it be done in mine. And he was right. But that wasn't where it ended. One morning, I woke up to his Bentley in my driveway and a text letting me know he'd taken my car to get an inspection since the due date was coming up shortly. He made sure to add that he would have just gifted me a new car, but knew I wouldn't accept such an extravagant and unnecessary gift.

Again, he'd been right.

He hadn't attempted to speak to me outside of text messages and explained that he wanted to grant me space and time to reconsider our relationship.

While I'd give anything to wrap myself around him, what my heart and brain wanted were two different things.

It was a quarter past seven, and there was no indication Derek would show up. Not that I wanted him to. While the rain had slowed in the past half hour, it was still coming down pretty hard; coupled with the darkness of night, it made for dangerous road conditions.

I set down my e-reader, intent on walking into the kitchen for some peanuts, when I saw lights flash across my window and the sound of tires over wet gravel.

My pulse began racing as I flew to the glass, Diego jumping up on the windowsill, obstructing my view.

"Move, Diego!"

Derek jumped from the driver's side and put his hands on his hips, as though contemplating his next move as the rain pelted him. The meals usually came in weatherproof packaging, so I wasn't sure what he was worried about.

"He's trying to figure out how to get to the porch." Diego glanced at me, and then brought his attention back to Derek.

Derek threw open the passenger side door and reached inside, pulling out a stack of containers in a tied-off plastic bag.

His hesitation suddenly made sense.

Making a run for it, Derek was about five feet from my porch when he slipped on the wet grass, sending the bag of containers into the air and into a muddy puddle.

The roar of obscenities that flew from his mouth pierced through the heavy patter of rain.

"Stay here."

Derek didn't notice when I opened the front door. He was standing over the ruined meal, facing away from me. Another string of expletives reached my ears as he bent over to examine the bag before kicking it across the lawn.

He set off for his car.

"Derek!"

His drenched figure froze and turned around slowly. The hood on his jacket served no purpose and sagged over his eyes. He tore it off, revealing his rage. His blue eyes pulsed with every heavy breath he blew out, droplets scattering across his mouth.

The soaked hoodie was plastered to his torso, and I couldn't help ogling those muscles and broad chest.

"Eva, I'm sorry I was late. Clyde, that bastard had a fucking family emergency. And what kind of name is Clyde anyway?" He pushed his hair back, away from his forehead, hands over his scalp out of frustration. "So I tried to do this all myself, and it was fucking hell. Took me all day. And that goddamn Deimos got into your lunch." Derek clenched his fists as he explained how he nearly dropped him off at the pound.

He was in a full-blown tirade, yet I'd stopped listening. My thoughts focused on what he'd said earlier.

The chef couldn't make it, so he decided to prepare the meals himself.

Tears sprung to my eyes. He'd spent all day determined to make this sweet gesture for me, and it all went to hell in the rain. My chest swelled with love and adoration, and for the first time since finding out the truth, my brain and my heart had finally synced.

"Derek," I whispered, my voice lost in the downpour. I tried again, but he was still venting and asking for forgiveness.

I shut my eyes and inhaled a deep breath, preparing myself for what I was about to do, for the decision I knew I couldn't take back.

I darted off the porch and into the rain, stopping a few feet in front of him.

"Eva, what are you doing? Get back inside."

"Is it true... what you said?" Hair stuck to the sides of my face as I squinted through the rain and strong winds.

"Eva, please. We can talk inside."

Ignoring him, I pressed on. "Answer me. Right here, right now. Do you love me, Derek? Would you wait for me as long as it takes?"

His jaw tensed, stormy eyes cutting through me. "I love you so goddamn much. And you're mine. Every part of you is mine, so I'll wait for you forever."

I hugged my body and lowered my head, my tears mixing with the rain as they slid down my face.

"I don't want you to," I said, my voice piercing through the storm. I looked into his eyes, and even against the downpour, I knew they were glistening with tears and emotions I'd never seen from him.

"Angel, please." His voice was thick, desperate.

"I don't... I don't want you to wait for me, Derek. I want you to take what's yours right now."

He stilled, as if processing my words or making sure he heard exactly what I'd said. For that moment in time, it was as if nothing and no one existed but us. Even the storm had faded into the background. It was just me and Derek, eyes on one another, afraid to blink away the droplets for fear the other would disappear.

A broad smile split his face, and we made a run for each other at the same time. I leaped into his arms, my legs circling his waist as he held me tightly to his chest.

"Baby, I'm so sorry."

"Stop apologizing and fucking kiss me already."

He laughed against my mouth. "I love you."

"I love you too."

Derek's lips slammed into mine with need and slight desperation and, instantly, I knew I was home.

"Say it again," I whispered between kisses.

"I love you."

"Again."

"I love you."

I held his face, my forehead pressed to his as the rain trickled between us, sliding over our lips. "One more time."

"Evangelina Cruz, I fucking love you, and I'll say it every day for the rest of my life."

I lifted my eyes to meet his, blinking away the water, and smiled.

"That sounds like a long time."

"That's what I'm hoping for."

He leaned forward and kissed me slowly, both of us taking our time to explore and taste this new depth of our connection, to rekindle the embers of what had been lost and left to simmer in the dark.

"Angel," he said, pushing back the wet hair sticking to my face. "I'm a flawed man. I've done things I'm not proud of. And I can't promise I won't slip. Or that there won't be obligations you won't agree with. But I'm doing my damndest to sever my ties. Just know it will take time and spilled blood. But I don't want any more lies between us."

I let my head fall onto his shoulder, gripping the wet fabric of his hoodie as I turned over his words in my mind. This was it. There was no going back. I had to accept Derek for who and what he was, with his past and the ghosts that would forever haunt him. He promised to find a way out, to sever his binds to that ring and all it encompasses.

And I had faith he would.

"I know your heart, Derek," I said, interlacing my fingers with his. "And I want to fill the parts of it that were left empty long ago. Just like I want you to fill mine."

He smiled against my lips and kissed me, the taste of our tears mixing with the rain.

"That's not the only thing I want to fill," he growled, tracing kisses along the curve of my neck. "I've missed you so damn much. The way you feel and the way you taste." Derek slowly set me on the ground. "I need you, Eva."

He pulled the wet hoodie up and over his head and tossed it to the side. I took a moment to admire his muscled chest, the ink canvassed on his skin. I'd memorized every stroke, every curve—every trace of his past painted on the planes of his flesh like a roadmap and timeline of his life.

Leaning forward, I pressed my lips to his chest. "I'm yours," I whispered.

Derek grabbed my nape and crushed his mouth to mine again. There was nothing gentle or sweet about how he was devouring my lips. It was primal, frantic—sexy as hell.

I wasn't sure how I ended up lying on the lawn as he peeled off the wet clothes from my body.

"Baby, I have neighbors."

He chuckled into my neck. "Well, then, we better make sure to give them a damn good show."

The playful rebuttal I planned died on my lips as he took them between his teeth, nipping and suckling until they were almost numb.

Having sex on my front lawn in the rain was never a check on my life's bucket list, but right now, there was nothing I desired more than to be taken and worshiped by this man in ways that would leave me walking with a limp in the morning.

My fingers slid through his wet hair as he licked across my breasts, lapping up the water as he made every nerve ending in my body sing and come alive. His mouth covered one of my nipples as his hand kneaded and squeezed the other. Gentle teeth grazed across the sensitive peak, and he looked up at me as he bit down with a little more pressure.

A hiss fluttered from my lips at the sensation, and I arched my back, offering all of me.

"You're so goddamn beautiful."

Derek traveled down my body, kissing and lavishing every inch. I let my thighs fall open, and he wasted no time in tearing the soaked fabric of my panties from my body.

"You know, you owe me at least two handfuls of underwear."

"I'll buy you whatever you want, angel, as long as I get to drown in this sweet pussy any time I want," he groaned, licking up my dripping slit.

There was just something so sensual about the extra layer of moisture, the silky way our bodies slipped against each other, the mixture of rain and the taste of his skin. Despite the slight chill in the air, the cold never reached me. Every part of me was covered by his heat and utterly consumed by the fire he was stoking hotter with every lick and flick of his tongue.

"Fuck, I missed this," he growled over my clit before suctioning it into his mouth. "So damn good." His hands gripped my hips, and he hauled me closer, drinking me down, slurping up every drop.

I threw my head back as an orgasm barreled through me. My mouth parted as he continued feasting, bringing me over the edge a second time. My legs closed around his head, unable to withstand another flick of pleasure, or I'd disintegrate into unrecognizable pieces. But Derek pried my knees open and took one last lick from end to end with the flat of his tongue before climbing over me.

"Eva, I don't have a condom," he said, nibbling on my earlobe.

Tracking my cycle had never been more useful than at that moment.

"It's okay. I want to feel every part of you. Fuck me, Derek."

His pants were off and tossed into a puddle in the next second, and he slid inside me with a groan. My eyes widened at the sudden intrusion, stretching me to nearly the point of pain.

"Are you okay?"

I nodded, a sated smile on my lips as I wrapped my legs around his body and gave his cock a squeeze. He chuckled into the hollow of my throat, pushing deeper, filling me so damn good he could have very well split me in half, and I'd die happy.

"You have no idea how much I missed this."

My nails dug into his back as he thrust forward, my body gliding against the grass with each powerful stroke.

"I love you, Derek. Fuck, I love you."

"Can't be without you again," he said, punctuating each word with a thrust of his dick.

I bit down on his chest as my climax crested. "Never again."

Derek pulled out and flipped me over, pulling my hips back before crashing inside me.

How his massive body covered mine, how he filled me so deeply, was enough to make me come undone. I broke beneath him, his name like the sweetest melody on my lips.

"Mine," he growled into my ear as he came, chasing my orgasm. His large arms gripped me tightly around the waist as his heavy grunts faded in time with his movements.

We lay there on the wet ground, me over his chest, tracing his tattoos.

The rain had slowed to a drizzle.

"Are you going to invite me inside, or you're just using me for lawn sex?"

I leaned my chin on his chest and laughed. "Oh, I'm definitely using you for sex." His laughter shook my whole body. "But you're right. It's chilly, and we're both absolutely filthy."

"You know that little bastard cat was watching us from the window the whole time. I'm pretty sure he has a voyeur kink."

It was my turn to laugh. Derek held my face, his expression suddenly serious.

"What's wrong?"

"I was just thinking, do you think Deimos and Diego will be happy about being roommates again?"

I couldn't suppress the smile stretching across my face. "What exactly are you saying?"

"Simple. Your place or mine?"

I leaned in and kissed him, brushing my lips against his. "Sounds like I'll be outnumbered."

Derek pushed wet tendrils of hair behind my ear and smiled. "You know there's a way to even those odds."

My heart hammered wildly in my chest.

"You… want a baby?"

He sat up and pulled me into his lap. "I never considered becoming a father. Never thought myself capable of that kind of love or worthy of it… I still don't even know if I am." Holding my face with both hands, he kissed my forehead. "But with you, angel, I want it all."

I tried to keep myself from melting into another puddle on the lawn.

We would be okay.

"You're just pulling out all the stops tonight, aren't you?"

We laughed in unison.

"Baby, I got about 100 different ways to make you swoon, moan, and scream for me. I'm not nearly done with you yet. But first, I need to get my bare ass off this ground."

Derek stood up with me wrapped around his waist.

"I'd like to put that to the test," I said, nibbling at his lips.

"You don't have to tell me twice."

With that, he thrust me over his shoulder, slapped my ass, and ran toward the house as I laughed and swatted at his back.

"What about the food? I'm kind of hungry. You were late, after all," I teased.

"Somebody wants to be punished."

"Do I need to say please?"

Another resounding slap to my ass cheek filled the night air before he closed the door behind us.

I'd worry about the neighbors tomorrow.

The End

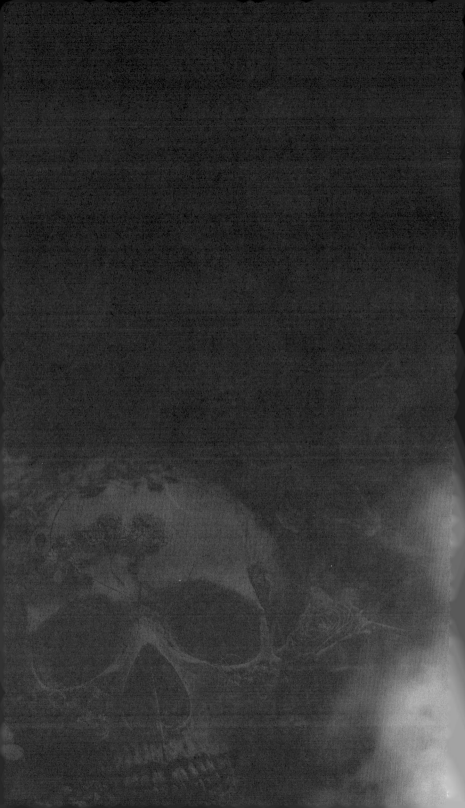

EPILoGUE
Derek

"I 'll kill them!"

I gripped the refrigerator handles and gritted my teeth, Eva's hand on my forearm, making me pause long enough before I tore the damn things straight off.

"No, you're not," she said, slipping underneath my arms and staring at the barren shelves. "Their flight was canceled, baby. We barely made it here ourselves." Eva turned to face me, throwing her arms behind my neck. "And you're not actually serious, are you? You know I brought my cuffs."

When she levered to kiss me, I scooped her into my arms and sat her on the kitchen counter.

"Mm, if that's what it takes to bring those out tonight, let me make a quick phone call. Kai wouldn't mind."

I nibbled down the column of her throat as she tipped her head back, fingernails on my scalp, and a sweet little moan on the wingtips of my name.

"Stop it. You're *not* going to call anyone, least of all your brother. Let him be. We're just going to have to go into town and pick up some things to tide us over before that two feet of snow hits the ground."

"I despise the grocery store," I said, groaning into her shoulder. "There are always people in there."

She laughed and jumped off the counter, walking toward the door and pulling on her boots. "That's the point. Besides, I have something I have to pick up, so this actually works in my favor."

I couldn't help smiling when she pulled a white beanie over her head. If she didn't need the fridge and pantry stocked, I'd take her upstairs and fuck her under the skylight wearing just those damn boots and beanie.

A year and a half later, I still craved every part of this woman like a starving man who couldn't ever satisfy his hunger.

"Later," she whispered, clapping my chest, knowing exactly how my thoughts stumbled and free-fell into the goddamn gutter.

My grin pulled wider as I followed her out the door, anticipating my prize, the only motivation for going out into this fucking weather and dealing with people.

God, the things I would do for this woman were limitless. Maybe it was unhealthy, but I didn't give a damn. Everything we'd gone through to get to this point was well worth the effort. She changed me. Changed the course of my life, and I strived to be a better man, maybe even a better human because of her.

Maybe.

Some days were harder than others to control what had been so deeply ingrained in me for so many years. But we loved each other and accepted the cards life had dealt us. Even when my departure from Ares demanded blood, she understood despite still holding a badge. She knew Ronan was still out there, and that my final body count wouldn't conclude until I tore his heart from his chest. Especially after finding out he was behind Eva's abduction. That son of a bitch had sold my girl. I never hid my hatred or the plans I had for his death from Eva. While she hadn't exactly given me the green light, she hadn't protested either.

Our love was unconventional, chaotic, passionate, and all-consuming. It didn't need to make sense to anyone but us.

All in all, the grocery store trip hadn't been the worst thing I'd had to do. Just a few more items, and we'd be on our way back home and under the cover of stars with my girl sitting on my face.

"Derek, I'm going to go grab that thing I told you about."

"I'll go with you."

She started to walk away backward. "No, just grab what's left on the list, and I'll meet you at checkout."

Eva disappeared around the corner before I could stop her. I questioned whether I should go after her. Something was off.

Had she been nervous?

"Excuse me, sir," a woman's chirpy voice broke my thoughts. Upon turning to find the intrusive voice, I was met with a redhead in a blue top that was probably three sizes too small. She certainly wasn't dressed for the weather. And not that I was interested, but the wrong move in any direction and her tits were guaranteed to pop out.

"I'm sorry to bother you," she continued, despite my lack of response, "but would you pass me that jar of peanut butter up top?"

Again, I said nothing and simply reached for the jar so she could be on her damn way.

As I grabbed said jar over her head, she made no effort to move aside. I could have sworn she moved in closer.

"Move."

She shifted uncomfortably, though not deterred in the least.

"Don't see many people like you around here."

The woman was shamelessly staring at my lips. Maybe two years ago, I would have taken her back to my cabin and degraded her in ways she'd never forgive herself for. Now, however, she was one drunken wink away from me telling her to fuck off. I wasn't a man of false pleasantries.

"Was that your girlfriend? She's very pretty. *Exotic*."

"My *wife*," I said, grabbing my cart and starting down the aisle.

"Hey, handsome?" Her hand landed on my forearm. "If you were looking to have a little fun after the wife's asleep, I own a little place down the road. I can keep you warm. I know a few things," she said, her tone low and breathy as she arched her back.

I suddenly feared one of those buttons becoming a projectile.

Catching her wrist, I opened my mouth to speak, intending to send her to hell in as few words as possible, when a loud crash and commotion had us both whipping our heads to the front of the store. She tried to latch onto me, but I tossed her ass and ran. Eva had told me she'd be waiting up front.

It had been six months since my last hit. For the most part, that life was behind me, but for her, I'd break that record without a second thought. The pit of my stomach bottomed out when I saw her on the floor on hands and knees, two bastards in a wrestling match behind her, arguing about who was next in line.

"Are you hurt?" I asked as I lifted her up and framed her face.

"I'm fine." She waved me off, and that's when I noticed her palm was bleeding, most likely cut on the broken glass she was pushed into.

My blood roiled as I set my sights on the two men, and fantasized about all the creative ways I could make them pay for every drop of my girl's blood. I stepped forward, reaching for my blade, when Eva's warm touch settled on my arm.

"No, Derek, let's just go home. Please," she urged, picking up a pink box.

A pregnancy test.

My heart was now racing for a whole new set of reasons.

"I'm sorry. I wanted it to be a surprise."

"Let's get the fuck home," I said, tugging her close.

Once I'd brought everything inside, I gave her no time to speak. I scooped her into my arms and brought her to the main bedroom. Where I would have usually tossed her playfully onto the mattress, I placed her gently over the white down comforter.

"I'm going to be… a father?" I asked for the fifth time. She nodded.

"I took a test before we left. But I forgot it, and I wanted to surprise you." Eva pulled me close. "Are you happy?"

"Am I fucking happy? Of course, I am, angel."

Eva had given me everything I never thought I wanted or would ever have. Happy couldn't even begin to describe what I felt at the prospect of becoming a father. But terrified was probably the loudest emotion. Maybe I needed a few days for that feeling to sink in all the way, because all I could think about was how goddamn gorgeous my wife was and how I needed her more than anything at that moment.

"Does your father know?"

She shook her head. "I wanted you to be the first. We can tell him together when we get back."

Franco and I weren't friends by any stretch, but we respected one another. Apart from Kai, he was the only man I trusted with Eva. And as much as he despised the core of who I was, he knew she would always be safe with me.

And I had to admit, he'd be the best grandfather to our child.

Our child.

"We have to celebrate. I'm hungry."

"What did you have in mind?"

"You, sitting on my face. Come here."

She laughed and let me undress her.

"So, who was that redhead I saw you talking to when I peeked into the aisle?" she asked, crawling up my body on all fours.

"She was fucking no one. Now bring me my pussy."

Eva laughed again, now straddling my chest. I reached up and squeezed her breasts, pinching her nipples and coaxing those sweet little noises from her I loved so much.

"She was practically attached to you like a strand of your DNA."

"Fuck her. I want your DNA all over me. Now, hold on to that goddamn headboard and sit on my face." I grabbed her hips and tossed her over my shoulders. "Wait, you're not bringing her up because you think I–"

"No," she said, cutting me off. "She doesn't matter. And I'm the one sitting on your face right now."

A soft moan broke from her lips as I ran my tongue up her slit. Eva rocked against my face, throwing her head back.

"That's my fucking girl."

If you're not ready to leave this deliciously dark world yet,
Helena and Silas
will be ready for you in November 2023
Tempted by Blood
Book two of the Severed Signet series is an enemies to lovers
dark romance.
He was supposed to be just another name on a contract.
A bounty to collect.
Until temptations of the flesh scorched the line between love and
hate.

https://books2read.com/u/47WwVj

About The Author

Elle Maldonado writes dark, contemporary romance. She lives in the U.S. with her husband and three kids and enjoys spending time with family, watching movies, and reading.

Subscribe to her newsletter for all upcoming releases, sneak peeks, giveaways, teasers, and extra scenes.

https://tr.ee/t5xCxlh6hc

Acknowledgments

I could not have done this without my husband's love, patience, and support. Thank you for putting up with me through the madness, late nights, and endless laundry baskets. I love you. Our love story will always be my favorite. This was just another chapter in our beautiful adventure. Until the next one!

My family's support was also an essential part of this project, especially my daughter, who sat and listened to all my ideas. Thank you to my main girls for not disowning me while I was in my writing cave and not taking part in our chats. I love you guys.

To my amazing author friends. I seriously would not have made it this far without you ladies. Your support, help, knowledge, and encouragement helped make this story possible. M.A. Cobb, Luna Mason, Darcy Embers, Katie B. Wright, M.L. Hargy, Linda B. Martins, Kat Neil, De'ahvion, and all the wonderful ladies in our romance group.

Marci, thank you for planting the seed and convincing me I could write a book.

To a special author who reached out and inspired me to go for it. O, thank you for your time, constructive criticism, and words of wisdom. I will forever be grateful.

Mackenzie, thank you so much for helping me polish this monster.

My PA, Margie Barr, you're the best! I'm always raving about how exceptional, helpful, and driven you are. Thank you for helping me with all my chaos, for all your beautiful creations, and for your expertise. You seriously rock.

Thank you to all my readers for your love, motivation, and support.